"Damn, damn,

Adam kicked at the la

"Quit swearing at the roof and hold still."

Adam wondered if he'd imagined the woman who appeared to be digging through the honeysuckle below and to the left of his swinging feet.

"Are you hurt?" a low melodic voice inquired.

"A few scrapes," he muttered. "Probably a bruised rib or two. If you can lift that ladder, sweet thing, chances are I'll live."

"Chances go down if you call me *sweet thing* again."

Adam couldn't see much of his Good Samaritan. But he fell instantly in lust with her sweet-as-sugar voice. Despite a downpour few women of his acquaintance would've ventured out in, this one had come from nowhere, raised his ladder and then climbed a few rungs to guide his feet to safety.

"Are...are you Jackson Fontaine?" she asked, her voice suddenly hesitant.

"I'm Adam Ross. I restore historic homes. I'm sorry," he said abruptly. "I didn't catch your name."

"Noelani. Noelani Hana. I'm...Duke Fontaine is..."

So this lovely woman was the secret daughter. Duke's little indiscretion. The illegitimate Fontaine heir.

Dear Reader,

One of the biggest challenges in writing linked books like the *Raising Cane* trilogy—especially a project involving three individual authors—is finding characters we love to love. Seeing the characters as people you'd want to know and live with for an extended period of time is essential to writing any book. When three writers carry over characters from each other's stories, it's like populating a small town.

Eve Gaddy, K.N. Casper and I met and brainstormed probably twenty scenarios and twice as many possible heroes and heroines before we decided to set our family in Baton Rouge, Louisiana, the heart of sugarcane country. Casey and Jackson Fontaine have roots in their ancestral plantation, Bellefontaine, stretching back to the Civil War. They've grown up in the sugarcane business and are itching to prove their worth to a controlling father. When their parents go off on an around-the-world second honeymoon, it seems the perfect opportunity. Except the Fontaine family has enemies and family scandals. Love interests show up, which further complicate their lives. It takes three books to solve the family's problems, bring in the crop of sugarcane and unite three sets of lovers. I hope you'll enjoy *Casey's Gamble*, *The Secret Daughter* and *Jackson's Girls*.

Sincerely,

Roz Denny Fox

P.S. I love to hear from readers at P.O. Box 17480-101, Tuscon, AZ 85731, or e-mail me: rdfox@worldnet.att.net.

The Secret Daughter

Roz Denny Fox

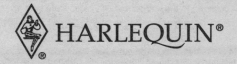

HARLEQUIN®

TORONTO • NEW YORK • LONDON
AMSTERDAM • PARIS • SYDNEY • HAMBURG
STOCKHOLM • ATHENS • TOKYO • MILAN • MADRID
PRAGUE • WARSAW • BUDAPEST • AUCKLAND

ISBN 0-373-71128-X

THE SECRET DAUGHTER

Copyright © 2003 by Rosaline Fox.

This edition published by arrangement with Harlequin Books S.A.

® and TM are trademarks of the publisher. Trademarks indicated with ® are registered in the United States Patent and Trademark Office, the Canadian Trade Marks Office and in other countries.

Visit us at www.eHarlequin.com

Printed in U.S.A.

CAST OF CHARACTERS

Duke & Angelique Fontaine: Owners of Bellefontaine, recently deceased

Cassandra (Casey) Fontaine: Bellefontaine plantation manager and daughter of Duke and Angelique

Nick Devlin: Riverboat casino owner and builder; married to Casey

Jackson Fontaine: Bellefontaine business manager and son of Duke and Angelique

Megan Fontaine: Jackson's four-year-old daughter

Esme Fontaine: Duke's opinionated sister

Noelani Hana: Illegitimate daughter of Duke Fontaine and Anela Hana

Adam Ross: Nick's friend and historic home renovator

Roland Dewalt: Long-standing neighbor of the Fontaines

Murray Dewalt: Roland's son and longtime friend of Casey and Jackson

Vivian (Viv) Pontier-Renault: Casey's best friend

Luc Renault: Jazz musician and Viv's husband

Tanya Carson: Megan's nanny

Betty Rabaud: Fontaine family cook

Bruce Shiller: Owner of sugar plantation in Hawaii where Noelani grew up

Denise Rochelle: Current Fontaine employee, romantically interested in Adam Ross

Chuck Riley: Copilot who flew with Duke Fontaine

Remy Boucherand: Police detective investigating suspicious events at Bellefontaine

In researching the trilogy, we discovered that everything we've ever heard about Southern hospitality is completely true. Our heartfelt thanks go to Kenneth and Mary Jane Kahao, longtime sugar growers in the Baton Rouge area, for squiring us around. Because of them, we were able to tour cane fields during cutting season and get an in-depth look at a working sugar mill.

Nor would our books be so rich with the history of the sugar industry if not for the generosity of Caroline Kennedy, Director, and Jim Barnett, Curatorial Assistant, of the West Baton Rouge Museum. (Caroline was quick to inform us she wasn't *that* Caroline Kennedy.)

Our apologies for any errors or bits of poetic license we may have taken in order to weave the fictional fabric of our linked stories.

I also want to thank my husband for driving us to and from Louisiana, and for the hours he and Mary Casper spent reading our stories for continuity. They're the best.

And thanks to Paula, Laura and Beverley, our editors, for their coordination, support and the insight needed to move this project from start to finish.

PROLOGUE

Baton Rouge, Louisiana

"BETTY! BETTY RABAUD. I thought it was you. Wait, let me catch my breath. I've been hoping I'd run into you one of these days. I declare, can anything *else* go wrong for Casey and Jackson Fontaine?" Ignoring a stiff October wind, Mary Louise Chastain ran up to her friend outside a local café. She used to be a cook at the Woodlands, owned by Roland Dewalt, the Fontaine family's nearest neighbor. And Betty was her counterpart on the larger plantation.

Betty Rabaud loved few things in life as much as she loved gossip. Her role as housekeeper-cook at Bellefontaine certainly gave her access to lots of the good stuff. She couldn't help it if her affluent employers had been involved in so many disasters—each one worthy of gossip—during the past few months.

Today it happened to be news that had somehow leaked into the community. The recently deceased Duke Fontaine had fathered an illegitimate child. Glancing both right and left before pulling the ever-present unlit cigarette from between her lips, Betty tucked it over one ear and said in hushed tones, "Ain't it something, Mary Louise? But how did *you* hear?"

"Murray Dewalt dropped by to see how I was getting on. I'd already heard rumors about the arson at Bellefontaine, how they had an expensive harvester go missing, and about

Casey Fontaine taking up with that riverboat casino owner. Murray's not one to talk out of turn, mind you, but I squeezed some information out of him. 'Cause he feels so bad for the way his dad fired me in one of his fits of temper. Not that I'd ever go back to the Woodlands, and Murray knows it.''

"Humph,'' Betty grumbled. "I figured maybe it was Roland spreading dirt about Duke's family, seeing how Duke stole the woman Roland had his heart set on marrying.''

"Isn't that water down the toilet? Oh, sure, Roland belly-ached to his old cronies, although he's a loner, that one. If you ask me—and no one does—Roland Dewalt's becoming a hermit.''

"Let's go inside where we can eat and chat some more, Mary Louise. Today's my day off, so I'm not in any rush.''

"Mine, too. Having a day off is new for me. Roland Dewalt expected me to work seven days a week, and for a lot less than I'm making working a shorter week for Baumgartner's.''

The friends went inside and sought an out-of-the-way back booth.

Mary Louise lowered her voice further, mostly to avoid being overheard by a chatty group seated at a nearby table. "Do you think Angelique knew her husband was playing around? Or would she ever tell you such a thing, since you're only a shirttail cousin?''

"Angelique didn't tell a soul. Truth is, I overheard Casey pitching a royal fit. I guess in some letter she and Jackson found, it more or less said their mother forgave Duke his little transgression. Know what else I heard, though? This tickles me pink.'' Betty gave a smug smile. "Esme Fontaine had no earthly clue.''

"My, my. Considering how hard it was for her to swallow the idea of Jackson's love child, that little girl, showing up to live at Bellefontaine, I'm surprised Esme didn't have a stroke over learning her brother had one of his own hidden away.''

''Well, she won't be hidden for long. She's coming for the reading of Duke's will tonight. I'd love to be a fly on the wall in *that* meeting. Which is why I'll bet you Esme arranged for Shelburne Prescott to read it on my day off. Mademoiselle Froufrou would like nothing better than to keep this secret inside the family. Mark my words, Esme'll have that girl in and gone again before she can do any more damage to Duke's reputation.''

''Doesn't matter whether you get along with Esme or not, Betty, you can't fault her for feeling like that. She's lived half her life with everyone in town snickering over the way Roland broke their engagement when he fell for Angelique.

''If this was just about Esme's feelings, I'd say tough. But Casey doesn't deserve to have this kind of shadow over her marriage. And poor Jackson. Now that Duke's dead, that boy's been left in charge of an operation his father barely let him touch.

''It's the same with Murray Dewalt, God love him. Duke and Roland, for all their petty squabbles, seemed to think a son proved their virility. Yet both of 'em were too stubborn and arrogant to equip their boys to take over if anything ever happened to them.''

''Ain't it the truth. But I'm sure Duke didn't plan on going.''

''Yep. I imagine he'd have done a whole lot of things differently if he'd had any idea he and Angelique were going to get killed in that plane crash. To make matters worse, the poor kids had to learn their papa was flying the plane that day.'' She shook her head. ''Still, any way you cut it, Duke left Jackson and Casey in a thorny situation.''

The women's friendly gossip session ceased abruptly as a waitress showed up to take their lunch orders.

CHAPTER ONE

Maui, Hawaii

"Hi, MIDORI." NOELANI HANA breezed full-tilt into the executive offices of Shiller Cane Company, the same way she'd moved through life for most of her twenty-seven years. Her long, straight hair settled like dark rain over her olive-toned shoulders as she skidded to a stop in front of Bruce Shiller's secretary. "What's so urgent to make the boss send a runner to the mill to get me? I'll have our vat computers running fine before the first load of cane's delivered, if that's what he's worried about."

"He didn't give a reason, just opened his door and told me to find you ASAP."

Noelani peeled off her leather work gloves and tucked them into the back pocket of her khaki walking shorts. "Guess I'd better go see. Oh—has he met with those truck farmers again? You know, the ones who proposed turning the cane fields into a tomato patch or some ridiculous thing?"

"Bruce hasn't mentioned them in weeks. He's still muttering about selling, though. You know this is the fourth year in a row our profits have dropped."

Noelani knocked on Shiller's door. Pasting a smile on her face, she burst gaily into his office. "You rang, oh great master?"

Seated behind a huge mahogany desk, a gaunt, sixtyish man, with a weathered face and white hair, glanced up. Probably for the first time ever, he didn't return Noelani's smile. "Take a seat." Rocking back in his chair, he idly twirled a pencil.

Unable to read his expression Noelani grew uneasy. "If this is going to be another lecture about flagging profits, Bruce—don't worry. I'll coax more from our worn-out equipment. We haven't given the new computer program I wrote a chance to show what it can do."

"Sit, Noelani. I didn't call you here to talk about the mill." Tossing the pencil aside, he peeled open a creamy envelope and removed an official-looking letter.

She did as he asked this time, throwing herself into a chair. Bruce's office was like home. Until her mother died of lymphatic cancer, Anela Hana had kept Shiller's books. Noelani had barely turned thirteen the day Bruce informed her Anela had died. It was the only other time she recalled seeing such deep sorrow in Bruce's eyes, and her stomach reacted accordingly.

"Noelani, it grieves me greatly, but I have the task of telling you that Duke Fontaine and his wife, Angelique, died in a plane crash." Bruce Shiller pushed the letter toward her. "This lawyer, Shelburne Prescott, says you're named in your father's will, along with Cassandra and Jackson Fontaine. They, of course, live at Bellefontaine. Duke's plantation…on the mainland," he clarified as Noelani stared at the letter without touching it.

"He had other kids? Well, if they're named Fontaine, I guess they're legitimate."

"Noelani!"

She crumpled the page and threw it back across the desk. "What am I supposed to feel, Bruce? Sorrow…for someone who didn't give a damn about me? I've never even *met* the man!''

"You should've gone there after your mother died.''

"I didn't need him. I had Grandmother. And I had you.'' She shook her head. "Did he come to her funeral or even send flowers? I know you notified him.'' Furious now, as she always was when she thought about the man her mother had thrown away her life for, Noelani twisted a lock of hair. The auburn streaks and her five-foot-six-inch height were attributes she'd probably inherited from Duke Fontaine. If Noelani felt curious about anything, it was what traits, if any, she shared with half siblings she hadn't known existed until this minute.

"Duke cared enough to name you in his will. His sugar-cane operation makes mine look like small potatoes, kid. You think it's not obvious that you're practically killing yourself in my mill, trying to achieve what Duke's children have by birthright?''

The initial shock of Bruce's news had begun to fade. In purely mercenary terms, Noelani considered what she could do with a windfall of cash. Do here—at Shiller's, she hastily corrected. Except…wasn't there always a catch when it came to money? In this case, she'd have to admit she was Duke Fontaine's bastard.

She eyed the balled-up letter belligerently. "I can't imagine that Duke's legitimate kids want me appearing on the scene to muck up their lives. How old are they?''

"Cassandra is thirty or thirty-one. Jackson's a little younger. Nearer your age. Girl, you owe it to yourself to at least go see what this inheritance is all about. Who knows, you may like Louisiana and Duke's family well enough to stay.''

"Never! If I have an inheritance coming, let them mail

it. Depending on how much it is, maybe we can upgrade our equipment.''

"Noelani, you're not sinking money into my operation.''

"Why not? You've been more of a father to me than Duke Fontaine ever was. I've made no secret of the fact that I want to buy you out when you retire. Please, Bruce, would you phone Prescott and ask him to mail whatever I have coming from the estate?''

The man across the desk sighed. ''All right. I'll ask. But then we have to talk about what's happening to the sugar industry in Hawaii, Noelani.''

Five minutes later, she'd heard enough of his one-sided conversation to know Prescott wasn't going to merely cut her a check.

Bruce confirmed as much after signing off. ''Duke's will states you have to be present at the property distribution settlement to inherit. His firm's wiring you a ticket out of Honolulu for tomorrow. So you'd better go pack. Your connecting flight leaves Kahului in five hours.''

"Forget it! Let them keep Duke Fontaine's guilt money. I don't need anything from him. I never have,'' she blazed.

"Noelani, do this for your mother. Anela never stopped loving him. Anyway, aren't you curious? Over the years you've asked questions about your biological dad. This is your chance to get answers.''

Vaulting from her chair, Noelani stalked to the door, angry tears glistening in her eyes. ''That's dirty pool,'' she finally said in a hard-edged voice. ''Okay, I'll go. But the minute his affairs are settled, I'm on the next plane home to Maui. Have Midori's son tend my computers while I'm gone, okay? If it was up to me, I wouldn't touch a cent belonging to Duke Fontaine. I will, though, because I want to buy Shiller's when you retire. Maybe this will allow us to be a contender in the world sugar market again.''

"Noelani…wait. I'm thinking seriously of sell—" Bruce heaved his arthritic bones from the chair and hobbled around the desk. She slammed the door, cutting off a statement she didn't want to hear.

NOELANI OPENED ONE EYE and was relieved to discover that the 747 she'd boarded at Honolulu International was safely aloft. This was her first ride in a jumbo jet. Not that she'd care to broadcast her inexperience. Easing her death grip on the armrests, she tugged at the short black skirt of a linen suit she'd worn to meet the family in mourning.

An elderly woman seated next to Noelani smiled. "I'm always nervous during takeoff and landings, too. Are you continuing beyond Dallas?"

"Uh…yes, I'm going to Louisiana."

"A vacation, how nice. I hear New Orleans is having a mild fall."

"It's not a vacation. I'm visiting family. Near Baton Rouge. They grow sugar." Noelani shocked herself by referring to the Fontaines as family. Then, uncharacteristically, bared her soul to a stranger. "Actually, they're my father's family. I lived with my mother, who was Hawaiian."

"So you're *hapa haoli.* Your Caucasian half must account for the lovely auburn highlights in your hair. They're quite striking, my dear. Is your father Scottish?"

"I don't know. We never met, and now he's gone." Noelani shut her eyes. "I was ten before my hair turned this funny color. My *tutu,* that's my mom's mother, said I was born with jet-black hair like all the other Hawaiian kids in our village—on Maui. My mother kept the books for Shiller's. The largest sugarcane plantation in the islands," she added proudly.

The woman's face fell. "Divorce affects so many families these days."

Noelani didn't bother to set her straight.

"It's a shame, dear, especially as sugar must've been something your parents once had in common. But I'm sure your father's relatives will appreciate that you've come so far to pay your respects."

"Hmm." Noelani mumbled something noncommittal as she recalled her first glimpse of Duke Fontaine's photo. She'd often seen Anela crying as she gazed at a snapshot of a stranger. Noelani recalled stealing into her mom's bedroom to get a better look at the picture one day, after kids at school had taunted her about her lack of a father. Instinctively, she'd known it was the man in the faded photograph.

Noelani's seatmate moved on to another subject. "Hawaii is a wonderful vacation spot. I own a time-share on Kauai and fly over for two weeks every year. Is it boring, living full-time on an island?"

"Boring?" Noelani was never bored. But then, she had nothing else with which to compare her life. "Ours is a seaside town. Two out of three adults work in cane. Shiller's office operates year-round, so my mother never really got time off, even though the mill shuts down for two months to overhaul equipment. Social life picks up considerably during that period. My *tutu* took me to all the *luaus, huki-laus* and *huli hulis.*"

"I'm familiar with *luaus,* where they pit-roast a pig. Locals net fish, I believe, at a *hukilau. Huli huli* is beyond my scope," the woman said, and then laughed.

"Mainlanders would probably call it a chicken barbecue. But we use a sweet molasses-based sauce. And islanders grab every opportunity to sing, dance and eat."

"I'll bet you do the *hula.*"

"No way. I'm a good kick-boxer, though."

''My, that sounds more like something men would do for sport.''

Because their lunch was served, Noelani let the subject drop. Her grandmother had believed it was a fitting outlet for a young woman's pent-up hostilities. She'd signed her only granddaughter up for lessons at age thirteen, insisting it'd help Noelani work through her grief and anger. A wise woman, her *tutu*.

Following lunch, Noelani's seatmate took a nap. The woman slept all the way to Dallas. Noelani barely had an opportunity to say goodbye, as she had to run to catch her connection to Baton Rouge.

Her arrival there was greeted by pouring rain. Thunder shook the baggage terminal. If this was mild weather, as her seatmate had intimated, Noelani hoped she didn't encounter bad weather during her brief stay in Louisiana.

And her stay here would be brief.

Gazing out at the ominous skies, Noelani was engulfed by a wave of homesickness. She watched people chatting with those who'd come to pick them up and felt more alone than ever.

In Dallas, she'd seen greeters carrying signs with the names of various travelers. She peered around, hoping to see someone displaying her name—maybe even one of her half siblings. Until now, Noelani hadn't realized how much she'd counted on being met by someone from Duke's family.

What were they like, these relatives she hadn't even known about?

As the carousel began to empty it became patently obvious that Duke's kids weren't imbued with the famous southern hospitality her mother had touted the one and only time Noelani succeeded in getting her to speak about the man she loved. She was always shuffled off to her *tutu* whenever she asked questions about her father, but on that one occasion Noelani refused to be ignored. In a rare unguarded moment, Anela described her absent lover as a dashingly handsome and charming southern gentleman. A hard man with a soft heart. Anela said then she'd love Duke Fontaine until the day she died. Noelani was sure she had.

It wasn't until much later that Noelani inadvertently learned that Duke had neglected to mention his marriage at the outset of his relationship with Anela. According to Tutu, Duke had also wanted to divorce his wife and leave his Louisiana home, but Anela refused to hear of it. It wasn't until after he'd left Maui that she discovered she was pregnant—a fact that never altered her decision to let him go.

Talk about decisions… After ten minutes of watching the baggage department clear out, Noelani collected her bags and went in search of a cab. If money to help shore up Shiller's mill hadn't been her prime objective in coming to this dreary place, she'd have asked the driver to take her straight to a hotel.

But according to a terse telegram from Jackson Fontaine that had accompanied her ticket, a room awaited her at Bellefontaine. It was that address Noelani reluctantly gave the cabbie.

Through a streaked window, she watched the skyline of Baton Rouge disappear in a mass of black clouds. Her cab crossed a wide, churning expanse of muddy water the driver said was the Mississippi River.

Never before had Noelani felt so out of her element.

Soon the city gave way to wet fields of tall cane. The knot in her stomach began to uncoil. As a child she'd played hide-and-seek in similar cane rows. Friends often broke off stalks and chewed them for the juice, but Tutu had warned it would ruin her teeth, so Noelani rarely sneaked a nibble. But, oh, how she loved the smell of burnt sugar that used to hang like mist in the air when they burned fields. More of life's changes, she mused, watching field after field slide past. Agricultural developers had introduced new cane that was too tough to chew, followed by better fertilizers, which made it more advantageous to plow under old ratoons. As well, environmentalists had forced an end to burning.

The driver pointed. "Up ahead, through those magnolia trees, is Bellefontaine. In French, Bellefontaine means pretty fountain. There are fountains all over the grounds. I'm not sure how many."

Noelani scooted forward as far as her seat belt allowed and craned her neck for her first look at Duke Fontaine's home. A home he'd purportedly been willing to give up for her mother. Right! The gift of a lei promised that its recipient would return to the islands, but Duke had never made another trip to Maui. Plainly, by the look of this place, he'd gone on with his life in grand style while Anela pined hers away.

Noelani counted four fountains on a huge manicured lawn. Not even the downpour detracted from the effect of tall white pillars and wide balconies supporting a mansion larger than Queen Emma's summer palace. As a special treat one time, Tutu took Noelani on a tour of their most beloved Hawaiian ruler's part-time residence. This home was more ostentatious.

Unable to catch her breath, Noelani didn't immediately realize the cab had pulled around to the back of the house. Awed by the home's magnificence, and heedless of the falling rain, she stepped out for a better look. The fresh, rain-washed scent failed to cloak an acrid odor of charred wood.

Standing several yards away from a jutting porte cochere, Noelani saw that a section of the mansion had burned. Recently enough so that a workman was even now attempting to spread tarps over a gaping hole in the roof. He leaned far out from the top rung of an extension ladder. The man was bare-headed, and dark hair lay plastered to his skull. Faded blue jeans and a gray T-shirt were molded to his wet skin.

Suddenly the ladder slipped out from under the man's sneakers and fell hard into a flower bed below. The man was left clawing at a sagging rain gutter. He managed to grab the tarp with one hand seconds before the gutter cracked and a large section canted crazily. If he continued to kick, the section would break and plummet him to the ground below. Granted, that section of the house was only one story tall, compared to three in the main structure. Nevertheless, the man could break his neck.

Heedless of her strappy leather heels and new linen suit, Noelani tore across the soft lawn, leaving her cabbie in the process of requesting her fare.

ADAM ROSS, WHO'D BEEN HIRED by Casey Fontaine to restore Bellefontaine to historical perfection, swore roundly at his ladder. He maintained a tenuous grip on the canvas tarp and had one elbow buried in a weak rain gutter that had sustained damage during a recent kitchen fire. It wasn't bad enough that this storm had blown in from the gulf, calling a halt to the job of his dreams; now Adam feared he'd break a leg or worse and lose the contract altogether. "Dammit to hell!"

He kicked experimentally to see if maybe the ladder hadn't fallen all the way to the ground. A warning crack and further sagging of the gutter forced him to freeze. Even at that, his hundred-and-ninety-pound weight was liable to rip the entire gutter from its shaky mooring.

"Damn, damn, damn, damn, damn!" He kicked again, only halfheartedly.

"Quit swearing at the roof and hold still."

Adam wondered if he'd imagined the woman who appeared to be digging through the honeysuckle below and to the left of his swinging feet.

"Are you hurt?" a low melodic voice inquired.

"A few scrapes," he muttered. "Probably bruised a rib or two. If you can lift that ladder, sweet thing, chances are I'll live."

"Chances go down if you call me *sweet thing* again."

Adam couldn't see much of his Good Samaritan. But he fell instantly in lust with her sweet-as-sugar voice. Lately, women hadn't figured in Adam's life. He'd been too busy building a business after working his butt off to graduate from LSU in restorative architecture. Certainly he'd never been smitten with a woman based solely on her voice. That was about to change, however, if this one got him out of his current mess.

Damn, any woman capable of standing his heavy ladder upright the way the Amazon below had managed with the ease of a seasoned construction worker definitely owned a big piece of Adam's heart.

Despite a downpour few women of Adam's acquaintance would've ventured out in, this one had come from nowhere, raised his ladder and then climbed a few rungs to guide his feet to safety.

"Thanks," he panted. "You saved my—" he'd been about to say job, but that sounded too parsimonious "—my life."

"Hardly anything so dramatic. But you're welcome."

Now that the dangling man was safe and her heart had stopped hammering wildly, Noelani retreated and squinted up for a clearer look at him. She judged the man to be in his early thirties. Even on this overcast day, she could tell that his eyes were very blue. The steaming T-shirt plastered to his broad chest sported the logo of a local university.

"Are you…Jackson Fontaine?" Her throat went dry as it struck Noelani that she might have given aid to her half brother.

Adam stared down on a mass of black hair framing a face that seemed to be all eyes. He also noted a lot of leg below a short black skirt. A very nice package from his bird's-eye view. "Stay put," he ordered, having more pressing matters at the moment than cataloging his helper's pleasing attributes. "Could you hold the ladder, please? I'll secure these tarpaulins so they won't blow away."

Either he hadn't heard or else he chose to ignore her question. The fool hoisted himself off his safe perch onto the roof and left the metal ladder vibrating under Noelani's fingers. She barely caught his request—or more to the point—his edict.

He must be Jackson Fontaine. Who but the lord of the manor would deem it his right to keep a woman standing in the rain while he covered his castle? Oh, well. She couldn't get much wetter. And it was a warm rain. Since she needed to speak to him, anyway, she might as well ensure he didn't break his fool neck.

"Hey, lady. How about you pay your fare and let me be on my way?"

Adam slipped again when he heard the rough male voice heckling his savior. He tied the last tarp and quickly descended the ladder. As he did, he saw that his helper was having trouble unsticking one of her spiky heels from the mud around the honeysuckle.

Skipping the last three rungs, Adam landed hard and grasped her elbow. He jetted her across the lawn to keep her from sinking those stilts she wore into the rain-softened grass.

She jerked away from his hold. "I can walk on my own."

But Adam didn't release her until they reached the asphalt

drive. "The least I can do for causing you a problem is to pay your cabbie," he said gallantly, peeling some bills off a money clip he'd dug, with great difficulty, out of the pocket of his soaking wet jeans.

Noelani wanted to get out of the rain before she squared the debt she now owed her host. As the driver snatched his fare and jumped back into the cab, she hefted her suitcases and again wobbled gingerly onto the wet lawn, aiming for the front door of the mansion. All at once she was left clutching air.

"We'll go through the back door. It's closer."

His second abrupt order in no way endeared him to Noelani. She stomped after him, kicking mud off her shoes and muttering darkly.

Striding across slick cobblestones, Adam halted beneath a high-ceilinged breezeway. He propped her large suitcase against the wall and drew a hand through his dripping hair. "If you're huffy because we're going in the servants' entry, sweet thing, don't think you're being slighted. This is where carriages used to deposit elegant women in ball gowns who visited the plantation during the social season."

"Really? Well, I'm going to drip water all over the ball-room floor."

Adam laughed. He was glad to see that this exotic-looking woman, who'd bowled him over with her competence, also possessed a sense of humor.

More used to giving orders than taking them, Noelani felt at a disadvantage. Flipping aside her soggy hair, she said, "If you'll tell me how much my fare was, I'll reimburse you." She unzipped her purse.

"Forget it. You saved my bacon. We'll call it even."

"I'd rather not. If you won't take cash, then I insist you deduct what I owe you from my portion of the inheritance."

Adam blinked. As a good friend of Nick Devlin, the new

husband of Casey Fontaine, Adam had observed the shock reverberating through the mansion when the siblings first discovered their father had a love child no one knew anything about. Adam recalled hearing that this secret daughter of Duke's was coming for the property settlement. But not in a million years would he have imagined that he'd foolishly develop a sudden adolescent crush on the illegitimate Fontaine heir.

Damn, the rumors floating around didn't do her justice. With her uptilted eyes and black hair falling halfway to a narrow waist, wet or not, she was a beauty.

But wait. She thought he was Jackson. A mistake Adam needed to rectify. "I'm Adam Ross, not Jackson Fontaine. At the moment, I occupy one of the family's two garçonnières." He jerked a thumb toward a squat tower Noelani had noticed and wondered about. "Jackson moved into the main house after his daughter came to live with him. Today he's in New Orleans on business."

Noelani gaped at Adam, feeling foolish but not at all sure how to extricate herself from this conversation. Certainly they were now both aware that she'd mistaken his identity.

"I restore historic homes," he said pleasantly. "I guess you saw the fire damage."

"As you aren't family, Mr. Ross, would you be so kind as to direct me to Cassandra Fontaine?"

"Devlin," he corrected smoothly. "Casey doesn't go by Fontaine anymore. She married Nick last week. She's out on the property overseeing the cane cutting. Their harvest was delayed but— That's beside the point," he muttered, getting a grip on his runaway tongue.

Noelani narrowed her eyes. This guy didn't have a clue. You couldn't cut cane in this deluge; it'd only mash the stalks into the mud.

"I suppose I could take you to Auntie E," Adam continued. "She's their aunt, uh…your aunt…not mine." Adam floundered as the woman to whom he spoke seemed slow to comprehend. "Esme Fontaine is Duke's sister. She lives here at Bellefontaine."

More blank looks from the dripping newcomer.

"Esme's the only one around right now. Megan's nanny, Tanya, left to collect her from preschool right before you showed up. Jackson's daughter, Megan—are none of these names ringing any bells with you?" he finally asked.

Shaking her head, Noelani rubbed her temples. She'd started out expecting to meet two relatives, and this man— Adam Ross—stood here blathering on about an aunt, a niece and a brother-in-law. Or would Nick Devlin technically be her half brother-in-law?

"I'm sorry, I didn't catch your name," Adam said bluntly.

"Noelani. Noelani Hana. I'm… Duke Fontaine is… My mother, Anela Hana… It's too difficult to explain," she said, blinking back tears. "Look, I've had a long flight from Honolulu, and I'm wet to the skin. Do you think I could see someone about getting a towel?"

"Damn. Excuse my manners." Adam reached around her and thrust open the screen, then the door. He grappled with her bags, accidentally brushing against her as he shoved his way inside, bellowing, "Auntie E! You have company."

Turning apologetically to Noelani, Adam added, "Jackson thinks Esme's losing her hearing. Casey claims Esme plays her TV so loud she wouldn't hear if dynamite went off on this level. Excuse me a minute, please. I'll go knock on her sitting-room door."

Adam hurried away. Noelani found herself gazing around a tall-ceilinged shotgun hall, twelve to fifteen feet wide, that ran from one end of the house to the other. Scarred hardwood floors were glossy black. Large oil paintings of flowers and landscapes hung on walls illuminated by three chandeliers, whose diffused light shivered through hundreds of intricate crystal prisms. Off to her left, she saw Adam lope up a sweeping staircase.

Tiptoeing over to double French doors, Noelani peered through beveled glass panes into a room too elegant to be livable. The furniture looked uncomfortable, and there were no pillows, books or toys lying around. Everything shone with polish.

A noise had her jerking back, turning toward the stairs where a stiff-backed elderly woman slowly descended. Damn Adam Ross. He'd abandoned her to this aunt she'd never met.

Yanking discreetly at her wrinkled short skirt, Noelani also attempted to straighten the damp collar of her blouse. If she'd dared hope Esme Fontaine would be plump and jovial like her *tutu*, she would have miscalculated. The aunt wore a jade crepe dress sprigged with yellow flowers, an ensemble made dressier by a citrine choker and matching earrings. Not a hair of her perfectly coifed auburn hair was out of place. Even the jeweled collar worn by the small gray dog prancing at her heels cried out pampered wealth. She crooned to the animal in French.

As her father's sister drew nearer, Noelani was faintly relieved to see curiosity and not hostility in the pale ocean-green eyes. She recalled her mother mentioning how captivating she'd found Fontaine's green eyes. Noelani took immense satisfaction in knowing she, at least, didn't share that family trait.

"So, you're Duke's secret daughter?" Esme murmured in a slightly nasal inflection, as if English wasn't her first language. Noelani found it reminiscent of the many French-speaking South Seas islanders. Anela had spoken French fluently, and Noelani had a passable command of the language.

"Oui," she murmured, considering whether or not she ought to curtsey.

"My dear, you are wetter than Adam indicated. I sent him to check the towels in your boudoir. We've hosted a round of guests this past week, what with two funerals." She shook her head without displacing even a hair. "Even though Jackson knew the property settlement meeting was scheduled for tonight, he gave Betty Rabaud, our cook-housekeeper, the day off. But come, we mustn't keep you shivering in the hall." Esme scooped up the yipping dog and started back up the curving stairs.

Noelani shouldered her purse and her overnight case. She gamely grasped the handles of her two larger bags.

"Leave those," Esme said sharply. "Adam will bring them. Won't you, *mon chèr?*" She fluttered an age-spotted hand. Fire shot from her many rings.

Glancing up, Noelani caught sight of Adam Ross striding down the stairs. His nut-brown hair curled over his forehead as it dried. The man she'd more or less dismissed suddenly had alarm bells clanging in her head as he closed in on her.

Noelani stepped aside. Even if he was about as perfect a specimen of manhood as she'd ever chanced to encounter, she hadn't come to Baton Rouge to dally with men. And if she *did* feel like indulging in a fling, she'd never choose some honey-voiced southerner. Her mother's bleak existence had taught Noelani that much.

Work. Hard work. She'd found that to be far more satisfying than either of her own brief romances. Both had occurred while she was attending college and were irrelevant to her life—then or now.

Dropping her bags at Adam's feet without a word, she

carefully skirted his broad shoulders and ran up the stairs to catch Aunt Esme of the poker back.

Esme crossed a hall at the top of the stairs and flung open a white door. "This will be your room throughout your stay at Bellefontaine. I must say you aren't what I expected. It appears your mother at least taught you to dress like a lady."

Noelani thought of the suitcase brimming with shorts and jeans. She'd brought one suit and two semidressy outfits in case she had to be here a week or two. But she wouldn't, not if the property settlement was tonight.

As she stepped into the room, everything else flew right out of her mind. "Oh! This room is beautiful. Look—carved pineapples on the bedposts. On the cornice, as well."

"I thought you'd like the pineapple bedroom." Esme seemed pleased.

"Oh—there's a pineapple carved on the ceiling medallion." Now Noelani saw that the bedspread, too, had been crocheted in a pineapple motif. "Do you grow pineapples at Bellefontaine?"

"Mercy, no. It's generally thought that early Louisiana plantation owners hosted visitors from the islands." Esme lowered her voice. "There's an old custom in Louisiana of delivering a fresh, whole pineapple to guests on their arrival. It's said that if guests overstayed their welcome, they'd wake up to a cut pineapple on their dressers, signifying it was time to leave."

"Uh, thanks for the warning, but I'm not planning to overstay my welcome."

Esme chuckled as she backed out the door. "You're Duke's daughter, all right. I do believe you'll give Cassandra and Jackson a run for their money. If you'd like a tour of Bellefontaine after you've had a chance to freshen up, I'm in the last room at the south end of the hall. Dinner is at eight. Cocktails at the table tonight. Except for Adam, you and I have the place to ourselves until seven. Tanya, Miss Megan's nanny, has taken the child to an after-school movie in town. Ah, here's Adam with your cases.''

She moved to one side, allowing him room to enter. "I know you're impatient to get back to work, Adam. However, I was telling Noelani we're dining at eight tonight. I trust we'll see you then?''

He gave a brief jerk of his chin, which sent a gold cross he wore around his neck swinging. Even though the room was large, he seemed to fill it as he entered and set her bags near the bed. Ignoring Noelani, he turned and went out again, chatting amiably with Aunt Esme about dinner.

Overwhelmed and more homesick than ever, Noelani flung herself across the crocheted pineapple spread. She blinked up at a frothy canopy hooked to the four corners of the tall bedposts. The tears that stung the backs of her eyelids didn't fall—but only by the sheer force of her will. She hadn't expected to be welcomed like a long-lost sister, but she didn't need hired help like Adam Ross slighting her as a blatant reminder that she didn't belong at Bellefontaine.

Vaulting off the bed, intent on changing out of her wet clothes, she made up her mind. By damn, she'd give Cassandra and Jackson a run for their money, just like Esme had predicted. *Their* money? Well, her portion of it, anyway.

They were divvying up Duke Fontaine's guilt money tonight, and all the people involved knew it.

CHAPTER TWO

ADAM ESCAPED NOELANI'S ROOM not a second too soon. Her light, spicy perfume seemed to follow him. He'd promised Esme he'd show up for dinner, but he doubted it'd be an enjoyable occasion given the vulnerability he'd noticed in their guest's eyes as they left her alone in the pineapple bedroom.

Once Jackson got back, maybe Adam would beg off. The storm had delayed his project; he'd had to cancel the roofers. It should be finished already, but he'd had trouble matching the mansion's old shingles. The historical society's rules for preservation made no exceptions when it came to building materials.

As Adam busied himself measuring for kitchen cabinet hardware, his thoughts kept straying—to Noelani Hana. He hadn't liked leaving her in that big old room where she looked so small and lonely. Maybe not so small, he mused. He'd assumed that as a rule Hawaiians were short. She had to be five-seven or eight. Still, short compared to his own six-two. And she certainly wasn't very big.

He *had* to stop thinking about her, had to keep his mind on his work. He didn't need distractions, Adam reminded himself. Refurbishing Bellefontaine was his lucky break. Not only because of the generous fee he and Casey had negotiated or the way this job would enhance his reputation, but because of Bellefontaine's proximity to Magnolia Manor, his old family home. His mom had been forced to sell it after a nervous breakdown that resulted in permanent hospitalization. Adam's goal had always been to buy it back one day.

Right before Nick invited him to leave Natchez and bid on this job, Adam learned Magnolia Manor might soon be offered for sale by the state. He couldn't help feeling the renovation of Bellefontaine had been an omen, bringing him within reach of his heart's desire. So no matter how pretty, lost or vulnerable old Duke's illegitimate daughter was, Adam had to forget her and stay focused on his objective.

Which proved easier said than done, especially as the afternoon wore on. Several times Noelani Hana's laughter interrupted Adam's work as she toured the house with Aunt Esme. *No, he wouldn't be skipping dinner tonight.* Even though he should…

NOELANI NEEDED TO REST after the tour. Aunt Esme had brought Bellefontaine's history to life, and Noelani's head throbbed with facts. While she might forget these facts in time, the pride with which Esme had imparted her family history would linger. Built in the early 1800s, Bellefontaine had withstood the ravages of the Civil War. Noelani knew little about that war, but Esme made it sound as if it had been fought yesterday. For the first time, Noelani was glad she didn't have what Esme called Yankee blood in her. Auntie E was a southern belle from the top of her coiffed hair to the toes of her designer shoes.

Rechecking her watch, Noelani thought she had an hour or two for a nap before changing for dinner. She drifted off quickly, and had no idea how long she'd slept when she awoke to voices and hurried footsteps in the hall. Her room was dark. Turning on a lamp, Noelani saw it was seven-thirty. She sprang off the bed in a panic. Her bags still sat where she'd left them after pulling out the slacks and blouse she'd hurriedly donned for her house tour. She felt rumpled again and pawed through the larger case, this time removing both of the dresses she'd packed. Why hadn't she asked how dressy people would be tonight? She eyed a sleeveless red linen shift. The other, a black crepe, was definitely dressier. The red, she decided, digging out red sandals. Faced with meeting Duke Fontaine's legitimate heirs, her spirits needed the bolstering red offered. She'd originally thought the family might be in mourning, but as Esme had worn a flowery dress today, Noelani doubted anyone expected her to wear black.

She splashed water on her face, then slipped into her dress and sandals. She started down the stairs with five minutes to spare. All the while, she prayed she wouldn't be the last to arrive.

She was. Talk stopped dead. The men's chairs scraped back the moment she appeared in the archway. Her knees knocked. Her palms were sweating. Determined not to show her nervousness, she breezed into the room. "Sorry I'm late. I fell asleep. Must be jet lag," she said as though she were a seasoned traveler.

Esme was slower to rise. "You'll sit here," she directed. Her miniature schnauzer, Toodles, lay curled on a velvet pillow under Esme's chair.

Noelani gripped the back of her assigned seat. A place mat peeked out from beneath off-white china. She spotted lead crystal and real silver. A soup bowl sat perfectly centered on her dinner plate, and a matching soup tureen steamed as it sat just so between etched, hand-blown glass fly-catchers. Esme had explained that before Bellefontaine was fitted for air-conditioning in the 1940s, the bottom of these globes were filled with sugar water to attract the flies that came into the house through unscreened open windows. Noelani tried to remember what the odd contraption hanging beside the light fixture above the table was called. Ah, yes. A shoo-fly fan. According to Esme, a slave child would sit out of sight in a corner and operate the fan with a rope pulley, which controlled the sweeping blades. It was impossible for Noelani to comprehend what life must have been like back then.

Anytime she felt as nervous as she was now, trivia tended to cycle over and over in her head. Aunt Esme had given her plenty of trivial facts.

"Noelani, you've met Adam. Jackson's at the end. His daughter, Megan, is to your right next to her nanny, Tanya Carson." Esme inclined her head toward a thin young woman. "And this," she finished breathlessly, "is Noelani Hana." Esme smiled through a series of greetings. At last, she suggested they all sit again, and she requested Jackson serve the soup.

Noelani detected a similarity between Duke Fontaine—as he looked in the snapshot she'd tucked into her purse at the last minute—and his son. Brown hair streaked blond by the sun had been recently cut. His navy eyes were shaded by indecently long lashes, which Noelani noted his daughter shared. Megan's eyes were gray, however, and her mop of curls a much richer brown. Athletically built, Jackson Fontaine appeared tanned, fit and stylish, although casually put together with that look only top designers could achieve.

Tanya Carson, young for a nanny in Noelani's estimation, had pouty lips and wore big glasses that gave her violet eyes a permanently myopic look.

Adam and Tanya had been discussing music, and they continued their conversation after everyone sat. Noelani deduced that jazz was Tanya's area of study. Although the young woman chattered nonstop with Adam, her eyes followed Jackson's every move. In fact, she gazed dreamily at him, although Noelani doubted he even noticed.

It was just as well that Adam and Tanya were talking, considering no one else at the table bothered. Megan was practically falling asleep in her soup. And no wonder, given the late hour. Noelani tried to draw her out several times to no avail.

Really, though, she was dying to inquire if what Adam had said about cutting wet cane was true. If so, what type of harvester did they use? Bruce's operation could benefit from cutting stalks beaten down by Maui's heavy rains. Maybe she'd have to wait until Casey joined them before she could ask. Since Jackson seemed preoccupied, and his silent wraith of a child didn't respond to her overtures, Noelani endured a tense meal except for an occasional word from the stiff-backed Esme.

The soup, a creamy yellow squash with just a hint of nutmeg flavoring, was delicious. Ravenous, Noelani ate every drop. By the time she finished the fresh spinach salad that came next, she was full. As she avoided red meat, she was dismayed to see the others load roast beef, potatoes smothered in brown gravy and creamed baby carrots onto their plates.

Declining the beef, Noelani dipped out small portions of the side dishes. At that point even Tanya and Adam ate in silence. The knot in Noelani's stomach grew.

Toying with her carrots, she glanced up once and found Adam staring at her. He gave her a warm smile, and she mustered a small one in return.

"Red is your color," he said offhandedly, as if he ought to make some remark, simply because she'd caught him staring at her.

"That's good. It's my favorite color." To her own ears, her voice sounded rusty from disuse. Understandable, considering how long it'd been since she'd mumbled hello to a tableful of folks who virtually ignored her.

Jackson set his fork down and used a napkin to blot his lips. "I have no doubt you are who you say. But did you by chance bring your birth certificate, Noelani?"

"Not by chance. Your lawyer requested it. But if you're hoping to verify your father's name on it, I can save you the trouble. It's not there. I'm Noelani Hana, daughter of Anela Hana, period." She lifted her chin and met his eyes without blinking.

Jackson's cheeks reddened under his tan. "Duke had a copy of your birth certificate in his files. You were born October 8, 1975, at Wailuku, Maui. The purpose of asking for the original is to match it to Duke's copy."

"Fine. It's in my suitcase. I'll get it and you can study it to your heart's content."

Esme arched an eyebrow. "It's plain the *jeune fille* has Duke's short fuse."

"The *girl* also understands French," Noelani muttered. "I throw that out so no one will assume they can talk around me that way."

Esme coughed discreetly. Jackson made no effort to disguise his scowl. "We aren't trying to dispute your cla—" He broke off as a three-toned doorbell played loudly up and then down the scale.

"Excuse me." Rising, he slid back his chair. "That's probably Shel Prescott. I'll take him to my office. Aunt Esme, will you phone Casey, then bring Noelani over after the two of you finish eating?"

"I'm through." Noelani folded her napkin. "Shall I help clear the table?"

"Tanya will stack dishes tonight. Betty will wash them in the morning. You run along and find your document. By the time you return, I'll have notified Cassandra of Shelburne's arrival."

Inclining her head, Noelani left the room and slowly

climbed the stairs. Had Jackson been about to say they weren't disputing her claim on Duke's money? She hadn't made any claim. *They'd* contacted *her.* She wondered if his comment implied they were looking for a way to cut her out of Duke's will.

She wouldn't put it past anyone raised by Duke Fontaine. Noelani knew Bruce liked the man, but what had Fontaine ever done to earn the love her mother reserved for no one but him until the day she died?

Noelani retrieved the certificate. She detoured past the bath long enough to press a damp washcloth to her face and put on lip gloss. Making her way downstairs again, she let out a surprised "Ack" and threw up an arm to ward off a bulky form appearing suddenly in her path.

"Careful," drawled a soft masculine voice. "Were you planning to karate-chop me in the old jugular?" Adam asked with a laugh.

"Yes, as a matter of fact." Noelani was a master kick-boxer. Had she not recognized him when she did, Adam Ross might have been flattened by a well-placed kick. Of course, she thought wryly, in the process she'd have ripped off every button from hem to waist of her red dress.

Adam eyed her, still trying to decide whether or not she was joking.

"Why were you sneaking around?" She deftly side-stepped him.

"I wasn't sneaking. I was waiting for you. Casey and Nick showed up two seconds after you left the table. They and Esme went on to Jackson's office. I've been appointed your escort."

"Aunt Esme showed me the office on our tour. I don't need escorting, but thanks, anyway. Or…were you instructed to delay me long enough so they can plot how to get rid of me?"

''Get rid of you? That's a pretty paranoid statement, don't you think?''

She lifted a shoulder delicately as they fell into step. ''I imagine the lawful duo wishes Papa had drowned the mongrel at birth.''

''Can't say you look like any kind of mongrel I've ever seen,'' he teased.

Their shoulders brushed as they walked down the hall. Noelani moved a step to the right to avoid touching him. The man was far too big—and far too quick with his flirtatious comments. Adam Ross made her uneasy.

''There.'' He pointed to a door at the end of the hall. ''I was going to offer to go in with you if you feel you need protecting. But you give the impression you can take care of yourself.'' Walking backward a short distance, Adam mockingly doffed an imaginary hat, then turned and left her on her own.

''Honestly,'' she muttered, feeling the doorknob slip under her sweaty hand. Darting a glance down the hall to make sure Adam wasn't spying on her, Noelani quickly wiped her palm down her dress. Taking a firmer grip on the knob, she threw back her shoulders and opened the door.

The instant she entered the room, her eyes landed on Cassandra Fontaine Devlin. Except for weepy, bruiselike smudges under her eyes, and a long, dark auburn ponytail, she shared the Fontaine look. A narrow face and foxlike chin proved a foil for her unsettling green eyes. At least they unsettled Noelani, because she sensed a vulnerability akin to her own in Duke's daughter. *His legitimate daughter.*

Jackson straightened away from an antique desk made of dark cherry. A white-haired, paunchy man sat behind it, swirling ice in a tumbler of amber liquid. The minute Jackson noticed Noelani, he came to greet her. "Casey. Nick. Shelburne. This is Noelani Hana."

Nick Devlin unfolded his rangy body from a chair to extend a hand.

Flustered by the hurt expression on her half sister's face, Noelani almost didn't shake Nick's hand. She did in the end, although she clamped her teeth tight to keep her chin from quaking.

"Shall we get on with this?" Casey abruptly demanded in a husky, scratchy voice. "Some of us get up at dawn to earn our keep."

Jackson frowned a bit. Nick sat quickly and slipped a bracing arm around his wife's narrow shoulders.

"Noelani, there's a vacant seat next to Aunt Esme," Jackson said.

Actually there wasn't. Toodles had claimed the brocade cushion. But Esme scooped the dog into her lap, allowing Noelani space to sit.

"Shelburne promised this won't take long." Jackson crossed the room again.

"It won't," the lawyer reiterated. "I already told Jackson that Duke and Angelique's property disbursement is fairly straightforward." Prescott pushed aside a stack of papers. Opening his briefcase, he removed a set of stapled documents.

"Cassandra and Jackson, Angelique made a list of her jewelry for insurance purposes. With the exception of her wedding set, which was previously earmarked for the woman Jackson will one day marry, she split the items equally between you. As she did the cash in her personal account. I must say, since she financed their recent trip abroad, it's a modest sum. Thirty thousand, give or take a few hundred."

Casey leaned forward, tension stiffening her slender back.

"Why would Maman finance their trip? Duke said he planned it as an anniversary gift—or more of a second honeymoon," she said, telegraphing Noelani a smug "so there" message.

"I'll get to that. Let me finish. Duke has allotted a yearly stipend for his sister, Esme. While technically the house passes to Jackson, a codicil gives Esme the right to live out her days at Bellefontaine. Wisteria Cottage, which belonged to Duke's mother, and its five acres, is in a separate trust for the use of current or future Fontaine heirs. I understand, Casey, that you and Nick are currently living in the cottage."

"Yes. Temporarily. What about the mill and the cane fields?" Casey asked, sliding to the edge of her straight-backed chair.

Shel again scolded her with a glance over his half glasses. Nick ran a hand up Casey's back and lightly massaged her neck. She automatically slumped sideways, curving into the hollow below his arm.

"The cane fields, outbuildings, mill, all warehouses and the refinery Duke purchased a few weeks before his death are to be divided equally among Jackson Fontaine, Cassandra Fontaine Devlin and Noelani Hana. I've prepared an inventory of all assets, liabilities and cash connected to the aforementioned properties. The bank has provided this independent audit, which Jackson requested." Getting up, Shelburne handed each of the three siblings a packet.

Noelani watched Jackson, Casey and Nick pore over the pages. She folded hers in half and cleared her throat. "Jackson, I…ah…don't know if you're aware that I knew nothing of this prior to Mr. Prescott's letter. It was never my intention to intrude on your lives. I feel the best thing for everyone would be if you and your sister cashed out my part and let me be on my way."

Casey sat up in a rush. "Finally, something that makes sense. I'm agreeable. Aren't you, Jackson?"

Jackson emerged from a stupor. "Casey, have you checked the bottom line? Except for the funds Maman left, which if we're lucky will cover this month's operating expenses, we're property rich but cash poor."

Casey flipped to the last page of the report. "How can that be?" She glared at Shelburne, while she repeated the question.

He set his tumbler aside. "Obviously Duke didn't expect to die on this trip, Casey. Both his banker and I advised against buying the refinery from Roland Dewalt. Duke wanted it. Thank God, he didn't second-mortgage the house to get it."

"No," Jackson snapped. "But he speculated on raw-sugar prices last season, banking prices would go up. They fell several cents a pound instead. We took a major loss. I had no idea until I saw the bank audit."

"Even so," Casey said stubbornly, "the last five years our yield has been up. Way up."

Noelani's head whipped back and forth as she tried to follow their talk. Among other things, Duke Fontaine had apparently been a worse businessman than he was a father. Well, to her, anyway.

Prescott held up a hand. "Duke always walked a financial tightrope. He gave you all free rein with spending. Angelique went overboard on clothes and cars for herself and you kids. She entertained lavishly—the Fontaines did everything first class. The upkeep alone on Bellefontaine is horrendous. Casey, you asked Duke to update the fleet of trucks and cane trailers. He bought everything new. You wanted the most expensive harvester. He bought it. Then you figure in college for three. To say nothing of the years he's subsidized Anela Hana and her child."

"Wait, a darned minute!" Noelani sprang up. "I went to Hawaii State on a full scholarship. My mother kept books for Bruce Shiller's company for her money. We took nothing from Duke Fontaine."

Prescott's eyes darkened sympathetically. "Duke allowed you to think that. He insisted on providing for Anela and you. He said she was a proud woman, and you were filled with anger. Through Bruce Shiller, Duke arranged to pay your mother's salary, including periodic raises. After she died, he continued the practice for you. He funded your scholarship, Noelani. Read the audit. It's all there in black and white."

Eyes suddenly awash in tears, she couldn't have seen the figures if she'd looked right at them. Shaking her head vigorously in denial, Noelani ran headlong from the room. She'd phone Bruce. They were lying! They had to be. This was all a trick to make her feel bad so she'd say they didn't owe her anything.

She'd seen a phone at the base of the stairs. She found it, figured out the time difference in her head, then dialed Hawaii. Bruce would still be in his office. "Hi, Midori, it's Noelani. Let me speak to Bruce. It's urgent." She tapped a toe impatiently until he came on the line. "Bruce, the Fontaines are trying to imply Duke paid Mama's salary. And mine. They claim he…he funded my scholarship."

There was a silence.

"Bruce? Did you hear me?" Noelani's hand tightened as the man at the other end sighed, then began talking fast.

"How could you?" she said in a hushed tone. "Guilt money, Bruce? You helped Duke Fontaine ease his guilty conscience. You let him trade money for Mama's broken heart. How could you?"

Shiller talked faster. Noelani chewed her lower lip to keep the tears at bay. And she cast her eyes toward the high ceiling. "I know the cost of shipping sugar from the islands has risen twentyfold in as many years. I've seen other growers sell out."

Noelani slumped against the wall. She was tempted to cut her losses and wash her hands of the Fontaines. But if she did, she could kiss her plan for Shiller's goodbye. "You said yourself this inheritance is mine by right of birth. I'm not leaving Louisiana until I have what's due me. I only wish you'd told me the truth before I had to hear it from Duke's legitimate kids." She couldn't stay angry with Bruce, the man who'd been more of a father to her than her own. Her voice softened. "Bye, Bruce. I'll keep you posted."

She set the receiver down gently, dried her eyes and lifted her head in time to see Jackson Fontaine hovering half in, half out of his office.

"Are you okay?" He stepped out of the room and she steeled herself to meet him.

"Your figures are apparently correct. I swear I had no idea my mother or I took one cent from your father. I'm sorry for my outburst."

Jackson rubbed his neck. "It's okay." His lips twitched. "Yours was nothing compared to the fit Casey threw when we first learned about you."

"I imagine it was a shock. Only I didn't ask to be born, remember?"

He spread a hand and invited her to enter the office ahead of him. "This is a situation none of us asked for. We're all in the same boat. And there's a lot at stake here, so we're going to have to make the best of it."

"You propose doing that how?"

"Well, you could go back to Maui and leave the resolution in our hands."

"Not on your life! Is it necessary for me to hire a separate lawyer?"

"God, no. In my experience, the more lawyers involved, the muddier a situation gets, to say nothing of tripling costs."

"So there you have it. I suspect you have a plan up your sleeve."

"Not up my sleeve, exactly. Would you be willing to sign an agreement to defer finalizing your portion of the property until Casey and I bring in this year's crop? Or at least until we settle the outstanding insurance claims?"

"I don't think I'm willing to sign anything. At least not tonight."

"Mind telling me why not?"

"When it comes down to it, Jackson, I know cane as well as you and your sister do. We all have a vested interest in bringing your crop in at a high yield."

"You say that now in the heat of the moment. Tomorrow you might feel differently." Looking unhappy, he returned to the desk where Shel Prescott still sat, having obviously refreshed his drink. Noelani returned to her seat beside Aunt Esme, who still stroked a snoring Toodles.

Jackson spoke up. "In spite of our denials, accusations and disbelief, I believe we can agree this problem isn't going away. I propose we sleep on it and meet again at breakfast, to see if anyone's been struck by some great revelation during the night. Shel's promised he'll recheck the status of our insurance claims."

Casey twisted her ponytail and lifted it off her neck. Sighing deeply, she deferred to her brother with a shrug.

"Sounds like a plan to me," Nick said. "Everyone's pretty emotional tonight."

Dropping her hair, Casey got to her feet. "It'll have to be early, Jackson. If saving our butts depends on bringing in the cane, that's all the more reason for me to be out in the fields rather than stuck in some meeting.''

''Betty's due at six. Is six-thirty okay with you, Noelani?''

''Sure. I've got nowhere else to be.''

''Aunt Esme. You're remarkably quiet this evening.''

''Bellefontaine has survived many ups and downs. It passed to my brother during one of its worst slumps. He built it into the voice of sugar in Louisiana—indeed, in the whole South. You're all of his blood. If the three of you pull together, I have no doubt we'll get through this.'' She stood, managing to look regal even after a long day. Carrying the yawning schnauzer, she marched to the door. ''Toodles and I will skip breakfast at that uncivilized hour. We'll see everyone for cocktails before supper.''

Casey and Nick followed Esme out after all good-nights were said.

Jackson remained by the desk. It was clear to Noelani that he wanted some time alone with the lawyer.

''I napped before dinner, so I'm wide awake. The rain's stopped. Is it all right if I change clothes and go for a walk?''

''Fine with me. There are night-lights in the upper and lower halls. Oh, and carriage lamps on the fence posts. The fence marks the perimeter of Bellefontaine.''

''Is there danger of falling in an abandoned well if I hike out to the cane? I love hearing the wind rustling through the stalks at night. It relaxes me.''

''Casey, too. Hmm. I guess you have that in common. But to answer your question—no wells. Feel free to wander. Except the rows aren't lit.''

''I won't go into the cane. I doubt your sister would approve of me touching her precious stalks.'' She gathered her papers and left the two men.

"Noelani," Jackson called before she disappeared. "Casey idolized Duke. He let her down. It's him she's furious with. Not you."

"My mother gave him up, you know. She only spoke to me about him once. She swore she never had any idea he was married when she first got involved with him, and when she found out, she sent him away. To the best of my knowledge, she never asked him for anything. No money. No contact. Nothing. But she never stopped loving him. Which made no sense to me, and I'm pretty furious at him, too. I'll see you at six-thirty tomorrow."

Noelani returned to her room, where she tugged on jeans, a tank top and a lightweight white cotton sweater. Pinning her hair into a loose bun, she tiptoed softly down the hall so as not to wake Tanya, Megan or Aunt Esme. In the aftermath of the squall, the night air was heavy. Too muggy for jeans, but Noelani was no stranger to the biting bugs that came out at night around cane.

Bellefontaine in all its glory made her catch her breath, not for the first time. She was used to living in a two-bedroom, single-story duplex. The bedrooms had no glass at the windows, but screens to let in cool ocean breezes.

The minute she stepped outside, Noelani dragged in a huge lungful of the heavy, humid air.

She wandered around front, where she paused and listened to the varied tunes played by the fountains. Closing her eyes, she let the day's tensions slowly seep away.

Noelani dug in her pocket and found a stray penny, then made a wish, tossing the coin at the top tier near a carved pineapple decorating the largest fountain.

Something scraped off to her right. Crouching instinctively, she whirled.

"Easy. Easy there." A rich, lazy voice reproached her from the darkened porch of the nearby garçonnière. Adam

Ross disconnected himself from the shadows and stepped into view. He wore jeans and a white T-shirt, and held a frosty beer.

"I've heard that people throw coins in fountains. I've never seen anyone actually do it. Is it more effective than wishing on the first night star?"

Noelani glanced upward. "I'd be out of luck tonight. There are no stars."

Adam leaned a shoulder against the rough siding and took another drink. He gestured with the bottle. "It's muggy as hell tonight. Want one of these?"

"Sure." She sauntered toward him. "Is the weather keeping you up?"

"Nah. I'm a night owl. Always have been." He bent, reached behind him, opened an ice chest and pulled out another cold bottle.

"Staying up alone, drinking the night away, seems a sure path to perdition," she said lightly. She accepted the bottle after he wrenched off the top.

Adam toyed with the idea of suggesting she come inside and keep him company —then he *wouldn't* be alone. He settled on a different tack. "Worried about my soul, sugar pie?"

"No. But I think you should be." The man was certainly glib with his cutesy endearments. Maybe it was the look in his eyes when he called her sugar pie that made it feel less insulting than when he'd thrown "sweet thing" at her. Anyway, she let it pass.

"If it'll ease your mind, two of these is my limit. Throughout the day I drink bottled water. How did your meeting go?"

She didn't know how to answer without going into the whole convoluted story. And the Fontaines had enough troubles without her spreading tales of their financial woes. Lifting her beer, she sipped, then rolled the cold bottle across her cheek.

"That bad, huh? I saw Shelburne Prescott peel out of here right before you came out. Figured something happened."

She shrugged. "I went up to change. He stayed to have a word with Jackson."

"Too bad you ditched the red dress. I liked it."

"Dresses aren't exactly conducive to walking in the cane. I'm on my way to have a look at it. Thanks for the beer." She wagged the bottle at him and made ready to leave.

"Does Jackson know you're out roaming the property this late?"

"He said it was fine. Why?"

"Doesn't seem too wise, considering the stuff that's gone on lately."

"What stuff?"

"Well, the kitchen fire was set. Plus, the arsonist cut all the garden hoses before starting the fire. Casey's new harvester mysteriously went poof one night. She's only recently taken delivery of its replacement. Stuff like that."

He'd managed to stop her cold in her tracks. "The Fontaines have enemies?"

Adam didn't answer.

"Who'd do such terrible things?"

"Maybe a disgruntled former employee. Casey also caught him in the greenhouse office where she keeps records on her hybrids. Supposedly he confessed to setting the blaze. He's in jail now."

"So, if they caught him, I should be okay. You're trying to scare me, aren't you."

"Call it erring on the side of caution. The guy swears someone hired him anonymously. There's no proof. Even so, I think I'll mosey along with you to be safe."

A thrill shot Noelani's pulse skyrocketing. But she'd be

darned if she'd let Adam Ross see she welcomed his attention. "How do I know I won't be safer alone than with you?" She gazed at him demurely through her lashes.

"You'll have to take my word for it, sugar pie. Or if you prefer, I'll escort you straight upstairs to your little ol' bed."

Noelani debated whether or not she should deflate his ego, and decided not to bother. She was more concerned about what he'd said. If the Fontaines had enemies, by virtue of her connection to Duke, they became hers, too. Come to think of it, Adam Ross had pretty free access to the property any hour of the day or night. Maybe someone should keep an eye on him. *Someone like her.*

CHAPTER THREE

JACKSON, NICK AND SHELBURNE rose quickly to their feet when Noelani entered the dining room the next morning. Casey stared at her over a mug of steaming coffee, her jade eyes still distant and cold.

"Coffee and juice are on the sideboard," Jackson said. "If you want what we're having, Betty's cooking on the stove out back on the screened porch. Most years it's used for canning during hot summers. But until Adam restores the kitchen, Betty will prepare our family meals there."

"Coffee's fine. I'm not big on breakfast." Noelani poured a cup and wondered whether to take a seat next to Prescott or one beside Casey. She chose to be nearer the sideboard, and caught Casey's unapologetic shift closer to her husband.

Noelani blew on her coffee to cool it. "You've got healthy-looking cane," she said casually. "Depending on how much acreage you have, your yield could be spectacular."

Jackson said "Two thousand acres," a figure large enough to impress Noelani.

"Stay out of my cane," Casey said, slamming down her mug. "The fields are *my* responsibility. Duke left me in charge before he went on the trip."

"Casey." Jackson and Nick cautioned her simultaneously.

Noelani wasn't going to be walked on. "I distinctly heard

Mr. Prescott say the cane, the mill, the refinery and everything to do with the business is a three-way split.''

''Maybe Duke wasn't of sound mind,'' Casey said, clenching her hands.

Nick stroked her tense arm. ''Let me figure a way to help you buy Noelani out.''

''No. You sank a bundle in the boatworks, and now with Moreau defaulting...''

''Casey's right. Thanks, Nick, but we'll manage.'' Jackson drank from his mug. ''So, Noelani. You slept on our last discussion?''

''Yes. I'm staying until the business is solvent. I hadn't planned to, but I phoned Bruce again last night. He'll send me more of my clothes and things.''

Turning to Prescott, who'd mopped up the remaining egg on his plate with a pancake, Jackson said, ''You reran those figures? There's no way Casey and I can cash out Noelani today with whatever Maman left?''

Wiping his pudgy face with a napkin, Shel tossed it down and tilted back in his chair, rubbing a hand over his portly middle. ''The way I see it, Jackson, you need every dime you can scare up to pay your crew. Plus, you'll have to borrow to meet the mill payroll.''

Casey came hissing out of her chair. ''We have money coming in from twenty-five growers and forty or so landlords who dump cane at our mill.''

Jackson scrubbed a hand over his face. ''Thank God for that influx of cash, since the insurance companies are delaying until the National Transportation Safety Board finishes evaluating the crash. Casey, we'll need those funds to buy supplies and to pay the landlords based on the core sampling of their loads.''

''That's your end, Jackson. Mine is to grow the best

damned cane in the state. I'm doing that,'' Casey said. ''My hybrids are thriving.''

A wiry woman of undetermined age, an unlit cigarette dangling from the corner of her mouth, stepped into the kitchen through a side door. ''Y'all want any more food before I dish it up and stick it in the warming oven for those lay-a-beds?''

''No thanks, Betty.'' Jackson spoke as he glanced around the table. ''Noelani?''

''I'm fine, thanks.''

''Betty, this is our…uh…Noelani Hana. You'll be adding a plate for her, maybe until Epiphany, which is when we tally our tonnage at the refinery.''

''I don't eat meat,'' Noelani supplied, smiling at the woman.

''Well, I ain't no short-order cook,'' Betty returned, propping her hands on skinny hips.

''I didn't mean…'' Noelani scrabbled to rephrase her intent. ''Don't add extra for me if you're preparing a meat dish.''

Everyone at the table skewered her with a glance. She glared back defiantly. ''I'll make do with salads and vegetables if you're serving them, anyway. If none of you eat fruit, I'll shop for some. I'm sure you must have a free corner in the fridge.''

''Not a problem,'' Jackson injected smoothly. ''Make a list. Betty can pick extra fruit up each week when she shops.''

Shelburne shoved back his chair. ''Since you're leaving Duke's disbursements in limbo for now, I'll be on my way. Good vittles as always, Betty. 'Course, my cardiologist won't thank you.''

''If you're gonna eat like that, you've gotta exercise,'' she said, then withdrew.

Prescott clapped a hand on Jackson's shoulder. "Say, Harold Broderick might be in jail, but he's some piece of work. Good thing Nick and Casey ID'd him as your vandal. I hear he's not giving in, though. Seems he's hired a pricey New Orleans defense lawyer. Who'd think selling a cane harvester on the black market would pay well enough to afford that kind of counsel?"

Jackson tugged at his lower lip. "Maybe Broderick got the proceeds from other robberies."

"Yeah? Could he. Well, like I said, I have to hit the road. No, don't get up, Jackson. I know the way out. I'm sure you have things to do."

Casey stacked her plate and Nick's. Reaching over, she added Shelburne's. "Are you finished?" she asked her brother. "Time I made my rounds of the fields."

Nick drained his cup. "I should've brought my car. I have an appointment with a company I may hire to do the interior of my next floating casino."

Jackson went to the sideboard and refilled his travel mug. "I've got a growers' meeting in town at eight. Afterward, several of us are taking a few of our D.C. lobbyists to lunch. We'd like them to bend somebody's ear on the Beltway. Get them to raise the cap on the three cents we get for sugar on the world market. Either that or tighten controls on Mexico to make sure they aren't shipping more than their quota."

"You know they are," Casey said with a snort.

"Apparently our friends in high places aren't aware of that. Or else they don't care."

Noelani found their discussion interesting. But she didn't want them to walk out and leave her twiddling her thumbs. "What shall I do today?"

"Your nails?" Casey said too sweetly.

Noelani displayed her short, efficiently clipped nails. "In

Hawaiian, the name Hana means work. I'm not sitting on my butt for five months when I have thirty-three-and-a-third percent interest in your operation.''

Casey all but lost her grip on the plates she'd gathered.

"You and Nick shove off," Jackson said quickly. "I have just the job for Noelani. What with the funeral, the wedding and the delay caused by the missing harvester, we put off our yearly *cochon de lait.* The workers are grumbling. So, Casey, I'm giving Noelani the file and putting her in charge of arranging a pigfest.''

"Like a *luau,* you mean?" Noelani straightened in anticipation.

"Brother!" Casey rolled her eyes. "This ought to be a farce and a half.''

Nick exchanged unreadable glances with Jackson, then aimed a kiss at Casey's neck. He hustled her through the archway into the makeshift kitchen.

"Top off your mug and follow me, Noelani. Our *cochon de lait* is similar to a *luau.* It's a party that usually kicks off harvest. Several whole pigs are roasted either on a spit or in a pit. We happen to use spits.''

"Then a *pua'a?* That's a plain pig roast." She shook her head. "Disgusting practice to a vegetarian—but I understand if it's your tradition.''

"Whatever. It's all spelled out in the file. But instead of ukuleles and hula dancers, we hire Cajun and Zydeco bands. We serve mint juleps." He opened his office door, crossed the room and pulled an accordion folder out of a cabinet. "If you need help finding caterers or musicians, or wording the flyer, Aunt Esme can advise you.''

"Is there a place you'd like me to work on this?" She gave a sidelong glance at his cluttered desk.

"There's a desk in the kitchen—the fire missed it. You can use it if you're not in Adam's way. There's another in the family room upstairs. Tanya and Megan hang out there, reading, playing or watching TV. That may turn out to be a little noisy if you're trying to talk on the phone. Oh, hey— speaking of Megan, I promised I'd get her up and read her a story before I leave for my meeting.''

''She's sweet. Do you have her full-time or do you split custody with her mom?''

Jackson stopped abruptly. ''Since you'll be living here temporarily, you should know Megan's history. Her mom and I were never married. Unfortunately, Janis fell in with a bad crowd. She's doing time. If she phones, she's not to talk with Megan. In fact, it's better if no one discusses her mother.''

''As you wish.'' Noelani put some distance between herself and Jackson. She'd been feeling more comfortable with him, but what now ran through her mind was *like father, like son.* Spawning illegitimate children seemed no big deal to the Fontaine men. No wonder Megan looked lost. Well, Noelani figured, she and the little girl had a lot in common. Still…Jackson tucked his daughter into bed at night and cared enough to read her stories. Perhaps he was a cut above his father, after all.

She hung back as he took the stairs two at a time. Turning left, she shoved open the door that led to the kitchen. As she stepped inside, she stumbled over Adam Ross. She dropped her folder and splashed coffee on Adam and a second man, who leaped away, but not fast enough.

''Did I burn you?'' she gasped. Putting down her mug and hopping across a tape measure the men had stretched in front of the door, Noelani left her papers strewn everywhere and found a tissue in her shorts pocket. She dabbed at coffee splotches on Adam's neck and arm. ''Hold still.''

''Stop, you're rubbing too hard.''

"Oh, sorry." She stepped back, only to bump squarely into the fair-haired stranger.

"Hi. I'm Murray Dewalt. I live next door at the Woodlands plantation. If you're one of Adam's subcontractors, I'm seriously going to consider a new occupation."

"Uh…I'm Noelani Hana."

"Ah. The thorn in Casey's side." Blue eyes assessed her quite thoroughly.

"Excuse me?" Noelani said coolly.

"Murray, after that comment I think it's time for you to go."

"Ah…gotcha. See you later, Adam. And you, too, sweet thing."

"Now you've really done it," Adam murmured just as Noelani took a deep breath. "Run, Murray, and if you value your life, don't ever call her that again."

Their neighbor left, but instead of running he sauntered out, chuckling all the while.

Adam stopped to scrape together some of the papers decorating the floor. The Fontaine letterhead at the top of one sheet gave him pause. "What's this? Are you making off with important family documents? Have I foiled your attempt?"

"Very funny. Ha, ha! Give me those. You and your friend are both too funny for words."

"Murray's Jackson and Casey's friend. Well, maybe not Casey's," he muttered. "And definitely not Nick's. Murray wanted to be more than friends with Casey. She *didn't* want that, and then he proposed and it got messy."

"Oh? Oh, I see." She paused. "Jackson put me in charge of arranging a *cochon de lait*. This file is my guideline. Darn, I hope these pages weren't in any kind of order."

She ripped a stack of papers out of his hand and stuffed them back into the collapsed accordion file.

In the act of rising from his knees, Adam was left staring at Noelani's bare legs.

He did what any red-blooded man whose tongue had just about dropped on the floor would do. He mustered enough spit to peal off a wolf whistle.

"Oh, grow up." Noelani leaned down to collect her mug from where she'd set it on the floor.

He slapped a hand over his heart. "May God strike me dead if I ever get too old to appreciate a woman's legs."

"And well He may. Hmm. I see you have stuff all over the desk. Jackson said I could use the phone here to make some calls." She began backing toward the door. "He said if I'd be in your way there's also a desk upstairs in the family room."

"Hey, you won't be in my way." Adam hurriedly gathered up blueprints from the desk. "I'll throw these on one of the counters."

"What's that racket?" Noelani tipped her head back to stare at the smoky ceiling. It sounded as if a herd of elephants had landed above and were tromping about.

"Roofers. They're tearing up burned shingles today. With luck, they'll have time to lay plywood, too. Then tomorrow, they can spend the day putting on a new roof."

She set her mug on the desk, wrapped both arms around the bulky file and plastered her nose against the window. "If those scattered bundles are new shingles, I can't tell them from the old ones—except for the charred spots."

"That's the idea, sugar pie. When I finish, this place will look exactly like it was before the fire."

She released a dark strand of hair caught on her lips. "Is my name too much for you to manage, Adam? *No-eh-lon-ee*. Four simple syllables."

He grinned rakishly. "It's a wonderful name, too. Straight out of James Michener's *Hawaii*. What a book."

"Actually, I was named after a Maui resort. It's where Duke Fontaine stayed when he and my mother met. Quite frankly, I'd rather be named for Michener's character."

"Did you ever pick up a phone to tell your father how mad he made you?"

"Don't be ridiculous." She stalked to the desk and slammed down the file.

"I'll bet it would have eased the load you're lugging around. And we both know I'm not talking about the folder you just took out your aggressions on."

"Thank you, Mr. Ross, for that two-bit psychoanalysis. But it hardly falls under the heading of historical restoration. I'm sure you have something important you're being paid to do."

"Ouch! I scored a direct hit on a sore subject, I see."

"You see nothing. You *know* nothing about me, and you have no idea what it was like growing up in my shoes."

Adam held up his hands, palms out. "That's right. We can rectify that over dinner. I'm talking about a meal in town. You ever had fried alligator? There's this cool Cajun place near the river. Alligator is their signature dish."

"I don't eat meat."

"They do a mean crab salad. Wait, wait, I see you crossing your eyes. Aren't crabs technically crustaceans and not mammals?"

"Did it never occur to you that I don't want to go out with you?"

He raised a shoulder. "That's plain enough. Tell me, did I say something last night to annoy you? I enjoyed our walk. I thought we'd hit it off."

Noelani shut her eyes and pinched the bridge of her nose between thumb and forefinger. Without uttering another word, she snatched up her file and mug, and left the same way she'd entered.

Adam watched the door swing forward and back on its hinges. Damn, but he'd never met such a prickly woman. He'd assumed, after last night's uncomfortable meal, that she'd jump at the chance not to repeat that experience. Somehow, he really doubted breakfast had gone better. Adam had been leaving the garçonnière and chanced to overhear Casey ranting to Nick about Jackson going soft on their father's little indiscretion. Adam thought if anyone could use a friend, it was Noelani Hana.

But if he offered an olive branch and all she wanted to do was wrap it around his neck, that was A-okay with him. He didn't need the distraction from his work. He had precious little free time as it was. Why waste it in the company of a bad-tempered, hotheaded woman who wasn't planning to stick around? Adam had heard Casey say to Nick that if they'd had the means, Noelani would take her money and run. With an estate of this size, surely it wouldn't be long before they had funds to send her packing.

Slamming outside, Adam shoved the whole kit and caboodle to the back of his mind and went to have a word with his roofing subcontractor.

UPSTAIRS, NOELANI SPREAD the information on previous parties out on the desk and tried to make sense of the various lists. She heard a noise behind her. It wasn't much, and sounded as if it came from behind the couch, which stood near a row of floor-to-ceiling bookcases.

She slipped from her chair and tiptoed across the room, aware of each creak in the old floor, wondering who or what had made that sound. She didn't expect to find Jackson's daughter, Megan, huddled in a corner behind the couch, hugging a tattered rag doll and crying. Not really crying, Noelani decided. More the kind of body-racking sobs that followed a crying jag. A child's book lay forgotten on the floor.

"Hi, Megan. It's Noelani. Do you remember meeting me last night?" Afraid of scaring the little girl if she hung over the back of the couch, Noelani walked around it and sat cross-legged on the floor. Not too near so as to appear threatening, but close enough for comfort.

Megan hugged her doll tighter. The girl wore a long, frilly pink nightie and fuzzy bunny slippers. Her beautiful dark curls were tangled from sleep.

"Does your tummy hurt?"

Megan shook her head until her curls bobbed.

"Did you get up to go to the bathroom and forget the way back to your bed?" Esme had skipped Jackson's end of the house on her tour, so Noelani wasn't sure if the child shared a bath with Tanya, or if she had one en suite.

Noelani sighed. "I'm not a good guesser. Maybe you should tell me why you're crying."

"I came to wave bye-bye to Daddy. And I fo…found Emmylou in a s-sack. In the trash." She pointed a quivering finger toward a waste basket tucked between a lamp and the bookcase.

"Mommy gave her to me. I lost Emmylou and Miss Tanya said she was gone. She said I could only sleep with the dolly Daddy bought me. But…but she's hard. Not soft like Emmylou."

Several thoughts as to how the doll might have accidentally ended up in the trash flitted through Noelani's mind. None made sense, especially since there was no denying that the crumpled plastic bag bore the name of a local boutique. Obviously someone had tried to dispose of the tattered doll.

Nanny Tanya, with eyes that coveted Jackson, fell several notches in Noelani's estimation. But would a young woman who was infatuated with her boss take anything so drastic upon herself?

But Noelani preferred to blame Tanya rather than Jackson. This morning he'd acted concerned about his daughter's transition into the household. He wouldn't sink so low as to dispose of a harmless toy.

"Did your daddy read you that book this morning?"

Megan nodded. Hooking the doll under one arm, she pulled the book onto her lap. "He woke me up. We read half. Then he had to go to a meeting."

"I see it's *Dragon Tales*. That's one of my favorite stories. Would you like me to read the second half now?"

Nodding her head, Megan lifted the large book and handed it to Noelani.

"Shall we go sit on the couch? The light's better, and I think we'd be more comfortable."

The child weighed that thought carefully. Finally, she got up and scampered over to perch on the very end of the sofa.

Noelani sat at the opposite end, near the lamp. She found the place where Megan's daddy had left off, and she began to read.

Little by little, Megan edged closer. Until finally she wriggled right up next to Noelani, who used various voices for the characters, from tiny to gruff to scary. Megan started out not smiling. Ten minutes later, she was giggling out loud.

They were both laughing when Tanya Carson rushed into the room looking as if she'd thrown on her clothes haphazardly.

"Megan! You gave me a scare, disappearing right out of your bed like that. It's time for you to dress and go downstairs for breakfast. Oh, my, how…where did you find that pitiful *thang?*" Tanya shoved her glasses up her nose and glared accusingly at Noelani.

Megan edged closer, shifting the doll, whose threadbare dress was badly torn and whose button eye was missing, into the space between her and Noelani.

"Isn't it lucky Megan found her favorite toy, Tanya?"

"But Jackson bought her a perfectly beautiful new doll. She has long blond curls, eyes that move and three changes of clothes. Oh, you don't understand. Jackson wants her to play with her new doll."

"Jackson wants his daughter to be happy here," Noelani said flatly. "This morning he asked if I'd seen this doll anywhere." She crossed her fingers below the book and silently begged forgiveness for such a blatant lie.

"He did?" Tanya blinked several times.

Noelani smiled at Megan. "Honey, I have a sewing kit in my room. If you'll leave your baby with me while you go with Tanya and get dressed, I'll mend her so she'll be almost as good as new."

Tanya stuck up her nose. "There's not enough thread in the universe to accomplish that miracle."

"You'd be surprised what a little cosmetic surgery can do. How about it, Megan, would you like me to sew up Emmylou's rips?"

The four-year-old gave her doll one last squeeze before placing her trustingly into Noelani's hands. "Please," she said in a very small voice. "Take good care of her. I was so afraid Emmylou got taken somewhere far away—like Mommy." Little face sober again, Megan slid off the couch and walked sedately from the room.

Even as Tanya flounced out and snatched the child's hand, Megan kept darting glances back at Noelani, as if checking to make sure her most cherished possession was safe.

Anger mounting for that poor, motherless girl, Noelani leaped up the second she heard the door at the end of the hall slam. Hurrying straight to her own room, she made a mental note to have another talk with her half brother. Megan needed to be able to ask honest questions about her mother. The child needed to know she hadn't been abandoned. Noelani could attest firsthand to the fact that avoiding mention of an absent parent only led to frustration, mistrust and outright dislike on the part of the child.

She found her sewing kit and stitched quickly. A button for the missing eye presented the biggest problem. Her kit had come with white buttons in three sizes and an assortment of safety pins. The doll's eyes were half an inch around and black.

The black suit she'd worn on the plane had exactly the right-size buttons on the jacket cuffs. "Emmylou needs this more than me." A snip of the scissors and Noelani had her button.

After she'd finished, she held the doll at arm's length and eyed her critically. With felt and yarn maybe she could fix the shoes and the hair. But she had none, and anyway, Megan loved the rag doll exactly as she was. Tucking the doll under her arm, she went off in search of the little girl.

It turned out she didn't have to go far. Noelani opened her bedroom door and practically fell over the child. Tanya leaned against the wall by the stairs. "There you are. Thank goodness! Megan refused to go have breakfast without her doll. Betty's going to throw a hissy fit 'cause we're so late."

Noelani tuned Tanya out. She focused in on the beautiful smile slowly blossoming on Megan's face.

"Emmylou's all well. You found her a new eye, No'lani. Oh, thank you. I've worried and worried 'bout her not being able to see so good."

"You're welcome, honey. Maybe one of these days, you and I can go to town and find yarn to spruce up her hair. Give her a new look." She smiled gently at the child.

Tanya pretended to stick a finger down her throat and gag, but Megan kissed her doll and nodded, making her own curls dance.

"Emmylou, it's time for us to go eat," she said, darting off ahead of Tanya.

Noelani buried her hands in her shorts pockets and watched them disappear down the stairs.

"That was a nice thing you did for Megan. First real smile I've seen outta her."

Noelani whirled and saw Adam standing quietly a few feet away, his fingers tucked loosely under his leather belt.

"Must you always sneak up on me?" she demanded. "Where on earth did you come from? We've been standing right next to the stairs."

"I came up the back steps. I had to check something for Jackson in his office. He phoned the kitchen wanting you, actually. I transferred him to the library, but you didn't answer. Now I see why. He'll be pleased, you know. He worries a lot about his kid. Cut Tanya some slack, though. She watches Megan okay. It's just that Auntie E is always harping at her, and those two clash. Tossing the doll was probably Esme's doing. I suspect she was trying to erase Megan's background."

"That child's hurting. Jackson should put his foot down. By the way, what did he want me for?"

"Oh, here." Adam took a folded message from his pocket. "He ran into Nick downtown. Nick said the White Gold has a new Cajun group performing a couple of nights a week. Jackson thinks you should check them out and maybe book them for the *cochon de lait.*" Adam grinned. "Nick said they can be had cheap."

Noelani read the message. "Is the White Gold a night club?"

"A riverboat casino. Building and staffing them is what Nick does."

"To tell you the truth, I've barely begun to read through the notes on what the family did in the past. I'd just noticed the date he gave me is only two weeks away. I'd hit panic mode when I heard Megan crying. She found her doll in the trash."

"So I gathered."

"Really? You spied on us that long?"

"I came down the hall about the time you left your room. You walked over to the stairs to talk to Tanya. I didn't want to interrupt."

"Likely story." She stuck the note in her pocket.

"That band's performing tonight. I'll run you downtown."

"Thanks, but you have your own work to do. I'll phone a cab."

Adam fidgeted. "We're talking about the waterfront. At night," he added.

She considered his subtle warning, glad he hadn't felt the need to make a big deal about her being a defenseless woman. In truth, she didn't know the area. They warned tourists against going into some parts of Honolulu at night. Her seat companion on the commuter flight from Dallas had mentioned that crime was on the rise in New Orleans. Perhaps it was also true for Baton Rouge. "If you're quite sure it won't disrupt your schedule, I may take you up on that offer."

"No problem. I can't do a lot until the wood for the cabinets arrives or the roof is finished. With any luck, both will be sometime next week."

"What time, then? Is it all right if I wear jeans? I may have packed a white pair, but my wardrobe leaves a lot to be desired. I hadn't planned to stay. Since I'll be here until they divvy up the property, I phoned Bruce and asked him to ship a better assortment of clothes.''

''Who's Bruce? I never thought to ask if you had a boy-friend or a live-in.''

She elevated an eyebrow. ''Not that it's your business, Mr. Nosy, but Bruce is a contemporary of Duke's. I work at his sugar mill, as did my mom and almost everyone else in our town. I live in one of his rentals. Bruce has a master key, and that's why he was the person I called. Although his secretary, Midori, would have a better eye for choosing shoes and accessories. Oh, well.'' She grimaced. ''It's already done.''

''So you worked in sugar? Doing what?''

''I set up Shiller's computerized vat and fermentation system. Most recently I developed a program to speed up the creeper feeders. They carry the cane to be crushed, in case you aren't familiar with the process.''

''I'm not. But it sounds interesting. Do Jackson and Casey know they have all this experience under their roof? I'd think they'd want you overseeing the mill instead of coordinating a party. Not that I have anything against parties, mind you.''

''I'm sure you don't.''

''What's that supposed to mean? I'm probably the least likely party animal you'll find living in the deep South.''

''Ri-ight,'' she drawled.

''It's true. I took over as man of the house when my dad, a pilot, went to 'Nam. My mother never worked outside the home until we got word that his plane had been shot down. She attempted retail, hoping to take her mind off his disappearance, but…she wasn't well.'' Adam's face reflected the state of his memories. ''The longer it dragged on without his being found, either dead or alive, the tougher it was for Mom.''

Noelani's demeanor changed at once from sarcastic teasing to total empathy. "That's awful, Adam. Was he okay when they found him?"

"He's MIA. The navy assumes he's dead." *So does Mom, when she's lucid.* He now had Charlotte Ross in a good sanatorium upriver. Shadows clouded Adam's blue eyes as he fingered a cross worn around his neck. He ran it back and forth along a gold chain. "Some mornings I still wake up thinking this'll be the day Dad walks through my door."

Noelani nibbled her lower lip. Finally, she squeezed his arm. "Stop. I can see that talking about this bothers you. I understand, because I hate talking about my—about the man who fathered me." She glanced at her watch. "We both need to get back to work. What time shall I be ready to go to the White Gold?"

"I'm sure Betty would be happy to have two fewer people for dinner. Remember the place I mentioned last night that has great alligator? It's near the casino. We can eat after you hear the band."

Having softened toward him in the aftermath of his sad tale, Noelani agreed. "I'm not eating alligator, Adam, but I guess I can see what else they offer."

"Good. Great." He galloped toward the stairs before she could change her mind. "I'll let Betty know. Be out front at six, okay?"

"Yes. Sure, I'll be ready."

She listened to him clatter down the stairs and slowly made her way to the library to start listing her duties as *cochon de lait* organizer. Adam was right; this probably was wasting her talent. On the other hand, she liked to excel at any job she did. So the Fontaines had better get set for the best darned party they'd ever experienced.

Noelani couldn't help it if her mind detoured every now and then. On paths that led to thoughts of Adam…

She was touched by what he'd said about his growing up—and what he hadn't. A boy, not very old, forced to deal with a mother who was sick and whose heart was probably broken, as well. Relatives and neighbors probably hadn't understood. She could be summing up her own life. The similarity between them was almost uncanny. It certainly made her take a different view of Adam Ross.

CHAPTER FOUR

THE MISSISSIPPI WAS SWOLLEN and brown with mud after recent rains. The night air pressed in, covering her body with a fine sheen of perspiration. Noelani was used to a bright moon suspended over a white-capped ocean. Here the moon barely cleared the rooftops, and it glowed an eerie, sickly yellow. Still, embarking on a new adventure, she could hardly contain a shimmer of excitement.

"There's a haze clouding the moon," she said. "It's like you're viewing the moon through gauze. In Hawaii, the moon and stars are clear and bright."

Adam squinted up through the windshield. "Used to be southern harvest moons were fantastic. But gas refineries have sprung up along the river. They pollute the air and belch smoke and carbons into the river and sky. Cane farmers and residents alike complain, but the powers-that-be look the other way. They want the tax revenues."

"Is there a possibility pollution will drive cane growers out altogether?" Her thoughts were on the declining Hawaiian cane industry as Adam found a place to park.

"You'd have to ask Jackson or Casey. I know Jackson's working with lobbyists." Adam held the door as she got out, and then locked his pickup.

"I heard Jackson tell Casey he had lunch planned with some lobbyists today," she said. "It'd be a shame if the cane fields wither away as they are in Hawaii. I intend to see Shiller's become what it was in my mother's day. If I envy Duke's kids anything, it's…well, never mind. You don't want me going on about that, I'm sure.''

"Duke didn't play square with any of you."

"You won't hear objections from me on that score."

Adam placed a hand on her waist as they navigated the first of a series of ramps leading to the White Gold—a replica of a paddle wheeler. The walkway was crowded with jovial people all headed into the boat.

Noelani moved closer to Adam. "Are all these people here to listen to the band?'' By now the catchy beat of a familiar tune spilled from the gently rocking boat.

"They're here to gamble. Music and liquor are perks to keep patrons on the boat spending money."

"Do you gamble?"

"I have better things to do with my hard-earned cash. But feel free to throw some of yours in the slots, sugar pie.''

"I've never been to a casino. I wouldn't know what to do. I have better things to do with my money, too," she said as they entered the dimly lit interior. The noise intensified; music and laughter now competed with the spin of slots and the clank of falling coins. Someone jostled Noelani, knocking her into Adam. She pressed both hands against his chest to remain balanced, and felt his heart pick up its tempo. Usually she shied away from closeness. Not this time. She maintained contact, liking the feel of his muscles under her hands.

Adam slid his arms protectively around her back. "Boy, it's packed tonight. There must be some big convention in town. Let's see if we can work our way upstairs to where the band is.''

She nodded but was reluctant to leave Adam's arms—certainly much more so than she ought to be. In marked contrast to the smoke, whiskey fumes and cloying perfumes rising from a row of women at the slots, Adam's shirt smelled of crisp, clean starch. His aftershave was a subtle mix of lime and some nice scent Noelani couldn't name. She liked it, though. A lot.

"Whew!" Adam stumbled with her out onto the upper deck, where the crowd was thinner. In place of slots, this deck offered roulette, craps and other game tables. A polished wood bar curved in a large horseshoe around a compact dance floor. Off to their right was a raised stage on which five musicians sat, belting out lively tunes.

"There's Nick and Casey. I wonder what they're doing here." Adam clamped a hand on Noelani's upper arm and literally dragged her across the room.

The men shook hands. Casey, who leaned against the bar, tightened her hold on her shoulder purse and stepped well to their right. "Are you about finished, Nick? You said this wouldn't take a minute."

"What's your hurry?" Adam asked, smiling at her.

Casually looping an arm around Casey's waist, Nick continued talking to a snazzily dressed older gentleman. A shrug was Casey's only response to Adam's question.

Noelani propped a foot on the rung of an adjacent bar stool. "Every time I see you, you're in a rush to take off. I have a question about your harvester."

Casey's head snapped around. "What about our harvester? I'm paying Len Forsen extra to keep an eye on it night and day."

"Adam mentioned you'd had one stolen. That's terrible. But I'm interested in learning the make, model and where I can get a brochure. I've been so concerned with increasing production on the mill end of harvest, I've paid no attention to the cutting process. In Hawaii, if it rains, cutting comes to a standstill. According to Adam, you cut the day I arrived, and it rained cats and dogs."

Casey looked her half sister up and down. "You really do work in cane?"

"At the mill." Noelani felt her temper flare. "The islands—Maui, in particular—were once the world's leading sugar producer. Didn't your father ever tell you about the month he spent on Maui studying Bruce Shiller's operation?"

"Leave my father out of this."

"Like he conveniently left me out of his life, you mean?"

"Ladies, ladies." Adam stepped between the two bristling women.

Nick interrupted his conversation to glance their way. "The band's taking a break, I see. Noelani, here's their card. I assume you've come to talk to them about performing. You'll want the guy with the accordion. He books all their gigs."

"What's she want with a band?" Casey peered around Adam.

"Short memory," Noelani said sarcastically. "Have you forgotten that at breakfast, Jackson put me in charge of your annual *pua'a?*"

"Our what?"

"Sorry. Your pigfest."

"Oh. I did forget. Nick, here's Viv, Luc and Murray. Let's go. You said you wanted Mr. Dardenne to meet Luc." Dismissing the others, Casey spoke to the man with whom Nick chatted. Linking her arm through his, the two of them left.

Noelani watched Casey flag down a handsome couple and a third party. She recognized Murray Dewalt as the extra male, the friend and neighbor she'd met that morning in the kitchen. The man she didn't know had midnight-dark eyes, killer good looks and carried a worn instrument case. His companion, a smartly dressed, racehorse-thin blonde, enveloped Casey in an effusive hug.

"Viv is Casey's best friend," Nick said for Noelani's benefit. To Adam, he said, "Henry Dardenne is considering picking up the casino contract Guy Moreau reneged on. Henry requested a meeting with Luc Renault, because he wants some reassurance that Luc will continue performing if he buys the casino."

"Um, excuse me." Noelani ducked away from the men and made a beeline for the band leader, now packing up his equipment.

Adam's gaze followed her. "Nick, I understand that Casey's suffering from the loss of her folks. But she's got to face facts. Noelani didn't write Duke's will."

"Don't push, Adam. For years Casey's poured her heart and soul into growing the best cane in the state—mostly to please her dad. Duke did more than die. He fell from his pedestal. And…this isn't for publication, but Casey had a miscarriage. The day before the property settlement meeting. Emotionally, she's going through hell."

"God, Nick. I'm sorry. For your sake, too. But maybe she'd benefit from having a sister at a time like this. Don't women connect over babies?"

"Casey needs time. I wish she and Jackson would let me help them come up with the money to get rid of Noelani."

"I hope you mean buy her out, rather than *get rid of her.* That sounds…sinister."

"You know what I mean. If Dardenne signs tonight, I could give them a loan. But my question is—why are you involving yourself, Adam?"

"From the vantage point of an outsider, it strikes me that Casey and Jackson were dealt a majority of the aces in this hand. They grew up with Duke's love. Noelani's the one who got shortchanged."

"Be that as it may, you can't force people to like each other."

"I'm not advocating force. Casey listens to you, Nick. It'd help if you put in a good word now and then for Noelani."

"I'll think about it. Meanwhile, don't forget who hired you."

"I know who hired me." Adam felt the sting of Nick's rebuke.

"Yeah? Well, you're awfully damn chummy with our foe for a guy who usually keeps his nose to the grindstone. Why are you out with her tonight?"

"Jackson expressly requested I escort her here." Adam's temper frayed as Nick turned and walked away without a backward glance. "For another thing, she's not the enemy," he muttered. But dammit, he couldn't afford to blow this job at Bellefontaine. And Nick knew full well that Adam needed the job if he had any hope of buying back Magnolia Manor.

Noelani paused a foot behind Adam. Close enough to catch the heated exchange that had passed between him and Nick. Adam's terse admission that he'd driven her to the casino at his employer's request cut deeper than any of Casey's recent barbs. Noelani froze. First shame, then fury buzzed in her ears.

As if sensing her presence, Adam glanced over his shoulder. *Damn! Had she heard?*

She blindly jammed a paper in her purse. "I signed a contract with the group for a hundred dollars less than Jackson paid last year. If you're reporting back to him, I think that news should please him."

Damn, she *had* overheard. Adam didn't know what to say to make matters better. "So, we're ready to head home, then?" He avoided her eyes.

Noelani read that as guilt. And had he forgotten about their going to dinner, or had he changed his mind? Darned if she'd ask. Obviously more had happened between the men than the few lines she'd heard.

That was doubly evident in the way they ignored each other as she and Adam walked by the huddled friends. There was no wave, no acknowledgment, nothing to indicate they were even acquainted.

She might have probed deeper, except that they were delayed by a commotion at the casino entrance. Security had a disheveled-looking man by the scruff of the neck. He'd obviously drunk too much.

"Take your hands off me, sonny. My credit's good here. Or it oughta be. I have wages coming from Duke Fontaine. His son-in-law owns this joint. If his wife won't pay me, by hell I'll take it out in trade." He wrenched loose long enough to snag a glass of whiskey from the tray of a passing cocktail waitress.

Noelani plucked at Adam's sleeve. "Who is that?" She rose on tiptoe to whisper in his ear. "Did you hear what he said about Duke?" Busily elbowing his way through the crowd, Adam forged ahead. And Noelani's voice carried farther than she'd intended.

The drunk, still evading the security personnel, fixed her with red-rimmed eyes. "I'm Chuck Riley. You wanna know about me and Duke Fontaine? I taught that bastard to fly. I went with him and the missus on their fancy European trip, but would he give me a turn at the stick? No. Said I'd lost my edge. I ask you, which one of us didn't make it home?"

Two hefty security guards grappled Riley, wresting him to the ground. "Sorry we let him get in your face, miss." Hoisting Riley, the guards carted him toward an office. When the door flew open, Noelani saw Nick, Casey and several others inside, looking anxious. Someone must have gone upstairs and gotten them.

Realizing they'd been separated, Adam hurried back to Noelani. "What happened with that guy? Did he grab you? I'm sorry—I let gawkers get between us."

"His name is Riley. Chuck Riley. He said he was in Europe with my fa—uh, with Duke." Her knees spongy, she dropped back behind a large group who were exiting the casino.

"The guy was plastered. Probably hallucinating. Why would a guy like that be with Duke in Europe?"

"Riley claimed Duke owed him back wages. I saw Casey and Nick in the office where security took him."

"Huh. Then they can handle him. Jackson and Casey always pay their bills."

"You'd know about that, I guess."

"Listen, I grant you Casey's been cross with you. But you might try being a little less abrasive, too."

"Me?" Noelani lifted the heavy hair off her neck, glad to emerge into less stale air. "Have I complained? I wouldn't dare since you've become her staunch defender."

"I would think you'd take her part over a drunk stranger. After all, you *are* a Fontaine."

"I'm a Hana," she flared. "If my mother had wanted to recognize Fontaine's blood, she'd have put Duke's name on my birth certificate."

"So his blood's not red enough for you, but his money's the right shade of green?"

They'd reached Adam's pickup. Noelani recoiled from his sudden attack.

"Buckle up," he growled. "We've got a mile to drive to the restaurant."

"If I was starving and hadn't eaten in a week, I wouldn't eat with you, Adam Ross. I've suddenly lost my appetite."

"Well, I haven't. I worked hard today."

"That's right. You've gone above and beyond the normal call of duty. I hope Jackson's paying you double overtime," she said, syrup dripping from each word.

Her jab hit home. Adam missed when he poked the key at the ignition. "God, Noelani," he said, at once sounding contrite. "Nick pushed a hot button of mine tonight. I'm taking my anger out on you, and I shouldn't. Forgive me," he said, finally getting his pickup started.

"Forget it. It doesn't matter."

"It does. I acted like a jerk."

"No argument from me there."

Adam glanced out his side window as he made a U-turn. "Nick reminded me that Fontaine family matters aren't my concern. He's right. But I'd already invited you out. I rarely take time off to date, and I'd really like to enjoy tonight. Anyway, we're almost at the restaurant," he finished off-handedly.

Noelani sifted through his stilted speech and ended up with conflicting clues as to what Adam was really saying. She decided he regretted asking her out, and wouldn't do so again. Yet—how different was that from her own repeated refrain? She intended to avoid him. So he wasn't far off. Not far at all.

She opened her mouth to request that he take her straight home. Her stomach had other ideas, growling long and loud. Blushing, she mumbled, "Okay, so I lied. I'm so famished I could eat an onion. Raw," she added sheepishly.

His quiet grin flashed as they passed under a streetlight. "Please don't go to that extreme. The restaurant's there on your right." Still smiling, Adam swung into the parking lot and jockeyed his big pickup into a too-small slot.

Noelani opened her door. Heat hammered her in sultry

waves, almost stealing her breath. Or was Adam's quirky smile to blame for the odd catch in her throat?

He vaulted out lightly, rounded the hood and helped her down. The minute her feet touched asphalt, she shook loose from his grasp.

The move didn't escape Adam, although he knew she had good reason to be touchy. His untimely irritation with Nick had hurt her. Adam felt bad about that. As blowups went, his tussle with Nick was minor. He should've kept quiet; he knew the whole family was under a strain. But he hadn't liked Nick's barb. After his mother had her nervous breakdown, the unscrupulous owners of her original sanatorium had coerced her into signing over Magnolia Manor and her military allotment under the ruse of paying for her care. Adam had spent too many years thereafter kowtowing to people who had money. He'd hated the feeling as a kid, and it didn't set any better now. The hell of it was, Nick probably hadn't meant anything by what he'd said. They'd both come out of a hardscrabble life, which was why they'd become fast friends in college.

But now Nick had someone to champion who meant the world to him. He was like a wild stallion fighting to save his mare. Logically, Nick might understand that Noelani couldn't help her circumstances. But the part of Nick's brain ruled by love had kicked in tonight. And maybe Adam was just a little envious of his old friend.

Dammit! Envy was unproductive. He knew that.

The restaurant was crowded, and they had a twenty-minute wait. Excusing herself, Noelani went to the ladies' room. While she was gone, Adam checked his phone messages to see if he'd heard back from a wiring inspector.

He was talking to a vendor when Noelani returned. "Ross, table for two," the hostess called. Adam hurriedly said goodbye and tucked his phone in his pocket. Placing his hand lightly on Noelani's waist, he guided her to a booth in a quiet corner.

After they were seated, she studied him over the top of her menu. "I heard you mention a wiring inspection. It started me thinking. With a house as old as Bellefontaine, they're lucky the fire didn't do more serious damage."

"This one would have if Casey hadn't seen the smoke. Esme had been knocked unconscious. Casey got her and Toodles outside, then phoned the fire department. She also ran upstairs and helped Megan and Tanya out. I guess Tanya was too rattled to function."

Noelani let the menu drop. "Gosh, that was brave of Casey. Was anyone hurt?"

He shrugged. "It all happened before I arrived at Bellefontaine. Nick was seeing Casey by the time they'd reached the point of assessing damage. He suggested contacting me. We met in college. Nick studied boat architecture, while I specialized in homes."

"You shouldn't have argued with him over me tonight. You all have to live here harmoniously. I'll be returning to Hawaii."

Adam turned away to watch the antics of a Cajun band. "I'll square things with Nick." Facing her again, he shut his menu. "Did you find anything that interests you?"

"A shrimp Caesar salad sounds good,"

"Not much food for someone hungry enough to eat a raw onion."

A glimmer of a smile found its way to her lips. "Are you kidding? You must not have seen the size of the portions the waitress brought to that table across the aisle."

"Hmm. I'm having eggplant and okra with alligator. It comes with onion rings."

Noelani thought he was kidding, but that was what he ordered when the waitress stopped at their table.

"Don't knock it till you've tried it," he said when Noelani wrinkled her nose. "Gator tastes like chicken, only better."

She declined to sample it. Granted, the alligator bits looked innocuous, but Noelani wasn't interested. "All I can say is I'm glad Jackson didn't put me in charge of an alligator fest. I wouldn't have been able to handle it."

Adam laughed. "Food likes and dislikes are all about what you're accustomed to. You probably love papaya. To me it looks slimy. As for alligator, you don't know what you're missing. By the way—how's your planning for the *cochon de lait?*"

"Good. I ordered pigs from the same man who catered last year's party. He provides four side dishes, plates, glasses, napkins and cutlery, plus he does the roasting, all for a flat fee. I booked the band tonight. All that's left is making flyers and ordering a keg. Oh, and the ingredients for mint juleps. Esme reminded me today."

Adam smacked his lips. "No prissy watered-down juleps for that lady. I accidentally knocked one of her drinks into a potted fern at Nick and Casey's wedding. Next day the sucker had shot up six inches and I watched the plant put out four new fronds—right before my eyes."

Noelani stopped with a forkful of salad halfway to her lips. She broke into a chuckle. "You southern men do love to exaggerate."

Adam laughed. Tipping back his head, he laughed. Any lingering tension left over from his encounter with Nick evaporated. Considerably mellowed, he found that the remainder of their evening passed far too quickly to suit him.

"Would you mind driving me past Fontaine's mill on the way home?" Noelani asked, somewhat abruptly. They'd lingered over dark chicory coffee about as long as they could. "Unless it's out of your way," she hurriedly added.

"It's not, but what can you see at night?"

"They're not hauling cane twenty-four seven?"

He paid the bill and took her hand as they walked out into the humid night again. "I'm no authority, but Murray's always hanging around, pontificating on what it's like to farm cane. He said the mill operates twenty-four hours a day, but they only haul the cane from seven to four, or something like that. I tend to tune Murray out."

"Wow, I wonder why they'd waste valuable hours."

"Beats me. Tomorrow you can ask Casey."

"I'll ask Jackson."

"Do you intend to spend the whole time you're here at odds with Casey?"

"Look, you heard me ask her a straightforward question about the harvester. Did I get an answer? No."

He separated out a key, weighing what he should say. "Uh, according to Nick, she's on emotional overload right now."

"And Jackson isn't? He's at least civil to me."

"You're asking me why women act more emotional than men? I have to tell you, I'm the last person who'd know how a woman's mind works."

Noelani fumbled with her seat belt. "So you're suggesting I should imagine myself in Casey's shoes?"

He started the pickup and shrugged. "You're poles apart on the subject of Duke. Is it even possible for you to look at the situation from Casey's perspective?"

She sat gnawing the inside of her cheek. "Yeah, it is. I had the advantage of seeing Duke's photo when I was ten. For seventeen years, I've been aware of the man who fathered me. I knew he was married. So while the news of Duke's death still came at me out of left field, it wasn't a total knock-me-off-my-props shock like learning about me had to be for Casey."

She leaned back and closed her eyes. "If our situations were reversed," she said in a small voice, "I'd probably hate me, too. I refused to speak to my mother for months after she finally broke down and told me about Duke. Poor Tutu." She glanced over at Adam. "*Tutu* is Hawaiian for grandmother, in case you didn't know. Anyway, Tutu tried so hard to make peace between Anela and me."

"At the funeral Nick said he thought Casey had finally managed to deal with Duke's betrayal. But maybe down deep she really hasn't."

"Seeing me in the flesh may have reopened an old wound." She sighed. "I wanted Anela to apologize to me for complicating my life. She never did. In fact, when she was very ill, she said that if she'd had a choice as to whether to repeat that month with Duke Fontaine or give up the time she'd spent with him, she wouldn't change one thing."

"Family matters can get tricky. I sometimes wonder if my dad's living in a remote Vietnamese village. And if maybe he has a new family to replace Mom and me. About the time I went to college, I read a report having to do with American soldiers in Vietnam who chucked their life here and took on new identities. Not long ago, a vet turned up in Australia with a second wife and passel of kids. He was the same age as my dad."

"At the time, did you know your father well enough to say how he might react?"

"No. I was fiercely loyal. I was furious at Mom for signing away our house. I'd go by there every morning and afternoon to see if Dad had come back. It was years before I understood how sick she actually was."

She touched Adam's arm. "Parents can sure screw up their kids' lives. I'll try to be more sympathetic to Casey. Like Jackson said, none of us created this mess, but we all have to try to make the best of it."

Adam toyed with mentioning what Nick had said about Casey having lost a baby. But as irritated as he was at Nick, his friend had said that wasn't for publication. Adam would respect Nick's wishes. "Hey, off to your right is the mill." He swung the pickup into a layby. "The gate's chained. Unless we climb over, you can't get any closer."

"That's okay. Under the lights, it looks remarkably like Shiller's. Well, bigger. Adam, thanks for stopping. After I complete the chore Jackson's assigned me, I'll ask him for permission to poke around the mill. Or maybe I'll see if he'll let me work there."

They talked sporadically on the drive home, sharing the small details couples like to exchange on a first date.

"I already knew you liked jazz from listening to you and Tanya talk," Noelani said during a discussion of favorite music. "Zydeco. I can't say I've ever heard it."

"If you're not from around here, you probably can't distinguish Zydeco from Cajun. It's a mix of Cajun with blues or rock. The band at the casino were playing Zydeco. They incorporated a saxophone and an electric bass with the standard fiddle and accordion. And some use odd—traditional—instruments like a washboard."

"Hmm." She yawned, then apologized for it.

"I can take a hint when I'm boring someone. Jazz and the old N'Awlins blues rev me up. I had a hard time deciding whether to renovate old homes or chuck it all and become an itinerant musician. Luc Renault did just that. You saw him at the casino. Luc struggled to raise younger brothers and supported them by playing in smoky, out-of-the-way night clubs."

"Music must pay better than raising cane." She grinned to show she was kidding. "If Viv is Luc's wife, she was dressed fit to kill."

"Viv comes from old Creole money. She's a product of

boarding schools and summers in France. Talk about a family uprising. Tanya said Viv's parents threatened all kinds of dire things when she announced her intention to marry Luc. Tanya is a fountain of gossip. Don't tell her anything you don't want the world to know.''

''I doubt that'll be a problem. I'm not exactly on her A-list of friends.''

Adam slowed his truck to turn right into the drive leading to Bellefontaine. He parked beside his garçonnière, shut off the engine and undid his seat belt. Resting his arm along the back of the bench seat, he picked up a thick strand of Noelani's hair and brushed his thumb back and forth across the blunt tips.

Suddenly nervous, she bent to retrieve her purse.

Adam released her seat belt and slid her toward him across the cool leather seat. His fingers brushed her stomach sending a shiver up her spine.

What was he doing? After all, he'd only asked her out tonight because Jackson ordered him to. Hadn't he?

''I had a good time, Noelani. I'm glad you let me off the hook for my surly behavior at the casino.'' Gazing fully into her confused eyes, Adam kneaded her shoulders. He'd intended to heed caution but was drawn to her by a stronger force.

''I'd, uh, better go inside.'' She fumbled behind her for the door latch.

To hell with caution! Adam seized the moment, angled his head and fit his lips over hers. Her purse fell to the floor, popped open and dumped the contents all over their feet.

She felt her hairbrush strike her ankle. A fleeting spark of rationality urged her to pick things up—so fleeting she hardly noticed the thought. Suddenly all that mattered was Adam's lips. Adam's arms. His solid chest. His...kiss. Heat built and built as her brain went numb and her body limp

Adam molded his chest to her soft breasts, and his hands memorized the curve of her waist, the gentle flare of her hips. His heart rate shot into high gear as her fingers slid restlessly up and down the buttons on his shirt.

Spicy ginger filled his nostrils. And her taste…her taste was more exotic than he'd dreamed in his most fanciful dream.

The slam of a car door cut through the odd gravitational force enveloping them both. Adam was the first to pull away. "It's Jackson coming home," he said in a raspy, winded voice.

"What? Oh. Oh!" Grabbing the drooping strap on her tank top, Noelani thrust unsteady fingers through her tangled hair. As she ran her tongue over her still-damp lips, she realized they tingled with the lingering pleasure of Adam's kiss.

"Jackson's heading our way," she hissed, her panic only adding to the whirlwind in her stomach. "I've got to go." Scrambling to the passenger door, she yanked hard on the handle several times, only to discover the door was still locked. "Unlock this now! Oh, jeez, my purse. Where's my purse?"

Adam grabbed her arm. "Calm down, Noelani. We're certainly over the age of consent. Besides, I'm quite sure kissing's not against the rules at Bellefontaine."

She was crawling around the floorboard, hunting for the contents of her purse that were strewn underfoot. Dimly she heard Adam roll down his window and hail Jackson. Muggy as the blast of air was, Noelani welcomed it because it restored some sense of balance. Crouched on the floor, she saw Jackson clearly in the yellow light falling from a carriage lamp. He had on a white shirt and skewed tie. His sleeves were rolled midway up his arms and he'd casually hooked a summer-weight suit jacket over one shoulder.

"You just getting back from your meeting with the lob-byists?" Adam asked.

"Yeah, those guys could talk an elephant to death. Who's bobbing around on the floor of your truck?"

Noelani tucked the last item into her bulging purse. She ducked and slid out the door. "I need a new purse. Darn thing fell off the seat and dumped all over creation." Turning to Adam, she murmured, "If you find any strange things under your feet, I can only hope they aren't embarrassing to either of us."

"I don't think I'll even ask what might fall into that category," he drawled, knowing she'd blush, which she did, but fortunately it was dark.

Jackson's voice rose over their banter. "Oh, it's you, Noelani. Did you connect with the band Nick recom-mended?"

"I did. We heard some of their performance. They're good, and they cost less than last year's band, so I signed them up. DuPree, who's catered your last two events, gave me a verbal okay for the date you picked. I got quotes from three printers. They all said I'd need to bring in copy. I'll be happy to type it up on your computer, if you don't mind running it into town." At last her nerves had begun to settle, although her tongue still had a thick, fuzzy feeling.

"You can take the copy by a printer. Feel free to use Maman's car. Or Duke's. They're both in the garage. I'll get you a set of keys. I have a state-wide growers' meeting tomorrow, so I'll be leaving home before daylight. It could last two days or more."

"Uh, sure. I was...uh...telling Adam good-night when you drove in." She darted a furtive glance at him and wished she hadn't. He'd climbed out to stand beside Jack-son. Adam's blue eyes smoldered, not hiding what had gone on between them. Noelani wondered if only *her* sanity had been restored. Surely he could see that there was no future in their embarking on a romantic liaison. None whatsoever.

But there he was—his thumbs tucked in the front pocket of worn jeans, his head cocked slightly to one side, eyes burning with...something she didn't care to name.

She told herself not to take a second look, but she darted one quick peek over her shoulder. Adam hadn't moved. He made an unforgettable picture silhouetted against the backdrop of a golden Louisiana moon. Wide shoulders. Not-too-bulky biceps. Just-right hips. Wavy brown hair gently ruffled by a welcome breeze.

Noelani spun forward, shifting her purse and twisting her hair into a knot to give the breeze better access to her hot cheeks and damp, sticky neck.

"I'll go get the keys and show you to the garage," Jackson said. "It'll take me only a minute if you'd like to wait here."

"Sure. Are the cars in an outbuilding? If so, I'll walk on ahead."

"They're in the garage behind the vacant garçonnière. Not Adam's. It's where Nick stayed before he and Casey got married."

"And now they live in your grandmother's house?"

"Yes. Wisteria Cottage. It's a grand old place. You'll have to get Casey to give you a tour one of these days."

Yeah, right! "I'll, uh, meet you at the garage."

She didn't know if it was her imagination, but Jackson seemed to leave her waiting for longer than she'd anticipated. When he finally appeared out of the darkness, she saw why he'd been detained. He had Megan wrapped in both his arms. She clung tightly to a doll Noelani had certainly seen before. The child's sleepy eyes, her Barbie nightgown and tousled hair told Noelani she'd at least been in bed, where four-year-olds belonged at this hour.

"Megan heard me come in. She's promised to go straight back to sleep when I take her back upstairs. So I've agreed to let her help me deliver the keys."

"Daddy, she's who fixed Emmylou's dress and gave her a new eye." Still hugging her father, Megan offered Noelani a shy, sweet smile.

"And we're going to give Emmylou a new hairdo, aren't we?" Noelani returned the child's smile.

Megan nodded, her curls scraping Jackson's five-o'clock shadow. The gaze he turned on Noelani showed more than scant surprise.

"Give me those keys before you drop them in the dirt," she said, plucking them out of his otherwise occupied hands. "I assume one of these opens the garage door?"

He pointed, and she undid the padlock. "Megan waited up because she wanted to tell me all about the doll. Thanks, Noelani. I gather she's had Emmylou forever."

"The doll's her talisman," Noelani said. When Jackson quirked an eyebrow, she added, "Jackson, I suspect the doll's disappearance wasn't an accident. You might want to let it be known that Emmylou has a permanent home at Bellefontaine."

"Yeah, Daddy. I cried when I lost her. She helps me remember Mommy."

Noelani wasn't sure how that news would affect Jackson. Some men would probably dispose of the doll without qualm. Jackson, however, hugged his child tight. Swaying her from side to side, he murmured, "I didn't know that, honey bun. This weekend, I'll see if I can find a picture of Mommy. She's had to go away for a while. But you should have a picture of her to keep by your bed."

Tears pressed the back of Noelani's eyelids as she felt along the wall for a light switch. All three of them blinked rapidly when she found the switch and flooded the interior with a blaze of light.

Noelani emitted a gasp. She'd never imagined such big cars. At home she drove a Jeep. Or on occasion, Bruce's imported compact. But these looked intimidating.

"The Cadillac was Maman's. Duke's is the Lincoln Town Car. He treated it like a baby. He had a newer model on or…der." Jackson's voice wobbled.

Faced suddenly with something that belonged to her father, something special to him, Noelani didn't think she could make herself touch it, let alone drive it. "I, ah, have never driven a big car. But I'm a good driver. So…maybe… I'll try your mother's."

"Maman loved the small Caddy. She bought a new one every year." Even though he had to juggle Megan, who'd dropped off to sleep, Jackson peeled two keys off a second ring. "The car key and one for the garage. Caddies guzzle gas, so I'll find a spare credit card. To be used within reason," he said as they left the garage.

"I understand, Jackson. I'm well aware of our lean finances."

"They're temporary," he growled. "Since I'm taking off before breakfast, I'll shove the credit card under your door."

They parted at the top of the stairs. Given all that had happened today, including those last few moments with Adam Ross, Noelani hoped the Fontaines' financial woes were indeed temporary. The sooner she got back to Hawaii, the better. For everyone.

CHAPTER FIVE

THE *COCHON DE LAIT* GOT underway at 10:00 a.m. Noelani had been up half the night checking and rechecking final details. She wanted it to go off without a hitch. Personal pride, she told herself. It wasn't because she needed to prove anything to Jackson and Casey. Although she admitted to herself that, deep down, proving her worth was what drove her. In her head lurked a little voice reminding her she'd been abandoned by her father and, in a way, her mother. When Duke Fontaine left, Anela Hana had lost her capacity to love. Her body bore his child, but her heart shriveled. And as the years passed, it died.

Noelani's *tutu,* a wise and practical woman, often said there were some things that just were. It was a hard concept for a kid to buy into. Because she couldn't help thinking that maybe if she tried harder or was smarter, prettier or…more perfect, maybe…

Blocking the old mental tape, Noelani exited the back door. Raising her head, she sniffed the steamy aroma of barbecue spices, saw Adam rounding the corner and tried to change her course.

He set down the folding table he carried on his shoulder so he could grab her arm. "Hey, sugar pie, what's your rush? Haven't seen you in over a week. I told Jackson that when he gave you Angelique's car, he created a monster."

She glanced guiltily away. In truth, he hadn't seen her since the night he'd kissed her because she'd purposely engineered her schedule to avoid him. Which was no mean feat. "I've, uh, been busy. And I need to go check on Mr. DuPree." Clutching her clipboard, she attempted to walk around him.

"Liar," he said softly. "You've been dodging me."

"You're right, Adam. I have."

A range of emotions crossed his face. "Mind telling me why?"

"I have my life. You have yours."

"Yeah. So? What kind of double-talk is that?"

"In a few months I'll be returning to Maui."

"Jeez, I figured since someone shipped you all your worldly possessions, it meant you'd decided to stay. I hauled four giant boxes up two flights of stairs and parked them outside your bedroom door."

"I—thank you, Adam. Bruce went overboard in what he sent."

"He did okay. I like the dress you have on. But what are these? I thought Hawaiians wore flower-things around their necks." He ran the tip of one forefinger down a long rope of polished black nuts draped to the waist of Noelani's flowing black-and-white flowered dress.

"The dress is a *holomuu* and these are *kukui* nuts. My grandmother hand-polished and tied them the old way for my high school graduation." She ran a reverent finger over the necklace, taking care to avoid contact with Adam's hand. "She passed away two days after she saw me graduate."

"Aw, sugar pie, I'm sorry. What family do you have left in Hawaii?"

"None. Grandmother's husband and sisters predeceased her. Anela was her only child."

"Then your only relatives are right here."

She looked startled, but only for a moment, then a wry

sadness stole over her. "I take it you missed the row Casey and Jackson had over my driving Angelique's car. Even if I wanted to, there's no hope of my ever bonding with Casey."

"Do you want to?"

"I'm not sure." She shrugged. "Yeah, I do. I've never been comfortable having people dislike me."

"Then persist."

"Like you? Aunt Esme told me often enough this past week that you asked why I quit eating with the family."

"Why did you?"

"I spent hours making the flyer. Also, Aunt Esme's car's in the shop. I drove her to the hair salon, the vet and to Toodles's groomer. She had meetings of the historical society, the garden club and her library committee. I did learn something interesting in the process of chauffeuring her around, though. Did you know she was once engaged to Murray Dewalt's dad?"

"Betty let it slip. She has no love for Esme *or* Roland Dewalt."

"I think it's a sad story. Aunt Esme brought Angelique, who was her best friend, home from the Sorbonne on winter break to help her plan a wedding. Roland and Duke supposedly both fell madly in love with Angelique. In the end Dewalt dumped Aunt Esme for nothing, because Angelique only had eyes for Duke."

"Yeah, well according to Betty, Esme's lucky she got dumped. Which says a lot. You've seen how those ladies bicker. But maybe you've never met Roland."

"We ran into him at the bank. He was rude to me, which was what prompted Aunt Esme's trip down memory lane. I gather the manner in which Roland broke their engagement caused quite a rift between the Dewalts and Fontaines."

"It didn't last. Murray practically lives at Bellefontaine.

He's sort of a know-it-all, but Jackson likes him. Casey and he had a major tiff recently.'' He made a careless gesture. "I'm not sure what he does for a living. He has a lot of free time, if you ask me.''

"Aunt Esme said Roland sold off half their plantation. I think they had pecan orchards and some cane. She said Dewalt used to own the refinery Duke bought.''

"Yeah. I did hear Murray discussing hybrid cane with Casey. She's growing some super-duper bug-and-rot-resistant cane for LSU's agricultural department.''

"I suppose Murray could also be involved in the development program.''

"Maybe. Hey, why are we spending our time talking about Murray? Before it gets too crazy around here, I want to put in my request for a dance with you.''

She flushed. "I won't be dancing, Adam. I'm the one making sure everything runs smoothly throughout the day and evening.''

"Are you kidding? When the music heats up, everybody dances.''

Noelani tightened her hold on the clipboard. "You were delivering a table, I believe, and I'm about to go check on our caterer.''

"Yeah. Auntie E said Betty needs a table for her desserts. If I don't get it delivered, Betty will accuse Esme of not telling me.''

"Talk about people who don't get along! Those two take the prize.''

"Or does each woman envy the other?''

"You obviously see something I'm missing.''

"Consider this. Betty slops around the house in jeans and rides a Harley. Does as she damn well pleases. Esme's every inch a lady. She still wears white gloves and a hat to church. She conforms to all of society's rules. Folks in town call her Miss Esme out of respect. Betty attended the school of hard knocks, not a finishing school in Paris, so she's jealous and gets in her digs. But maybe Esme's tired of being a straight arrow all the time.''

''Anything's possible. For a guy, you have deep insights into human failings.''

''You wouldn't be calling me an armchair psychologist, would you?'' Adam squatted to lift the six-foot folding table again. His well-defined biceps and back muscles bunched as he hoisted it to his shoulder. ''If so,'' he grunted, taking a few steps to balance the heavy load, ''just remember how remarkably shortsighted I am when it comes to identifying my own faults.'' He started down the path, but slowed when he drew abreast of her and winked broadly before taking off at a trot.

She found herself grinning at his foolishness just as Esme left the house. ''Mercy, I told Jacque DuPree you left fifteen minutes ago. Is something wrong? Who are you smiling at?'' Esme swung in a circle.

''At Adam. He can be so annoying one minute and so charming the next.''

Esme raised a carefully made-up eyebrow. ''His mother came from good stock. She was a delicate thing. The poor dear's life went from bad to worse after she married that Yankee pilot. Tragic, really, the way she lost the family home.''

The women walked together toward the floating smoke from the barbecues. ''No family is immune to problems, Aunt Esme. Vietnam wreaked havoc in a lot of lives,'' she said, as if Adam's mother needed an advocate.

''Nothing like the Civil War, Noelani. That war pitted brother against brother. I dislike talking about it. What I meant is, Adam has enough of his grandfather Ormond in him to counter the Ross blood. He's a good boy. Oh, does that pork smell delicious. A *cochon de lait* is exactly what we need to get beyond the unpleasantness of the last few months.''

"I haven't seen Jackson since his meeting at the bank yesterday. Is everything okay? Whenever I've run into him lately, he seemed pretty stressed.''

Esme fluttered a hand decked out with three rings, all set with impressive stones. "Duke's insurance carrier is being tedious. I'm sure it's routine to investigate a plane crash, but this is preposterous. My brother would *never* take his life or Angelique's. Oh, they had spats. What couple doesn't? But…Duke loved life. He loved the plantation and his family. I wish they'd settle the claim so things here can get back to normal.''

Noelani seconded that notion. She worried about what was happening with Bruce's harvest. He'd sounded rushed the last few times she'd phoned. Noelani trusted her programs to keep the mill running and yet—it would be nice to verify that all was well.

Esme broke into Noelani's private thoughts. "We part company here. I have to go see if that woman followed my instructions on mixing Mama's mint juleps.''

"That woman? Ah, you mean, Betty.'' Noelani remained somewhat confused. "I thought she's made the juleps for the last five years?''

"Humph! It'd be just like her to leave out an ingredient to spite me. Honestly, I wish Jackson would fire her. Hiring that woman is the only disagreement I ever had with Angelique. When the cook who'd been with us forever up and died, my sister-in-law brought in her twice-removed cousin without so much as consulting anyone else living under her roof.''

"I'm no gourmet, but Betty's meals certainly get eaten.''

Esme sniffed. "In public, she's a fright. I shudder to think what the neighbors say behind our backs when she rides that awful bike to the store to do our shopping."

Noelani remembered what Adam said about Esme secretly envying Betty her joie de vivre. "I wish I had the nerve to ask her to take me for a spin. It looks like such fun, don't you think?"

Esme appeared to be so thoroughly shocked, Noelani decided Adam was way off base. "Well, I'd better dash. People are starting to gather and it's barely nine-forty-five."

"Mill workers and field hands arrive in shifts. Normally we do this the weekend before harvest begins. Frankly, I'm surprised Jackson didn't cancel it altogether."

"He said it's tradition, and workers had begun to grumble. He probably made a wise decision. Happy workers are a lot more productive than unhappy ones."

"Yes, but whatever happened to loyalty for loyalty's sake? That horrid Broderick man who hit me and set our kitchen on fire claims he was getting back at the family because Casey fired him. When our papa ran Bellefontaine, the locals lined up and begged for work. To work at Bellefontaine then meant something."

"In Hawaii, cane growers spend huge amounts of time and money in labor negotiations."

"It's a crying shame, and that's the last I'll say on the subject." She lowered her voice. "Lord knows I'd hate to risk another discontented employee overhearing us."

"I should go, anyway. Jackson asked someone to spell the band I hired. We'd worked out a deal, but they forgot to tell me they take longer breaks over twelve hours. Speaking of labor problems." Noelani flashed a grin.

"Jackson twisted Luc Renault's arm to fill in. I'll grant you the boy is brilliant with a saxophone, but...there's a case where one of our old Creole families had a daughter marry beneath her. Viv's poor mother is still weeping over her marrying that *Cajun.*''

"Viv—she's Casey's best friend? I've seen them dashing in and out of Wisteria Cottage all week. If marrying beneath her presents a problem, it's not visible.''

"Cassandra and Nicholas are choosing colors for a house they're having built. Viv has a fine eye for design. Too bad she let love blind her.''

Noelani frowned. "How do you view my mother?''

"All families have their scandals,'' Esme said. "Duke and Jackson, at least, had the good sense not to marry their dalliances. Having you turn up is nothing compared to the people who've shown up at the doors of some of our other fine southern families.'' She rolled her eyes before marching off, leaving Noelani with her jaw hanging.

Noelani didn't know whether to laugh or be furious. Had Esme complimented her or insulted her? In either case, she decided to let it go. She could talk until she was blue in the face and never change the view of a woman as set in her ways as Esme Fontaine. Noelani had learned long ago to choose her battles with care. As her *tutu* said, some things a body couldn't change.

People of all sizes, shapes and skin tones began spilling onto the grounds of Bellefontaine. Many spoke a dialect of French Noelani found enchanting but hard to understand. Those were Acadians, she learned. Or Cajun, which was a more colloquial term. Esme had been right in one sense about Luc Renault. He played a mean saxophone. He could make that alto sax wail and cry like a baby.

The sun had peaked overhead before Noelani was satisfied the day was going well. She stood at the edge of the crowd, raptly listening to Luc jam with a trumpet player who'd hopped onto the makeshift stage. The two were playing what she heard a man in the crowd refer to as free jazz.

"There you are." Jackson dragged her aside. "No one's seen Casey in over an hour, including Adam and Nick. They're both over there pulling beer for the second wave of workers." He kept rising up to scan the crush of people circling the stage. Noelani thought he looked more frazzled today.

"I saw Casey earlier with Viv. But Viv drove off alone when I went to the house for a new supply of paper products. I let DuPree store them on the porch. He said otherwise folks help themselves to two or three plateloads of food at a time. What's up? You seem on edge."

"I am. There's a problem at the mill. One of the boilers has overheated. I told Marc to take it off line and shut it down. Duke hired the firm who installed the software, but I can't find their name or number in either the mill office or his files here. I thought Casey might know how to reach them. Dammit, I wasn't able to raise her at the cottage. Did she go to the fields? She hadn't planned to."

"Is her truck gone?"

"No. It's parked under the carport alongside Nick's car."

"If she'd gone to the fields, you'd think she would've told Nick."

"Yeah. Well, hell. I don't know what to do. There's no danger of it blowing up since we shut it down, but it slows production at peak season. And I'd like to be sure the others aren't going to go flooey, too."

"Want me to have a look? I've worked with several of the canned programs, and I wrote the one we use to run Shiller's cookers."

Jackson did a double take. "You wrote a program?"

"Yes, for the vats, and also one to operate our creeper feeder. I hate to brag, but I speeded up crushing our cane by ten percent."

"I should've known that."

"I told Casey. In fact, if you hadn't been rushing hither and yon these last few weeks, I intended to ask if you needed help at the mill." Noelani hesitated, then decided to take the bull by the horns. "Actually, I hoped that if I did a good job planning this party, you'd let me pitch in at the mill. I'm not one to sit idle."

"I'd like to have someone in the family overseeing the mill. I'm concentrating on the refinery Duke bought, plus trying to keep on top of meetings and the finances. It's no secret that we've had a rash of bad luck lately. I'd…ah, rest easier with someone I trusted on site."

"Has there been other trouble at the mill?" Noelani's ears perked up at the worried inflection in Jackson's voice.

"Landlords and growers are grumbling about being told their core samples are too dirty. But I guess they always gripe. Come on," he said, taking her arm. "Aunt Esme said she had Adam take her favorite rocker up on Casey's porch. We'll tell her we're going to the mill, so she can keep an eye on things here."

Adam cornered them before they reached Wisteria Cottage. "Hey, where are you two going in such a hurry? The band's starting up again. I was just coming to claim a dance, Noelani."

Jackson almost ran Adam down. "Afraid that'll have to wait. Noelani knows something about mill computers. We're on our way to put Aunt Esme in charge here, then I'm taking Noelani to the mill. Do me a favor, Adam. Tell Nick if he touches base with Casey, to have her meet us there."

"Sure. So will you make it back before the party ends?" Adam's eyes rested briefly on Noelani. His tone reflected his disappointment at having her spirited away.

"Depends on whether or not Noelani fixes the problem," Jackson said.

Adam nodded. "If I knew more than how to operate my own CAD system, I'd offer to lend a hand. Designing cabinets on my laptop is the extent of my know-how."

"Well, if Noelani pulls this off, she's got my undying gratitude."

"Stop!" she said. "That's a surefire way to jinx things before we start. I see Aunt Esme on Casey's porch where you said. I'll run and tell her, shall I?"

Jackson nodded. "And give her the message for Casey in case she returns to the house before she sees Nick."

Esme sat in an oversize wicker rocker, holding court on Casey's wide porch. At least that was the term that came to Noelani's mind. The older woman even sat regally. As workers came up the broad steps—both men and women— Esme extended the tips of her fingers, as if she were the queen and they her minions. Given what she'd said earlier, Esme probably did fill that lady-of-the-manor role.

Not inclined to get in line with those waiting to pay homage, Noelani hurried to the end of the porch and up the side steps. Gliding behind Esme, she bent and murmured Jackson's instructions.

Esme sneezed several times in a row and fumbled for her lace hankie.

Noelani noticed she seemed quite flushed and she smelled overwhelmingly of rose talcum powder and hair spray. "Aunt Esme, are you catching a cold?"

The older woman gazed at Noelani with a kind of beatific expression that suggested she might have sampled her mother's julep recipe more than was judicious. "It's too bad you have to leave, child. This is a splendid party. Splendid." Esme dismissed Noelani with a flip of her pale hand, causing a rainbow flash of gems.

Nodding, Noelani took a different route back to Jackson.

Once again she crossed paths with Adam, who hadn't yet returned to see Nick.

"Adam, I spoke with Aunt Esme. I, ah, suspect she's had too many mint juleps. Or she's taken a chill. She's sneezing her head off. Would you mind keeping an eye on things—and on her—while we're gone? I hate to impose, but..."

"No problem. As long as you hunt me up when you get back. Even if it's after the party, okay?"

"Sure. If you were me, Adam, would you tell Jackson his aunt's a little tipsy?"

"Nah. At Casey and Nick's wedding, she knocked back a few toddies. I think she sneezes when she's reached her limit. It slows her down because sneezing in public embarrasses her. Esme's not really a lush. As a rule she drinks tea."

"Good. I didn't know. Thanks, Adam. I see Jackson checking his watch. He's getting antsy, and I need to change into more appropriate work gear before we can leave."

Adam pounded a fist lightly against his heart. "Dammit, woman. Every time you have me drooling over some dress you're wearing, you manage to dispose of it before I can get you alone." He waggled his eyebrows.

"Ri-ight," she drawled. "Some things in life just aren't fair, Adam." As he smiled, Noelani rejoined Jackson. "Give me a minute to change? I talked to Aunt Esme. And Adam's promised to watch for any problems."

"I guess you do need to put on something you don't mind messing up. I don't have to tell you how sticky a mill gets. Oh, and wear tie-on shoes. We'll be traveling on catwalks."

"Where shall we meet? Here?"

"No. The Jag's out front. While you're changing, I'll track down Tanya and Megan. I want to be sure Megan's enjoying herself, and that she knows I'm gone."

Jackson was a conscientious dad, Noelani thought as she

went up to her room. She'd had a few conversations with Megan about her own childhood. During their next talk, she'd tell the girl how lucky she was to have one parent who cared for her welfare.

Noelani didn't waste time combing her hair or rechecking her makeup, but simply skimmed off her dress and dived into shorts, sturdy shoes and a T-shirt. Still, Jackson was pacing near the car when she came out. "Sorry. Have you been waiting long?"

"As a matter of fact, I just got here."

"What's that on your face? Barbecue sauce?"

He rubbed where she pointed. "Chocolate, from the fist-ful of chocolate-chip-pecan cookies Megan was chowing down. I told Tanya she absolutely had to make sure those were the last she ate. The kid'll be up half the night with a stomachache."

"They were delicious. I grabbed a couple myself. Betty must've made a million."

He took out a handkerchief and wiped his face. "It's the only way she knows how to make cookies. Maman finally had to ask her to bake only for special occasions. She took pride in her figure. Plus she didn't want Duke to end up paunchy like Roland Dewalt, Shel Prescott and half the other men their age."

"Aunt Esme let me leaf through her albums one day last week. Your parents were a handsome couple," she said wistfully.

He glanced up sharply as he shot the Jaguar out of the lane onto the main highway. "Duke's your parent, too," he reminded her gruffly. "And if you're at all like your mother, it's little wonder Duke was swept off his feet."

Noelani felt heat prickle up her neck. "Thanks. I think Mama was quite beautiful back then. But from my earliest conscious memory of her, she was too thin. She had a slow-growing cancer for which she refused treatment. Maybe living without Duke was more painful than suffering through a ravaging illness. She died when I was thirteen.'' Noelani plucked restlessly at her T-shirt.

''I won't make excuses for Duke's behavior. He and I had our disagreements. Like most sons of hard-charging fathers, I could never please my dad. I thought he pushed me too hard. But Roland always put Murray down, which was worse. Murray and I both rebelled for a time. I did some things I'm not particularly proud of. Basically, though, Duke did okay by us. Like I said, Casey thought he hung the moon.''

''I'm not placing the burden of his sins on you, Jackson. You're the first one here, outside of Adam, to ask about my mom. People who remember her from when she was young and carefree described a person I honestly never knew. I…guess I'd like you to understand she wasn't the type to deliberately seduce a married man.''

''No, probably not, or she wouldn't have stood silently by all those years. When I first found the letters Duke sent her, which had all come back unopened, I admit I wished to hell I knew what had gone wrong between Duke and Maman. Something, obviously, as I'm a mere three months older than you.''

''Duke didn't learn about me right away. From things Bruce Shiller let slip, he notified your father after Anela went into the hospital to deliver. She had a terrible labor. Ultimately the doctor did a cesarean, but she teetered between life and death for several weeks.''

''That would explain why the letters postdate your birth. There were four in all, and most of them were Duke inquiring about Anela's health. The date of the last one corresponds with Shelburne's account of when Duke changed his will and began to pay a monthly stipend via Shiller for Anela's keep, and yours.''

''If I'd known, I doubt I'd have come for the property settlement.''

''Why? It's nothing more than what you're due. I'm only sorry the settlement's turned out to be such a royal pain in the ass. I promise we'll get it sorted out. Ah, here's the mill. If you can make heads or tails of the problem, I'll be indebted to you, Noelani.''

''Before you start going all soft on me, Jackson, let's see if I can read the code.''

He parked a distance from a small outbuilding. They hiked to the mill, where he got hard hats and safety glasses for them both. ''This isn't the office where we house the computer for the vacuum vats. That's three levels up, near the boilers.''

Noelani looked carefully around as Jackson hustled her through the lower part of the mill. ''Your creeper feeder should travel faster, Jackson. If your computer has the capacity to handle greater speed, I can maximize that part of your operation. When Bruce sent my gear, he included my laptop and all the disks I'd left in my desk. I was annoyed with him for shipping so much, but maybe I should thank him.'' She pulled a small plastic case of disks out of her handbag, as well as printouts, which she unfolded.

''All that chicken scratching means something to you?''

Glancing up, she laughed. ''Those are codes to run an entire system.''

''Okay, this is it,'' he said, unlocking the door to a dark office. ''Marc, a guy the original analyst trained to watch the gauges, knows nothing about this end of the operation. He couldn't even remember the name of the company that trained him.''

''Most mill programming comes from one of three sources.

Yes,'' she exclaimed after sitting down, booting the system and ripping off her hard hat and goggles. ''This is the same basic program we use. I'll bet Bruce recommended these folks to Duke, or vice versa.''

Jackson lifted a series of black notebooks off an overhead shelf and set them beside Noelani. She clicked through several frames and flipped to corresponding pages in the book, frowning as she worked.

Clearly growing restless, Jackson prowled the room. ''How do you have the patience for that?'' he asked after approximately forty minutes.

''What? Oh, I love troubleshooting. It's what I do best. That, and writing new programs. I have a degree in computer science, with a minor in chemistry.''

''I wish I'd taken more computer classes.''

''My interest in computers is limited to improving output at a sugar mill.'' Silence descended on them again for a time.

''Here. I think I've found your glitch,'' she exclaimed after twice tracing a finger over a line of jargon in the book and matching it to what had come up on the screen.

''Really?'' He bent over her. ''How can you tell?''

''An entire string of code is missing.''

''Like—destroyed by a virus, you mean?'' Jackson straightened, his expression one of puzzlement.

''Gone, as in kaput. I doubt it's a virus, or more would be garbled.'' She propped the book up at an angle and began typing. When she'd finished, she saved it and tracked through another ten or twelve pages.

''That was probably enough to cause the steam to build,'' she said, closing the book with a snap. Pushing her chair back, she twisted her hair up off her neck. ''Shall we go kick it online again and give it a trial run? Depending on what stage spinning the sugar was in when everything overheated, you may be able to save the juice. If it's at *masse-cuite* stage, you can recook the batch and at least get black-strap molasses for cattle feed. How quickly did your guy, Marc, tumble to the problem?''

''We can ask him. We run three shifts in his position. I don't know if the problem started during his shift or the one before.''

They left the office with Jackson in the lead.

''Wait!'' Noelani grabbed his arm. ''Aren't you going to lock the door? As a matter of fact, who all has keys to this office?''

''The technicians who work up on the fourth level in the sterile lab, I think. To tell you the truth, I'm not really sure. Duke hired and managed the mill. He had the computer installed maybe five years ago. Does it matter?''

''It does if someone went into the program and deleted the line of code.''

They were still standing outside the office, discussing the likelihood of that possibility, when Casey pounded up the metal steps and stopped a foot away.

''What's wrong, Jackson? Nick said we had a problem with the cookers.''

''You did,'' Noelani answered as Jackson still tugged his lower lip perplexedly. ''I found a code wiped out and re-placed it. We're on our way to see if that's enough to get you up and running again.''

''Wiped out? Deliberately?'' Casey's eyes immediately cut to her brother.

''Noelani and I were just talking about that.''

''You know this how?'' Casey switched her laser gaze to Noelani.

''Lighten up, sis. Noelani has a degree in computer sci-ence. You won't believe how easily she waltzed through that mumbo jumbo.''

Noelani held up a hand. "Like I said, Jackson, hold your thanks until we test the system."

The three siblings climbed up a half level to an area where all but one vat spewed steam. Jackson introduced Noelani to Marc over the clatter of machines. They discussed the valves and gauges, then Marc flipped two breakers and several switches. All of them watched anxiously as pressure began to build.

"Hey, I don't know what miracle you worked," Marc said, half an hour later. "The vat reached proper centigrade temp and recycled exactly as designed."

Casey was the one who acted shaken. "I've gotta say, I'm impressed." She yelled to be heard above the noise from below. "You saved us the expense of lost time and also a service call. Neither of which is cheap." Surprisingly then, she stuck out her hand.

Noelani shook it, but when she drew back, she motioned Jackson and Casey a few feet away from where Marc fiddled with his gauges. "For that entire string of code to disappear, it'd take someone who knows his or her way around the program. You don't have to listen to me, but I advise getting someone out here to change the lock on the office door. I wouldn't keep any more than two keys around—one for each of you."

Casey Devlin shut her eyes. Then, in her smoky whiskey voice, she said, "Make that three keys. That night at the casino, I know I acted like a jerk when you said you knew sugar, Noelani. Now I'm thinking, since we're all in this sinking boat together, maybe it'd be a good idea for you to hang out here until harvest is done."

Noelani wanted to raise her fist in triumph. Instead, she said gravely, "I could, I suppose. Will you order a new lock?"

"Adam's downstairs with Nick. He can probably change

the lock in a jiffy. Noelani, stay and show him what you need. Jackson and I will send him up.'' Linking arms with her brother, Casey hauled him along the catwalk and down the steep steps.

Noelani followed more slowly. Peering over the railing, she saw their two heads together and wondered if they were discussing her. Shrugging, she decided she had no reason to be paranoid. Casey was right. They were all in the same boat.

And if Noelani had anything to say about it, that boat wasn't going to sink.

CHAPTER SIX

NOELANI EYED THE MILL critically while she waited for Adam. The equipment was old, but it all appeared to be chugging along. She breathed in the smoky scent of burnt sugar and felt truly at home for the first time since leaving Maui.

Glancing over the rail, she saw Adam before he noticed her. Still dressed in jeans and a white T-shirt, he bounded up the sticky stairs with ease and strode comfortably along the narrow mesh walkways. Someone, Jackson probably, had provided him with a hard hat and safety goggles. Noelani realized she'd left hers in the office. She disliked anything on her head, and glasses tended to get gummy with sugar residue.

"Hey, is it a bird, a plane or superwoman up there?" Adam called out as he topped yet another perpendicular set of steps wearing an audacious grin. "I'd begun to think I took a wrong turn below. Wow, is this place a maze or what? Do people really work up here in the nosebleed section?"

"Say again who I found dangling off a kitchen roof?"

"Okay, but you've got to admit working here could deafen you."

"It's no noisier than the power saw I've heard you using in the kitchen."

"Except that's sporadic, not constant. But hey, I didn't climb up here to argue. I'm more interested in learning all about how you saved the day. And unless my ears deceived me, I'd say you patched things up with Casey.''

The smile she'd withheld earlier blossomed now. "The problem with the computer was simple to fix. What's really a biggie, Adam, is that they're letting me work here. Jackson didn't specify duties, but having Casey suggest I tend the mill computer is more than I ever hoped for. If Jackson agrees to let me try, I know I can speed up the feeders that send cane through the crushers. Increased output is our primary goal.''

Without warning, Adam stopped her run-on chatter with a well-placed kiss.

She swallowed her next sentence. As she reeled from shock, it struck Noelani that she'd never been kissed at a mill before. She gave herself permission to absorb and savor the moment. Adam's shirt carried a faint odor of leftover barbecue smoke. His lips tasted pleasantly sweet of sugar mist. A familiar taste, but one combined with the headiness of risk. Around them forty tons of machinery whirred and clanked. The catwalk swayed. Boilers steamed. Any fool knew an operating mill could be a dangerous place, where you needed to keep your eyes wide open. Hers were closed. Definitely closed.

Adam eased out of the kiss not knowing what reaction to expect. It made his heart rush to see her blind attempt to follow his lips.

He covered her hands where she'd tangled them in his shirt. "Much as I hate to bring this up, we'd better go have a look at that lock." He spoke directly into her ear. "I'm all for continuing on as we were, mind you. But if you're going to be working here, you may not want to deal with the fallout from the interest we've sparked."

"What?" Her eyes snapped open in time to see several employees dart out of sight. She quickly backed away and yanked down her T-shirt, which had ridden up under Adam's seeking fingers. Charging headlong down the steps, Noelani took refuge in the shadows near the office, which was tucked beneath a bulwark of overhanging machinery. "Did Jackson give you his key?"

"Casey gave me hers. I see it's a standard lock. Shouldn't take half an hour to install a new one. Come to the hardware store with me and pick out the one you want."

"Isn't it a case of, if you've seen one lock, you've seen 'em all?"

He shrugged as his gaze swept the shrouded catwalk. "There are options. You may want to add a dead bolt."

"I'm only going to be here temporarily. Adam. These are questions you probably ought to ask Jackson or Casey."

"They went home. You were right about Aunt Esme sampling too many juleps, by the way. Shortly after you and Jackson took off, she came by sneezing like crazy. Considering how badly she wobbled, I decided to walk her to her room."

"If you and Nick brought Casey to the mill, who's in charge at the party?"

"DuPree. The guy's big as a house. Would you mess with him? Oh, and Nick cornered Luc and Viv. They promised to keep a lid on things. People were having fun—no hint of anyone getting out of line. Why are you so nervous? Were you expecting trouble?"

"Expecting it? No. Worried something might go wrong? Yes. You said yourself stuff's been happening around Bellefontaine. But since Jackson and Casey went back to the house, there's no reason I shouldn't go to the hardware store with you. If you promise not to make any sudden moves on me, that is. Out of curiosity, why did you kiss me up there?" Her eyes shifted to the catwalk above.

"You looked so kissable. And…it's been on my mind all

day. Do you need another reason? This is the first time since our last kiss that I've seen you without that damned clipboard you brandish like a shield.''

"That's ridiculous! A shield against what?''

"You tell me.''

"Did you ever think it might be *your* problem? That you can't handle the fact not every woman you flirt with is going to fall at your feet?''

He choked on a laugh. "You're mixing me up with Jackson and Nick. Although Nick's been out of the running since he first set eyes on Casey.''

"I think all of you honey-tongued southern boys have a habit of sweet-talking your way into the beds of foolish women. I don't happen to be foolish.''

"And I don't recall inviting you into my bed,'' Adam said clearly, but mildly.

That shut Noelani up for a second. "Isn't that what you're doing with your onslaught of kisses?''

"I like kissing you. Since you kissed me back, I assumed it was mutual. If I'm wrong, hey, tell me to get lost.''

She glanced warily around to see if any of the mill workers might be within hearing distance of their personal and not altogether flattering conversation. Admittedly she *had* returned Adam's kisses. And if she was honest about it, she did enjoy kissing him.

Because she was too shy to speak outright about any of this, she mustered some of Esme's starch for her backbone. "This is far too intimate a discussion to have where staff might eavesdrop,'' she said. "Anyway, if we're going to the hardware store, shouldn't we go?''

In spite of the dim overhead bulb that shed scant light in the secluded alcove, Adam saw the truth in Noelani's eyes. He'd given up on the notion of tending to his work and ignoring her. While he saw some reservation, the fact that she hadn't told him to get lost offered all the encouragement he needed. Grinning happily, he made a sweeping gesture with his hand, allowing her to lead the way out.

Once they reached the parking lot, she stopped and sent him a helpless look. "I rode with Jackson. Where are you parked?"

Adam grinned again as he dangled a set of keys in front of her face. "I came with Nick and Casey. Jackson rode home with them and left me the Jag."

"He's trusting, considering the insurance nightmare he outlined the other day at our meeting. I have no idea what Jaguars cost, but I'll bet it's a bunch."

"You've got that right." Adam unlocked her door and waited for her to climb inside before he closed her door and jogged to his. He adjusted the driver's seat and ignited the powerful engine. "What insurance nightmare?" he asked abruptly. "Didn't the company pay the fire claim?" In the back of his mind, Adam recalled Casey calculating what the insurance would pay before she'd signed a contract for his services. If those funds were in question and Casey had to delay his next installment, it could wreak havoc with his bidding on Magnolia Manor. An information update said the closed-bid process would likely start before month's end.

"I don't know about the fire, Adam. Jackson said Duke and Angelique's life insurance claims won't be paid until some sort of investigation of the crash is complete. There might be a holdup with the harvester payment, too. I'm not sure."

"I suppose this rash of claims could arouse curiosity at an insurance agency. I imagine Duke kept all his insurance under one umbrella."

Noelani shook her head. "I probably should've asked this already. I'm aware they crashed in Italy. Aunt Esme mentioned a funeral. But...was it a memorial service? If they held up the claim, were the bodies released?'' The face she turned toward Adam had lost a great deal of color.

''It was a nightmare, but Jackson managed to have their remains shipped home. That all took place while I worked up my initial proposal. I attended the joint burial service, of course. Jackson had it especially hard, since Megan had barely met her grandparents before they left on their trip. That poor kid lost her mom and her grandparents in a really short time. On top of everything, they learned about you when Jackson combed the files looking for Duke's policies. Casey was a basket case even before that. But I doubt you'd believe she's the type to go to pieces.''

''Give me a little credit, Adam. When I met her, I sensed she was covering a lot of pain with her anger.''

''It's rough losing someone you love without warning.''

''Loss under any circumstance is hard. Do you know where they're buried? Duke, anyway? It feels as if I should at least know where both of my parents have been laid to rest. Anela's in Hawaii.''

Adam's strong features relaxed. ''You're not as tough as you try to let on, either. You and Casey share that trait, even if neither of you admits it.''

''Jackson pointed out a few other things she and I have in common. Or are there universal reactions to birth, death and betrayal that women share?''

''What I know of women you could inscribe on the head of a pin,'' he said firmly enough for Noelani to glance over at him.

Adam's mind had scrolled backward to recall what losing his father had done to Charlotte Ross. Unlike his mother, neither Noelani nor Casey had withdrawn from the real world in their grief.

''I'm sorry, Adam. I've reminded you of your dad. Maybe those feelings I mentioned aren't universal only to women.''

"How did you know I was thinking about my past?"

"Because you suddenly got this distant expression. The same one I noticed the first time you mentioned your dad. Both times you fiddled with the cross you wear around your neck. Did it belong to him? Your father, I mean."

"I bought it with money I earned from a paper route. The jeweler engraved Dad's name on the back, along with the date his plane went down. Most friends and family of MIA victims wore commemorative bracelets. I thought a cross might…well…" Lowering his eyes, he shrugged. "Uh, there's the hardware store. If we're quick choosing a lock, I can install it today. We should still make it to Bellefontaine early enough to help wind down the *cochon de lait*."

And they did. But not before Adam had detoured past the above-ground cemetery where Duke and Angelique lay buried in vaults shared by a long line of Fontaine ancestors. The sun-bleached concrete tombs belonging to maybe fifty families were arranged between cane fields that stretched as far as the eye could see. Compared to the peaceful but traditional resting place of Noelani's *ohana*—the Hawaiian part of her family—the Fontaine crypt unsettled her.

So much so that Adam felt compelled to explain. "The Mississippi often rises and floods the bottomlands, Noelani. I assumed you were already aware that's why we bury aboveground in this part of Louisiana."

"I had no idea." Noelani couldn't seem to shake her unrest. Imagine how difficult it must be for Casey, having to plant and harvest cane so near the vault where her loved ones would spend eternity. Not ancestors, but people she'd kissed, hugged and seen every day, probably right up to the day they left on a simple trip. A second honeymoon, apparently.

She and Adam were both wrong about Casey Fontaine Devlin. The woman had grit through and through.

"Are you okay?" Adam asked after they'd rejoined the dwindling party. She hadn't said three words since they'd left the cemetery. "The band's actually playing a tune I think I can dance to," he said, and smiled warmly. "How about it? Shall we lose ourselves in the music? Otherwise, if I know you, you'll get involved in cleaning up."

Her sober eyes rested on his face a moment. "You *don't* know me, Adam. No one here does. The cane, the *roulais-ant*—that whole milling process I understand. The peo-ple…we're so very different. Even if I wanted to, I'd never fit in here."

"I only asked for a dance, sugar pie. I wasn't proposing marriage." Adam tapped a finger on the tip of her nose. He ended up brushing his thumb back and forth over her bottom lip. His goal had been to lighten her mood. Something—he wasn't sure what—had stolen the sparkle from her eyes. Eyes that enthralled him with their changing colors. Nor-mally her huge dark eyes expressed her every thought. Not this evening. Now they were bottomless and troubled.

"I'm sorry. I wasn't referring to your question. Yes, let's dance. Remember I warned you that it's not true what they say about all Hawaiian women having rhythm."

"Damn, then we'll be falling all over each other's feet. I kid you not, this is probably the first time I've danced since I left college."

"Get outta here. You tell such whoppers, Adam Ross."

"It's true." He gathered her close for the skin-shivering, bluesy tune a man on an electronic keyboard and one with a mournful slide trombone were playing to set a new mood. A going-home, taking-your-lover-to-bed mood. Adam felt it the moment he took Noelani in his arms. Even as he tucked her silky hair beneath his chin and she curled against his chest, he realized he was a goner. His heart thudded in time to the bass licks, but it was the woman in his arms who stirred to life a long-dormant part of his anatomy. It'd been years since anyone had affected Adam with such immediacy. He lost his concentration and landed squarely on Noelani's toes. "Jeez, I'm sorry. Did I hurt you?" He pulled back, grateful that they were on the outer edge of the dancers, in deep shadows cast by several huge live oaks.

She laughed and pressed three fingers to his lips. "As dancers, I swear we'd make better pineapple pickers."

"I spoiled the mood," he grumbled. "Are you sure you aren't crippled for life?"

"I'm sure. It's probably my own fault for changing into sneakers. They're good for running the catwalks at the mill. Not so good for tripping the light fantastic."

"Thanks, Noelani." He caught her hand again when she tried to shake loose and slip away. Bringing her knuckles to his lips, he kissed them one by one, then whispered in a husky voice, "The first day we met I remember being impressed with your sense of humor."

"Some sense of humor. I remember getting uppity when you paid my cab fare. Come to think of it, I still owe you."

"If you want to pay me back, sneak away with me now. There's something I want you to see."

Noelani studied him warily. She saw nothing but boyish eagerness reflecting from his guileless blue eyes. Maybe she'd been mistaken when, during the dance, she thought he'd reacted sexually to her. "Adam, this isn't something in your garçonnière, is it?"

"Sorry, no etchings—but, I could be persuaded to change my plans and give you a guided tour of my quarters."

"Maybe one of these days I'll take you up on your offer. I'll bring Megan over—say on an evening when Tanya has class. Neither of us has been inside a garçonnière."

He tipped back his head and laughed. "Okay, I had that coming. What I really have in mind will take about ten minutes. If I ever do coax you into my bed, Noelani, I guarantee you'll be there longer than ten minutes.''

"Ten minutes, huh?" She could feel heat washing over her face. "Okay. I'll give you that much. Then I'll have to get back and begin picking up around here. Betty is looking weary, and Auntie E must have retired already.''

"Meet me at my pickup. I need to grab an industrial flashlight from my toolbox.''

He intrigued Noelani with that statement. She tried to worm out of him where they were going as he boosted her into the pickup. But he refused to say. He drove to the end of the lane and turned right rather than left, which would take them toward town.

They'd traveled two or three miles along the winding road when Adam suddenly pulled into a driveway she hadn't even noticed because it was so overgrown. Stopping, he yanked on the emergency brake.

"Where are we? Who lives here?''

"No one now.'' There was a thread of eagerness in his voice. "This is Magnolia Manor." He got down from the cab, then helped her out, snapping on the powerful flashlight. The beam cut through the darkness, revealing a heavy chain looped around a warped gate. "We can't go inside. Another time, perhaps. The bank or whoever owns the property has cut off the power." He moved the light slowly over a two-story dwelling that stood fifty or so yards off the road. The once-green lawn had been taken over by weeds. The house was less than half the size of Bellefontaine. Ten upright four-by-fours separated the upper and lower stories, and three cupolas jutted from a gray shingle roof. Dark mysterious areas between the uprights probably contained windows or doors. Adam's flashlight, though powerful, didn't reach quite that far.

"This is where you grew up?" Noelani stepped closer to Adam along the peeling white split-rail fence.

"Yes. I'm hoping to buy it back. I've heard from a reliable source that it'll be auctioned by the state through closed bids sometime this month."

"Really? How much land is in the parcel?"

"Thirty acres. I have the plot figures. The backyard slopes to the levee. Otherwise there's not a lot of land beyond that line of trees." He shone the light from one edge of the house to the other.

"No fields for growing cane? Bellefontaine sits on five hundred acres, and has two thousand more cultivated. Adam, why on earth would you sink good money into nothing but an old house?"

Adam felt as if she'd punched him in the gut. He blinked several times at her, saying nothing.

"I'm sorry, I know the house has sentimental value. But I honestly can't understand why you or anyone would risk hard-earned money on a structure that will only drain you. Raw land gives back everything a person puts into it and more."

Adam abruptly snapped off the light. "The ten minutes you were willing to give me are probably up," he said stiffly. "Come on, let's get you back to Bellefontaine."

Noelani settled into the thick silence inside Adam's pickup truck. Clearly she hadn't reacted the way he'd wanted or expected her to. But for the life of her, she really had no idea why anyone would work as long and hard as Adam had for a mere house. Yet she knew he'd been saving to do exactly that. Auntie E and Tanya had both said that buying back his family estate was Adam's big dream. Naturally, she'd assumed Magnolia Manor included cane fields, since all the old plantations in the area did.

Nothing she said on the short trip back to Bellefontaine penetrated the wall Adam had thrown up between them.

"Thank you," she said hesitantly, after he swung in next to the garçonnière and parked. "I hope you successfully outbid everyone else, Adam. I mean that." Suddenly miserable, she figured wishing him luck was the least she could do.

Adam slammed out of the car. He didn't want her good luck, dammit. He couldn't say *why* it mattered how she felt about the home he loved, but for some reason it did.

Manners were ingrained in him, so he assisted her from the pickup, even though she wouldn't blame him if he left her to fend for herself.

"Are you going back to the party, Adam?"

"Nope. I have things to check in the kitchen. Then I'm hitting the hay."

Noelani hadn't imagined his cool attitude would affect her so profoundly. All along she'd tried to be honest. She'd said her stay here would be short. And God knew she didn't need the extra pressure of an entanglement. Neither did he, if truth be known. Then why did she feel so guilty trudging back to the remains of the party, where a few diehards continued to goad the band into playing yet another *last* tune?

Head down and hands stuffed in her back pockets, Noelani didn't see Casey and Nick walking arm in arm along the path. She almost bumped into them.

"Jackson's been looking for you," Casey said. "He's wondering if you gave the band a set time to quit."

"Their contract is for twelve hours with six breaks. That's nine o'clock based on my calculations." She checked her watch. "Oh, it *is* nine. Wow! Well, I have their check on my clipboard. I'll run upstairs and get it. I left it in my room when Jackson invited me to run out to the mill."

"Have you been at the mill all this time?" Casey's eyes widened in surprise.

"More or less," Noelani mumbled. She didn't want to talk about her side trips with Adam. Not the one to the graveyard Duke was buried or the more recent visit to Adam's boyhood home.

"Adam didn't have any trouble changing the lock, did he?"

"No." Noelani dug in her pocket. "Do you want the spare keys? The new lock came with three."

"That's good. I'll take one, and you can give Jackson the other." Casey accepted a key, but acted as though she had something else on her mind.

Noelani didn't give her time to say whatever it was. "Did Jackson mention whether or not he has time to introduce me around the mill tomorrow? I can't imagine the crew will be overjoyed with me poking my nose into their work all on my own."

"He'll have to give you a title and let everyone know. If…uh…you had to make an educated guess, what do you think happened to that vat program?"

"I'd say somebody pulled up the operating files like I did, paged forward and deleted a row of code."

Nick stroked a lightly stubbled cheek. "In other words, someone willfully caused a slowdown. But people with that kind of knowledge could have destroyed the system if that had been their aim. Right?"

"They could have wiped the disk clean and shut down all the cookers. If they'd wanted to mess things up long-term, they'd have wrecked or stolen the code books and backup system disks." She frowned thoughtfully. "The company that installed the system probably gave someone a backup operating disk. Who'd know where it's stored?"

Casey stirred. "Duke handled the entire installation. He

may have brought such a disk home. If so, it'll be in his office. Otherwise, it's probably lying around the mill office. He wasn't the most computer-savvy person in the world.''

Hearing his wife's voice tremble, Nick drew Casey closer. "There's no chance the string of code disappeared accidentally?" he asked Noelani.

"Sure, it's remotely possible. If somebody was playing on the computer, happened on the program and accidentally leaned on the delete key.''

"A lot of coincidences," Nick said, expressing the worry on Casey's face.

Noelani nodded. "Precisely. Yet, coincidences can occur. If you don't mind a suggestion, it'd be better not to make my title anything to do with computers. That is, if your objective is to find and catch anyone who might have fiddled with the program on purpose. If your object is to simply discourage them from messing with the system, then call me an analyst.''

Casey rubbed her forehead. "I've had trouble getting a handle on any of the things going on lately. We've fired employees before, and a few have even made threats. Broderick is in jail for carrying out awful deeds that were never even threats. If someone's attacked the mill, it means we have another warped person who hates us.''

"Or it means Broderick didn't act alone," Nick said. "You know Jackson and I never thought he had the brains to engineer all the stuff he's charged with.''

"And he claims some unknown man hired him. But the police are sure he's lying about that, Nick.''

Noelani listened raptly. "It's probably none of my business, but Adam and I were at the casino when a man by the name of Chuck Riley caused a commotion. He said Duke owed him money.''

"It's possible. Riley was too drunk to listen when I said

the NTSB hasn't yet given us the plane's log. Chuck may have flight pay coming. I suppose we could take his word and cut him a check. Jackson would prefer to wait until we have proof of the number of hours he actually flew.''

''Jackson isn't willing to give that bastard a cent more than he's due.'' Casey's brother walked up behind Noelani. ''Riley hasn't drawn a sober breath since he returned to Louisiana. I want to see Duke's trip log. Chuck swore Duke insisted on flying the day of the crash, but I wonder if Riley was actually drunk, in which case he forced Duke to fly. If that's what happened, he'll never get a red cent out of me. Casey, speaking of pay—did you ask Noelani about the check for the band?''

''I was on my way to get it, as well as the second half of DuPree's money. Sorry, we started talking about the mill.''

''That's okay. We'll sit down and draft a plan of sorts for your duties there. Casey? Nick? Shall we go say good-night to our hangers-on? Nick, if you'll help the band dismantle the speakers, I'll give DuPree a hand loading up his barbecues. Casey, I don't know if you feel up to helping Betty cart pots and dishes back to the house but—''

''Why wouldn't I?''

''You've been looking pale this week. I thought with the miscarriage and all—'' Jackson saw her quelling glance and swallowed the rest of his statement.

''You suffered a miscarriage?'' Noelani, who'd turned toward the house, spun around, her face a mask of sympathy. ''On top of everything else you've had to deal with? Heavens.''

''Yeah. I wasn't very far along. We'd just done the strip test, in fact.'' Unexpected tears shimmered in Casey's green eyes. She bit down on her lip and fanned her face rapidly. ''Damn, I hate women who cry over every little thing.''

"Losing a baby isn't a little thing," Noelani exclaimed, reaching without thinking for Casey's free hand. "Please go put your feet up. I'll be right back. After I dispense the checks, I'll help Betty."

"Where did Adam get off to?" Jackson asked, changing the subject.

Noelani tensed. "He…ah…said he had a couple of things to check in the kitchen. Then he planned to go to bed."

"Casey, are you okay?" Nick gathered both of her hands.

She bobbed her head repeatedly. "I'd be great if Jackson hadn't mentioned the ba-baby." Tears pooled along her lower eyelids again. This time she pulled away from Nick and used the heels of her hands to scrub at them furiously.

Nick herded her toward the porch and the old kitchen. "Why don't you fix a pot of coffee? I'll go see if Adam's hit the sack yet. If not, he can help lug tables and chairs back to the shed. With three of us, we'll be able to clean up in nothing flat. Then we'll join you ladies and hammer out a plan for this mill situation."

They split up, going in different directions.

Had Adam gone to bed or was he sulking on his porch with a beer? Noelani wondered if he'd discuss her with Nick. Or maybe guys didn't do stuff like that—maybe they didn't gossip about the women they dated. And maybe the sun didn't rise in the east.

She found the checks where she'd left them. The second floor was quiet except for someone snoring. Auntie E or Toodles? Noelani smiled, imagining how horrified Esme would feel over being caught snoring.

Obviously Tanya and Megan were asleep. No light filtered under either door. Since the backstairs were closer to the path leading back to the party, Noelani sped off down the dimly lit hall. She met Tanya on the landing.

The young woman cracked her gum as she flattened herself against the wall. "Where are you headed so fast? The band's quit, and the party's over."

"I have the band's check. Where's Megan?"

"In bed. Like I'm stupid enough to keep a kid up this late? But I suppose you'll run and tattle to Jackson that I snuck back out to dance."

Noelani hesitated. "You shouldn't have left Megan alone."

"Aunt Esme's in her room."

Sleeping off the effects of too many mint juleps. Noelani didn't feel like sharing that with Tanya. "Aunt Esme isn't being paid to care for Megan. You are."

"Yeah, well the kid was upset because you took off with her dad. And that old poop promised me a dance, which I never got. We saw you climb into his Jag. The two of you were gone for hours. Megan asked a million times where you went. Where *did* you go, might I ask?"

There was no reason not to tell her, except that Noelani thought Tanya was a ding-a-ling who was more interested in Jackson than Megan. "He and I have an early-morning mission, too. Tell Megan I'll have her dad bring her a surprise from town." Deliberately skirting the nanny, Noelani ran lightly down the stairs. Tanya's hostility followed her. But honestly, if the girl was too dense to realize there couldn't possibly be any hanky-panky between Jackson and his half sister, she deserved to be left in the dark.

Back at the site, Noelani thanked the band and DuPree. "My pleasure, little lady," the big man said, shifting an unlit cigar from one side of his mouth to the other.

Betty materialized out of the shadows, her arms laden with dirty dishes. Finding the cook had been next on Noelani's list. "Ah, Betty, let me take those. How many more pots and dishes are out here?"

"This is it. I'll let you have 'em, though. Rufus and me

are going for a moonlight spin on my Harley. Unless he chickens out,'' she said, jabbing DuPree in his beer belly.

"I told you, Betty, I'll go if you let me drive. Otherwise I'd be laughed clean out of Green Water Bayou if any of the guys see me perched on that little ol' buddy seat.''

"My bike. I drive.''

"Aw, dammit it, woman. Think about my image.''

"Think about mine.'' Betty flicked her unlit cigarette into the trees. The two sauntered off, still arguing. Noelani couldn't help but smile at the unlikely pair.

"Did you forget which direction you were going?'' Adam came up behind her, jolting her out of her reverie. His voice alone left her longing for the camaraderie she'd witnessed between Betty and DuPree. Adam balanced a table on his shoulder.

"This is déjà vu,'' she quipped. "Is that the same table you carried out this morning?''

"Not quite déjà vu. You're missing your clipboard. Nick says y'all are gonna have a powwow. What's that about?''

"My work schedule at the mill, and maybe devising a plan to catch whoever caused the glitch in the computer program.''

Adam's eyes locked with hers for several long, troubled moments. "Is that wise?'' he finally ventured. "The police term for that would be *sabotage*. And folks who mess in treachery of that nature generally aren't your friendly boy or girl next door.''

"Or it could be nothing,'' she said, brushing aside his concern.

"Uh-huh,'' he drawled. He didn't sound convinced. "Shoot the dead bolt I installed anytime you're in the office, will you? And have Jackson get you a cell phone.''

"I thought you were mad at me, so why do you care?"

"Damned if I know," he muttered, hoisting the table higher on his shoulder. "I just do," he said, loping along the path. She stood there with her mouth open.

CHAPTER SEVEN

NOELANI'S NOSE FOLLOWED the scent of fresh coffee. Casey's head jerked up when the door opened, but her expectant smile faded the minute she saw who walked in. Although the women had buried the hatchet as far as business was concerned, Casey Devlin remained aloof. Or uneasy. The men hadn't yet arrived.

"The coffee smells heavenly." Noelani helped herself to a mug, poured it full, then added a dollop of cream. "I skipped breakfast and lunch except for two of Betty's cookies. This is the first I've slowed down all day."

"Everyone enjoyed the *cochon de lait*." Casey stirred sugar into her coffee.

"Good. I hardly slept a wink last night for worrying."

Casey licked her spoon. "You stressed out over a party? Why?"

"Would you be asking that if it'd flopped?"

"Touché! I'd have pounced all over you."

Noelani fiddled with her cup and sighed. "I'm sure you'd like me to have two heads and a forked tail. But as I told Jackson, nothing any of us does or says will change the circumstances of my birth. So, if you want to hate me, hate me."

"I don't want to hate you. I want to know why Duke put us all in this predicament, dammit! I thought he and Maman had the perfect marriage."

"My grandmother blamed it on the *menehune*. Those are

the Hawaiian equivalent of leprechauns. They're purported to have great magical powers.''

Casey smiled crookedly. ''So, you're saying I shouldn't bother placing blame?''

''Far be it from me to flog you for doing something I've indulged in for years.''

''Weren't you ever curious about us? Jackson and me, I mean.''

''I only learned about you when Bruce received Mr. Prescott's letter. You don't want to know my first reaction to that, believe me.''

''Nick insists there are two sides to every coin.'' Casey uttered a semichuckle. ''I closed my ears when he said it, but damn, he's right as usual. Speak of the devil, I hear him and Jackson now. I'm glad we had this chat, Noelani. If nothing else, you've been incredibly candid. The guys let me vent, but they simply don't see things the way a woman does. And my good friend Viv shrugs off other people's opinions. She can't really understand why I'd be so angry at Duke. I think you can.''

''Can what?'' Nick walked in and dropped tiredly into the vacant chair next to his wife.

''Nothing. Were your ears burning? I told Noelani you're always right.''

A grin slashed his very masculine face. ''Hey, deal with it, princess.''

Jackson set a steaming mug in front of Nick and pulled out a chair between the women. ''Go ahead and crow. She admitted it in front of witnesses, Nick.''

''Before we start,'' Noelani said, turning to Jackson. ''We ran off today and Megan's feeling neglected. I told Tanya to let her know you'd bring a surprise from town tomorrow. Anything is okay. Kids love little trinkets. Even small gifts say *I care* to a kid.''

The other three gaped at her. She frowned at each. "You think a gift has to be expensive? Oh—you obviously think I'm presumptuous to commit money we can ill afford. Don't they have dollar stores here?"

"It's not the money," Casey said. "I don't know about Jackson, but I'm amazed you'd bother with Megan."

"Why? Because you think I'm a bitch? Since there's only family here, let's put our cards on the table. What, exactly, do you all think of me? Expect of me?"

Jackson stirred uncomfortably. Nick kept his eyes trained on Casey's face. She clasped and unclasped her hands around her mug. No one spoke for a moment, then finally, she cleared her throat. "Okay, here goes. Jackson and I have been involved in the day-to-day running of Bellefontaine since we were teens. To say we were horrified to learn that Duke would divide it with a stranger—at a time when we were already devastated by the news of our parents' deaths—is an understatement. You accused me of hating you and I said I didn't. But you're still something of a mystery. *Bitch* might be a stronger term than I'd use, but I *have* called you a gold digger. And I assumed you couldn't care less about any of us—including Megan. After all, you came here asking us to bleed our funds to buy you out. That's the truth as I see it. Take it or leave it."

Noelani didn't shy away from Casey's spitting eyes. "If my goal was to bleed Bellefontaine dry, I'd have hired a lawyer and demanded you liquidate your holdings to pay me. And I would've had that right. But from the outset I agreed to wait until the crop's in. I'm volunteering my time and experience to help speed the process. As far as my being a mystery, I notice you don't ask a lot about my past. I grew up walking, talking, living sugarcane. I've never pictured myself doing anything else. One day, I hope to buy out Bruce Shiller."

Jackson glanced at first one woman, then the other. "You may kill me for saying so, but you're both a chip off the old block. Duke faced adversity head-on and he never backed down from an argument. Thank God I'm more like Maman. A negotiator sort. It strikes me that we're all reasonably intelligent people who have basically the same short-term goal. Namely, get this year's sugar to market."

Casey settled back in her chair. "Agreed."

Noelani nodded, and Nick remained quietly sipping his coffee. "We don't have to love one another to accomplish that end," Noelani said.

"We do have to present a united front to the employees," Jackson shot back.

"I'll buy that," Casey said. "Noelani impressed me today in an area we're deficient in, Jackson. I can run a canned program to track growth of my hybrids, and Jackson, you have a layman's knowledge of computers. Noelani has a computer science degree."

"And one in chemistry," she said with a lack of modesty. "I have to say I like the way you two have handled a rash of setbacks that would intimidate a lot of others."

"There's your common ground," Nick said, putting in his two cents' worth. "Respect and a united goal is more than a lot of marriages start with. Not ours," he rushed to say when Casey came forward in her chair.

Leaning his elbows on the table, Jackson rubbed his hands together. "Duke oversaw the whole operation by himself. Casey elevated Len Forsen to field manager not long ago, in order to devote more time to her hybrids. I'll tell old-timers at the mill that I'm investing my time and energy in rebuilding the refinery, which is why we've elected to let Noelani manage the mill."

"Jackson, that's brilliant." Casey rose, yawned and tugged Nick to his feet. "It sets the stage, allowing Noelani to poke her nose into everyone's station. I hate to sound wimpy, but frankly, I'm beat. I've gotta go home to bed.''

As if to confirm the lateness of the hour, the old grandfather clock in the corner of the kitchen chimed 3:00 a.m.

''I'll only keep you another minute,'' Jackson said, stalling their departure. ''Next weekend is the Sugar Fest.'' He elaborated for Noelani's benefit. ''The West Baton Rouge Museum is housed in an early 1800s French Creole home, where they've preserved the history of sugar. The fest is designed to educate locals and tourists alike regarding the importance of what we do. I told the coordinator we'd all be happy to attend and support the festival this year in Duke and Maman's absence.''

''Murray left me a note today asking if we're participating.'' Casey sighed. ''Can't Aunt Esme represent Bellefontaine? She has all those period costumes she wears during the historic home tours. She and Maman loved re-creating yesteryear. It's not me, Jackson. The New Iberia festival is more my style. I deal better with the Mardi Gras atmosphere.''

''I know.'' Jackson expelled a breath. ''But I want Megan involved. Kids get a kick out of seeing how they cook the cane in open kettles the way they used to. I think she'll enjoy the working replica of the old mill, too. Noelani, you'll find it fascinating, I'm sure.''

''Sounds like it. I've never been to a museum devoted to our industry.''

''Take Adam,'' Nick suggested. ''He loves poking around among moldy antiques.''

Noelani felt herself blush without meaning to. ''I doubt he'll spare the time from his work. But count on me. Just draw me a map. You guys have a ton of events associated with cane harvest, don't you? It's big business on Maui, but that's all it is. And even that's dwindling,'' she said, a certain sadness creeping into her tone. Rousing slightly, she turned to Jackson. "I probably should follow you to the mill tomorrow in your mother's car. That way, you won't have to hang around waiting for me."

"You're right. I have a full day of appointments on my calendar."

"Ouch. Now you have to rearrange your schedule to introduce me around the mill. To say nothing of finding time to buy Megan some little gift. I'll run out during lunch hour, if you'd like. It seems the least I can do, since I volunteered on your behalf."

"No. In fact, I need to get in the habit of bringing her surprises now and again. I always provided money for her clothes and toys, but I can't be sure Janis told Megan, or that she spent the money for what it was meant. I visited Megan when I could—or rather, when her mom said it was convenient."

"You tried, Jackson. That's to be commended." Whether Noelani intended to let her expression reflect her old resentments or not, it did.

Casey immediately flew to her father's defense. "Duke sent support money every month. His account logs every payment to your mother. And Janis at least allowed Jackson to be in Megan's life. You yourself admit your mom wouldn't even talk to you about Duke, let alone encourage contact. Maybe it wasn't his fault."

"Anela died fifteen years ago," Noelani said. "Bruce notified Duke. He more or less told Bruce it suited his purposes to have me living half a continent away. Not that I'd have come here if he'd begged me on bended knee." But of course she would have. She was the only one who did know that well-kept secret. She'd have given anything if the man who'd fathered her had thrown her the smallest crumb of affection.

"Here we go again," Jackson said, slicing a hand through the air. "Sniping at one another over things in the past. Things out of our control. Noelani, we won't leave the house until seven tomorrow. All this arguing makes me realize I need to cement a relationship with my daughter before it's too late."

"I'll be ready. If I don't make it down for breakfast, don't worry. I sometimes prefer an extra half hour of sleep over food." Inclining her head ever so slightly at Casey and Nick, she set her mug on the sideboard and strolled out.

SHE DID WAKE UP EARLY ENOUGH to go down for breakfast. Mainly because the prospect of immersing herself in the mill excited her.

Though they were all sleepy-eyed, everyone sat around the table. Megan and Tanya were on either side of Jackson, regaling him with tales of *cochon de lait* and the parts he'd missed. Adam and Aunt Esme sat at the opposite end of the trestle table. They, too, were deep in conversation. The way Toodles licked his chops, Noelani figured Esme had fed him a tidbit off her plate, as she often did but swore she didn't.

Esme noticed Noelani first. Or rather she noticed the frayed jeans, hiking boots and a faded red T-shirt Noelani had on. Work gloves also poked out of her back pocket. "Sakes alive, child, there's no need for you to help clean up from the *cochon de lait*. Our gardeners have already seen to that. Or else they will shortly."

"Jackson didn't tell you I'm starting work at the mill today?" Noelani picked up a mug and went about her routine of filling it with coffee and adding cream.

Esme glared at Jackson. "It's not bad enough that Cassandra sees fit to disgrace the family showing up in town dressed like a field hand? Now you've corrupted Noelani?"

"No one's corrupted me, Auntie E. I've practically run

Shiller's mill since I graduated from college. It's what I do.''

Esme sniffed. ''Lord only knows what this world's coming to. In my day a woman had soft hands a man wanted to hold. And skin he wanted to kiss. You and Cassandra, your complexions will be boot leather before you're forty.''

''That's what good hand creams are for.''

''Humph! Homes like ours need a woman devoted to keeping them beautiful and running like clockwork. I don't advocate that women sit idle, mind you, but men's work should be left to men. What's wrong with you, Jackson? Or Nick? Or you, Adam? Why would you encourage such foolishness?''

Jackson smiled. ''How did I get drawn into this conversation? I'm talking with Megan and Tanya about the *cochon de lait.*''

Adam drew back. ''Don't involve me in this feud, Auntie E.''

''Now, Adam. When we first discussed the kitchen renovation, I recall you telling me that whoever you marry will make maintaining Magnolia Manor a top priority.''

''Brother, talk about archaic thinking!'' Noelani snorted inelegantly.

Unmoved by her theatrics, Adam said patiently, ''You're jumping to conclusions, Noelani. I wasn't putting women down but elevating them to the status they deserve. If you knew the history of the South, you'd see that our women were capable and strong. During the Civil War they fed the troops, bandaged the wounded and more. Yet in the process of caring for their menfolk, none ever lost her dignity or beauty.''

''We're not in a war, Adam. During World War II, women in Hawaii did all those things. Plus they flew planes, serviced engines and reported activity of enemy aircraft.''

Esme daintily broke a buttered biscuit in fourths. "The difference, Noelani, is that after the Second World War, women continued to work outside the home. They quit teaching their daughters to quilt, play the piano or set a proper table. Today they hire virtual strangers to fulfill a wife and mother's role. If the money a woman earns goes to pay those expenses, what's the point?"

Noelani gathered her ammunition to fire back, but Tanya interrupted. "I agree with Miz Esme. What woman, given the opportunity to be the queen bee of a hive like Bellefontaine, would drive miles on the freeway every day to...say, get all grungy in the fields or equally grubby working in the sugar mill?"

Tanya was so obvious in the way she batted her big eyes at Jackson. Opening and closing her mouth twice, Noelani finally decided there was simply no way to combat people who didn't want to understand that modern marriages were partnerships and that equality meant women had choices. "Uh, Jackson, my watch says five after seven. Last night you said we should get under way by seven."

"Right." Rising, he picked up his plate and prepared to carry it and his mug to the screened-in kitchen porch. "Adam, my friend, all I can say is you're either a brave, brave man, or one who places zero value on his life. The only way I'd venture a comment on this subject would be if I wore a full suit of armor. Even then, I'd have second thoughts." Jackson clapped Adam on the back and left, chortling.

Noelani refilled her mug and left, period. She was surprised when Adam followed her outside. "Adam, Jackson made a good point. If you've come out to continue the argument, it'll be one-sided." She juggled her mug while she fished car keys from the tote she'd slung over her shoulder.

Adam relieved her of the mug. "Why don't we just let

Esme ramble. It's obvious she misses the way life used to be when she was growing up at Bellefontaine. I think most of us occasionally wish we could turn back the clock.''

"Yes—occasionally. But in Hawaii I saw women Aunt Esme's age play eighteen holes of golf and then go dancing. Eighty-year-old women run marathons and swim the English Channel. We can be far more than domestic creatures.''

"I agree." Passing back her mug, Adam slipped the key from her hand and bent to unlock her door. He opened it with a flourish, stepped aside to give her room to climb in, then he returned the key. "I really didn't come out after you to continue a pointless argument.''

"No? What then?''

"Before you arrived for breakfast, Jackson told everyone about the museum's weekend event. I'm not altogether sure what takes place, but I gather it's a fair they have every year to commemorate the history of sugar in this parish. I thought it sounded like something you'd enjoy. I wondered if you'd care to go with me. If so, I'll find out more about it.''

Just when she was prepared to cut him out of her life, he had to come up with an offer of this sort. He knew she'd be interested in anything to do with sugar. But, did he also know how much she detested going to new places alone?

"Last night, during our meeting, Jackson talked a little bit about the Sugar Fest. I *would* like to go. Are you sure it's something that would interest you, though?" Then she remembered Nick's saying that Adam loved poking through antiques.

"If you're there, how could it not interest me, sugar pie?''

"Adam…it's comments like that—" She broke off. "Never mind. I'm beginning to see through your southern nonsense. Saturday or Sunday? And what time?''

"I didn't know if you'd be working at the mill on Saturday, so I thought Sunday. Jackson said he asked Betty to prepare them a picnic. Why don't we do the same.''

''A picnic? In this weather? It's ten after seven and already too muggy to breathe.''

''There's a cooling trend forecast for the weekend. Even if we have to eat in the truck with the air running, it'll be different. Fun.''

''Okay. And thanks for the invite. Goodness, there goes Jackson. The way that guy drives, I'll have to step on it to catch up. I don't think he even saw me. Drat, he must think I've gone ahead.'' She wedged her mug into the holder and thrust the key in the ignition with her right hand while jerking shut the heavy Caddy door with her left.

''Hold on. What's the rush? Since the object is for Jackson to introduce you around the mill, he's not going to start without you.''

Feeling the car surge under her foot, Noelani flexed her fingers on the wheel and hauled in a deep breath. ''You're right. I'm suddenly very nervous. What if the mill workers don't like me, and some long-trusted employee complains to Jackson?''

Adam reached through the open window and feathered his fingers through her hair. ''People won't show open resentment. You're part of the family, Noelani.''

Noelani read between the lines, understanding what Adam hadn't said. That employees who held any resentment for the Fontaines might act *behind* the scenes. Covertly, like wiping out a computer code—or setting fire to the mansion.

He leaned in the window and nibbled on her lips. Pulling back slightly, he murmured, ''I didn't say that to frighten you more. Only so you'll be cautious.'' Straightening, Adam held her gaze as he retreated and tucked his hands loosely in his back pockets.

Briefly, she had second thoughts about going. Then her

stomach dropped back into place and her legs stopped shaking enough for her to press the gas pedal. Still, her fingers shook when she gave a semblance of a goodbye wave. She was miles down the highway before her heart stopped pounding and her lips no longer tasted the whisper of Adam's kiss.

That man. She'd never met anyone who blew her good intentions all to bits the way Adam Ross did.

She reached the mill later than planned and was forced to fall into line between a row of three-quarter-ton trucks pulling cane trailers up to a window where the trailers were weighed and core samples taken.

Jackson stood near the scale house, chatting with two men. One wore bibbed overalls, the other had on splotched coveralls. His hands were gnarled and his face bore traces of grease. He probably worked with some of the mill machinery.

Her half brother looked almost relieved to see her drive in. He waved for her to turn in the opposite direction from the slow-moving trucks. She saw the Jag, and that he'd left a space next to it for her to park.

"I thought you were in front of me," Jackson called, trotting up to her car. "When I didn't see you anyplace, I was worried that you might not remember how to get here."

"I have a good memory for directions. If I go someplace once, I can usually get back there on my own. Frankly, I'm glad all the worry I saw on your face was because you were afraid you'd lost me. I saw you talking with one of the mill employees, and for a minute I was afraid something else had gone wrong."

"It did. But it's nothing major. Well, at this point anything is major if it involves money." He half laughed, half groaned. "That was Wally Minton. He's in charge of waste management. I'm talking about our bagasse, not sanitary waste.''

"Yesterday I noticed the stockpiles. Most have sat there awhile. How are you marketing waste, if you don't mind my asking?"

"We burn bagasse to fire our cookers, like every other sugar mill I've ever visited. Wally came to report that the flu's been hitting us the last couple of weeks. He has two men down. They shovel waste into the carts that dump into our fire pits. So as soon as I introduce you around, I need to run past the union hall and see if I can hire some day laborers. Either that, or Wally says we'll have to let one of the fires die. I'd come and shovel, but I've got a bunch of meetings today.''

"I'm ready anytime you are. Jackson—getting back to my question. Even with burning, aren't your bagasse piles growing? I'm wondering... Well, surely Duke explored other avenues.''

"Like what? I'm not sure he did.''

"For one, we bag and sell it to local nurseries. It makes fair mulch. We also installed a system, and during peak production, Shiller's sells excess energy to the city at a reduced rate. A project I'd begun exploring before I left is a method used in Australia. They have quite a lucrative side business marketing their bagasse as home insulation.''

"Hmm. I read about that in one of the monthly journals. I think Duke decided it was too costly to implement. He thought we'd be better off to buy and renovate the refinery.''

"Maybe so. At the moment the refinery is an albatross. The bagasse sits there doing nothing. With a mulch bagger, the plastic bags work out to a few pennies each. I know you're busy as all get out, but I'd be happy to phone around and compile costs. It's a no-brainer to operate. You can pull people in off the street and teach them the job.''

"Get me some figures, then. Although I thought you were going to devote your time to writing a program to speed up our creeper feeders."

She patted her tote. "I brought the disks here for the program I wrote for Shiller's. Remember I told you yesterday? You both use the same computer system."

"I forgot. Okay, have at it, Noelani." Reaching around her, he opened a door. "We'll start your introductions in the core sample room. Don't expect much chitchat from these women. The trucks are rolling in hot and heavy today. They'll be busy collecting samples, weighing them, cooking them, extracting the *brix* and measuring the percentage of sucrose in each batch."

"Jackson, I've been around a sugar mill my entire life. I cut my teeth on core sample counters. Just establish my presence so the next time anyone sees my face, no one calls the cops and has me thrown off the property."

He grinned, and for the first time all morning, Noelani saw his shoulders relax.

"You run how many shifts in the core room?" she asked a group of busy women.

"Two," the youngest of the women said. Noelani tried to store their names, which were Rose, Denise and Sue Ann. "We rotate shifts to keep fresh," Rose volunteered.

Noelani removed a notebook from her tote bag. She jotted notes to remind herself to come back and meet the second shift, saying to Jackson, "They seem nice."

"Rose has a brother my age. We used to pal around. Sue Ann's worked here since she got out of high school. Denise didn't. Her dad used to work for us, but he had a problem with booze. Denise worked for Roland Dewalt, instead. When he closed the refinery, Duke offered to hire her. She'd recently lost her dad, and Duke felt sorry for her. She's working out, as far as I can tell."

"Adam said, or rather I understand he learned from Murray, that the mill only operates twelve hours a day."

"Sixteen. We run two full eight-hour shifts. That's the only way we can keep ahead of the tonnage. Even pushing with every ounce of oomph we've got, there are times our Dextran readings show some inversion. I guess I don't have to tell you that when bacteria sets in, we're paying for cane we have to scrap."

"Speeding the feeders will give some relief. How are you doing at the back end of the operation?"

"I'll have to show you the refinery I'll be refurbishing. It's about five miles down the road. It and the mill are equal distances from Bellefontaine. Eight miles at most. Having our own refinery will cut down on the warehouse space we need. We're storing way too much raw sugar. Every morning the refinery lets us know how many batches they'll accept. Currently I'm renting warehouses for millions of pounds. Sometimes, we end up paying rent on empty buildings."

"Yeah. That's how we do it at Shiller's, too."

They traversed the noisy building from side to side and back to front. Finally after two hours, Jackson said he thought she'd met everyone on first shift.

"Have you got time for coffee, or do you need to take off? Betty dug around in the cupboards and found a six-cup coffeepot. I brought it to use in the office. I saw there's a sink. I'll run back to the car to grab it and a few other things I collected."

"You do know mill workers run on caffeine," he said, laughing. "Sorry, I have a meeting I'm probably going to be late for now."

"Will you swing past again this evening to introduce me to the second shift, or do you think the rumor mill will have announced the news?"

"It's up to you whether or not I come back. People accepted you well, I thought."

"You're right, everyone seemed friendly. No one threw darts, anyway. I guess I can handle meeting the next crew on my own."

"I know you expected flak." He paused. "What all did you write in your little green book? I saw how discreetly you logged notes each time we changed areas."

"I think best when everything is cataloged and sequenced. In high school, a teacher steered me toward computer science in college, saying my mind operates in logical steps." She pulled a baseball cap from her bag and stuffed her long hair up under the cap. "Yuck. I should have done that sooner. My hair's already sticky."

"You've been away from a mill for a few weeks. You've forgotten the sugar floating in the air. You'll get back into the swing in a day or two."

She nodded. "I'll walk out with you. I probably need two trips to haul in boxes."

At his sidelong glance, she smiled faintly. "Don't worry, I'm not moving in permanently. No pictures for the wall or pink carpet or anything. I have blank disks, my favorite pens, the coffeepot and various odds and ends. Frankly, I don't know why Bruce shipped me so much, but since he did, I like the idea of surrounding myself with a few familiar things."

"No problem. Put pictures of your family on the desk, if you want."

They'd walked outside and he'd immediately donned sunglasses. Noelani could no longer see his eyes, which was a shame, since she had no idea what compelled her to say, "You and Casey are the only family I have left. Oh, and Aunt Esme. But I'm sure she wouldn't appreciate me lifting her photos from the Fontaine archives."

A moment passed during which neither spoke. Jackson finally cleared his throat. "I know you think Casey and I are callous for not asking more about your mom or your past. The truth is, I had Shelburne order a background check on you between the time I turned up your birth certificate and when he sent you the letter via Shiller."

"*That's* callous." Whatever tiny hope she'd developed over the past weeks of developing some kind of future, be it by phone or e-mail, with her half siblings, evaporated in the hot rays of the Louisiana sun.

"There was a lot at stake, Noelani. Can you honestly say that, if our situations had been reversed, you wouldn't have done the same?"

"We'll never know, will we? So, what dirty little secrets did you uncover—or think you uncovered?"

"None. It wasn't that kind of check."

"What other kind is there? I'm sure you looked into my bank account to find out whether or not I had any outstanding debt. Also what I did for fun, maybe even who I dated. Tell me, were you disappointed to learn I lead such a boring life?"

"The opposite. Noelani, I'm sorry. I shouldn't have brought it up. But since you're offering to help us out at the mill, I thought you deserved my honesty."

"It doesn't matter," she said flippantly. "I'm only here until January. Then I'll take my money and run. I've been saving for years, hoping to buy Bruce out when he retires. The background check you did—is that why Casey considers me a gold digger? Or were you two worried I'd try to muscle my way into taking over Bellefontaine? You were! Casey's surprise when I told her I'd worked at a sugar mill was pure baloney. You knew *exactly* what my job was at Shiller's."

"I did. But Casey was so broken up, I didn't share the

information with her. Shelburne and I discussed a lot of possibilities. Remember, we were operating in the dark. We assumed you knew Bellefontaine existed. Shiller certainly did. After all, Duke funneled money for Anela's maintenance and yours through him. I even thought it was possible he'd groomed you so the two of you could take over our operation.''

Noelani laughed, but with scant humor. "I'm surprised you didn't blame me for the kitchen fire and the harvester going missing,'' she said, folding her arms.

Jackson looked so guilty so fast, it jolted her. "You suspected me of underhanded, even criminal, acts? I can't believe it!''

"I'll admit it crossed my mind when I confronted Shelburne with your birth certificate, and he said Duke and Maman had changed their will to include you. But it wasn't anything I mentioned to Shel or Casey. It was all my silly notion.''

"Are you sure you want to trust me now? Maybe I'm more clever than you think,'' she said scathingly.

"Can't we clear the air? Spending time with you, I can see I was off base. Eventually, I hope you'll forgive me. I swear it wasn't personal. Casey and I saw our world collapsing. I grasped at any and every straw that might tell me why.''

"Now, *that* statement I can identify with. My world's been upset a few times. It's hard to view anything rationally when that happens.'' Noelani rubbed her hands back and forth across her elbows, all the while studying the toes of her boots. At last, she sighed and stuck out her right hand. "Truce? I pride myself on acting mature in most circumstances. I'm afraid I haven't managed so well when it comes to anyone named Fontaine. I'll try to change, if you will.''

Jackson clasped her hand in both of his. "I'd like to say

this will be the last time we'll ever clash swords. I'm not that naive, however. Not anymore. I probably ought to have coffee with you, so we can lay any other ghosts to rest. Except that my first meeting is with our bank president. He's balking over extending our line of credit. I really need to convince him the three of us are united.''

''Will he contact me? Shoot, even if he does, Jackson, he won't find any crack in our facade. Not from me.''

''Good. And thanks, Noelani. If we can make it over these next four months or so, I predict we'll be home free.''

''Music to my ears.'' She watched him climb into the Jag and wave. ''Hey!'' she called. ''Don't forget to buy Megan something before you go home.''

He nodded that he'd heard and flashed her a thumbs-up.

CHAPTER EIGHT

FOUR DAYS INTO NOELANI'S venture as mill manager, she arrived home around midnight to a pitch-dark house. Ravenous after having squandered her lunch hour at a gym she'd discovered not far from the mill, she made a pit stop at the refrigerator in the partially renovated kitchen, where she'd stored a few food items.

She didn't need to turn on a light, but merely juggled her tote while rummaging in the cheese drawer. All at once light flooded the room. Noelani shot straight up, banging her head on the shelf above the drawer. Spinning, she squeaked, "Adam! Holy cow, you scared me out of my wits. Why are you prowling the house at this hour?"

"I might ask you the same," he said, stepping fully into the room. "Are you just coming in, or are you scaring up breakfast before you leave again?" Sleepy-eyed and shirtless, he wore shapeless cotton pants with ripped pockets that might have passed at one time as cargo shorts.

"I'm just getting home. Last night, during the late shift, a couple of departments had accidents. One brought production to a halt. The other severely curtailed progress. Tonight, I decided to stay late and study the sites where the problems occurred. Now, let's hear *your* excuse for sneaking up on me in the dark and frightening me out of ten years' growth."

Shrugging, he propped the four-foot piece of one-by-two he'd been holding against a corner cabinet. "I couldn't sleep. My quarters are hotter than hell tonight. I'd been watching TV and got up to adjust the window air conditioner. I saw a light bobbing in the kitchen and was afraid maybe a friend of Broderick's had come back to take another stab at the job he botched.''

''I didn't see any light bobbing.'' She glanced uneasily over her shoulder and into the dim recesses of a kitchen in various stages of repair.

''It was probably your shadow I saw as you searched through the refrigerator. Remember, I was looking through two sets of beveled windows.''

''Ah. Well, I'm sure glad you turned on the light and identified it was me before you bopped me over the head with that big stick.''

One side of his mouth quirked a little. ''I couldn't find anything heavier, but believe me I wanted the biggest weapon possible, just in case you were somebody messing with all my hard work. Which leads me to ask—what were the accidents at the mill? Have you notified Jackson?''

She shrugged. ''They could be nothing. When you work with machinery day in and day out, stuff happens. People get careless. If I'd found any reason to suspect otherwise, of course I would've called Jackson. In this instance, I decided not to worry him.''

''Why don't you go ahead and eat? While you do, we can talk. By the way, no one mentioned you'd stocked this refrigerator. I wish Betty had told me. I periodically cut the power to this room. Now I'll know to shut it off for briefer stints.''

''Betty doesn't know I put stuff in here. She keeps the smaller refrigerator on the back porch chock-full so there's no room for anything else. This week I haven't been home for supper at all, and it seemed easier to keep cheese, peanut butter and salad in here.''

"You're subsisting on cheese, peanut butter and salad? Better not get too close to one of those turbines I saw at the mill, or their wind will blow you clean off the catwalk."

"Very funny, ha, ha! I eat. I have a canned breakfast drink." She hauled out a six-pack of thin cans and wagged them at him. "I joined a…a…gym, where I spend my lunch hours working out. But I keep apples and energy bars in my desk." As she talked, she opened a loaf of whole-wheat bread and removed two slices. Rummaging in her tote, she emerged with a small sandwich spreader and proceeded to spread crunchy peanut butter over each slice. "I usually take the food to my room. Where shall we go? Did you want to talk about something specific?"

"Like I said, it's hotter than—well, it's extra muggy to-night. Normally our temperature cools off by now. This has been a weird fall all over the south. Thank God we've had no major hurricanes to add to Bellefontaine's problems." He paused and gazed at her with amusement. "How can you eat that gluey stuff without honey or jelly? You don't even wash it down with milk."

"Jelly and honey are too sweet. Water, that's what I for-got to get out." She opened the fridge and removed a bottle of water. Then she reached in again for a second one, which she tossed to Adam.

He caught it neatly.

"Good reflexes. Let's stay right here, Adam. The kitchen's cozy now that the burned smell is gone." She scanned the area as she hopped up on one of the counters. "These cabi-nets are going to be great when you finish. I'll bet no one will be able to tell them from the originals that weren't dam-aged. But…I guess you know you do good work."

"It's always nice to hear." Adam leaned against the op-posite counter. After taking a long pull from his water bottle, he dashed a hand through his sleep-mussed hair. "I shouldn't keep you up if you're planning to head out early again. Maybe there's nothing for us to discuss if you're confident the incidents weren't out of the ordinary."

She finished chewing the bite she'd taken, then carefully folded the peanutty sides of the bread together. "I said they *could* be routine. Monday, Jackson made it clear to everyone that I'm managing the mill for the family. Yet getting anyone to open up about the accidents was like pulling teeth."

"The workers resent you, you mean?"

"Maybe. I don't know. I can't explain, really." She set her sandwich on a paper towel. "No one purposely distorted facts or denied they were in the area. Both episodes were written up in the daily log. Oh, shoot, I'm probably making a big deal out of nothing. All because I can't accept that what happened to the computer program last weekend was accidental."

"Other than the computer, what exactly has occurred?"

"A piece of metal jammed the creeper feeder, for one. A huge piece. Uh...are you familiar with how the feeders operate?"

"Only what I saw the other afternoon as I walked through the mill. Jackson directed me through a veritable maze, but no one explained the equipment."

"The device I'm talking about moves billets of cane through the washing and shredding process. It's not uncommon for the field cane to carry in rocks or small branches. But this was an inch-thick, two-foot-long piece of steel. It could've done a lot more damage than it did. Especially as I'd been testing my program to speed up the feeders. It so happened I'd returned the creeper feeders to the old program before I left for home, so they were running slower."

"Anyone act unhappy about your tests...?" Adam's voice trailed away as his eyes paused on Noelani's mouth.

The way she licked peanut butter from the sides of her sandwich had begun to have an effect on him. Afraid Noelani would notice, he shifted from one hip to the other, very aware that the thin shorts he wore hid nothing of his wayward thoughts.

Or she might notice if she was paying any attention to him. But unlike his, Noelani's attention seemed to be entirely on her work. In contrast, Adam found it next to impossible to concentrate on what she was saying.

She stopped licking the oozing peanut butter. "No one grumbled within my hearing. It's one woman's job to sit up in a crow's nest and spot debris. Duke had four people covering two shifts, because it's so boring sitting there staring at cane for eight-hour stretches. The woman whose shift it was has worked the same job for ten years."

"Are you going to eat that food or play with it?" Adam growled. "If you're just going to play with it, for God's sake, throw it away."

"Wh-what? Oh, sorry. It's a really bad habit, isn't it?" She wrinkled her nose.

"No. Don't listen to me, Noelani. It's my reactions that are bad. I envisioned you doing other…things with your tongue. Sorta got to me."

"Adam!"

"Can't help it, sugar pie. That's how men are. Our brains are connected directly to the male part of our anatomy. Don't you ever just…fool around?"

"Not if by *fool around* you mean what I think you mean. In college, everyone I knew slept with a bunch of different guys. I felt totally out of step."

He leaned his elbows on the counter alongside where she sat and stared at her. "Are you trying to tell me you have no experience with, uh, you know…sex?"

"Huh? Oh, no." She jumped off the counter and made a

production of looking in the fridge again. Mostly to cool the heat suffusing her face. "I, ah, had a couple of not-so-hot experiences. I've decided some people aren't made for it."

Bent over the way she was, with her worn jeans clinging to every inch of her long legs, and a half moon of soft skin showing at her waist where her T-shirt had slipped out of her jeans, Adam thought he'd never seen a woman more made for sex. Unless he wasn't a good judge. Maybe he was simply horny from doing without for so long. He'd enjoyed his fair share of women in college, but afterward, work had taken precedence. Even he found it hard to believe how fixated he'd been on building his business. He'd hate to think he wanted to have sex with Noelani for no other reason than her proximity, or because she was the first woman to attract his interest in more years than he cared to count.

Thrusting out his chin, Adam massaged the tight cords running up one side of his neck. "There's no need for you to crawl into the ice box to get away from me. I'd argue with your assessment of yourself, but Mama taught me to respect a lady's wishes, so you can relax. I'm not going to pounce on you, Noelani."

She slammed the refrigerator shut. "I never thought you were, Adam."

"Well, good. I'm afraid I've forgotten what we were talking about. Want to walk in the moonlight and take another stab at it?"

"It's very late, and as you pointed out, extremely hot and muggy. Both of us are going to be rummy in the morning if we don't get a few hours' sleep. Nothing really happened at the mill. So it won't help for us to rehash a few minor glitches. Particularly since you don't know how a mill operates. Shall I turn off the light on my way out, or will you?''

''I will. As long as I'm here and having trouble sleeping, anyhow, I may do some hand-sanding on the cabinet doors.''

Noelani tossed the remains of her sandwich, gathered her tote and her water bottle. At the door leading to the interior of the house, she hesitated. ''Tomorrow's Friday. Are we still on for the Sugar Fest on Sunday?''

''Oh, I meant to tell you. Jackson would like us to go on Saturday, instead. Casey opted out, as you know. Jackson decided to take Aunt Esme, Megan and Tanya on Sunday. He said it'd be better if Bellefontaine's represented both days.''

''Did he say it was okay for me to miss a day at the mill?''

''Not in so many words. But you can't be in two places at once, and he made it clear he'd like you to be at the Sugar Fest on Saturday.''

''Huh. Okay. What time?''

''Here's my thought. I have an early-morning meeting in Baton Rouge with a sub-contractor. If it's okay with you, I'll give you a lift to the mill and pick you up at noon. That way you'll get in a half-day's work.''

''I can live with that. But Adam, if changing to Saturday puts you in a bind, I can drive there by myself.''

''I want to take you, Noelani. Damn, you're a difficult woman to date, you know that?''

''Date? No…I—'' She averted her eyes, marshaling her thoughts and her words, but she wasn't quite able to kill her frown. ''Good night, Adam. If I don't see you between now and then, I'll see you early on Saturday.''

Noelani didn't know how to take Adam Ross. One minute he spoke plainly and directly about wanting more than a simple date. Just as fast, he reversed and pulled completely away from her. She hadn't imagined the distance he'd put between them a while ago; she was sure of it. Yet, when she'd tried to give him a graceful out, he'd called her difficult.

But how could she blame him when she ran hot and cold and hot again? Her problem—she *enjoyed* spending time with Adam. She enjoyed simply looking at him. And tonight, half dressed and rumpled from his bed, he'd taken her breath away.

From the outset, the man set wild fires licking through her body. But the logic she'd told him she possessed kept intruding. Part of her recognized the futility of forming a romantic attachment with someone whose goals and objectives tied him to a part of the country she couldn't wait to leave. Once in while, like tonight, she felt so homesick for Maui, she honestly didn't know if she'd be able to stick it out here for the length of time she'd told Jackson she would stay.

ADAM WRAPPED A PIECE of the finest-grade sandpaper around a block of wood and started lightly sanding a cabinet door he'd placed between two sawhorses. Working with wood had become his escape. Coaxing the beauty from a particular grain usually let him blank his mind of all worries and troubles. Over the years there had been many. This mood had settled over him when he'd turned the calendar and discovered tomorrow was the day he'd scheduled to visit his mother. Her doctor had suggested a regular schedule for visits. In the beginning, Adam went twice a week. Then once a week, which later shrank to twice a month. At first her team of psychiatrists had given him reason to hope she'd fully recover. As the years dragged on, and the likelihood of finding his father dimmed, so, too, had his mother's mental state declined.

He blew off the wood dust and smoothed a hand over the oak. Adam was strongly tempted to go up and knock on Noelani's door. If he asked nicely, would she come back downstairs and keep him company? Just to talk. Nothing more. He'd been a jerk to hint at more. He'd frightened her—the very last thing he wanted.

His sleeplessness, his need to be close to someone tonight, was all tied in with seeing his mom sometime the next day. And it probably had something to do with tomorrow being opening day for submitting sealed bids on Magnolia Manor.

Adam stared at his hands, usually so steady. Just now they weren't. He set the sandpaper block aside. Dusting off his hands, his shorts and then his bare legs, he left the room and slowly climbed the stairs.

At the top, he tiptoed across the hall and knocked softly on Noelani's bedroom door. If she didn't answer, he'd go back to the garçonnière, get dressed and go for a drive. If she did answer, that would be something to consider, too.

The door opened a crack. "Adam?" The crack widened. "Are you okay? You didn't hurt yourself, did you?" Noelani asked in a whisper.

"I...no, I didn't hurt myself. I shouldn't have come up here and bothered you. It's...do you ever have nights when you just can't sleep?"

She heard a hesitation, a tremor in his voice she didn't recall ever hearing before. Adam's voice, a rich baritone, always sounded sure, decisive and upbeat. This time she definitely noticed something else.

"I haven't changed into my pajamas yet. As a rule I don't have trouble falling asleep. Guess I'm keyed up tonight, too. You aren't exactly dressed for a walk through the cane, but listening to the rush of wind through the rows generally relaxes me.''

"Like I said, it's hot tonight. I've never been around cane. Music relaxes me. Jazz, in particular.''

"Oh. I don't even have a radio in my room. Sorry.''

"I've got a CD system set up in the garçonnière. I travel pretty light, but music is one thing I take to every job site.''

She opened the door wider, slipped out and closed it softly behind her. "I've never seen the inside of a garçonnière. Since we're both wide awake, you may as well give me the grand tour.''

"It's functional. Primitive by today's standards. That may be why I like it.''

They talked in low voices as she advanced ahead of him down the stairs. "I remember thinking it unfair when Aunt Esme said garçonnières were bachelor quarters for the teenage sons of plantation owners. Sons had the freedom to come and go at an early age, while girls were often sent to convents. Or lockup wards, which is what I'd call them.''

Outside now in the sultry darkness, with only the moon and the carriage lamps to light their way, Noelani missed the eyebrow Adam spiked upward. "They're schools, not prisons. Many young southern women still attend all-girl Catholic schools. I'm not sure if Casey went to one, but her friend Viv did. The old Creole families still place a huge importance on old-world manners. A number of people in the neighborhood where I grew up also preferred private religious schooling for boys as well as girls. Not only for the education, but because the nuns drilled social skills into the students.''

Noelani stepped aside and let Adam open the door to his quarters. If she hadn't been so interested in what they were discussing, she might have felt a ripple of apprehension at walking into what could be his bedroom. "Are you Catholic?"

"Not practicing, but technically, yes. Thanks to the Spanish and French influence, Louisiana is largely Catholic."

"People tend to think of Hawaiians as pagans. Actually, we're an eclectic mix. My grandmother was Buddhist, but my mother never adhered to the faith. As a result, I'm sort of in religious limbo." She blinked as they moved inside, then glanced at Adam to see how he'd reacted to her news. Clearly, it didn't seem to matter one way or the other to him.

"This is it, Noelani. There's not much to see."

She studied the room. Wood-paneled walls, a beige carpet, indirect lighting from old-style wall sconces gave the space a warm feel. Modern touches, like a futon couch, a TV, stereo system and a counter with a microwave, reminded Noelani of her duplex at home. "What's upstairs?"

"The rudiments of a bedroom and a remodeled bath. A shower stall. I'm sure it was added without consulting the historical society. There's a half bath off this room."

Spotting a corner fireplace flanked by full-length bookcases, Noelani crossed the room.

"The fireplaces here and in the main house look like marble. It's really hand-polished cypress," Adam said.

"This is wood?" She ran her fingers over the shiny surface; it still seemed like stone. "Well, it's not cool like marble, though, is it?"

He laughed. "It's wood, all right. What's your pleasure in music?"

"Anything that suits your fancy." She leaned in to read the titles of the books. There were old and new ones. Hardcovers and paperbacks. Mysteries, thrillers, spy stories, mixed in with nonfiction, mostly popular history. Two entire rows of books were devoted to architecture, mostly architecture in the deep South. "Do all the books on these shelves belong to you, Adam?"

He turned from where he knelt, adjusting the volume of a tiered sound system. The room was suddenly filled with the mournful wail of a muted saxophone, joined with the layered rhythms of snare drum and piano. "The stuff on the top shelves was here when I moved in. The rest are mine. Remember I told you I'm an insomniac?"

"You also said you travel from job site to job site. This is a lot of stuff to lug around. Why don't you visit the local libraries instead?"

"Most people want to know why I rent as I go and don't own a home somewhere in one location where I can store all my junk."

"That's easy." She trailed a finger along the tops of the books. "Two reasons, I think. You like having solid, tangible things around you. And you've been saving a long time to purchase your family home. So why waste money making payments and paying taxes on another place when money in the bank earns compound interest?"

"You do understand." Rising, he crossed to where she stood and simply stared deep into her eyes, which had softened to a dark caramel color in the yellow lamplight. "The other night when we drove by Magnolia Manor, I was positive you didn't have a clue what I felt for that old house."

She lifted a hand and laid it against his bare, warm chest. The music seemed to fill her head and whisper along her bloodstream. "The house. Is that why you're edgy tonight? You put in a bid?"

Adam covered her hand with his. "Tomorrow, maybe. The bidding process opens then. They'll accept bids for thirty days."

She'd held her last breath, and now let it out slowly. "Your chances are excellent, aren't they? You've worked on similar homes for years. Who better to know their value?''

"That's what I keep telling myself. But it all boils down to dollars and cents. Well, dollars. The information I picked up at the courthouse says the winning bid has to be one full dollar over the next highest figure submitted. It goes without saying that the forms have to be filled out correctly. I've seen contractors lose bids because they missed something as simple as checking a box.''

"Will there be a lot of competition?" Noelani found it difficult to believe a lot of people would want a home in need of a major overhaul, particularly since it had no land attached. That was really her problem with Adam's plan. Land—plantable soil—meant everything to her. Houses weren't a waste, exactly, but...

"I don't really have any idea how many people might enter bids. I've talked to builders who've bought homes by a bidding process, but I've never done it before. I *have* studied the records of similar auctions in Louisiana and I'm assured no two are ever alike.''

She started to move away from him, but Adam tightened his hold on her hand, and caught her free hand, too. He tugged her lightly into his arms. "We don't have much room, but you owe me a dance. I asked for one at the *cochon de lait,* remember?''

The CD he'd put in earlier had slipped from its mournful sax music into an R and B number with the low throb of kettledrums in the background. The sultry, sexy beat begged for two bodies to touch and move together. More athletic than musical, Noelani was surprised by how much she wanted to do as Adam asked. She felt the tempo in her feet and uttered no objection when Adam placed her hands on his shoulders, then spread his wide palms across her back.

His touch remained light, and the night was too warm for the shiver that sneaked up her spine.

"This is a first for me—dancing alone with a man in his room."

"Shh," he murmured near her ear. "Go with the flow. Feel the beat." Ever so subtly, Adam edged her closer until their bodies barely brushed. A lock of hair that perpetually fell over his forehead tickled her ear. Noelani let her tension give way as Adam's lips skimmed her neck. She didn't even realize she'd tilted her head. Nor was she really aware of gliding her arms around his neck and funneling her fingers through his thick brown hair. In the low light cast by the old wall sconces, the whole experience seemed surreal. The room breathed the slow, teasing notes, and their two bodies reacted accordingly. So, when the horns kicked in with a sob, Adam was already hard, erect and ready. Stirred by him and the electrifying music, Noelani practically purred and rubbed against him like a happy cat. Her body felt weightless while a hot heaviness claimed the lower part of her abdomen.

Adam might have suggested going upstairs. Certainly Noelani read need in his eyes. She preceded him willingly up the iron steps, although her legs were shaky, whether with arousal or nerves, she didn't know.

The loft seemed to be all unmade bed. Pillows and sheets were a tangle of wine red. In spite of a window air conditioner, the room radiated enough warmth that when Adam faced her and stripped off her damp T-shirt, Noelani welcomed the faint touch of cooler air against her skin.

Always, always, the music. More muted now, it filled her head and her heart. But she wanted Adam to fill her soul. It was a need that was suddenly so strong it shocked her. Rushing, she unzipped her jeans and let them drop. They pooled around her feet and lay trapped by the sneakers she'd worn to work that day. With her heart thundering in her ears, Noelani sat on the bed and frantically tried to untie the knotted laces.

Adam knelt before her and stilled her fingers. "At the risk of spoiling the moment," he said in a voice so thin it almost didn't sound like him, "I have to hear you say you want this as much as I do."

She leaned over and kissed his eyes closed. "Hush. I want this to be my dream. My illusion." In spite of sitting at the edge of a strange bed in her panties and bra, her jeans shackling her ankles, she took the lead—a definite first for Noelani Hana.

The scrape of her fingertips along his rib cage was featherlight as her lips joined briefly with his, then skipped away to explore his chin, his neck, his chest, his navel.

Because it'd been so long for him, and because his control threatened to crack at any minute, Adam thrust her away as gently as all his rough, frantic feelings would allow. "There's something I have to do before this goes one step further," he said through teeth clamped tightly together. Stumbling to his feet, nearly falling over a comforter that had slipped off the foot of the bed, he disappeared into the black interior of the loft.

Noelani heard him muttering, and it sounded as if things were falling into a sink. It dawned on her that he'd gone into his bathroom, no doubt to secure protection for her. *For them,* she thought, a rush of pleasure flooding a heart that had begun to knock erratically with a case of nerves.

She made short work of her sneakers. By the time he reappeared, smiling visibly thanks to a sliver of light spilling from the room he'd so recently left, every last stitch of her clothing sat folded in a neat pile. She lay in the center of his wide bed, her body pale gold against the dark red of the sheets.

Adam had lost count of the times, since he'd met her, that he'd pictured her long black hair spread over his pillow. Seeing her welcome him with a shy smile and uplifted arms rocked all that remained of his intention to take things slow.

He sank to the bed on one knee, tossing down a handful of small gleaming packets.

"Adam," she squeaked, partially rising to blink and gasp at the pile of condoms.

"These come courtesy of whatever kind soul lived here before me," he growled, gathering her into his arms with a sigh. "I'm afraid I made a mess of the medicine cabinet. I knew I'd seen the stash when I moved in, but I couldn't remember which shelf they were on. Tell me it's not going to throw a wet blanket on your illusion."

"No." She shook her head and wriggled closer, giving the mood a chance to settle over both of them again as their lips met, and her nipples hardened from the merest friction of rubbing against his bare chest.

Noelani had always thought Adam had a nice body. Never more so than when, after a few minutes of mutual exploration, he skimmed off his raggedy shorts and she caught a glimpse of him fully aroused. "Oh, my," she exclaimed, her breath catching.

Then talk ceased. Only the distant echo of music—the wail of a sax, the spasm of trumpets and rolling drums— which, in time, climaxed in perfect synchronization with the couple upstairs. They were, during that moment, two people locked together in a secret world known only to lovers.

Breathing faster and harder than the bossa nova tune that followed the earlier jazz piece—which Adam knew would forever after have cataclysmic importance for him—he nevertheless managed to muster the strength to roll off Noelani.

She groaned. "Am I alone in thinking *wow?*"

"You can think?" Adam propped himself up on one elbow and pressed a kiss to the rounded part of her shoulder.

She laughed nervously as she turned toward him. She hadn't been a quiet lover, and that was new territory for her. Noelani wished he'd said it was a *wow* experience for him, too. "Should I apologize for screaming?" she asked, then pulled her upper lip anxiously between her teeth. "I'm afraid I'm not good at this sort of thing. Not good at all."

"If you were any better, we'd probably both be dead." Adam traced a finger over her plump lower lip, then stretched up to kiss her, forcing her to release her upper lip.

The music on the floor below shifted to a melancholy, haunting tune. Again, their lovemaking matched the tempo. Slow as the bow drawn over a violin as a fiddler coaxed out the high notes with loving care. This time Adam took the same care to see to his partner's pleasure first. This time they changed places and, never having been given such total power over a man, Noelani couldn't hold back her tears when they climaxed.

Adam felt those tears trickle down his chest where she'd collapsed. "God, did I hurt you?" That was his first thought as he stirred and sat them both up so he could look into her eyes.

She wasn't able to voice her feelings, was only able to shake her head over and over.

Thinking he understood her silent message, Adam smiled, plumped the pillows at his back, and held her close until her tears stopped.

Her breathing slowed, and after a time, he realized she'd fallen asleep. Careful not to wake her, he smoothed back her tangled hair and slid down the bed with her, until they rested side by side, heads on the same pillow.

Watching her sleep, something he'd never done with another woman, he wondered if she was dreaming of him. Or was she dreaming of the time she'd return to Hawaii?

Had this experience moved her as it'd moved him?

He wound one of the dark curls, shot through with traces of auburn, around his forefinger. Damn, he was beyond the stage of indulging in one-night stands. Noelani had been straightforward about cutting her losses here and returning to Hawaii the moment Duke Fontaine's property distribution was settled. And she'd shown little excitement over his desire to buy and refurbish Magnolia Manor. Although tonight she'd seemed genuinely supportive.

A growl of frustration rose in his throat as he released the curl and let it spring loose and drape along the curve of her breast.

Lying flat on his back, staring at the play of light across the ceiling, Adam heard the end of the last song on the CD he'd put on an hour ago. The system clicked off, bathing the garçonnière in silence except for Noelani's quiet breathing.

He felt more than the sense of lethargic well-being that followed in the wake of good sex. And he wanted more than one night with Noelani. She was smart, funny and tough, yet he'd seen her softness and compassion. Knowing she was here beside him vanquished the vague dread that had stalked him earlier.

He drifted off to sleep planning to talk to Noelani in the morning. He'd speak honestly about his feelings, and...

Disturbed some time later by movement on the bed, Adam fought to stay asleep, and simultaneously attempted to wake completely.

"Sorry, Adam. Go back to sleep. I'm dressed. All I have to do is tie my second shoe and I'll be ready to leave."

"Leave?" He struggled to rise, but she pressed him down again with a hand in the middle of his chest. "What time is it?'' he inquired with a yawn. ''I'm not sure I've even slept.'' He rubbed a hand over his gritty eyes.

''You probably haven't been asleep long. It's not quite 4:00 a.m.''

''Then why are you getting dressed? Come back to bed. It's pitch-black out,'' he said, catching her arm.

''No, Adam.'' She pulled from his loose grasp. ''I don't want anyone in the household to see me leaving your place in the morning. This way I'll be back in my room and have time to shower and change before Betty arrives to start breakfast.''

The mattress shifted as she rose and started for the door.

''Wait! I hoped we could talk before breakfast.''

''About what? Didn't we decide the accidents were just that?''

''I mean, talk about us. About a…future.'' This time he did sit up, and he didn't like the sudden tension in the air.

''Adam—maybe we should just admit we got carried away. I hope we don't let what happened interfere with our being friends. Once you stop to think clearly, I'm sure you'll agree with me. Your future is here, restoring your family home. Mine lies with a sugar plantation on Maui. We won't even be within commuting distance. So…'' She took a deep breath. ''Let's just agree to meet on Saturday as friends, and leave it at that.''

Her footsteps echoed as she hurried down the wrought-iron steps. Adam hurtled out of bed, planning to follow her and talk some sense into her. He couldn't find his shorts. Then he heard the click of his front door and realized he was too late. He fell back on the rumpled bed, not altogether sure what had just happened. She wanted to be friends, but he'd been considering way more than friendship.

''Well, hell,'' he muttered, knowing he'd had all the sleep he was going to get for this short night.

CHAPTER NINE

ADAM SHOWERED, OPERATING in a fog. While coffee brewed, he downloaded e-mail onto his laptop. He thought he'd been quick about it, but as he trekked to the main house he noticed the Caddy wasn't parked where it'd been last night.

"Betty?" Adam yanked open the screen door. "Have you seen Noelani today?"

"She came in looking for coffee two seconds after I arrived. I hadn't even got out the beans, let alone ground them. Now here you are with your mug in hand. Don't nobody keep civilized hours around this house anymore?"

"I made coffee at my place, Betty. Damn, that must be why I missed her. Did she say if she planned to put in an appearance at supper?"

"Didn't say. Snatched a banana from the batch I bought yesterday. When I let her know a banana wasn't a fit breakfast, she said she'd grab a breakfast drink from the other fridge, then dashed off. It wasn't a minute before I heard the gravel spit from the Caddy's tires. Gotta hand it to the girl, she drives that monster the way it was built to be driven. Angelique—bless her soul, and I don't like speaking ill of the dead..." Betty crossed herself as a matter of course. "But we wuz related, so I can say Angelique drove like a pansy-ass woman."

Adam took a big gulp of hot coffee. He didn't know why he attempted conversation with Betty, especially when he wasn't hitting on all cylinders himself. The woman tended to talk in riddles. "Thanks, Betty. Is Noelani aware of the family gathering tonight?"

Betty shrugged. "She'd better show up."

"Well, I now have another reason. I need to see everyone. The firm I got to put in the security system Jackson and Casey wanted plans to shoot juice to it at noon. It'll change how people are able to come and go. Especially people who fly on and off shift the way Noelani does."

"Big expense for nothing, if you ask me." Betty threw a handful of beans in the coffee grinder. "Duke wouldn't have handled this with no 'lectric folderol. He'd have loaded his double-barreled shotgun and put out word around the parish that anyone settin' foot on Bellefontaine without sound reason had better plan on leaving here with a butt full o' buckshot."

"Jackson and Casey would rather let the security company and the police deal with crooks and crazies. However, they won't want to bail family members out of the pokey. Never mind, Casey'll be up by now. I'll go over there and let her handle dispersing the information."

Adam had to admit it was a fine morning. A slight breeze took the edge off the far-reaching tentacles of a fiery sun beginning its slow ascent. He loved this hour of the morning when the buildings and landscape glittered like gold. His mood was much improved by the time he reached Wisteria Cottage.

Nick and Casey were breakfasting at a wicker table on their screened porch.

"Adam, hi." Nick rose.

Casey glanced up and waved. "What brings you calling so early? Something about tonight's secret celebration? Aunt Esme said everything's all set." She gestured with the coffee carafe, indicating Adam should fill his mug.

"Thanks, I brought my coffee. It's something else about tonight. I got an e-mail this morning from Art Rafferty. The security system's in place. He'll activate it at twelve noon today, unless one of us leaves a message at his office to the contrary."

"He worked fast," Nick acknowledged with satisfaction as he bent and kissed his wife. "But he couldn't have been too quick for my peace of mind."

Adam sank into the offered chair. It creaked under his weight. "Outside of the mill, there hasn't been another incident since the harvester, has there?"

"No. At the mill? Adam, what incident?" Casey narrowed her eyes.

"You've forgotten asking me to change the office lock?"

"Oh, that. I've been on such a treadmill lately, it slipped my mind. We're not even sure it *was* an incident. Murray said one of the techs who pulls core sample data off the computer could've hit a couple of keys by mistake and erased a line of code."

Adam sipped from his cup. "Noelani's pretty sure it had to be deliberate. Too bad we can't monitor the mill with a closed-circuit TV system of some kind. That way you'd know if the two accidents the night before last were really accidents."

Casey and Nick both pounced at once. "Accidents?"

"Noelani said two, but only gave me particulars on one. Somebody fished a piece of steel out of the creeper feeder. She said it shut the whole operation down for several hours while they checked for damage."

"Junk is always getting mixed in with cut cane. Noelani ought to know that, since she claims to have so much mill experience."

"She knows her stuff, Casey." Adam immediately came to Noelani's defense. "The size of the metal bar was significant. So far, she's calling it an accident, and she decided there was no reason—yet—to worry you and Jackson. But what if it's not? That's all I meant about wishing there was a way to monitor the mill.''

''Security costs big bucks. Our bad luck's the result of one ex-employee. Broderick has a screw loose. He's locked up tight, and there's been nothing since the harvester. Everything's back on track now,'' Casey said with conviction.

''I sure hope so.'' Adam extended his hand to Nick. ''Anyway, I'll leave you with the responsibility of informing the family how the security system works.''

''We set 11:00 p.m. as the time for locks to activate, didn't we? Glass breakage sensors go off whenever a window's breached, but to come and go after eleven, a visitor either has to phone us or key in?''

''Correct. Art gave you and Jackson the codes, didn't he, Casey? In his e-mail, he recommends setting the outer-perimeter sensors to coincide with seasonal changes of sunrise and sunset, rather than tie it to a twenty-four-hour clock.''

''He and I discussed that. I meant to talk it over with Jackson and Nick. Art says to be effective, it's advisable not to operate the system with any predictability.''

''It's your call, Casey,'' her husband said. ''Adam chose Rafferty's firm because they're the best.''

Casey frowned. ''I hate letting that weasel Broderick curtail my freedom. I mean…we have a right to come and go as we please on our own property.''

''Personal safety comes at a price,'' Nick muttered.

''I agree with Casey,'' Adam said. ''When I was a kid and lived a mile or so from here, my mom never thought about locking doors. Back then, the Fontaines were like royalty. None of us lesser mortals would've dared step on the property without invitation. Today, you're installing gates with sensors.'' He shook his head.

Casey rose and walked to the porch steps with Adam. ''I read a notice in last night's paper that the bids on Magnolia Manor open today. Is yours prepared?''

''Yes, but I'm thinking of hanging on to it until I do some more up-to-date real estate analysis. I only have one shot at naming the right price. I'd hate to underbid by a few bucks.''

''Sealed bids are a crapshoot,'' Nick warned. ''You know what I think, Adam? Go with your gut feeling. Submit the amount you can afford and forget it.''

Casey turned an appraising gaze on her husband. ''That's all well and good, Nick, unless some court clerk sneaks a peek at the bids and then feeds the information to a bidder who may pay under the table for such a tip.''

''I swear, Casey, I've never met anyone as paranoid as you.''

Adam thumbed his lips thoughtfully. ''Sadly, Casey may be right. Which is why I'm leaning toward turning my bid in at the eleventh hour.''

''What bid?'' None of them had seen Murray Dewalt enter the screened porch from the side. He helped himself to coffee before joining them at the steps. Casey, uneasy around him since the day he'd shocked her by proposing she marry him instead of Nick, deftly put Nick and Adam between herself and her one-time best friend.

Adam would've been inclined to say it was none of Murray's business, and even Nick glowered. Casey, though, brought their neighbor up to date. ''When we were kids, Adam's family owned Magnolia Manor. It's about a mile down River Road, closer to your plantation, Mur. The estate's going up for sale via sealed bids, starting today.''

''You're that Ross?'' Murray took a second look at

Adam. "I never connected you with a local family. Jackson said you'd come down from Natchez. Did you used to hang out with a bunch of kids who rode bikes through my dad's cane rows?"

"Probably," Adam admitted with a shrug.

"My dad had fits over you guys popping wheelies in front of our cane trucks. So did Duke, now that I think about it. They just knew one of you would get hurt or killed and then your folks would sue us."

"I'm afraid my carefree days ended when I was twelve. I only rode my bike to deliver newspapers after that. To help put food on the table," he added, intentionally pointing out the difference in their circumstances.

Murray carelessly hiked a shoulder. "I lost touch with everyone except Jackson and Casey after dear old dad shipped me off to boarding school." He turned to Casey. "Most of those neighbors moved on after the big hurricane wiped out our crops. Duke cut fifty percent of the mill's workforce and my dad did the same at the refinery. All the plantations laid off field hands. Growers' kids cut and hauled their own cane. Man, I hated that job."

"You and Jackson griped, but I always loved working in the cane," Casey said.

Adam tried again to leave, but Murray's next statement affixed weights to his feet. "Good luck on your bid, Adam. You'll be going up against my dad."

"*What?* Why would Roland want another house? And with the work the place needs, it wouldn't pay to make Magnolia Manor a rental."

"Oh, he doesn't want the house. In fact, he said he'll tear it down. He wants the thirty acres for a new pecan orchard."

"Magnolia Manor's on the historical register." Adam didn't try to contain his anger at the very idea of demolishing the house. "You must have it confused with some other property."

"No. Dad called it by name."

Adam tossed out his coffee and stormed down the steps. By God, he'd check to make sure it was still on the register. In Natchez, he'd seen a case where the wrong physical coordinates were put on a court manifest. A historic home was torn down before the mix-up could be resolved. If dozers razed Magnolia Manor, Adam vowed it'd be over his dead body.

His mood had soured, and he still had to visit his mother.

THAT EVENING, THE MASSIVE dining table had been set to include all family and household staff. Once those present had claimed their spots—except for Noelani, who hadn't yet shown up—Adam noticed there was an extra place setting. "Besides Noelani, who's missing?"

"Murray." Jackson glanced up from a drawing Megan was doing. "He's in and out of here more often than Casey and Nick. I want him to be aware of the security."

"He's like his father when it comes to tardiness," Esme said, sighing. "We could've extended the cocktail hour rather than sit here twiddling our thumbs." She bent and patted the velvet pillow under her chair. Toodles scampered over from Betty's chair, where he'd been begging for a handout. At Esme's command the schnauzer dropped his head between his paws, looking contrite as he licked his chops.

"Betty, I've asked you repeatedly not to let Toodles snack on table food. It's obvious you don't heed a word I say."

"If that's not the pot calling the kettle black, what is? At least I just give him meat. You sneak him sweets, for crying out loud."

Esme flushed all the way to her newly colored roots.

Jackson interrupted his aunt before she could snipe back. "I hear the Caddy. That engine is so distinctive. Are we sure Murray's coming?"

Casey made a face. "Murray never turns down a free meal. Especially not since Roland fired their cook."

Esme swung round. "Roland fired Mary Louise Chastain? Mercy, why she's an institution! Furthermore, she's the one who kept that household from ruin."

"You didn't know Roland let her go?" Casey sounded surprised. "You'll have to ask Murray when it happened, exactly. It's been a while—I think around the time Duke and Maman left on their trip. I only recall the timing vaguely because I had a lot on my mind, what with Duke insisting I fill a notebook with everything he wanted done— stuff I'd already been doing. Murray was underfoot griping about how Roland's temper was making him go hungry. I'm sure Murray will tell you I was less than sympathetic."

The door from the back porch swung inward. Noelani skidded across the polished dining room floor on bare feet.

"Noelani, where on earth are your shoes?" Esme scowled. "A lady never comes to supper barefoot."

Before Noelani could answer, all eyes swung to the man waltzing in behind her. Murray had obviously heard Casey, because as he passed her, he gave her ponytail a yank. "It's no secret that you're a hardhearted woman, Casey Fontaine."

"She's Devlin now," Nick said coolly, but Murray paid no attention.

Instead, he asked, "What did I do this time? Am I being raked over the coals for showing up late? Here I thought that since I ran into Noelani outside, I'd be safe from Esme's usual lecture."

Esme gazed on him with the same indulgence she reserved for Megan. "Cassandra said Roland let Mary Louise go. I wish we'd hired her," she said, plainly to needle Betty.

Betty returned the fire and Noelani grabbed the opportunity to slip into the chair next to Tanya. She almost broke her neck to avoid sitting beside Adam, which didn't escape him. After the night they'd shared, he was more hurt than irritated.

Noelani spoke directly to Jackson. "Sorry I missed your phone call—and sorry I'm late. I'd taken printouts of today's core samples upstairs and stayed to tour the lab. They have a neat setup. The microscopes your techs use are superior to Shiller's, but I think our lab is freer of contaminants."

"Really?" She'd garnered Jackson's attention.

"Yes. Are you aware the ladies from your sample room go all the way upstairs to have their break with the techs? They don't wash first or put on smocks. I'm unpopular at the moment. I said the techs can't play host to every Tom, Dick and Jane who'd rather eat where it's quiet. That's their excuse—they claim the break room is too noisy. Do you know if Duke set rules that are being broken or ignored? Or did he let workers do as they please?"

Jackson tapped Casey's shoulder. "Do you know, sis?"

"Nope. My responsibility ends with planting, cutting and loading our cane. Duke handled everything to do with the mill."

"There you have it, Noelani. Notify me if you give anyone the heave-ho. Otherwise, the mill operation is your bailiwick."

"Jackson, that puts her squarely in the line of fire of anyone perpetrating mischief at the mill," Adam said.

"I realize you came onboard at a dicey time, Adam, what with the arson and the stolen harvester. But I can't see people who've worked for us for years going postal just because Noelani makes them switch where they eat."

"I agree." Noelani darted a mind-your-own-business glare at Adam.

Aunt Esme rapped her knife blade on her crystal wine goblet, making it ring. "We don't discuss work at supper. In fact, this is a celebration supper to wish Noelani a happy birthday!" Everyone sang as Betty appeared, carrying a flaming cake.

Noelani gasped aloud. And Megan hopped around excitedly. "Blow out the candles, Noelani! Hurry. Make a wish."

Noelani clapped a hand over her mouth. Her eyes glossed with tears as almost everyone at the table magically produced wrapped gifts and set them in front of her. At Megan's insistence, she mustered breath enough to blow out the twenty-eight candles in one long puff. "Betty, that cake looks wonderful. Did you make it yourself?"

"Anyone can make a cake," Esme said. "It's for after supper. But go ahead and open your gifts now."

"I don't know what to say." Noelani fussed over the prettily wrapped packages. "Being an only kid, I've never had so many gifts at my birthday. I was prepared for no notice at all." Her happy smile said how pleased she was to be wrong.

"Around here, we tear packages open without a lot of talk," Casey said.

So, Noelani ripped into Casey's package first. She and Nick had given Noelani a red silk blouse. "You said red was your favorite color," Casey mumbled.

"It is. The blouse is beautiful. Thank you so much." She blotted away tears.

Jackson and Megan's package produced a flowered tote.

"Megan noticed your old one's wearing thin," Jackson said offhandedly.

Slipping out of her seat, Noelani caught Megan close and gave her a big smoochy kiss. Before sitting again, she hugged Jackson, Casey and Nick.

Esme's offering was a book of historic southern homes. "I'll cherish it," Noelani declared. To her surprise and delight, Tanya gave her a CD by a local jazz artist.

"Someone should've told me it was Noelani's birthday," Murray complained.

"We realized it sort of last minute," Jackson said. "Sorry, buddy. Next time, okay?"

Noelani had gone quiet as she traced a finger over the foil paper of the last gift. A label simply read *From Adam*. "Can I help open that one?" Megan asked. Noelani pulled the child onto her lap and let her untie the satin ribbon. Inside bubble wrap, they unearthed a clear glass paperweight shaped like a pineapple. Noelani held it aloft for all to admire, then turned teary eyes toward Adam. Her soft thank-you hung on trembling lips.

Betty clapped her hands. "Supper's ready. You can celebrate more later. I'll remove the candles from the cake. Meanwhile, here's a spinach soufflé I made specially in honor of Noelani. Eat up, folks, or it'll get cold and fall."

They all laughed and joked as they dipped into the fluffy casserole. Noelani gathered the warm feelings about her like a mantle. She felt—included.

After the soufflé and a salad that included chicken, pecans and chunks of sweet potato in a garlicky dressing, Betty brought the cake in again. Noelani cut generous pieces. When everyone had a slice, Esme again struck her water glass to gain everyone's attention. "Jackson or Casey, I suppose, you'd better explain our new state-of-the-art watchdog. It's nearly time for a program I want to see on the

Home and Garden channel. Could we get this over with? I'd like to take my cake and coffee upstairs."

Eating stopped as Casey produced booklets and plastic cards she passed out to all family members. "The cards open the main gate after it locks at 11:00 p.m. Don't lose it and don't lend it. We've installed a voice phone at the entry for delivery people or guests. Betty, Tanya and Adam, you have temporary codes you'll have to key in."

"Does that include me?" Murray queried, sounding grumpier than he had over being left out of the party plans.

"Sorry, Murray, but no," Jackson interjected. "Art Rafferty, who built the system, recommended restricting use of gate codes to those living on the premises. In fact, he insisted on it. However, I wanted you to be aware of this new system, since you're over here a lot."

"I'm practically family! More so than Adam. He's merely an employee."

"At the moment, Adam lives at Bellefontaine."

Clearly disgruntled, Murray slumped and crossed his arms.

"How will this affect people who pay to take the Historical Society's tour of homes in December?" Aunt Esme asked.

Jackson smiled. "It'll make them conform to the hours set in the Society's brochure. The ones who show up outside the hours listed always irritate you, Auntie E."

"Because they're rude and so often pushy. I…suppose you're right." She finally capitulated with a small expulsion of breath.

"Is there anything special I need to do if I come in late, as I did last night?" Noelani put the question to Jackson, taking care to avoid looking at Adam. "From work," she hastily added.

Jackson swung toward her. ''What time did you get in last night?''

Exceedingly flustered, Noelani stammered a bit, then mumbled, ''Af-ter midnight.''

''Midnight, huh? Well, there'll be those occasions for everyone. Tanya's class sometimes visits nightclubs so students can report on jazz artists. Those nights, she'll key in. If you're ready, and if Murray's taking off now, I'll demonstrate the keypad.''

Murray pushed back his chair. ''What was the point of inviting me over for this enlightening bit of nothing? I get the message.'' He aimed his glare at Casey. ''From here on out, I'll call before I drop by. *If* I drop by. Excuse me…'' He stalked toward the door.

''Murray, as our nearest neighbor—and someone who saw the fire—I thought you of all people would understand our need for security,'' Jackson said.

''I don't. I agree with Esme. If you feel you need a watchdog, buy Dobermans. They're friendlier than locking out your true friends.'' They all winced as the screen door banged shut behind him.

''Whew! He's pissed,'' Nick muttered.

Jackson rubbed his chin. ''Poor Murray. His mom died when he was seven,'' he said, obviously for Noelani's benefit. ''Since then, he's run in and out of Bellefontaine like he lives here. I asked Art about giving him free access, and he strongly advised against it.''

''Is Art aware it was Murray and Roland who assisted us the night of the fire? Well, Murray did, anyway. I can't say Roland did much but get in the way. He's useless in a crisis,'' Casey said, turning to Noelani.

''The man is rude. I met him at the bank one day when I drove Aunt Esme to town. I don't know that I'd want him having access. While Aunt Esme was tending to business.

Dewalt waltzed up to me and made an uncalled-for remark about Duke and my mother.''

Aunt Esme handed Tanya some empty plates to carry to the kitchen. ''He finally felt vindicated by publicly pointing out Duke's indiscretion. I explained to Noelani how insanely infatuated Roland was from the moment he set eyes on Angelique.''

''That wasn't exactly yesterday,'' Noelani said, flipping back her hair. ''Considering how he behaved toward you, Aunt Esme, he had some nerve acting as if Duke had committed a mortal sin.''

Esme touched her lips with her napkin. ''I'd be the last person to stand up for Roland, but his rivalry with Duke goes back to their boyhood. It was always a game of one-upmanship with them. When it comes down to it, they're neither one a saint.''

''Enough.'' Jackson dipped an eyebrow toward Megan, who took everything in. ''I'm going to an Elks breakfast tomorrow, and I'm giving Murray a lift. Five will get you ten, he'll be over his snit by morning.''

Adam waited until after talk of the Dewalts had died. ''Auntie E, tomorrow Noelani and I are going to the Sugar Fest. Do you need us to deliver anything? We'll be leaving the house early, since Noelani's working till noon and I'm meeting a subcontractor in town.''

''I'm glad you jogged my memory, Adam. The museum director gave me name tags for everyone. When I go up-stairs to watch my program, I'll tuck an envelope with your tags under Noelani's bedroom door. Since you're representatives of Bellefontaine, the director may ask you to help in some manner.''

Noelani bobbed her head. ''I don't mind. But Adam, if you'd rather not get roped into some boring chore, I can go alone.'' She'd suggested this before, and wondered if she sounded too…eager.

''It's not the first time I've been roped in. I doubt it'll be the last.''

''Uh…fine, then. Jackson, I hate to rush you but could you explain the keypad? I planned on going back to the mill. Aunt Esme, that's what I started to say…before all of this.'' She indicated the gifts she'd carefully stacked. ''I left my boots on the stoop because I accidentally stepped in a puddle of molasses.''

Esme looked aghast. ''You ought not to have cut your arrival time so close, child. How long has it been since you put in an appearance at our cocktail hour?''

''Sorry. I've been tied up at the mill.''

Jackson intervened before Esme could respond. ''No need to apologize, Noelani. It's just that Auntie E remembers life at Bellefontaine when people weren't so busy and moved at a slower pace.'' He tugged one of Megan's curls. ''Speaking of busy—honey, after we finish our cake, run and get your bike helmet. Daddy will take you for a ride along the river.''

The child's eyes glowed excitedly.

''That sounds like fun.'' Tanya beamed at Jackson. ''Darn, I'm signed up for one of those pub crawls you mentioned earlier. I don't mind skipping it, though.''

Jackson stopped her. ''Megan's with you all day. It's important she and I spend some time together, Tanya.'' He folded the security system's schematic and rose. ''If we're all ready, I'll explain the secret to sneaking in late.'' He laughed, but Noelani thought his gaze settled a moment too long on her. She worried that maybe he'd seen her sneaking out of Adam's garçonnière in the dawn hours.

But why would that matter? She was an adult and didn't answer to Jackson or anyone. Her guilt stemmed more from the fact that she hadn't intended to go to bed with Adam.

And when she did, she certainly hadn't expected to enjoy the experience so much she'd like to repeat it. Therein lay her real concern. As she'd told Adam before leaving his bed, it was pure foolishness for them to form an attachment. But the way he'd gazed at her tonight only showed that he hadn't listened. And Noelani was awfully afraid she didn't have what it took to be strong enough for both of them. She'd fallen more than a little for Adam Ross.

NEXT MORNING, SHE HAD EVERY intention of addressing the subject frankly when they met. But Adam burst out of his garçonnière carrying a picnic basket and wearing a boyish grin that shot her resolve all to hell.

Her heart remembered how good his lips had tasted. Her hands itched to feel the silky softness of his still-damp hair. And there was the little matter of his birthday gift. She had just the place for it on her office desk, and was taking it there now in her new tote. He couldn't have chosen anything that would please her more.

Placing the picnic basket in the bed of his pickup, Adam opened Noelani's door. "It's a beautiful day. The weatherman promises it'll only get to seventy-nine. Perfect picnic weather."

She caught his enthusiasm. "I brought clothes to change into. Aunt Esme insisted I wear a dress to the Sugar Fest, as there'll be other growers' families present."

Adam draped her garment bag over the bench seat. "By chance, is it my favorite red dress?"

"Sorry, it's blue."

"I like blue. With your skin, you can wear anything and look good. Or nothing," he added, purposely ducking his head as he started the pickup.

He'd provided the opening Noelani needed to caution him about their getting involved. In the end she said nothing. It must've had something to do with a feeling of enchantment in the air. Something to do with traveling a tree-shaded lane seated next to a drop-dead gorgeous guy, while the morning breeze tangled her hair. If she wasn't already committed to Shiller's, Noelani could imagine herself content to stay at Bellefontaine. *Whoa!* Where did that idea come from?

They spoke very little on the trip to town. Both seemed comfortable listening to a CD Adam had selected right before they left the house. Celine Dion's latest. If Noelani thought it an odd choice for a man whose collection consisted mostly of jazz, she wasn't sufficiently moved to comment. In truth, the love songs added to her mellow mood.

The album had two songs to go when Adam pulled into the parking lot at the mill. "I'll be back at twelve sharp. Shall I come up, or would you rather meet me here?"

"I'll meet you." Grabbing her garment bag and her new tote, she hopped out before he could assist her.

Adam sat with the pickup idling until she disappeared into the noisy mill. Smoke from two tall stacks billowed into the blue sky. Another skinnier one spewed steam. Adam thought Noelani looked small and delicate against that backdrop.

Six hours had slipped away before he again pulled in between the area where cane trucks unloaded and the mill sat. It surprised him to see Noelani still in her work clothes, gesturing wildly to Jackson and Murray Dewalt.

Even when Adam walked toward them, loud machinery blocked their voices. As he joined the trio, Noelani acted surprised to see him. "Golly, I had no idea it was so late."

"No problem. We aren't on a set schedule. Jackson. Murray." Adam reached across Noelani to shake hands with the men. "You all look so grim. Is there trouble in River City?" Adam tried to make his query lighthearted.

"Maybe." Noelani's eyes remained dark and fathomless.

"I contacted Jackson around ten. I believe someone deliberately jammed the mud roller, which is an essential step to removing waste from the evaporator," she told Adam. "I was on normal rounds when I saw a workman pull a crowbar out of the rollers. Even he was baffled. That equipment hasn't had a work order on it for months."

"Sounds to me as if the problem's remarkably similar to the steel bar you found in the creeper feeders the other night."

"Yes," Noelani murmured. "But when Jackson arrived and questioned the men who work with the evaporator, one insisted he saw me leave the area not ten minutes before the rollers bound up. That would've been nine-fifteen. I was in my office until nine-thirty. I remember checking to see if I had time for rounds before meeting you at noon."

"So he's obviously lying."

Jackson paced back and forth in front of his maroon Jaguar. "Bobby Castille, who's positive he saw her, is one of our oldest, most trusted employees."

Noelani looked unhappy. "Thing is, Bobby's Cajun, Adam. And he's very superstitious and mistrustful. He's sure I brought the mill bad luck."

Murray leaned nonchalantly against Jackson's sedan. "I don't know if you recall how superstitious some Cajuns are, Adam. Several workers pulled Jackson aside as we walked through the mill, basically calling Noelani bad *mojo*."

"Hogwash." Adam whirled to confront Jackson. "Why would you even give credence to anyone's word over that of your sister?"

"Half sister," Murray and Noelani said in unison.

Jackson's navy-blue eyes remained locked with Adam's. "To my knowledge," he finally said, "the mill's never experienced labor disputes. Perhaps I made a mistake putting Noelani in as manager."

"Just Noelani? Or any woman?" Adam asked. "What if Casey had stepped in? Would they trust *her?* I think you should ask yourself if what's happening here is an extension of the recent trouble at Bellefontaine."

Jackson raked a hand through hair needing a trim. "You think I haven't asked myself that? Murray says it's probably coincidence. Lord knows our equipment's not new. Maybe someone on the night shift used a crowbar to unjam the rollers. He could've set it on a ledge and forgotten it. The vats vibrate. Maybe it fell."

"That's my guess, too," Noelani said. "Jackson, I already told you any of these incidents could be accidental. I'll bet if you go back over Duke's logs, you'll see similar reports. Removing me will be like saying you believe in bad omens."

"You're right. Next thing you know, someone will be blaming all our trouble on voodoo. Black magic has power in the bayous. I can't let it catch hold here."

Noelani hooked her thumbs in her back pockets. "So, I can run up and change into the dress I brought to wear to the Sugar Fest? And you'll go in and set Bobby Castille and the others straight about who's boss?"

Jackson nodded. He took Noelani's arm, and the two of them went into the mill, leaving Adam and Murray standing by the Jag.

"Bellefontaine didn't have problems until Nick Devlin blew into town. Or should I say paddle-wheeled into Baton Rouge."

"Stuff it, Murray!" Adam scowled. "If that's not sour grapes because Nick got the woman you wanted, I don't know what is."

"I'm merely stating facts," Murray said curtly. He yanked open the passenger door, climbed into Jackson's car and slammed it in Adam's face.

Adam dismissed Murray's charge as pure jealousy. Still, he was glad to see Noelani return when she did—before he punched Murray Dewalt in his aristocratic nose.

Noelani's royal-blue sundress accentuated her golden skin. From the moment she exited the building, Adam's mind emptied of everything except her.

He rushed to relieve her of the garment bag.

"Do I look all right?" She twirled in a circle.

"Let me stop drooling long enough to say that if Auntie E finds fault with you now, she's going blind."

Laughing, Noelani linked arms with Adam. The pleased expression he wore more than validated what she'd seen in the tiny office mirror. As a result, her earlier festive mood was restored. Until Adam drove the circle back out to the highway and she felt the whisper of a chill sneak up her spine.

She hunched to ward off the feeling that someone who disliked her intensely was watching her departure. Glancing out the passenger window, she saw nothing amiss. Two of the core samplers stood in the shade, smoking. Rose and Denise. Noelani would understand if it'd been Sue Ann— she'd pitched a fit over the change in their break schedule. Rose and Denise had seemed to accept it with equanimity.

As Adam completed the circle, Noelani's gaze collided with Murray's. He acted as if he thought Adam might side-swipe Jackson's car. Other than that, when he noticed Noe-lani, he smiled. She returned his smile and waved.

The chill had been so fleeting that once Adam had pulled onto the highway, excitement about the day ahead again filled her with anticipation. She surprised Adam by moving her garment bag and scooting closer to place her hand on his knee. "Hi!"

The unexpectedness of her action shocked Adam so much

his foot slipped off the gas pedal. The pickup slowed dramatically, so he leaned over and kissed her square on her mouth. "Hi, yourself," he said, smacking his lips loudly enough to make her laugh out loud.

CHAPTER TEN

"I VOTE WE EAT BEFORE WE GO to the Sugar Fest," Adam said. "I'm starving, and if we're asked to help out, the day could get away from us."

"That suits me, Adam. I have to admit that picnic basket's calling to me. Do you know of a park near here?"

"There's a jogging path along the river, with benches every so often. I never tire of watching Old Man River roll on."

"Oh, please, let's sit by the river. I haven't seen much of the Mississippi, except for when I cross the bridge."

Adam found a parking place. He carried the basket and handed Noelani two bottles of water he pulled from a cooler. They passed a few joggers as they walked. Adam ultimately settled on a site that looked out beyond a bend in the river. Nick's White Gold Casino was moored directly across from them. Downtown Baton Rouge provided an interesting skyline along the opposite shore. As they sat down on the bench, a barge chugged upriver, pushing a platform loaded with wooden crates.

"Did Nick or Casey ever mention if anything came of their interview with that pilot—Chuck Riley?" Adam opened the basket he'd set at their feet and passed Noelani a checkered tablecloth.

She left it folded in a square and placed it on the bench between them, watching while Adam pulled out containers of fruit, sandwiches and chips. "I asked Casey about Riley.

He was so disagreeable. She said he insists Duke owed him money for the hours he flew the plane. But Jackson refuses to pay until he can look at Duke's trip diary. The authorities are holding it, pending the crash investigation. Is the casino what made you ask about Riley?''

''Yeah.'' Adam offered her a dill pickle, then crunched on one himself. Noelani declined the pickle, but sorted out grapes, sliced apples and melon balls.

''Do you think Chuck Riley might be behind the mill accidents? I mean, if he's angry at Duke's family, maybe he's striking back. I heard Nick's banned him from the White Gold.'' Adam unwrapped a turkey sandwich and handed Noelani one filled with cucumber, tomatoes and sprouts. The bread was homemade wheat, crusted with pecans and pine nuts.

Noelani ate a quarter of it, then kicked off her sandals and dug her bare toes into the grass.

''Be careful doing that,'' Adam cautioned. ''I don't know if you have chiggers in Hawaii, but we have a lot of the little suckers here. If you don't want to itch for a week, put your shoes back on.''

Dutifully, Noelani obeyed. ''I'm not familiar with chiggers. On Maui, we have stinging jellyfish that wash up on our beaches. And a lot of flying insects that bite. The usual bores and fire ants around the cane. Talk about sting! Fire ants can eat you alive. Well, almost.''

''Noelani, you're sidestepping my question about Chuck Riley because…?''

''I'm not ignoring you, Adam. I'm turning your question over in my mind. There's no doubt that he was angry enough to cause trouble. But mill accessibility is where I see your theory falling down. Our staff knows who belongs on-site. Someone would've seen him skulking around and reported it to me.''

"Yet Bobby what's-his-name claimed he saw *you* in a work area when you were actually in your office."

"Castille. Bobby Castille. That does puzzle me. On the other hand, if Bobby's convinced I'm bad *mojo,* he may have purposely lied in hopes Jackson would get rid of me."

"Possibly. But in this part of the South, superstitions aren't to be taken lightly. Voodoo can be dangerous. A lot of bad people practice the black arts."

She laughed nervously. "You're scaring me, Adam. The river's nice, but if you're through eating, I'll clean up and we can go on to the Sugar Fest."

"Sure." He capped his bottle of water. "My aim wasn't to frighten you, Noelani. Promise me you'll stay alert, though."

"I promise," she said solemnly. "I'm not used to having anyone worry about me, Adam. Frankly, it's nice," she said, gazing at him through her thick eyelashes.

Pleased, Adam kicked around the idea of telling her he cared for her a lot, and that was why he worried. But all at once she withdrew, becoming so remote, he decided not to mention it.

As they walked back to where he'd parked, Noelani abruptly skipped to a new subject. "I almost forgot. Did you hand in your bid today?"

"No. I'm going to hold on to it for a while. I've been so caught up in my plans for Magnolia Manor, I never gave a thought as to what I'd do if someone outbids me."

"You knew other people would bid, Adam."

"Yes. But before, they didn't have a name. According to Murray, his dad wants the thirty acres of land where the house sits."

"Murray must be mistaken. Thirty acres is a drop in the bucket when it comes to farming. Besides, you said Magnolia Manor is on the historical register."

"It is. I did some snooping in the court records and found that Roland's pecan orchard butts up against the west end of Magnolia Manor's property line. Thirty added acres of pecan trees could yield him as much as forty thousand dollars a year in profit."

"That much?"

"Afraid so. And a courthouse clerk confided, off the record, that there are a number of reasons to bump old houses off the register. For instance, if there's so much wood rot it's not feasible to restore," he said, stowing the basket while she climbed inside the cab.

Noelani buckled her seat belt before she said earnestly, "You're a builder, Adam. You said the house was sound."

"What if Dewalt has an inspector in his pocket? He could dummy a report to say the house is falling down. Another thing the clerk said with a wink and a nudge was that I should check the record to see how many old homes have gone up in flames—coincidentally, she said, soon after a new owner buys the place for a song. Apparently if a buyer carries an umbrella insurance policy, any property purchased is automatically covered for the first sixty days."

"But that's insurance fraud!"

"Right, and how does anyone prove or disprove that? The clerk said it's usually blamed on homeless people, or on kids out playing with matches."

"Adam, that's awful. I can't believe an upstanding member of the community, like Dewalt, would stoop so low."

"I hope you're right. Roland may figure he's getting prime land for a lowball price. Or maybe he thinks the house should be condemned."

"In that case, won't your bid win? I mean, you aren't planning to lowball."

"So much depends on what a court assessor decides Magnolia Manor is worth. But the court isn't required to post an assessed value before bidding starts. I'm limited by the amount I've managed to save. I can't afford to bring the house up to code if I have to borrow to buy it.''

"Do you think you have enough saved?" She reached across the seat and clamped a bracing hand over his wrist. "I have some money set aside. But not knowing how much I'll get out of Bellefontaine, I may need what I have to buy out Bruce.''

"I wouldn't take money from you, Noelani. You didn't even like the house.''

"I liked it." Her fingers tightened on his arm. "Only to me, a house is secondary to its land. If you own land capable of growing crops, you're independent. You never have to depend on anyone else for your livelihood.''

"Ah. You like being your own woman?" Adam teased.

Noelani withdrew her hand. "Make fun of me. But take my mom, for instance. If she'd owned land instead of being Bruce's employee, she'd never have been beholden to Duke Fontaine. And there's Aunt Esme. Despite all the time and love and effort she's invested in making Bellefontaine a showplace, technically she owns nothing but the clothes on her back and a few pieces of furniture her parents left her.''

"She doesn't seem to mind. In her day, property always passed to a male heir. Jackson may own the house on paper, but as long as he holds on to Bellefontaine, Esme's assured of a place to live. Duke broke the mold by willing the fields and the business to all three of his kids. If you ask me, he gambled that the three of you wouldn't split up the operation.''

"I'd rather not talk about Duke Fontaine. Let's take Jackson's role as owner of the house and immediate land. What if he marries someone who hates Aunt Esme? Do you think Jackson—now, I'm picturing a Jackson goofy, slobbering in love—do you think he'd hesitate in shuffling Aunt Esme and Toodles straight off to a retirement home?''

"First of all, you have an unflattering opinion of what it means to be in love. And until you face up to the fact that Duke Fontaine did his best by you and your mom, you're not likely to fall in love yourself anytime soon. Do you really think Jackson would be interested in a woman incapable of loving Megan, Aunt Esme and Bellefontaine?''

Noelani thrust a hand through her long hair, avoiding direct contact with Adam's serious blue eyes. "God save me from self-appointed preacher men.''

Adam tipped back his head and laughed. "Sorry. I guess I did sound like a soapbox psychologist.''

She pleated and unpleated the skirt of her dress. "Still, you're dead-on when it comes to analyzing me. The last man I dated said practically the same thing, only he didn't know about Duke, so he called me a career-driven bitch.'' She brushed off Adam's objection. "I hope you're right about Jackson. I'd like to think he's a more compassionate man than his father. Because from where I sit, Duke didn't do the best he could by us. A checkbook's a poor substitute for a heart.''

"There's no getting around the fact you've been hurt, Noelani. But Duke's dead, so there's no going back. There's no asking him to explain why he didn't pick up the phone and call you. Only he never tossed out the letters he wrote to your mother. It seems to me a totally heartless man would've burned them and washed his hands of the two of you.''

"I said I don't want to talk about Duke.''

"This is about us, Noelani.''

"There is no us in that sense, Adam.'' She raked his face with sad, brooding eyes. "I like you too much to lead you on. You need a woman who can devote her life to keeping

Magnolia Manor spit-polished like the grand old showplace she used to be.''

"I want a wife who loves me, and wants to be the mother of my children. Somewhere on my list, I suppose, is the hope that she'll take pride in Magnolia Manor, should I be lucky enough to win the bid. I'm not looking for anyone to fill those roles tomorrow. And I'm sure as hell not looking for a housekeeper. So can we proceed, and just play it by ear?''

"You're wasting your time romancing me, Adam. After today, I'm not an available date. But there's a whole town full of eligible women out there.''

Appearing to tune her out, Adam slowed to search for a spot to park. They'd reached the museum and both the lot and the street were crowded with cars. "I hope those shoes are comfortable enough for hiking. We might have to park some distance away.''

Noelani craned her neck to study the families wandering the museum grounds carrying plates of food. Kids with balloons chased after dogs. She didn't see any parades or bands, but laughter drifted in Adam's open window, along with the burnt sugary scent she loved.

"Oh, someone's cooking cane. There! There, Adam. That Lincoln Continental pulled out. I think your pickup will fit into the slot he left.''

"You have sharp eyes. I would've missed seeing this place.'' Adam managed to parallel-park the oversize truck on the busy street in one try.

"You're going to have to show me how you did that,'' Noelani exclaimed, clearly impressed. "I need a city block to park Angelique's Cadillac. My vehicle of choice is a small Jeep. It may have stiff suspension, but you don't need the length between two telephone poles to park it.''

Adam got out, then set the picnic basket inside the cab

before he locked up and pocketed the keys. "I'm trying to picture you roaring down the road in a Jeep, wearing that dress," he said, eyeing her obliquely.

"I've done it lots of times. See, you don't really know me."

He shook his head. "I know more about you than you think. For instance, I know how kind you are. You went out of your way to console Megan. You didn't have to take her to town to get yarn for her doll's hair. Also, you can laugh at yourself, and you aren't quick to jump to conclusions. Instead, you prefer to think things through. You have a feminine streak that lets you indulge in perfume even when you wear jeans and boots to work at a grubby mill. And you choose to work long hours, even though you could sit back and do nothing." He smiled. "How am I doing so far?"

"Well, I learned something new about you, Mr. Ross. You have keen powers of observation."

"I do when the subject's interesting."

"Here, pin on this name badge. Aunt Esme described the museum's curator. She'll have on a wide-brimmed hat and an 1840s burgundy-colored gown with a handmade lace collar. We need to find her and introduce ourselves."

They found the woman in question teaching a group of children how to make ice cream using an old-fashioned hand-cranked oak freezer.

"Noelani. Adam. Miss Esme phoned me yesterday and said I should arm-wrestle you into helping out this afternoon." She thrust a large box full of museum brochures at Noelani. "Plant yourself inside the front door or outside on the porch. Anyone who comes past gets a brochure. Adam, making ice cream is hard work and takes someone with a strong arm. If you'll finish this batch, I'll go mix another. Oh, good, Tess," she cried, leaping toward a young woman hauling two grocery bags. "You found more junket. With the weather turning nice today, twice the number of people we expected have shown up. I'll locate someone to spell you both in an hour or so,'' she promised her two new volunteers.

"Isn't junket a Chinese boat?" Adam asked in an aside to Noelani.

"That's a junk." She chuckled. "Junket is sweetened milk that can be used for making ice cream. In the summer, my *tutu* mixed the ingredients for ice cream, and since we didn't have a machine, she sealed it in a plastic bag, put the bag inside a can, and then packed it inside a larger can with rock salt and ice. All the kids in the neighborhood came over and rolled the can back and forth over Tutu's kitchen floor. Presto, before long we were eating ice cream."

"Your grandmother more than made up for the love your mother couldn't give you, Noelani."

Her eyes suddenly got misty, and she blinked rapidly. "I miss her so much. All these kids running around without a care in the world. That's how I was as a young child."

"It's hard when life forces you to grow up early," Adam said, his tone slightly gruff.

"Yes. Well, I'd better go handle my assignment. I'll catch up with you later. When someone relieves me, I want to see all the displays. It says on the schedule there are slave cabins to tour out back, plus a replica of a working mill in the next room. And somewhere they're cooking down sugar the old way in open copper vats. I want to see *everything*."

"We'll meet up in an hour or so," Adam yelled over the children who clamored for him to churn faster.

It turned out to be more like two and a half hours later before anyone came to spell either of them. Adam thought his arm might fall off. "The curator said making ice cream was hard. She's right. I can't think when I've worked harder."

"My feet are killing me from standing so long on a concrete floor. You warned me about wearing shoes for vanity's sake. I should have listened. And remind me to quietly strangle Aunt Esme...that dear sweet lady," Noelani drawled. "It was her bright idea for us to wear Bellefontaine badges. There was hardly anyone here who didn't take one look and instantly peg me as Duke's indiscretion. The people who *didn't* know about me when they arrived soon found out. I want a tour, but first, I'm getting rid of this darned badge."

"In their place, wouldn't you be curious?"

"Curiosity killed the cat."

"Ah, but satisfaction brought him back. Cats have nine lives," Adam said lightly when she made a face at him. "Come on, everyone in the county probably had dealings with Duke Fontaine. He was *the man* when it comes to sugar. If any of his friends won't admit you do Duke proud, they're lying, Noelani."

"You're full of compliments, aren't you, Adam?"

"I speak nothing but the truth. Auntie E probably figured let them get a look at you now. So when the end of harvest rolls around and Bellefontaine throws its annual Christmas ball, you'll be universally accepted as one of the family."

"I *am* one of the family. Who gives a damn if people in the community accept me or not?"

"Don't you care? At least a little?"

Noelani unpinned her badge and stuck it in her purse. She did care, dammit. More than she wanted Adam to know. She envied the closeness evident in the easy way Jackson and Casey interacted. They grew up in the protected bosom of a prominent family, yet Casey certainly didn't trade on the Fontaine name. She'd earned the right to be called a top area grower. Jackson, while more the family politician, did okay at making lemonade out of the lemons life had handed him, too. He didn't shirk his duty to Megan. Come to think of it, he could have contested his dad's will.

A month ago, she'd never have believed she might covet anything her half siblings had. A month ago, she preferred to stand on the outside looking in. The longer she spent working with Casey and Jackson, the more she'd begun to wish she was one of them. Too often now, Noelani caught herself vowing to earn her rightful place in the family business.

But that was silly. When the time came for Auntie E to throw her annual Christmas ball, Noelani would probably be on a 747 winging across the Pacific.

Lifting her chin, she stared straight at Adam. "It's already mid-October. That gives you plenty of time to figure out who you'll escort to the Fontaine ball. With luck, by Christmas, I'll be well on my way to owning Shiller's. *Hana Sugar*. Has a nice ring, doesn't it?"

Adam let her say her piece. Maybe she thought he was slow, and that he wasn't getting the message. Unfortunately, her statements were about as subtle as a two-by-four upside the head. Noelani Hana had no interest in him, and no plans to stay in Louisiana. He had a hard head, but he wasn't a masochist. If she wanted him to get lost after today, get lost he would.

Their last exchange sapped much of the joy he might have experienced in touring the museum. History, though, was solid and real and constant. Sugar had played a huge part in shaping lower Louisiana's political and economic climate. As they wandered around, looking at old photos and reading the captions, it became increasingly evident how influential the Fontaine family had been in the history of this territory.

"Jackson and Casey must be really proud of the contributions their family's made to the state," he murmured.

"To sugar," Noelani said without hesitation. "It's not an easy business now, but the early cane farmers operated in primitive conditions. That workman's shack is devoid of the slightest convenience we take for granted today. I'm glad to see the Fontaines freed their slaves voluntarily. Just think, those families must have descendants living in and around the area."

"Quite possibly some still work at the mill," Adam pointed out.

"Have you ever stopped to think how you might react to a current plantation owner whose ancestors could conceivably have owned yours?" she asked.

"No. Have you? Wait—you're not hatching some theory that all the stuff happening to Jackson and Casey is a result of some long-standing grudge dating back to before the Civil War?"

"You're right. I'm going off the deep end here."

"If I recall, the longest recorded feud in American history took place in the Appalachians. It ended before you and I were born."

"Someone recorded a feud? Wow, that's amazing." Noelani shrugged. "I didn't really suppose Bellefontaine's problems had anything to do with slavery or the Civil War, but reading all this history, I happened to think what if—and my mind went wild shooting off ideas."

"Hmm. Maybe you ought to concentrate on appreciating how many times Fontaines took leadership roles over the years. Look how often they've underwritten agricultural programs whose purpose is to find better ways to farm and harvest cane."

"Have you ever seen Aunt Esme's family scrapbooks? They're impressive. I have so few pictures of my family," she said, sounding pensive.

"Ditto. I have one picture of my dad in his uniform, and a small one of my parents at their wedding."

"I never thought to ask about the antiques and such that must've been at Magnolia Manor when you lived there. Are any of them left?"

He placed a hand at her waist and moved her out into the fading afternoon sun. "As far as I know, when Mom fell on hard times, everything was auctioned off to pay our creditors."

"As far as you know?" Noelani turned. Her mind had probably skipped some bit of information Adam had already given her.

"Mom suffered a series of nervous breakdowns. The worst happened when I was in junior high. Our football team went to conference up on the Mississippi line. It was before the days of cell phones. Looking back, I'm not sure the authorities would have tried to reach me, anyway. After all, I was a mere kid. Anyway, I arrived home in the middle of the night to the news that she'd slit her wrists. By then the asylum had pushed through a court order committing her and seizing Magnolia Manor as payment. Later, they auctioned the contents. It took years before I learned the truth. I assumed she'd willingly signed it over. Of course, at the age of thirteen or so, how could I have made a difference? I was sent to live with a great-uncle, who has since died. No one knew the sanatorium would require Mom to sign over the house and her military allotment before they'd agree to admit her."

"Good Lord, Adam. Your mother...died in some horrid state mental institution?"

"She's not dead."

"But I assumed—so, where is she? Not still in the place that fleeced her?"

"No. I got her moved to a private facility before I spent one cent on college."

"Do you see her often? Is she better? Oh, I hope for both your sakes that she's improved."

"She has her ups and downs. I used to visit weekly, but then she got it in her head I was my dad. The doctor had to sedate her heavily. Now I go twice a month to check on her. If she's having a good day we sit in the courtyard and have lunch. I've given up on the idea of bringing her home to Magnolia Manor. Unfortunately, she has fewer and fewer good days." *Like yesterday, which had been really bad.*

"Her care must be very costly, Adam. No wonder you've had difficulty saving up enough to bid on the house."

"She's my mother, Noelani. And I don't have a lot of other expenses. Still, I really appreciate Jackson letting me stay free of charge in the garçonnière. I should be able to apply most of what I earn on this job to my bid. So save your pity."

"I didn't mean—sure, Adam." Noelani pulled back from his ferocious scowl. She knew what he meant about pity. She hated feeling pitied, too. Lordy, but she had a ton of baggage. So, apparently, did Adam. Another reason why they simply shouldn't hook up for even the short time she'd be here.

Noelani absorbed the sights and sounds of a southern evening as Adam drove back to Bellefontaine. He was either doing the same or felt too irritated with her to make conversation. Nor did he bother to put in a CD. Had she upset him so much that he couldn't even find refuge in the music he loved?

They'd almost reached home—in fact Adam had signaled to turn onto the property—when the gates swung open and Jackson's Jaguar shot out onto the highway.

He slammed on his brakes and threw the car into reverse. Adam stopped and rolled down his window.

"Is that Noelani with you?" Jackson yelled.

She released her seat belt and scrambled across the bench seat to poke her head out Adam's window. "I'm here. What's wrong?"

"There's been an accident at the mill."

"Is it bad? What happened?"

"Come on, ride with me. I'll tell you about it on the way."

Noelani flew across the seat and opened the passenger door. She grabbed her purse, then patted at the floor, hunting for the tote bag that held her work clothes.

"What are you looking for?" Adam asked.

"I'll need to change into my jeans and boots again. I can't tromp through the mill in heels and a dress."

"I tossed your bag in the back with the picnic basket. Tell Jackson we'll follow him. You'll save time if you change in the pickup en route."

"Okay. Thanks. Except then how will I learn what happened?"

"When we get there, I guess."

"All right. But can you hurry and grab my bag? Jackson looked positively haggard. Maybe he shouldn't be driving."

Adam missed the last of her message as he'd left the cab. He soon returned, tossing her the tote. "A truck driver's been injured. Jackson said his cane box didn't release when the crane went to pick it up. The driver hit the release a second time, but the crane operator thought the box was stuck, so he applied more leverage. The box separated too fast, tumbled end over end and landed on the cab of the truck, pinning the driver inside."

"You got all that in the few seconds you were retrieving

my tote?'' Noelani glanced at him in amazement as she extracted her jeans, shirt and boots from the bag.

''Jackson talks fast. The fire department's on the scene trying to free the driver. It remains to be seen what condition he's in. Of course, the windshield's broken all to hell. If he didn't duck, he might've been crushed.''

''Stop, already! I can do without worst-case scenarios.'' Noelani kicked off her heels, hiked up her skirt and began wiggling into jeans stiff with the sugary substance that permeated the air inside the mill.

Adam gave a long, low wolf whistle.

''Keep your eyes on the road, buster. You're driving, and it won't do anyone any good if we have a wreck on the way.''

''Story of my life. A striptease going on right under my nose and I don't get to watch.''

''Aw, gee. Give me a minute. As soon as I get out of my dress and back into this yucky T-shirt, I'll find my violin.''

''I'm only trying to take your mind off the accident.''

''If it *is* an accident, I'll feel better. I'm trying to decide if there's a way someone could have jimmied the hydraulic release on purpose.''

''I'm sure Jackson's worried about the same thing.''

''We find the slightest evidence to that effect, and I swear I'm going to camp at the mill day and night until I catch whoever's doing this.'' Her voice sounded muffled, coming as it did from under yards of dress material.

She emerged with her T-shirt on backward. Cursing mildly, she pulled a quick change without exposing anything but her back and midriff.

Adam grinned. ''Nice moves, Hana. Sure you worked in a mill in Hawaii and not some girly bar?''

''I should've ridden with Jackson. He's not so hung up

on female body parts.'' Bending, she squirmed around, doing her best to pull on her boots.

''Yeah, Jackson Fontaine is a saint. And I'm not referring to our beloved pro football team, either.''

''I don't doubt he's a womanizer, too. All you southern men are. Oh, I see the fire truck. Pull over, Adam. I'll hop out at the gate. I don't think you'll be able to find a parking space in the lot. If you want to make a U-turn and head out again, I'll catch a ride home with Jackson.''

''I'll park and see if there's anything I can do. I don't want to get in the way, but, it looks as if a fair-size crowd has already gathered. What's one person more or less?''

Noelani released her seat belt and leaped from the pickup while he continued to ramble. She left her dress and her tote on the seat, and took only her purse—in case she needed her office keys for any reason.

She elbowed her way through onlookers and hurried over to stand beside Jackson as he talked with a fireman. An aid car pulled through the crowd with lights flashing and sirens blaring.

The quick glance Jackson shot Noelani was one of relief. ''Mason says Rob Dvorak's alive and alert. He was the driver. Our crane's involved, but the truck's not one of ours. They're transporting Rob to Emergency. If you'll have Adam take you there, I'll stay behind and wind up with reports and such. Mason tells me Rob's wife has been notified. She's meeting him at the hospital. Either phone me on the cell with the doc's verdict, or else I'll join you as soon as we get things back to normal here.''

''Consider it done.''

Adam had no sooner poked a foot out of his truck than Noelani shoved him back inside and scrambled in next to him. ''Can you drive me to the hospital?''

He didn't even fumble for his keys. The pickup roared to life.

She relayed to him everything Jackson had said. "Keep your fingers crossed that Rob's injuries aren't serious."

Adam stuck to perimeter roads and was soon parking outside the hospital.

When they finally got someone to direct them, they found a tall, well-built, swarthy man in his late twenties busy informing the doctor he didn't need skull X rays. He insisted that what he needed was to check on the condition of his truck. A pale blond woman clutching the patient's hand tried to get him to listen to the doctor.

"Mr. Dvorak, er…Rob. I'm Noelani Hana, manager of Fontaine's mill."

"I've heard of you." He ignored her proffered hand. "Some of the guys are saying that screwy things have been happening on-site ever since the man put you in charge."

Adam stepped forward to stand hip to hip with Noelani. "Rob, you strike me as too savvy to buy into superstitions about Noelani being bad *mojo*. Didn't I see you one night hanging out with Tanya Carson's college crowd?"

"Yeah. I'm going to night school. I've got a wife and a kid to support. I don't plan on driving a cane truck for the rest of my life like my daddy."

"A family man who wants to get ahead is to be commended. So why don't you tell Ms. Hana exactly what you think occurred."

"I don't have to think. I know. The truck and cane I was hauling belongs to Junior Mandeville. I've complained to him for weeks. The hydraulics on that old crate needed checking. Junior pinches a buck so tight, you can hear the eagle scream."

"So it wasn't the fault of our crane operator?" Noelani

asked. The sharp pains that had been slicing though her stomach started to ease.

"Nope, Ray Dee Plover, he's the crane operator, hooked on to my cane bin like always. And that's the story I gave Mason Trotter, who cut me out of the cab."

Jackson walked over just in time to hear the last. He lightly punched Rob's unbandaged arm. "Glad to see your pretty face wasn't cut, pardner. Scared me, seeing all the blood on the steering wheel. I'm about to invite Junior to dump his cane in a different mill. Before I do, I came to tell you Casey has a truck available if you'd like to drive for us."

"I'll be on the job in the morning. Tell me where to collect the truck. And Jackson, thanks. I knew you'd fill Duke's shoes."

Jackson grimaced. "Rob, get an X ray, all right? Take tomorrow and Monday off for good measure. Noelani, would you and Adam swing by Wisteria Cottage on your way home? Ask Casey to put Rob Dvorak on the payroll, and make it retroactive to the beginning of this month."

"I'll phone her from work. Adam can go on home. If it's not out of your way, Jackson, would you drop me at the mill? I know how antsy workers can get after any accident. I think management should be on-site to answer questions, don't you?"

"Yeah. Probably a good idea. Okay, bunk there tonight. I'll swing by in the morning and take you home to get the Caddy."

As they went out to the parking lot, Adam had the distinct feeling Noelani had neatly excised him from her life. He didn't like it, but what could he do except lump it? He had no intention of playing second fiddle to a sugar mill. Already, though, he hated the thought of watching her walk away.

On the lonely drive home, Adam tried but never managed to shake from his mind a spectrum of vignettes. Most featured Noelani as she'd been today, looking like a million bucks, chatting easily with people from the community. *Looking as if she belonged here in Baton Rouge.*

CHAPTER ELEVEN

As Noelani predicted, many workers were shaken up by the accident. Walking with Jackson past Rob's wrecked truck, she felt unease ripple outward in waves from groups of workers who had yet to return to their jobs. "If your work isn't directly affected by this accident," she shouted, "it's time for everyone to return to his or her station."

Realizing far too many of their personnel stood idly by, Jackson seconded Noelani's directive. "Here comes Ray Dee," he said, turning her attention to a workman coming toward them. "I know his take on the accident matches Rob's, but we should make sure he knows we're not blaming him in any way."

Ray Dee Plover, a lion-maned fellow with a beer gut and a lot of tattoos, seemed unaffected by the whole thing. "Not the first bin to fall, Mr. Fontaine. Probably won't be the last. Mostly they bounce on the cane pile and it's a matter of straightening 'em out with the front loader so I can hook onto 'em again. Rob's a lucky sumbitch. Junior Mandeville oughta fix his equipment or be drummed out of the business."

Jackson rested the toe of one polished boot on a sticky ledge. "We'll be minus Junior's cane from now on, Ray Dee. Noelani's and my main concern is that the accident doesn't spook the crews. I don't mind telling you Fontaine's has dealt with enough accidents this year. We'd appreciate you helping us keep a lid on the tension building around here.''

"You're the boss. Junior Mandeville ain't gonna be a happy camper. I advise watching your back.''

"Noelani manages the mill. And Junior's a blowhard. He doesn't worry me. Maybe next season he'll listen if one of his drivers says a truck needs servicing.''

"Don't hold your breath. Well, the wrecker's here to haul the truck away. Time to blow the whistle and get that line of cane trucks moving again so we can send all these lazy bums back to work.'' The whistle to which Ray Dee referred was an internal system devised to be heard above the noisy machinery. All workmen were required to learn a code of long and short blasts developed to save machinery from damage, or to summon help fast if a worker needed assistance.

"I'm fighting city council over the big whistle we blow at noon and 6:00 p.m.,'' Jackson remarked as he and Noelani left Ray Dee to go inside. "Newcomers to our parish complain in letters to the editor and at council meetings about the loud noise. On the other hand, old-timers set their watches by the whistle. I'm for progress, but even I believe losing it would be like saying goodbye to an era.''

"You sound like Adam,'' Noelani said. "A couple of weeks ago he was lamenting all the changes in and around Baton Rouge. He said the moon isn't as bright as it used to be. The river's dirtier, and its course is altered. In general, a whole way of life is slowly being eroded. I told him change is happening in Hawaii, too. Jackson, do you envision a time when there won't be sugar grown in Louisiana?''

"Yeah, next year if we don't pull our fat out of the fire.'' His tone was teasing, but his eyes had bleak shadows hovering at the edges.

"My program's working well. A trial run speeded our

intake of cane by more than ten percent over twelve hours. Give me the go-ahead and I'll make the permanent switch tonight. The timing is perfect since I plan to be here, anyway. Sometime around midnight I should be able to reset the computers that drive the conveyors carrying bagasse to the fire pits, too. At 6:00 a.m. I'll cut in an accelerated program to control the vats. Voila, by noon tomorrow, we've increased our across-the-board output.''

''Will you have to tell staff? I'm wondering if we shouldn't give them a breather following Rob's accident.''

''The crew handling the liming tanks are aware I'm running tests. They like the idea of firing up the two empties. Same with the men in charge of the vats.''

''I hear a *but* coming, don't I?''

''The core samplers, who are already peeved at me over the lunch changes, will have to run two added batches per shift. That equals four full sets of data for the chemists to analyze. I'm prepared to pitch in during the transition if they bog down. Nothing I can do about the core samplers, though. Their room is cramped, plus the ladies are territorial as it is. Not that I blame them. They're doing a good job, but I believe they can work faster.''

''You're expecting them to give you flak?''

Noelani smiled as they climbed the steel-mesh stairs to reach her office. ''You read between the lines, Jackson. I can handle flak if I'm sure management supports me. Duke had absolute control here. However, I sense everyone thinks they can go over me and gripe to you or Casey. Like Ray Dee, for instance. He looked right through me and spoke to you. If I make changes, I need to be confident you and Casey are one hundred percent behind me.''

''We are.'' Jackson stood with his hands buried in his pockets while she unlocked her office. ''Have you calculated how many added tons of crystal we'll get under your new program?''

"Implement it today and by Christmas, oh, an extra fifty thousand pounds.''

In her office, Jackson dropped into what had been his father's favorite leather chair. "Duke picked up a couple of empty warehouses from Roland Dewalt in the refinery transaction. I hung on to them because Casey's excited about the prospects for her new hybrids. She said her yield may be up seventy-five percent. The hybrids are all planted on land we own and were funded by us, not by coalition advances.''

Noelani didn't understand the significance, but she could almost see his brain running calculations. Less familiar with the warehousing and marketing end of the business, she didn't know what that meant to overall profit and loss. "When will Casey begin cutting the hybrids? I heard her say the stalks are stronger, but that hybrids mature more slowly than the old established breeds.''

"I think she hopes to cut the week after next. She's anxious to see the core samples. If they do as well as she predicts, we'd benefit from faster processing. So, implement away, Noelani.'' After clapping his hands on his knees, he stood. "Time for me to hit the road. On my way out, I'll detour past the core sample room and tell Rose we're stepping up production. I'm not going over your head, Noelani, but she considers me a friend. Her brother and I closed a few bars together in our younger days. I can't decide if I should alert Rose to look for some high-grade cane or not. I'd hate for her to think she's getting false readings.''

"You're expecting miracles from Casey's hybrids,'' Noelani exclaimed. She might have said more except the phone on her desk rang. Because Jackson was closer, he answered it.

"For you, Noelani. Eugene Blanchard, from Blanchard

Garden Center." Jackson covered the mouthpiece and grinned. "Gardening in your spare time, are you?"

She snatched the receiver. "Mr. Blanchard? This is Noelani Hana. Ah, you've read the proposal I dropped off the other day? Good. You're interested? Great. A trial from now though the end of November works for us. I should be able to deliver the first product to you by Friday."

Jackson headed for the door but, unable to hide his curiosity, he stopped and waited for Noelani to finish her call.

She didn't keep him in suspense long. "Eugene Blanchard wants to stock our bagasse clinkers and our shredded bagasse for landscape materials. All we lose in giving it a try is a few man-hours and possibly a truck and driver for two or three hours a week. We're ahead if the stuff sells in his nurseries."

"Somebody might actually buy sugar rocks?"

"I got the idea from the grounds at Bellefontaine. Your gardener lined all the flower beds with bagasse clinkers. They look like lava rock, but they're far cheaper."

"Maman's doing, I'll bet. I never paid attention to the landscaping," he muttered. "Well, except when Maman twisted Casey's and my arms to pick a site for the fountain we're expected to add. Maman loved the grounds and the fountains. She was fascinated with the concept of each Fontaine generation building a new one. Casey and I always told her we had years to think about our design." His voice cracked. Indeed, their time to decide on a new fountain had come much sooner than they'd envisioned.

Rallying, he eyed Noelani. "Technically you have a vote in the next fountain. I think Casey has a few possibilities Maman got from a landscape architect."

"I love the three-tiered fountain with the pineapple. Now I understand why they're all different. I'd like a voice in choosing the next one, Jackson. Shall we pencil it on our to-do list before I go back to Hawaii? After harvest? And maybe one day I can even come back for a visit and see it operating.''

''I should hope so.''

Noelani said nothing. At times she had difficulty separating her current life from the one she'd left behind. The life she'd return to once they'd settled Duke's estate. It often seemed far removed from the here and now—like a misty dream.

Jackson, ever pragmatic, dug his day planner out of his pocket and jotted himself a note. They parted with Noelani promising to update him on how the new program was doing the next day, when he dropped off Angelique's car.

Some women would do anything to avoid spending the night in a noisy, sticky mill. Noelani never felt more comfortable than when she heard the hiss of steam, smelled the ever-present odor of toasted molasses, or felt the very floor beneath her feet vibrate from the steady hum of hundreds of conveyors. This was the world she'd grown up in. The only world she trusted.

She carefully tucked disks from the old program into her back pocket. She'd switched to the new system, and now had to run a check on the lower floors to make sure everything was working smoothly. At Shiller's, she would've left her door unlocked and probably even left the old disks lying on top of her desk. Adam's repeated warnings about being careful had made her wary.

His face lingered in her mind as she peered over the narrow catwalk to the machinery below. She remembered how at home he'd looked the day of the *cochon de lait* when Casey sent him up to change the office lock. Other men might be ill at ease if asked to walk strange catwalks high above hot and dangerous machinery. Not Adam. He sauntered with a certain swagger, no matter what the environment. A swagger that never failed to clutch at her heart.

Noelani's T-shirt began to cling to her skin as she remembered the humid night they'd spent making love in Adam's bed. When she caught herself smiling and slowing her steps, she knew she needed to shift gears and flush all memories of Adam from her mind. Accidents happened when people let their attention drift. And even if she was in no danger of causing an accident, dreaming about Adam Ross was pointless. She'd cut him loose. If visions of his broad shoulders, narrow hips and rugged face intruded, she had to mercilessly excise them, too.

An exercise made more difficult the next day by her half brother.

Ten o'clock, and Noelani had no sooner returned to her office after a satisfying check of all the systems, when her telephone rang, startling her.

"We're two blocks from the mill," Jackson said.

"We who?" Noelani yawned in his ear.

"Jackson and Adam, sleepyhead. Did you forget I said I'd bring you the Caddy?"

"I expected you. But Adam…?" Her voice faltered.

"Yeah, poor guy. I dragged him away from sanding counters. It crossed my mind that you might not be in a position to drive me home. So I asked Adam to take the Caddy, while I've got my Jag. That way, I'll run him back to Bellefontaine and pick up Auntie E, Megan and Tanya for our outing to the Sugar Fest. I phoned because I'm running late. Can you meet us in the parking lot and fill me in on the new system?"

"I can update you now. Park the Caddy and leave the keys in the core sample room. I'll get them later. Jackson…. Jackson?" Noelani frowned and depressed the switch several times, but ended up with a dial tone. Flipping through the card file, she hunted for his cell number. Nothing. Apparently Duke had kept the family phone numbers in his head.

"Well, damn!" Not only didn't she want to lock up and dash down three flights of slick steps, but Noelani didn't care to cross paths with Adam on the heels of severing their ties. But wasn't that dumb? They didn't *have* ties. They were adults, and adults fell in and out of relationships all the time. *Not true!* She ran a fingertip over the glass pineapple—Adam's gift. And a persistent little voice pulsed inside her head. *He made you feel something you've never felt before. Cherished.*

Doing her best not to listen, Noelani slammed her door and shook the handle to make sure it was locked.

The men were climbing from their respective vehicles about the time she exited the building on the lower level. She caught her breath the moment she glimpsed Adam, backlit by the sun—tall, bronzed and ruggedly handsome, even dressed as he was for work. She wished for a moment that she could sneak him into her suitcase and take him back to Hawaii. *Impossible.* Adam would no more walk away from his dream of owning Magnolia Manor than she'd give up hers of owning Shiller's one day.

Jackson noticed her before Adam did. He hailed her and leaned against the Jag, dropping his sunglasses over his eyes as he waited for her to reach them.

"Hi. You don't look any the worse for spending all night working," Jackson said. "Remind me before I go that I've got some stuff for you. Aunt Esme had Betty fix you a salad. She put it in a small cooler. And she sent a washcloth and towel." He winked. "If she didn't consider it an invasion of your privacy, Aunt Esme would've packed you clean undies, I'm sure."

Adam approached the Jag, circled around and climbed in

the passenger side without acknowledging Noelani. The slight bothered her, and Jackson noticed.

"What's with Adam?"

"Do I look psychic? Ask him, why don't you?"

"I will. On the way home. Did you two have a falling out?"

"Did we have something to fall out about?" Noelani asked sharply.

"Come on, Noelani. It's not my imagination that Adam watches you like a lovesick Romeo."

She rolled her eyes. "Brother! You need your eyes checked. I thought you said you were in a rush to go. What else can I tell you about the new program?"

"Aunt Esme will be disappointed to hear you and Adam are on the outs. She's lost the battle trying to change Casey into a genteel lady. Just yesterday I heard her say if you married Adam, she'd talk you into opening Magnolia Manor for the historic home tour. And then you'd forget all about working at the mill."

"Ma-rry Adam? Auntie E needs to lay off the mint juleps."

Jackson grinned. "I promise I won't tell her you said that. She hates anyone noticing an occasional overindulgence. So, Noelani, I've teased you enough. How's the program going? All right, I assume, or you'd have said so."

"I couldn't get a word in edgeways. But it's working like a dream. If you've got no objections, I'll take a nap during lunch, then spend another night monitoring the whole works. After forty-eight hours with no bugs, I'll be ready to say we're home free."

"Never let it be said I stand between a woman and her work. I'll be in and out at the house next week. The coalition is meeting with national committee people in New Orleans. Australia is angling for a bigger slice of the European market, as is our neighbor to the southwest. If we can't block their votes, we may all be planting pecans next spring.''

"Ouch. You don't really think that's possible, do you? I know Australia has fine-tuned their mills. They're forerunners with some innovative systems. In fact, I've been talking to Bruce about trying some of their equipment. Wow, Jackson, if they speed production again, it could spell market disaster for all U.S.-grown sugar.''

"Thanks for the prediction of gloom and doom. I didn't need that, Noelani.''

"You do. So you'll go into the meeting and talk harder.''

"Yeah, yeah! I'll do my best to rally growers around the red, white and blue. You haven't seen me in my cheerleader mode.'' Grinning goofily, he made a few rah-rah moves that cracked Noelani up.

She smiled all the way back to her office, in spite of the fact that she'd made a special effort to wave goodbye to Adam and he'd pretended not to see her.

Increasingly restless, Noelani failed at her attempt to nap over lunch. Finally she gave up, grabbed her workout clothes and whiled away an hour at the gym. Given her mood, her assigned kick-boxing opponent never stood a chance. But she did leave the gym energized and somewhat more optimistic.

OVER THE NEXT FEW DAYS, Adam saw little of anyone in the family except for Esme, Betty, Tanya and Megan. A couple of nights, well after midnight, he sat out on his porch nursing a beer and watched Noelani roll in. He watched her climb from the Caddy, roll her neck tiredly, then sneak in and rummage through the fridge. He wanted to intercept her, but each time stubborn resistance held him back.

His work was on hold again. The lumber company

couldn't find the cypress he needed to match the dining room flooring. In his spare time, he helped Esme rearrange furniture in the historic portion of the house, which included sending the heavy Oriental rugs out for cleaning. The woman had turned into a whirling dervish preparing for the eventual tours that preceded the Fontaines' elaborate holiday ball.

Adam didn't like thinking about the Christmas ball. Noelani had said point-blank she'd be gone by then. Although he hated feeling like a voyeur, he'd taken to hovering in the dark, waiting to catch even the smallest glimpse of her.

Friday, he reworked his bid on Magnolia Manor until he couldn't look at it any longer. Still, he didn't turn it in.

Aware that his project at Bellefontaine would be done well before Esme's upcoming events—and that was taking every possible delay into consideration—Adam used his downtime to seek out other renovations in the area.

Monday of the week following his reluctant decision—to let Noelani go her way while he went his—he met with a prospective client. Shortly before noon, he handed the owners an estimate, and on his way home stopped at the hardware store to pick up replacement chandelier bulbs for Aunt Esme. He noticed a woman about his age ahead of him in the check-out line. She seemed to be eyeing him. She had light-brown eyes and streaked blond hair. He tried to recall if he'd met her through Casey and Nick, or Jackson, but came up blank. She left without speaking, so Adam decided she'd simply been checking him out.

After he'd paid for his bulbs and walked out of the store, the same woman appeared out of nowhere. "Adam Ross, right?"

"Yes. I'm sorry, maybe we've met, but I'm afraid I can't place you."

"I'm not surprised. I've changed a lot. Last time you saw

me, I sat in front of you at St. Francis Elementary. Sixth grade. I'm Denise Rochelle.'' Shifting her purse and hardware bag, she thrust a hand toward Adam.

Frowning, he took it. ''Rochelle? Elementary school was a lifetime ago. I hope I've changed from the gangly kid I was then. How did you ever recognize me?''

She laughed. ''I have the advantage. I saw you at Fontaine's mill. I do core sampling there. You looked so familiar, I asked a co-worker for your name. Rose Doucet knew it. She said you're restoring Bellefontaine.''

''Yes. You probably heard about the fire someone set in their kitchen.''

''Yes, well, Jackson Fontaine and his snotty sister can afford to have their whole mansion rebuilt from the ground up. Unlike the poor folks Duke screwed.''

Her terse comment took Adam aback. He measured the distance to his truck, wondering if she was another crazy bent on harming the Fontaines.

''You still can't place me, Adam? Our families both fell on hard times. Arlen Rochelle, my pa, used to run Duke's cookers. There was an accident. Someone said Pa was drunk, but he wasn't. Fontaine fired him, even though Pa suffered bad burns. We lost our car and our house. Mama literally died of shame—the same year your daddy went missing in 'Nam and your mama took sick. You and I had lunch together and talked about what we'd do if we were bigger.''

Adam studied her as she talked. ''You had freckles and reddish pigtails then.'' He didn't say the grown-up Denise looked harder than the sad child he remembered. They reminisced about other classmates for a few minutes. ''You say Roland Dewalt eventually bought your family home and the Chenard place as the site for his refinery?'' he finally asked.

''Yep. The Fontaines own that now. Roland gave Pa a

chance when no one else would. I quit school my senior year and worked for Dewalt's, too—until their equipment got so outdated, business fell off.''

"Is your father working for the Fontaines now, or has he retired?''

"Pa's liver gave out five years ago. But he never worked again—also thanks to Duke Fontaine. He passed the word, and no grower would hire my dad.''

"I'm sorry, Denise. It doesn't sound as if life treated your father well.''

"I'm sorry your daddy never turned up.''

"Yeah, well, time eventually dulls the pain.''

"Does it?'' Denise's clasped her sack with both hands and glanced away.

Adam shifted his purchase, too, preparing to say goodbye. "Hey, it's good catching up, but I've got to run. I've been out all morning and I still have to check on some flooring.''

"Before you get away, Adam, let me jot down my address and phone number. Old friends should keep in touch.''

"Almost everyone I knew as a kid has moved away from here. I've been up in Natchez.''

"I'd heard that.'' Denise handed him a scrap torn off her bag. "You know, instead of leaving a second meeting to chance, we should set up something firm. Next weekend kicks off the New Iberia Sugar Fete. There'll be food, drink, fabulous jazz and Zydeco bands in the park. If you don't already have a date, we could go together. Hang out for old time's sake.''

"Uh, a couple of weeks ago I, ah, went to the Sugar Fest.''

"Oh, well, the Sugar Fete's way different. It's more of a carnival atmosphere. Complete with floats. But I say if you've seen one float, you've seen 'em all. I go for the music and the dancing. You look like a man who could use a little fun, Adam.''

He smiled, thinking Jackson had said the very same thing the day they rode home from the mill together. ''Okay. Sure. Why not?'' Adam glanced at the slip of paper, saw he could read it okay, then tucked it in his shirt pocket for safekeeping.

''Really? Hey, great! Friday I work a graveyard shift till 8 a.m. I can change clothes at the mill if you'd like to swing by there and pick me up.''

Mere mention of the mill brought Noelani's exotic face into focus for Adam. ''Uh, no. I...can't get away that early. How about if I collect you at your place at ten-thirty?''

''Ten? Otherwise we'll miss some of the best jazz groups. Come earlier if you can. I'll ice a six-pack. Do you have a preference?''

''Not really. Shall I bring anything?''

''Just yourself and a hearty appetite, big fella.'' Denise touched one of his shirt buttons before she wiggled her fingers at him and scampered off.

Adam stood for a moment, wondering why he'd agreed to go out with an almost-stranger. But then, he'd asked Noelani Hana out knowing even less about her. And she'd been the one to insist he circulate.

Driving off, Adam dredged up memories of Denise Rochelle as a sympathetic kid. They'd probably have fun.

At the lumberyard he discovered his planking had come in. It was hard not to get excited by the beauty of the rare wood. Adam couldn't wait to begin laying the aged cypress, and made arrangements for next-day delivery.

A phone call from the client he'd visited earlier in the day interrupted his cheery whistling. They wanted him to start their renovation the day after he finished the Fontaines' kitchen. Things were really beginning to look up.

The date with Denise totally slipped Adam's mind until suppertime the next night. Noelani put in a rare appearance, which served to jog his memory. Adam entered the dining room and stopped dead, surprised to see the whole family gathered, including Casey and Nick. Pulling out a chair, he whispered, "Are we celebrating another birthday? If so, I didn't get the message."

Noelani unfolded her napkin. "I asked Aunt Esme that very question when she phoned the mill and said I had to be here tonight. She refused to clue me in as to the reason for our command performance. Where's Jackson? Does this involve him?"

Megan bounced all over her chair. "Auntie E's got a s'prise for my daddy and she won't tell nobody what it is."

"A surprise for Jackson?" Casey's interest went up a notch. "How long do you plan to keep us in suspense, Aunt Esme? I can't, in my wildest imagination, come up with anything involving Jackson that requires so much secrecy."

Jackson moseyed in and heard them bandying his name about. "Who's keeping secrets? Megan, did you lose a tooth?"

"No, Daddy. Ask Auntie E. She knows the secret."

Jackson glanced around at the blank faces as he slid in next to his daughter. "If we're all in the dark, it must be something outside the family."

Esme Fontaine rose, her face wreathed in smiles. She moved her plate and picked up a folded letter they'd all missed seeing. "Ripley Spruance dropped by this afternoon. Jackson, this year the growers have voted you King Sucrose." Esme held up the half glasses she wore on a chain around her neck and read the official decree.

The majority of people at the table looked bewildered. Only Casey rammed an elbow in her brother's ribs. "Hallelujah, Jackson, you've finally been recognized as somebody in Louisiana sugar. Except for that dorky robe and crown, I'm envious as hell.''

"Cassandra!" Esme handed Jackson the letter even as she scolded her niece. "Being selected King Sucrose is a time-honored tradition in our trade. There are precious few traditions left. We must celebrate the way the festival was meant to be celebrated. I had Ripley book us a front table for the 11:00 a.m. presentation. Next Saturday, you will all clear your calendars. We'll pay homage to Jackson as a family unit.''

"Tell us more about the festival, please, Auntie E," Noelani begged.

"Wait. First a toast." Casey tried for a properly contrite expression as she lifted a glass of red burgundy. "The committee will pick you a pretty young woman as Sugar Queen, Jackson. You'll get to squire her around all day on your arm. Hear, hear!''

Once everyone had clinked glasses, Casey said for Noelani's benefit, "Usually the king is a much older, more established sugar grower. For that reason, Jackson, I truly salute you.''

"That's better, Cassandra," Esme said approvingly. "Noelani, to answer your question, the coronation kicks off a week-long event that recognizes how important sugar is to our state's economy—although some people see it as little more than an excuse to recycle their Mardi Gras floats. Creoles and Cajuns alike are big partiers. But the festival was designed as a tribute to those who grow and produce sugar.''

"However, I won't expect y'all to bow and scrape more than once a day," Jackson said. "As for squiring the queen, Megan's my best girl. Will someone see she gets a special new dress?''

"I'll take her shopping," Tanya volunteered immediately.

Adam realized this was the event Denise Rochelle had invited him to attend.

"Betty." Esme beckoned the cook, who'd popped in to drop off a steaming dish of shrimp *rémoulade.*

"Yah?" Betty skidded to a stop a foot short of the door.

"Next week…all week, growers and their wives will drop by to congratulate Jackson. We need to have trays of hors d'oeuvres on hand. I know you weren't here when Duke was king, but guests are always offered food and drink. Of course you're invited to the coronation, Betty. Please don't show up on that horrid motorcycle. I'll ride to New Iberia with Jackson, Megan and Tanya. Perhaps Cassandra and Nick, or Noelani and Adam will have room for you, Betty."

Adam cleared his throat. "I, uh, can't go with the family. I…already have a date for the event."

All eyes at the table zeroed in on him, especially Noelani's. She didn't want to appear curious, but she was dying to know who he had a date with. At the same time, she battled a hard lump that lodged in her throat, making her meal less palatable.

Nick had no compunction about asking Adam to name names. "Spill it, pal. Who's the lucky woman?"

Adam feigned interest in the shrimp stew Esme had ladled into his bowl. "I don't know how lucky she is. I ran into an old friend at the hardware store. Denise Rochelle. We went to the same elementary school." He'd been about to say she'd asked him out, but he glanced up and saw a flicker of irritation on Noelani's face. *Jealousy? Wouldn't that be interesting?*

When she noticed him watching her, she instantly lowered her eyes.

Esme broke the tension that had begun to swirl between her niece and Adam. "Rochelle? The only family I recall by that name caused my brother prob—but, my goodness.

Anyone involved in that unpleasantness is gone by now. Cassandra, if you and Nick invite Viv, and the four of you ride together, perhaps Jackson can drive Duke's Town Car. That way we'll have space for Noelani.''

"I'll get myself there.'' Noelani hated the thought of being shuffled around like so much excess baggage. All because Adam had a date.

"Parking is at a premium near the park. It makes sense to double up. Although…'' Jackson combed his fingers through Megan's dark curls. "Snicklefritz here may run out of gas before it's time for the dance. Festivities go on till 2:00 a.m. Also the growers often hang around to talk. We used to.''

"I won't run out of gas, Daddy,'' Megan insisted. Even as the promise fell from her lips, the child emitted a huge yawn.

"Yeah, sure,'' Jackson teased, making everyone laugh.

"As King Sucrose, you're expected to stay to the end,'' Casey pointed out. "It's considered your kingly duty.''

Folding her napkin, Noelani rose and began to stack her dishes. "Before I go back to the mill, Jackson, I'll solve one problem. I'll drive. That way, if Megan gets tired or if anyone else wants to cut out early, I can take them home.''

They all knew she was referring to Aunt Esme, who simply wasn't as young as she thought.

Adam opened his mouth to volunteer to bring Megan or Esme home so Noelani could stay. He enjoyed good jazz, although he wasn't crazy about the idea of dancing half the night with a woman who was practically a stranger. But for all Adam knew, maybe Denise hated kids.

He could hardly subject Megan to that possibility.

So he held his tongue, instead letting Noelani and Jackson hammer out an agreement. But curiosity got the better of him. He excused himself and followed her outside.

"Hey, wait up. You acted unhappy at my news back there."

"Surprised, I suppose." She still sounded miffed.

"Why? You made it plain enough that I need to find another woman. Are you, by chance, having second thoughts?"

Was she? Well…yes. Even so, she couldn't admit it. "I hate to disappoint you, Adam. If you only invited Denise out to make me jealous, it's not working. I hope you have a good time." Jerking open her car door, Noelani climbed in and started the engine. She drove off, leaving Adam in a cloud of dust.

For a long time, he stared at the spot where her car had disappeared from sight. Hell, for some reason, he still had a feeling she was more upset than she'd let on.

CHAPTER TWELVE

PARKING AT THE SUGAR FETE was even worse than Jackson had said it would be. Noelani drove around the block five times before enlarging her search. Several blocks past the square where everything was happening, she chanced on someone pulling out of a slot on a side street. She didn't mind stretching her legs after the drive from Bellefontaine. Better prepared today than she'd been at the museum, she'd worn comfortable sandals.

In choosing what to wear, she'd passed over the red dress Adam liked and had picked a golden-yellow sundress. The gold muted the auburn streaks in her hair. It was a dress she felt good wearing. And since she was nervous because this had been declared a family-on-parade day, looking her best was important.

Noelani worried about finding the family in the dense crowd. But as she entered the room where the coronation would take place, she spotted Jackson and Megan. In his white shirt and black pants, and with his athletic build, he did the family proud. And Megan's pale-pink organza dress set off her violet-gray eyes and her mass of dark curls. Someone, Tanya or Esme, had pulled the ringlets high atop her head and secured them with a pink satin bow.

"Well, don't you look like a little princess," Noelani exclaimed, catching hold of the dancing child's hand.

Jackson turned from the huddle of men. "Ah, Noelani, you made it. Aunt Esme's been fretting. Our table's at the front of the room. It's almost time for the program. Do you mind taking Megan with you?''

"I don't mind at all. Come on, honey, let's go dazzle them with our charm.''

"What's *dazzle?*'' Megan hopped from toe to toe on new white patent shoes held to her feet by a thin rhinestone strap.

"See how the light winks off the diamonds in your shoes? That's dazzle.''

"Oh.'' Megan laughed happily and kicked high so she could see the sparkle. "They're not real diamonds,'' she said, pulling Noelani's head down in order to whisper in her ear.

"I won't tell anybody, if you don't,'' Noelani whispered back.

"'Kay. Noelani, if my daddy's a king, will he hafta go live in a castle?''

Noelani dropped to one knee and gathered the girl close. "Gracious, no, honey. This is all pretend. King Sucrose is…'' She started to say a title, but a four-year old wouldn't understand that, either. "King Sucrose is make-believe. Today your daddy plays the part of a king, but tomorrow he'll be plain daddy again.'' Loosening her hold on Megan, Noelani started to rise, but as she idly scanned the crowd hunting for the Fontaine table, her gaze accidentally lit on Adam Ross. She caught herself seconds from taking a backward tumble.

As she stood and took Megan's hand, she saw that Adam and his *date* sat two tables away from the Fontaines. Thank goodness. Spying an empty chair at the very end of the family table, some distance away from him, she left Megan with Tanya and quickly grabbed it. A mistake, she saw at once, as it placed her facing Denise Rochelle. Noelani had a passing acquaintance with the woman who worked as one of the mill's core samplers. Surely it was her imagination that Denise was staring at her with animosity.

She was saved from dwelling on *why* by the arrival of Casey, Nick, Viv and Luc. Viv Renault glowed, as usual. Casey, while beautiful in her summer white pants and emerald shirt, still had shadows lurking deep within her eyes. They'd barely taken seats when the ceremony started.

Casey and Viv chatted companionably throughout. Nick and Luc did the same, occasionally giving Jackson a hard time until one of Aunt Esme's famous scowls curbed their tongues.

If not for Megan dashing over to report every last detail to Noelani, she wouldn't have felt like a part of the family.

"Auntie E said my daddy makes the handsomest king she's ever seen, except for her brother. Her brother is my grandfather who went to heaven," Megan announced as the ceremony wound down.

"The four of us are going to skip the parade and go somewhere for brunch," Casey said. "We'll catch you all later. If not in the park, then back here for the dance."

She and Viv moved briskly away. Nick hesitated. "Luc's group is performing in the square at three. You all ought to try and stop by to hear him."

"Uh, sure." Unconsciously, Noelani was checking Adam's whereabouts. He and Denise had melted into the crowd. Sharp disappointment filled her as she dredged up the energy to stand. All at once, Tanya and Megan plunked down across from her.

"Aunt Esme said I shouldn't ask. But since you don't have a date, Noelani, would you take Megan to the parade and on the rides?" Tanya's big eyes beseeched Noelani to say yes.

"What are your plans?"

"Several of my school friends are performing in the park.

And there are some groups from New Orleans that I've never seen. Megan doesn't like hanging around with my friends.''

Megan underscored that remark with a vigorous bob of her head.

''So we're all splitting up? What about Aunt Esme?'' Noelani craned her neck.

''She has friends who own a home on the parade route. They've invited her to sit on the balcony with them. She figured Megan would rather sit on the curb where she has a better chance of grabbing the candy and beads they toss from the floats.''

''It looks like it's you and me, kid.'' Noelani grabbed Megan's hand. ''In this crowd, promise you'll stick right with me. Last thing I want to do is tell your dad I lost you.''

''Can we go see Daddy and the queen first?'' Megan tugged Noelani down to her level again. ''Daddy's not gonna marry that old queen, is he?''

''Heavens, no. And she's not old. In fact, she's closer to being your sister.''

''A sister?'' Megan skipped along. ''I'd like a sister.''

''Honey, I didn't mean *your* sister. Big people do a lot of joking around when they talk. Remember? I said this whole day is pretend.''

''Do all big people pretend?''

Noelani thought back on her life; when all the layers were stripped away, it had indeed been one pretense after another. Maybe that was why she had a difficult time letting anyone get too close. ''I'm afraid most adults pretend things are different than they really are,'' she said.

''Oh. Well, I won't do that when I get big.''

MEGAN LOVED THE PARADE. So did Noelani. She'd never seen anything like it in Hawaii.

"Look, Noelani. We both got lots of pretty beads."

Noelani's three strands came from a swashbuckling pirate who swung down from a float. He kissed her before he laughingly dropped the beads over her head. She giggled, then glanced up to see Adam watching. Tossing her long hair over one shoulder, she gave the pirate a big hug.

Adam had no right to deliver that smoldering evil eye when he had Denise crawling all over him.

For the rest of the day it seemed that every time Noelani turned around, she and Megan ran into Adam and Denise. First, at the arcades, where Adam had apparently won Denise a garish stuffed dinosaur that Megan coveted. Noelani patted herself on the back for maintaining a smile all the way through Adam's introductions. Denise was the one to say rather rudely that they'd already met. Then she dragged Adam away.

Noelani immediately addressed Megan's wish. "I'll try to win you a dinosaur, honey." Twenty dollars later, Megan proudly carried the ghastly green toy she promptly named Dino.

The next time they met up with Adam and Denise, Noelani was trying to help Megan juggle the huge dinosaur with a big tube of cotton candy.

Adam made a one-handed catch and saved the tube seconds before it hit the ground. "Careful, there, cupcake. Hey, we're just heading out to put Denise's stuffed animal in my truck. Would you like me to take yours as well, Megan?"

The child studied the woman with the similar toy, who seemed glued to Adam's left arm. Megan edged closer to Noelani. So close, her sticky fingers brushed Noelani's skirt, leaving a pink smear across the gold. "I wanna put Dino in No'lani's car."

Adam's shrug said fine. "I guess you guys bought him in one of the booths."

Megan shook her head. "Noelani won him for me."

"No kidding?" Despite Denise's pout, Adam reached out and squeezed Noelani's biceps. "Who'd have guessed you had muscle enough to knock down three sets of pins in a row."

"Gee, I thought you'd put all my muscles to the test already," she said sweetly, before she jerked loose and circumvented the couple. She wasn't sure why she felt so inclined to remind Adam of their intimate night together.

However, she refused to look back to see if her barb had hit home. But of course it had. Because she heard Denise ask Adam what she'd meant. He stuttered and sputtered, then ended by clamming up in typical Adam Ross fashion.

The five-block jaunt to her car helped to neutralize her irritation. Darn it all, though, she'd ordered Adam to find someone else. But it was *who* he'd found that set her teeth on edge. Although, why did the *who* matter? She'd resent anyone.

Megan chattered a blue streak as she skipped along. It took Noelani a minute to realize the girl expected a response to her last question. "Can we get some lunch, Noelani?" Megan repeated patiently.

"Gracious, it's later than I thought. I guess you're hungry for real food. Let's drop Dino off and find a place to wash your sticky hands first."

Once they'd accomplished that goal, they wandered the food booths, running into Jackson and his pretty young queen. Megan threw herself into her dad's arms. "Hey, sugarplum, I wondered where you got off to." Turning to the blonde, he said, "Trish, this is my daughter, Megan, and my…uh…sister, Noelani Hana."

"We're after food," Noelani babbled, not fully absorbing the significance of Jackson having declared their family ties.

"Us, too. Although Trish plans to eat with her boyfriend.

We saw Adam and Denise, and I said I'd grab a burger and sit with them. Why don't you two join us? Noelani, I gave Tanya money for Megan. Let me buy your lunch and here's some extra for her afternoon.''

''I have money, Jackson.''

''Which you don't need to spend on my daughter. Aren't you saving every cent to buy out Bruce Shiller? By the way, how's he doing?''

''I haven't talked to him in a couple of weeks. Should I be calling him?''

''I heard the coalition mandated another hike in shipping. Stuff like that hits Hawaiian and Australian growers especially hard.''

Noelani didn't respond as she took the money Jackson handed her. ''Megan, you said you wanted a hot dog. Here's the booth. Tell the man what you'd like on it.'' She chewed her lip as they waited. Tomorrow, she'd try to reach Bruce. Another shipping increase was not good news.

She followed Jackson to a table and began nibbling on an apple she'd brought. She let their chatter swirl around her. Even so, it was a relief when they were joined by Casey and Nick.

''We were going to wait for Viv and Luc, but Nick's starved.'' Casey took a seat across from Noelani. ''So, how are you liking your first Sugar Fete? I see you picked up some beads.''

''No'lani got kissed by the pirate who gave her the beads,'' Megan said loudly, making Noelani blush.

''Ooh.'' Casey, Nick and Jackson all teased her at once.

''Adam!'' Denise tugged on his shirt until he turned. ''We'll miss the blues singer at the south end of the park if we don't leave now.''

''I haven't taken two bites of my po'boy, Denise.''

''Can't you carry it? I'm eating my catfish as we walk.''

Jackson and Nick shared a smirk as Adam got up and stepped outside the bench seat. No one said a word until after the couple had disappeared.

"What do you suppose he sees in that little tart?" Casey muttered.

"Careful, she works for us at the mill," Jackson cautioned. "They weren't here long enough for me to form an opinion. What do you have against her, sis?"

Casey shrugged. "She certainly has Adam jumping through hoops."

Noelani thought so, too. And it nagged her all afternoon. She didn't want to run into them at the dance and wished there was some way she could just leave. Unfortunately, she'd been more or less told by Esme that attendance at the dance was a command performance.

By 6:00 p.m. the building where they'd held the crowning ceremony had been transformed into a ballroom. Thankful that it was dimly lit, Noelani took a seat with the family. Aunt Esme introduced her to her friends. Their son asked Noelani to dance.

After one dance, Noelani escaped to the ladies' room. While in a stall, she realized Denise and a couple of her friends had come in to use the mirror. Denise made a disparaging remark about Casey. Noelani knew then what Casey had against Denise Rochelle. This wasn't the first derogatory remark the woman had made about the family who paid her salary. Noelani battled a tug-of-war within herself. She wanted to go out and say something, but maybe Denise was hoping to provoke her in order to bring shame to the family. Keeping silent, Noelani outwaited them.

But from then on, her eyes constantly tracked Adam.

She had no way of knowing that, across the room, Adam did the same with her. He tried several times to break away from Denise. But every time, his date clung to him, or dragged him onto the dance floor. Adam gnashed his teeth whenever some new man swung Noelani out for a dance. Dammit, he wanted to hold her at least once before the night ended.

After the band's break, he said, "Denise, excuse me, but I'm going to go claim these last few dances with the Fontaine women."

"Why? You're only a lowly employee," Denise drawled. "They're not like us, Adam."

"That's crap, Denise, and you know it."

Adam found Casey and Nick alone at the family table. He'd already seen Jackson dancing with a grower's wife. "I'm here to claim my dance," Adam said. "I expect to take a turn with all the beautiful Fontaine femme fatales."

Casey glanced up. "You'll have to settle for me, Adam. Noelani left to drive the others home. Tanya wanted to wait and ride with Jackson, but Aunt Esme pointed out that it's her job to put Megan to bed. The others were more than ready to go. Anyway, I somehow doubt it's me you're dying to dance with. You think we haven't noticed the way you've been keeping tabs on Noelani?"

"What?"

Nick laughed. "You two aren't fooling anyone. It couldn't have been more obvious to anyone that you and Noelani would rather be with each other."

Adam straddled a vacant chair and rubbed his face with his hands. "You're wrong. At least from Noelani's perspective. Every time I saw her, a different guy had her in his arms."

Casey made tsking noises. "Take it from me, she was pea-green over your bringing Denise. But Adam, jealousy only works so long. Then you have to declare."

Nick leaned toward Adam. "Best friend or not, you dance

with my lady and I'll break your face." Nick's devilish smile took the edge off his threat.

"Go soak your head." Rising, Adam socked Nick in the shoulder for good measure, and they all laughed as he twirled Casey away in a fast two-step.

Rejoining Denise after the number ended, Adam yawned. "Esme and half the family has gone home. I've gotta say, that idea has merit. Going home," he reiterated, yawning again. "It's been a full day. And we've got a ways to drive."

"Please let's stay one more hour?" Denise begged. "My favorite band in the whole world takes over from this one."

Adam agreed to one hour, which turned into three. The last band quit at two, otherwise, Adam figured he'd never have pried Denise away.

She cuddled up to him on the seat and fell asleep, which was fine with Adam. He woke her up when they arrived outside her apartment.

"Ugh, I'm zonked. You must be, too, after that drive. Come on in and spend what's left of the night, er... morning," she purred, stretching and rubbing catlike against Adam.

"It's not that far to Bellefontaine."

"Sure. I understand if you're squeamish about going to bed on a first date. Shall we set up a second one now?" she suggested, tugging Adam forward by his shirtfront.

He untangled her hands from the material. "Ah, Denise. I, uh, enjoyed today, but I'm...interested in another woman," he said in a rush.

"Duke Fontaine's bastard." She scowled. "I'm right, aren't I, Adam?"

"It's late, Denise. We're both tired. Accept that we had a nice day for old time's sake."

She flounced from the pickup into her apartment, slamming both doors. Adam winced at the noise, half expecting lights to pop on in her neighbors' apartments. Or maybe they were used to such outbursts. He left the moment he saw her lights go on.

Adam brooded all the way home about Casey's advice.

DECLARING HIS FEELINGS for Noelani had sounded like a fine idea when Casey needled him at the dance. But a week later, Adam still hadn't managed to talk to her. If he stayed up late, she showed up later. Days he rolled out of bed with the chickens, she was already gone, leaving little but a trace of her perfume in the vicinity of the refrigerator. Too close to where Adam had to spend the day working.

His one true satisfaction came from seeing the antique cypress floor blossom under his hands. Once it was down and polished, however, he had only the counters left. Then he'd be on to another job. And he couldn't very well continue to live in the garçonnière once he'd collected his final check from Casey.

A check that brought him ever closer to his goal. With those funds banked, he had to get serious about placing his bid on Magnolia Manor. He ought to just do it. What did waiting get him, really? It wasn't as if he had a source at the courthouse willing to feed him inside information.

He pounded a square antique plug into a hole in the hardwood with enough force to split the plug and had to dig it out with his pocketknife. Adam was on his hands and knees muttering darkly when the back door flew open, and a wild-eyed Casey Devlin rushed in, shouting, "Have you seen Jackson? Do you know where he is?"

"I saw him leave with Murray. They took off right after he put Megan to bed. Is something wrong? Where's Nick? Do you need help?" Adam fired question after question at her, never giving her time to answer.

"I got a phone call from the mill as I quit cutting cane for the night. Noelani slipped on one of the catwalks and fell down a flight of stairs. The workman who called said she'd been knocked unconscious. He said it's possible Noelani's arm is broken. A paramedic team arrived and took her to the hospital." Casey bit her lip. "Jackson seems to have his cell phone turned off."

"What are we waiting for? Let's go." Adam closed his pocketknife and leaped to his feet.

Casey, who'd pulled out her cell phone, held up a restraining hand. "Murray? Is Jackson with you? No? Adam said he saw you leave together."

She waited, pursing her lips as she listened.

Adam fidgeted by the door. He had it open before she'd shut her phone.

"Jackson and Murray took separate cars to the refinery. Murray just got home. He said Jackson should be here any minute. Nick's waiting for me outside. I hate to ask this, Adam, knowing how you feel about Noelani. But since I'm family, the doctors may need authorization from me before they treat her. Can you stay and wait for Jackson?"

"Sure, but if he doesn't show up in five minutes, I'm out of here."

"Please, Adam. Don't let Jackson drive. This is yet another insurance claim for him to worry about. On top of that, he'll blame himself for letting Noelani manage the mill. I don't want him on the road driving like a maniac, maybe having an accident."

"Okay. As long as you promise that if we're more than fifteen minutes behind you, you'll phone me with an update."

"You've got it. And Adam, she may be perfectly all right. Aunt Esme lost consciousness in her accident and she came out of it fine and on her own."

Not mollified, Adam paced the width of the driveway. As Casey and Nick roared off, he scanned the lane for any sign of Jackson's headlights. Thinking it'd save time, he hiked to the gate to wait.

Luckily, Jackson slowed to make the corner about the time Adam reached the gate. Flagging down the Jag, Adam quickly relayed the information Casey had given him.

"Get in," Jackson ordered.

"Casey would prefer you not to drive. I gather she's afraid you'll go ballistic or something about the fact that you'll be facing another insurance claim."

"Oh, for Pete's sake. Get in," Jackson roared. "I'm not that unstable."

Adam wasted no time jumping into the passenger side. "I didn't think so, but I have to admit you've had a run of bad luck."

"I'm beginning to wonder if our stars came up in the wrong quadrant this year or something."

"Jackson, is there a possibility this wasn't an accident? I mean…Noelani told me she grew up playing at Shiller's mill. She's not the careless type."

"At a sugar mill, it only takes one misstep. The stairs and railings are coated with syrup. She wouldn't be the first to slip and fall. I've stumbled a few times myself." Jackson stopped for the light before turning onto the main highway. "Did Casey say something to make you think the fall wasn't accidental?"

"No. But when Noelani and I were…loosely dating, she was worried about a couple of mishaps. She wasn't sure whether or not someone had thrown a piece of metal into one of the feeders on purpose to slow production. Then there was a later incident involving a crowbar. She promised me she'd call you if anything else occurred. But Noelani and I—well, we haven't talked much since then."

"To put your mind at ease, she and I did discuss it and came to the conclusion that there was no serious cause for concern. A few old-timers resented her filling Duke's shoes. I had a heart-to-heart with the employees and let it be known that Noelani's an experienced member of the family team. She hasn't mentioned any complaints since."

As they entered the hospital emergency lot, Jackson parked the Jag. He and Adam were out before the engine died.

Inside the emergency room, they were directed to a waiting area where Nick sat thumbing through a classic car magazine.

"Where's Casey?" Jackson asked at the same time Adam demanded, "Any word on Noelani's condition?"

"Whoa, you two. The doctor's in with Noelani now. I imagine Casey has everything under control. Noelani came around before they got here, and I heard her asking Casey to take her home."

Casey walked in as the men were talking. "I convinced Noelani to let them X-ray her arm. She's sure it's not broken. I'll grant you she can wiggle her fingers, but she cried out in pain when the doctor rotated her arm."

"Did she say how she happened to fall?"

"Golly, Jackson, you guys broke speed records to get here. I wasn't with her five minutes. Well, maybe ten at most. We—"

Adam cut Casey off. "Jackson drove—sanely, so don't worry about that. I walked to the gate and flagged him down as he pulled in. That gave us a jump start on getting here."

"Why don't you come with me to X-ray, Adam? They said I could be with her, but I decided I'd better report to Nick. I knew you'd be rolling in soon and that you'd be just as impatient as you are."

Adam didn't need a second invitation. "Where's X-ray?"

He left at a trot the moment Casey pointed down the hall. Halfway there, he nabbed a technician. "Would it be okay if I went in with one of the patients? Noelani Hana," he said, giving the young nurse his best smile.

"I told Mrs. Devlin she could stay with Ms. Hana until I take the films." It was only then that Adam realized Casey had stopped to speak with someone in the hall.

"Uh, we're all friends of Ms. Hana."

The tech directed him to the room. Slipping inside, Adam tiptoed toward Noelani, who lay flat on a black table. "Hi," he said softly when she opened an eyelid.

"Adam? What are you doing here? Casey said she'd be right back."

"She'll be along shortly. I wanted to see for myself that you were awake and kicking."

Noelani reached for Adam's hand. He gave it willingly and used his free one to smooth her long hair away from her face. "What happened? Jackson tells me he's slipped at the mill on occasion. But your boots have nonskid soles, right?"

She closed her eyes again. "It all happened so fast, Adam. I'd left my office to run up and check the day's core samples. I noticed the light outside the lab had burned out. I had my clipboard, and I think I stopped to jot a note to myself to have someone change it. The whistle tooted, indicating an equipment failure. I turned to see where, and…uh…someone hit me from behind. I tumbled headfirst down the steps."

"Are you sure? Could you be thinking that because of the crack you took on your head?"

"Oh, Adam. I'm so mad at myself. Right before the whistle, I heard a…footstep. I should've reacted faster. For crying out loud, I hold a master's belt in kick-boxing."

Adam blinked. "Noelani, are you—"

"Think back to the night I arrived, when you surprised me in the hall and I went into fight stance. You joked about me karate-chopping you, but...I could have."

"Why didn't you tell me?"

"I'm sorry, Adam. In light of the problems at the mill and elsewhere, I decided to let it remain my secret. For all the good it did," she said bitterly. "A beginning kick-boxer who let this happen would get chewed out."

A noise at the door had both Noelani and Adam glancing up. Casey, Nick and Jackson huddled in the entry. "I just got off the phone from talking to the workman who saw you take the nosedive," Casey said. "He swears there wasn't a soul anywhere near you on the catwalk. Probably the knock on the head scrambled your mind, Noelani."

Nick rubbed his jaw. "Let's not dismiss her claim so fast. It's no secret I've never been comfortable with the cops' insistence that Broderick worked alone. I tell you, that man simply isn't the brightest match in the box."

Casey threw her husband an odd look. "That's why I believe Broderick *did* work alone, as does Remy Boucher—and, my friend, the detective who's been working the Broderick case. Surely you agree it's crazy to think the guy would hire out to some nameless, faceless person."

Nick pursed his lips, saying nothing.

"Does your family have other enemies?" Adam aimed a look at Jackson, then at Casey, who supplied a resounding "No!"

Jackson's silence claimed their attention. "None I can name. But I'm beginning to doubt the likelihood of so many coincidences. Up to now, I haven't said much about the investigation into Duke and Maman's crash. In spite of Shelburne's numerous requests, no one's releasing their personal effects to us. Lately, I get the runaround when I phone the carabiniere."

"You told me those investigations take time," Casey said.

"They do." Jackson scraped a thumb down the side of his neck. "Call me paranoid, but dammit, we need those claims paid. I hate to sound mercenary, but we're real close to robbing Peter to pay Paul."

Casey stared from one somber face to the other, then threw up her hands. "If you think there's the remotest chance someone at the mill shoved Noelani down the stairs, why aren't we on the phone to Remy?" She peeled her cell phone from its pouch.

Noelani objected feebly. Adam, slightly more vociferously. "Hold on. It's my belief the cops botch as many cases as they solve. Jackson, I'd suggest you, Nick and I nose around the mill. Maybe one or more employees—not necessarily the guy who found Noelani, but someone else— saw or heard something they didn't think significant at the time. We'd be looking at the larger picture."

Noelani tried to sit up, but fell back with a groan. "I run the mill. You guys aren't going without me."

A doctor strode into the room, his white lab coat flapping. "Out, everyone except my patient. Yvonne," he said, turning to the tech who'd begun to slap film trays into the X-ray machine, "Give us PA, lateral and oblique shots of that right shoulder and clavicle. Whichever of you needs to know this, I'm admitting Ms. Hana overnight for observation. She took a mean bang on the head and has a mild concussion—mild so far as I can tell. I don't want to chance her building up cranial fluid. If no one objects, we'll go down the hall to talk and let Yvonne take her films."

"Wait," Noelani protested. "I object."

"You don't count," they all chorused.

Adam hesitated at the door. "I'll find out what time

they're planning to release you tomorrow. I'll be back to get you myself," he said before following the others out.

The pretty technician winked as she pulled the camera close to Noelani's shoulder. *"Galee, cher, dat man be purty, en effet."*

"Sure enough he is," Noelani replied, agreeing with Yvonne's Cajun assessment of Adam's good looks. She'd picked up a trace of the local dialect working at the mill—enough to know that Yvonne had said something along the lines of "Golly, that man sure is pretty to look at." But laughing hurt, so Noelani closed her eyes and clamped her teeth over her lower lip. What didn't hurt was remembering how happy she'd been to open her eyes and see him standing there, concern etched on his handsome face.

CHAPTER THIRTEEN

As PREARRANGED, THE THREE MEN met at six o'clock the next morning at the mill. They split up and each took a floor. It was a frustrated threesome who rendezvoused an hour later outside the core-sample building.

"Every person I spoke with on the first floor heard about Noelani's accident secondhand," Jackson informed Nick and Adam. "No one saw her fall or remembered anyone saying they'd witnessed the accident personally."

"Same story on level two," Nick lamented. "The guy who reached her first is sticking to his story. He says he looked up because her keys landed at his feet. If she hadn't dropped them, no telling how long she might have lain there passed out."

"The lab where she was headed is off by itself. A tech verified that the lightbulb in the alcove had burned out. He replaced it this morning." Adam searched the others' faces. "I have to say I don't believe anyone on level three is concealing evidence. The men in charge of the evaporation vats, and those operating the vacuum tanks, all seem to respect Noelani."

"So, we came up with a big fat zero," Jackson declared flatly.

A door opened behind them and two women exited the core building. They stopped when they saw the men. One produced a pack of cigarettes. She stuck one in her mouth and lit up, blowing smoke over the head of her companion.

Jackson waved. "Hi, Sue Ann. Denise. Break time? Don't let us interrupt. We're heading out to grab some breakfast."

Denise shaded her eyes. "Adam, what are you doing here?" She ran up to him, wearing a bright smile. "I've tried calling you. Luc Renault is headlining a jazz concert in the park this weekend. A friend gave me two tickets she can't use. Would you like to go as my guest?"

Adam felt put on the spot. Two days ago, he'd bought tickets to the same concert to surprise Noelani. But now, with her having a cracked clavicle, she probably wouldn't want to sit on the ground all evening. He'd considered giving his tickets to Nick and Casey. "Thanks, Denise. But I'm too backlogged with work to get away."

Nick nudged him. "Hey, Adam, why not go? Luc does a bang-up performance."

Denise continued to gaze expectantly at Adam.

Adam brushed Nick's hand aside. "I said I can't spare the time."

Plainly disappointed, Denise shrugged and returned to Sue Ann, who was stubbing out her cigarette. The two women talked for a bit, then went back inside.

"Why did you turn her down?" Nick asked when the men were alone again.

"Not that it's your business, but I'm not interested in Denise the way she's interested in me. I thought you'd figured that out at the Sugar Fete. Besides, I already bought tickets for Noelani and me. She probably can't go. Would you and Casey like them?"

"We have tickets. And I only suggested you go with Denise because it occurred to me that on a date she might confide if she'd seen or heard stuff going on behind the scenes. I know that in casinos the dealers hear all the dirt first."

Jackson studied his friends. "It might have been opportune, but if Adam doesn't want to spend an evening with the woman, he shouldn't have to.''

Nick backed off. ''Hey, it was a thought, that's all. Let's go eat. I'm starved. Meet you guys at Frank's on the lower floor of the White Gold. I can already taste his smokehouse ham.''

Jackson caught Adam's arm. ''Did you call and ask when the doctor's releasing Noelani?''

''Any time after ten. I talked to her. She wants me there on the dot. Said she's climbing the walls. I gather the doctor said no work for a week. You can imagine how she took *that* news.''

The three friends discussed that before climbing into their respective vehicles. They met again at the casino entry and walked in together. Adam remarked on the musical sound of the rolling slots. ''What kind of people gamble at 8:00 a.m.?''

''All kinds,'' Nick said. ''Vacationers, mostly. The restaurant will be full, too.''

They'd barely made their way through the door of Frank's when they noticed a disturbance near the cash register at the end of the buffet.

''Excuse me.'' Nick stepped out of the food line. ''I'd better see what's up. The White Gold's still mine—until Harry Dardenne signs the contract.''

The other men followed him. ''I recognize that guy,'' Adam muttered to Jackson. ''It's that Riley character.''

''So it is.'' Jackson's face turned grim. ''As usual, he's three sheets to the wind. And up to his old tricks.'' Riley was attempting to get a meal on the house by insisting Duke Fontaine, and Nick by association, owed him.

''Call security,'' Nick ordered the cashier. ''Or maybe I'll take care of this bum myself.'' Clearly angry, Nick grabbed Riley by the shirtfront until Adam and Jackson closed in on either side of him.

"Nick," Adam said quietly. "Why not call the cops and let them read him the riot act?"

As if by magic, casino security showed up and relieved Nick of the drunk. Nick tucked his own shirt back in his pants, smoothed his hair, then stepped directly in front of Riley. "You come in my place and harass my staff again, and I'll press charges."

Jackson pointed to the door. "Here come the cops now. They'll handle him. We're blocking people whose food's getting cold."

Nick paused and flashed the customers his famous smile. "You guys go on and grab a table," he said. "I'll have a word with the police and join you shortly."

AT FIVE MINUTES TO TEN, Adam took a seat in the hospital lobby where a woman at the information desk directed him to wait. She said a nurse would be bringing Noelani from her room. It was a good twenty minutes before they appeared.

"Adam, hi! I didn't realize you were here. I thought you'd come upstairs. I phoned Casey and asked her to have you bring one of my muumuus. The way my arm's bandaged, I had to stretch this T-shirt out of shape to get it on."

"Sorry, but I never saw Casey. I left the house early. Jackson, Nick and I met at the mill, then went on to breakfast. I came straight here from the restaurant."

"It's okay. A stretched out T-shirt is the least of my concerns. Walking's a bigger chore because my balance is off."

"Jackson took my pickup and gave me his car. He thought it'd be easier for you to slide into the Jag."

"That was nice of him. Did you guys find out anything at the mill?"

"Nothing. We concluded it must've been a freak accident."

"I know what I heard and what I felt, Adam. I was pushed." She spoke with such conviction, she drew glances from nearby nurses.

"They're waiting to release you," he said patiently.

"You think I imagined the whole thing, but I didn't."

Adam let the subject drop. While she signed release forms, he excused himself to bring the car to the patient-loading area. He waited beside it until a nurse wheeled Noelani out. Careful not to bump her bandaged arm, Adam assisted her into the low-slung car. "Thanks," he told the nurse as she turned to leave.

"Do you need anything before we head out of town?" he asked Noelani. "Did the doctor give you a prescription?"

She'd leaned back with her eyes closed. Now she opened them and tried to focus on Adam. "Something for pain. A nurse had me take a pill already. I think that's why I'm woozy. I hate how painkillers make me feel. I don't think I'll fill the prescription. It's only a hairline crack of my collarbone."

"You should probably get the pills, Noelani. Then you'll have them if you do need something to take the edge off. You fell quite a distance and hit the ground hard."

"You're right." She tried to reach for her purse, but let out a yelp as the seat belt tightened around her injured shoulder.

"Here, let me get that. Dammit, you don't always have to be Miss Independent. It won't kill you to ask for help on occasion."

"I know. I'm just so used to doing everything for myself.

The prescription's in my purse. Thanks, Adam. I'm feeling rockier now than I did earlier.''

"Try to nap. I'll take this to the drugstore.'' He brandished the prescription. "Jackson's gone to a meeting at the courthouse. It's over at one-thirty. I'll phone and ask him to pick this up on his way home so you won't have to wait around now.''

"Courthouse? Oh, did you turn in your bid?''

"Damn, it slipped my mind completely. Yesterday I decided to quit stalling. I'd planned to submit the forms today. But then Casey raced into the house like a wild woman looking for Jackson and said you'd fallen. That's the last I thought of my bid.''

"Isn't time getting short?''

"One more week. I'm still debating how high to go. Which is dumb. I can only bid what I can afford to shell out in cash. That's rule number one.''

"When you phone Jackson, have him flirt a little with the courthouse clerks. I realize the bids remain sealed until the deadline, but maybe one of the women overheard figures being mentioned.''

"Jackson will probably tell me to do my own flirting. Then again...I may suggest he give it a whirl. What have I got to lose?''

She closed her eyes again and might even have drifted into sleep. She jolted awake when Adam returned after dropping off her prescription. "I reached Jackson. He's happy to pick up your medicine. He's also agreed to chat with a clerk he knows. For all the good it'll do. Roland Dewalt isn't going to tell a lowly clerk what he bid.''

"Get Jackson to pump Murray. I gather there's no love lost between him and his dad. At the Sugar Fete, I came away with the distinct impression that Murray had more respect for Duke Fontaine than for Roland.''

"About the Sugar Fete, Noelani…"

She abruptly turned her head away from him.

"We need to talk," he insisted. "All last week I tried to make sure our paths crossed. But you whirled in and out of the house like a phantom."

"You're a free agent, Adam. You don't owe me any explanations."

"I do. I tried to explain already. The truth is, Denise is just someone I knew as a kid." He paused. "Listen, I bought tickets to Luc Renault's concert in the park this coming weekend. I'd intended to invite you. But the way you're trussed up, I guess sitting on the ground for several hours is the last thing you'd want to do."

A wary expression entered her eyes. "Is Denise busy?"

"Damn it, Noelani! As a matter of fact, she asked me to go with her and I said no. She invited me to the Sugar Fete, too. That's the only reason I went with her. She stopped me at the hardware store, and at first I didn't even remember her. She reminded me that we'd gone to elementary school together, and that her folks had fallen on hard times the same year my dad went MIA. She thinks that gives us a lot in common."

"You had fun at the festival, didn't you?"

"Truthfully? No. All I thought about was you. I left her with friends and went to ask you for a dance. But you'd gone."

"Probably just as well. The last time we danced…"

"Was pretty damned fantastic," he said, finishing for her.

"Uh…putting that aside, if you and Denise both lost your homes during childhood, I'd consider that a solid connection."

"Magnolia Manor holds good memories for me. Denise doesn't seem to have a lot of those as far as I can tell. We may share similar losses, but our assumptions about life are different. I can't explain it more clearly than that, Noelani.''

''I do understand. You feel about Magnolia Manor the way I do about Shiller's. For you, success or failure is tied to a house. For me, it's the cane. I guess our dreams come from a similar source. Something in here.'' She rested a hand over her heart.

''I don't think I'd consider myself a failure if I don't get Magnolia Manor.'' Adam shrugged.

''You will. Magnolia Manor offers closure to a portion of your past you can't resolve. Be honest, Adam. Nothing means more to you than that house. You need it to prove you can do what your father couldn't—make a safe haven for your family. A place he can come back to if he ever does return.''

Adam slowed to make the corner into Bellefontaine. Her relentless probing made him uncomfortable. Perhaps he *was* trying to prove to an absent father that he could rebuild the Ross standing in the community. A standing tarnished by his dad's Yankee roots, as well as his mom's mental breakdown.

''Do you need help getting up to your room?'' he asked gruffly after he'd pulled Jackson's car into the family garage.

''I'm a little shaky.''

Rounding the hood, Adam scooped her out, into his arms.

She opened her mouth to object, then shut it again and slid her good arm around his broad shoulders—where she felt oddly cherished.

Aunt Esme, apparently awaiting their arrival, flung open the side door. Toodles bounded out, barking wildly and tangling himself in Adam's feet.

''Toodles, come here.'' Aunt Esme snatched up the high-strung animal and fussed over Noelani's bandage. As if sensing something amiss, the dog strained to give Noelani a welcome-home lick.

She laughed, and quite suddenly it did feel like a home-coming. Enveloped in affection, she let Adam carry her all the way up to her bedroom. She also allowed Auntie E to turn back her bed and remove her shoes. After that, she couldn't keep her eyes open.

THREE DAYS LATER, HOWEVER, Noelani'd had enough of being cosseted and coddled. Although she still wore an Ace bandage, she'd taken off her sling. "I'm going stir crazy," she confessed to Adam as she paced the kitchen while he laminated counters.

He tightened the last butterfly clamp, then straightened and wiped Mastic off his hands. "The inlay has to dry for several hours." Dropping to one knee, he piled his tools neatly in the toolbox. "Would you like to go for a drive?" he asked out of the blue.

"Would I ever! Let me go tell Auntie E and Megan. Lately, they've become my self-appointed guardians." Noelani spoke softly, so neither of them could accidentally over-hear. She wouldn't hurt their feelings for the world. In fact, these last few days, she'd developed a closer bond with the older woman, who loved teaching her about Bellefontaine.

During her recovery, Noelani had learned much of the history attached to individual pieces of furniture. Before, she wouldn't have been aware that the desk in Jackson's of-fice—formerly Duke's office—had reportedly belonged to the other *Duke*. John Wayne. The cherry-wood piece dated back to the Civil War. To get the desk, Esme said her brother had outbid a host of other movie buffs.

Noelani returned to the kitchen. "Betty said supper's catch-as-catch-can tonight. Tanya has a test. Jackson and Auntie E are going to a program at Megan's preschool. I don't know where you'd like to drive, Adam. Shall we get wine, bread and cheese, and stop somewhere for a picnic?''

''That'd work well for the place I have in mind.''

''Oh, so you've decided we're not just taking an aimless drive through the countryside?''

''Nope. And don't be nosy, either.''

''A surprise, huh? You know dangling a surprise over a woman's head is like offering a carrot to a horse you're coaxing out of the barn.''

She might as well forget attempting to pry their destination out of Adam. His lips were sealed. And he could be mighty stubborn.

After they'd raided Betty's fridge, Adam stopped by his garçonnière to change, collect a blanket and a bottle of wine. As they drove through the gate, Adam turned in the opposite direction from the one they usually took. A rapidly falling sun painted the trees overhanging the road a murky violet. Content not to know their destination, Noelani settled back to enjoy the transformation of day to dusk.

But Adam only drove a few miles along the highway before he killed his lights and swerved onto a badly rutted side road.

If it even was a road. Noelani grabbed the dashboard with her good hand.

''Potholes,'' Adam said, frowning. ''Am I jarring you too much?''

''Cracked all my back teeth,'' she teased. ''But don't let that influence your plans. Adam, where are we? And why are the lights off? What's out here in the boondocks?''

''Hang on. I know what I'm doing. This is an old cane road.''

''That accounts for the washboard ruts. Growers don't usually invest a lot of money in improvements.'' Her voice shook as the pickup bounced over a series of deeper furrows. They passed a weathered outbuilding. Noelani gasped when Adam swung around behind the structure, yanked on his emergency brake and turned off the engine.

"Okay. I said I needed to get out of the house, Adam, but—"

"Shh." He touched a finger to her lips. "Last week I found this back way into Magnolia Manor. I wanted to take some measurements and get pictures of the interior. You know—in case Dewalt tries to make a case for tearing it down. I was also curious to see if anyone had trashed the inside."

"Oh, Adam, they didn't?"

"No, thankfully." He got out and went to give Noelani a hand climbing down. Plucking the picnic basket from the bed of the pickup, he handed her the blanket and anchored his free arm around her waist. "Stick close, Noelani. I brought a flashlight, but I'd just as soon not use it where a neighbor driving past might see."

Stars had begun to pop out overhead before they reached the house. It was the dark phase of the moon, and Noelani felt as if she was walking blind. They climbed warped steps to what she surmised was a porch, and Adam set down the picnic basket. He quietly and persistently rattled the handles on a set of French doors until the left one sprung ajar.

"Adam, can this be classed as breaking and entering?" Noelani hung back as he retrieved the basket and urged her forward.

"Technically, I suppose. But I've been here three times and I haven't been caught. I don't intend for us to get caught tonight, either."

She shuffled along in his wake, taking small steps. Still, she walked into him once they were inside because he'd shut the door, and the smoky gray of the dusk outside became an inky black interior.

Feeling Adam vanish, Noelani stopped dead. Then she heard a hiss and smelled the sharp odor of butane. The glow from a dual-mantled lantern threw grotesque shadows on a stark white wall.

Little by little her eyes adjusted to the light. They were apparently in a large dining room, or drawing room. A row of crystal chandeliers marched down the center of a tall ceiling. She realized it was the shivering of the crystal pendants dangling from the chandeliers that added weird shapes to the room's shadow.

"Look at this floor," Adam said, drawing her attention to dark planking that showed few scars. He held the lantern above his head. "Check out the lacy plaster frieze work. It's repeated in the living room. The doorknobs throughout the entire place are hand-painted porcelain. I can't believe a later owner never replaced those."

Noelani caught a little of his excitement. The blue of his eyes reflected the lantern light, and his black pupils were intense. Something in the way Adam ran a hand lovingly over the walls and doorknobs affected her deeply. To him, this place was far more than merely a place to hang his hat.

"Come upstairs." He motioned to her eagerly. "We'll use the old servant route, which keeps to the back of the house. That way our light won't shine through the upper windows, and we won't risk being seen by passersby."

She started to leave the blanket, but saw he intended to carry the picnic basket upstairs, so she clamped the blanket under her good arm again.

Adam led her through an intricate, dank warren, leaving Noelani out of breath. "This house is larger than it looks from the outside," she panted. "Either that or I suffered more residual effects from my fall than I realized."

"It's roughly half the size of Bellefontaine. Quite livable

as a private residence. We're only going a little farther down this hall. Want me to carry the blanket?''

''I'm fine. Are we going to see your old room? I mean, the one you occupied as a boy.''

''I can't show you that room or the master bedroom, because their windows face the road. There are five bedrooms and three baths on this level. The one we're visiting, my folks used for guests. Judging by the decoration, a subsequent owner made it a nursery. Probably due to its proximity to the playroom. It's really changed. I remember wallpaper covered with toy soldiers. Everything looks girly now.''

He opened the door on a cozy room painted soft pink. The walls above white wainscoting were papered with a delicate rose print. A burgundy-colored carpet covered the floor. The anteroom, which reminded Noelani of Megan's play area, had bare floors, creamy white walls and frilly pink-and-cream curtains of some light, frothy material. ''You're right. This room belonged to one lucky little girl. Oh, Adam, wouldn't you love to know what happened to them? Why would a family who owned this place allow it to revert to the state?''

He set the lantern and basket on the floor, took the blanket from her and spread it out over the carpet. ''That can be researched. I haven't taken the time to do it,'' he said as he knelt on the blanket and held up a hand to guide her. ''Things just happen, Noelani. Jobs dissolve, families move. Lives change.''

She sank down beside him. ''That's so true. The islands have been virtually overrun by resorts and vacation playgrounds. Our beautiful cattle ranches and fruit farms on the Big Island are a thing of the past. Bruce says sugarcane and pineapples can be exported a lot more cheaply from South America than from Maui. But I'm positive that if he hangs on, we'll prove our sugar can compete in the world market.''

Adam pulled the cork on a bottle of semisweet white muscadine wine. He poured a small amount into a glass, swirled it several times, then tasted it. "Ah, good! This is from a local winery. The owner runs a tasting room. He said his business is growing." Adam filled both their glasses, recorked the bottle and set it aside.

Noelani removed a loaf of French bread from a bag. The smell of fresh yeast permeated the stale air in the window-less room. They'd brought three kinds of cheese and a bottle of spicy mustard.

Smiling quirkily, Adam leaned back on his elbows and watched Noelani assemble sandwiches.

"You're enjoying my stab at domesticity a little too much, Mr. Ross," she said, slapping a finished sandwich on a plate and shoving it toward him.

She lifted her wineglass. Raising it higher, she waited until he joined her in a toast. Noelani found the ping of crystal against crystal satisfying. She was glad she'd insisted they bring real wineglasses rather than plastic.

"What are we toasting?" Adam asked, holding his glass aloft.

"We'll drink to you realizing your dream." Since he didn't move, she elaborated. "Here's to you becoming the new owner of Magnolia Manor."

"This toast should be to us." His brow puckered.

"Okay." Noelani elevated her glass again. "May we each attain our heart's desire." She went to touch his glass with hers, but he jerked away.

After a lengthy pause, he downed his wine and put his glass aside.

"Adam? What's wrong?"

"I hadn't planned to tell you. The real reason I wanted to come here tonight is to say goodbye to this grand old lady." He scanned the room with carefully hooded eyes.

"You were a good sport, not pressing me too hard about our destination. Thanks, Noelani."

"Goodbye?" She placed her glass on the basket and slid closer to Adam. "The bidding's not over, for pity's sake. You said you haven't turned in your forms yet. I don't understand. Isn't there still a week to go?"

"Remember you suggested having Jackson make a few inquiries at the courthouse? Well, he did. He was able to guess at a range of figures based on what two clerks said. I could beat the lower bid, no problem. The top bid, according to them, is a solid thirty thousand over the highest I can go, and that's a stretch. It depends on me finishing at Bellefontaine and collecting my final payment, which might not even be possible with the insurance mess. But what the hell. I guess I always knew that owning this place was a long shot."

"Adam, thirty thousand or even a little more is nothing when you're talking to bank lenders or real estate brokers."

"It might as well be a million. Noelani, you know that if I borrow for the bid, I either won't be able to do essential repairs or it'd take me years to furnish the house. This room looks fine, but the plumbing's old, and the wiring needs updating to be safe."

"I know Jackson can't lay his hands on any additional cash right now. But what about Nick?"

"If he hadn't been stretched thin with the boatyard, don't you think he'd have bailed you guys out?"

Noelani touched a trembling finger to a deep, bitter slash bracketing one side of Adam's mouth. "Adam, I can't bear the thought of you coming so close to your dream and losing it. I have more than thirty thousand saved. That's above and beyond what I'll get from my share of Bellefontaine. Let me write you a check."

He didn't pull away, but he shook his head savagely. "No

way. Not an option. I won't take money from you, sugar pie. It'd be different if you were going to stay here and make Magnolia your home as well. But you say that's not in the cards.'' He folded her hand in his and pressed a kiss to her knuckles.

That kiss wasn't enough for Noelani. Circumstances, the house, Adam's nearness—it all weighed heavily on a heart that was aching for him. Leaning close, she kissed him on the lips.

He didn't deepen the kiss right away, but slowly, ever so slowly, he gathered her into his arms. Adam was mindful of her injury as their lips touched, and contact grew more urgent. Neither had planned this moment. Both accepted that it was as inevitable as taking their next breath.

She licked the sweet taste of wine from his lips. Unhurried, he reclined on one elbow and let her do it.

Noelani only had one hand that worked well enough to unbutton his shirt. She managed because neither of them was in any rush. It was as if Adam's saying goodbye to the house somehow meant they were saying goodbye to each other.

"I don't want to hurt you," he muttered. "The floor isn't soft. I brought nothing—"

"Shh." She kissed away his protests. "I want this night, Adam. I want you."

His reserve cracked, and he could no longer hold his desire to possess her in check. Adam wanted to take things slow and make this a memorable experience of love. He was desperately afraid it'd be the last time for her. For him. For them.

Her fingers brushed lightly over his skin, heating him to flash point. Adam wasn't sure he could last until he removed the rest of their clothing.

He wanted to take time peeling away each layer until he

exposed every inch of Noelani's olive-toned skin. That thought allowed him to be both reverent and gentle.

At a certain point, Noelani wanted no more of reverent or gentle. She tumbled him backward on the blanket and straddled his hips.

Adam entered her in one thrust. She sank over him with a delighted cry. The room blurred, and even small troubles disappeared as they joined in the wildest ride either had ever undertaken. The house that had lived so long and seen so much was silent. And when the ride ended, they sank together, content to breathe in the warm scents of wine and love.

Replete. Content. Neither wanted to bring back the reality of everything they'd left behind. This was a time out of time. It existed separate and apart from their everyday worlds.

Adam lazily stroked her bare back. Noelani nestled her cheek against the smooth contours of his damp chest.

As she'd been first to initiate their lovemaking, so, too, was she first to break the silence. "Tell me about your ideas for restoring these rooms, Adam. I've seen the miracle you worked on the kitchen at Bellefontaine. I want to close my eyes and envision what Magnolia Manor could be."

"Let me show you instead." He helped her sit up and dress, then slipped into his own clothes. "I don't care who sees our light, I'm giving you a grand tour of the house, Noelani."

He held the lantern in one hand and her good hand in his other. They began in the master suite and wandered from room to room. In a hushed voice, he sketched in words what he could see so vividly in his mind for each empty room.

The house took shape and came alive inside Noelani's head. She was painfully aware as they walked that if Adam submitted his bid—a mere two sheets of paper—he had a chance to lay claim to his dream.

She hadn't had the heart, before tonight, to admit that her own hopes of owning Shiller's had faded into the realm of fantasy. Her last three calls to Bruce had gone unreturned. Days ago, she'd dragged out of Midori that twice in recent weeks Bruce had met with the truck farmers. Clearly he was evading her attempts to pin him down. But he hadn't sold yet. Maybe he wouldn't before she could get back to Maui.

"Well, that's it," Adam said as they ended back at the servants' stairwell. "You let me run off at the mouth for nearly an hour. What do you think? Can you see yourself living here for the next fifty or sixty years?"

"I can certainly see *you* spending the rest of your life here, Adam. You describe the rooms in such detail, I look around and I'm surprised to see bare walls." The smile accompanying her words felt strained even to Noelani.

More so when she watched the sparkle in his eyes disappear.

"Yeah, well, they were some of my better ideas. Those plans earned me straight As in design at college. Shall we go back and eat our bread and cheese?"

"All this running up and down stairs wore me out, Adam. Do you mind gathering our stuff so you can take me home?"

"I'm sorry. It's probably smart to leave now. Either people driving by will be telling ghost stories about this place for weeks, or someone will call the cops. It won't do your reputation any good to be caught in an empty house guzzling wine and scarfing bread and cheese with a man charged with burglary."

"Stop, Adam. We didn't burgle. And I'm not worried about my reputation."

"The Fontaines might feel differently," he said, leaving

her in the dark as he mounted the stairs. "As if they need a scandal on top of their bad luck."

Thankful for the darkness, she managed to wipe away the tears trickling down her cheeks before he reappeared. She gathered the blanket tight to her chest and said, "You can't bring this blanket on Saturday, when we go to Luc's concert in the park. It holds too many memories. I'll ask Aunt Esme for a quilt."

"You're still willing to attend the concert with me?"

"Of course. Wait!" She caught up with him as he blew out the lantern and held open the door he'd jimmied earlier. "What part of our evening made you think I'd changed my mind about going out with you?" she asked sadly.

"None. All. Hell, I don't know. You play havoc with my mind, Noelani. But that's not your fault. It's mine." He barely touched her as he locked the door and led the way to his pickup. "I've always hankered after the unattainable. Pay no attention to me, I'm rambling. We'll have a great time listening to Luc blow his brains out on his sax."

Noelani hoped Adam's mood would improve so that when they got back to Bellefontaine they could raid the refrigerator and maybe sit and talk some more about dreams. But he walked her to the door and without fanfare offered an abrupt goodbye. He went straight to his quarters while she climbed the stairs to her empty room and even emptier bed.

CHAPTER FOURTEEN

TWO THINGS BROUGHT NOELANI'S week to a tolerable climax. One, the doctor told her she was fit to return to work on Monday, and two, Denise Rochelle saw her and Adam at the concert. And she was chartreuse with envy.

The bad part was, she sat with two friends who apparently had no compunction about making catcalls at Adam and otherwise heckling his party.

Halfway through the program, when the men went to buy cups of beer, Viv glared at the disruptive women. "When the guys get back, let's move."

"And give them the satisfaction of having driven us off? No way!" Casey said. "Ignore them. Or better yet, when they bug us, smile your sweetest. If they think they're getting to us, they'll have achieved their goal."

"Adam and I could move," Noelani said. "It's us they're goading. Denise invited Adam to the concert. He told her he was too busy and yet he turns up with me. I should probably feel bad about it."

"*C'est la vie!* Adam decides who he wants to be with," Casey said. "I keep trying to remember what it is that's nagging me about her. Denise, not the others," she said, darting a veiled glance at the trio.

Murray plunked himself down next to Casey. She edged closer to Viv, but Murray butted into the conversation "Denise once worked for Dad at the refinery."

"Maybe that's it. I sometimes picked you up there, I

might have seen her. I rarely went inside, though. I don't know, maybe she has a universal look or something.''

Nick made his presence known when he returned by deftly making Murray scoot over. ''Luc's combo's doing two more numbers. After that, he suggested we run down to Vermilion Parish where his cousin, Darnell, recently opened a seafood joint. That suit you, princess?''

''You know it does.'' Casey threw her arms around him.

Viv perked up. ''Darnell makes a shrimp omelette to die for.''

Noting Noelani's silence, Adam declined for them. Always intuitive where she was concerned, he saw her immediate disappointment. ''We can go if you'd like.''

''No. You paid a lot for these tickets, and you love jazz. We'll stay.''

''I didn't refuse for that reason,'' Adam said testily. ''I thought you might be getting tired. You keep rubbing at your bandage.''

Casey put her fingers to her lips and whistled. ''Hold on. I hear an argument brewing over nothing, guys. We'll all go, or we'll all stay.''

They all went, all crammed into Murray's big SUV. Noelani had the time of her life. She loved the atmosphere in the cramped diner, right down to its tacky, hodgepodge decor. Darnell made her a personal vegetarian omelette. *''Ahm gone call it Noelani, and put it on the menu, me,''* Darnell said in his lilting Cajun accent.

Everyone got in the act of teasing Noelani. Instead of blushing like she would have a few months ago, she enjoyed the attention.

An impromptu jam session thrown together by half a dozen talented musicians, including Luc, turned out to be an even better show than the one they'd heard in the park. Their group closed the place down at 2:00 a.m.

On the drive back to Baton Rouge where they'd left the remaining cars, Noelani snuggled in Adam's arms and let the pleasant chatter weave a spell around her. The city was less than ten minutes away when it struck her—she could spend the rest of her life with Adam Ross, tucked against his side, just like this. In fact, she couldn't bear the thought of leaving him.

Startled by the revelation, she slowly began to absorb what was being said. The topic under discussion centered on the series of unlucky events plaguing her family.

Her family! Gosh.

How could she be so callous as to walk away at the end of the season and let her half sister and brother face an unknown enemy alone? Casey, Jackson, Aunt Esme and Megan weren't strangers anymore. Somehow, some way, they'd become entrenched in her heart, alongside Adam. She shot up, suddenly terrified.

"What is it?" Adam shifted and yawned. "Are you in pain? Did I hurt your shoulder?"

"No and no." She shook her head, afraid to say more. Afraid Adam would hear her heart pound and demand an explanation. She couldn't give one. She needed time to sort it all out in her mind. "I, ah, think I fell asleep," she mumbled.

Indeed, she did exactly that after they all split up and climbed into their respective vehicles.

At home, she woke up long enough to deliver a sleepy good-night and a thank-you kiss to Adam. He walked her to her room. If she hadn't heard Jackson tramping up the backstairs, she might have invited Adam in to spend the night. As it was, she slipped inside to unscramble the tangled feelings she'd just identified. Ultimately she concluded that Hawaii was her home. She had to detach her feelings from this place, this man, and go back there.

She slept a good share of Sunday, except for a few hours spent taking Megan to the zoo. Noelani had offered Tanya a study break, which the nanny snapped up almost too fast to suit Noelani. Organizing her last weeks in Baton Rouge, she jotted a note to herself to have a word with Jackson about Tanya. Aunt Esme already thought the nanny was irresponsible. Maybe if someone seconded her opinion, Jackson would seek a more motherly role model for his child.

By Monday, Noelani made a positive decision about something else. Today was the last day Adam could turn in his bid on Magnolia Manor. She intended to give him a reason to follow through. Rising very early, she hiked over to see Casey, and got right to the point the minute Casey opened her door. "As things stand now, Adam isn't quite finished with the kitchen. But without his last payment, he doesn't feel he can bid on Magnolia Manor. In his mind everything's connected to your insurance problems. Can the accounts afford to pay him early or not? You know he'll finish the job."

"No problem." Casey yawned. "He should've said something. Our insurance covered his estimates. Just a second, I'll write him a check and you can deliver it."

While she waited, Noelani took out her own checkbook. With absolutely no qualms, she emptied her account of everything except the price of a plane ticket home. She also wrote a brief note to include with the checks.

Pausing only to hug Casey and thank her profusely, Noelani dashed back to the house to beat Adam to the kitchen. She tucked both checks and the note into a toolbox she'd seen him open first thing every morning. Then she calmly drove off to work.

ADAM CAME OUT OF THE garçonnière as she backed around and pulled into the lane. He waved, but she didn't see him.

Damn! If he could've stopped her, he might have started the day with a kiss.

The last kiss was on his mind when he set down his coffee cup and opened his toolbox. Three pieces of paper fluttered out onto the new wood floor. "What the hell?" He picked them up, digested the amount on each of the checks, and then unfolded and read the note. Howling at the ceiling like a wolf, Adam kicked his toolbox so hard it hurt his toe. Noelani had written that she'd decided to go back to Maui at the end of harvest, as originally planned. Even if her share of the estate wasn't enough to fully buy out Bruce Shiller, she was certain the bank would extend a loan on the land until Adam was in a position to pay her back.

He picked up the tools that had scattered, too angry to see anything but red. Whatever gave her the idea that he was the kind of man who'd take her money and let her walk away? "Dammit to hell!" Uncovering the phone on the desk, Adam almost ripped the cord from the wall in his fury. He'd say to hell with his dream of owning Magnolia Manor rather than accept her money. The knowledge burst in his head as he punched in her office phone number.

He paced as the phone rang. Someone picked it up. He heard a breath before it clicked off. He slammed down the receiver, jerked it up again and repeated the process. So did the person on the other end of the line. *Noelani.* She knew damn well he'd be calling, and it was clear she didn't intend to talk to him.

NOELANI HAD NO MORE THAN PUT her purse away than her phone rang. *Adam.* She picked it up and set it down again. It rang a second time, and she did the same. Plainly, she had to get out of the office or go nuts.

The last thing she expected was that Adam would show

up at the mill. She was truly shocked when he stormed in, catching her knee-deep in soggy cane. She and two workmen were fishing through the muck of the creeper feeders. *Ack, she must look a mess.* Although he didn't seem to care.

Avoiding his hot, angry eyes, she wiped her hands on her jeans and turned to one of her helpers. "Excuse me, Beau. I need a private word with Mr. Ross." She climbed off the teetering conveyor. "You caught me off guard, Adam," she said. "A magnet fell into the feeder. We have to locate it before it does major harm."

"You're the damn manager," he snapped. "Let someone else dig it out." Grasping her good arm, Adam hustled her toward the stairs.

"Three sets of hands are better than one." But since the set of hands in question were covered in sticky gunk, Adam thrust open Noelani's office and stepped aside to let her pass.

Her steps faltered. She could have sworn she'd locked up when she left. Adam was too irritated to notice her concern. And after all, maybe she was mistaken.

"What's this?" he demanded, slamming the two checks down on her desk, looking beautifully male in his indignation.

"Offhand I'd say it's enough money to give you a bona fide shot at owning a house down the road from Bellefontaine."

He paced for a few minutes like a wild animal in captivity. She watched warily as she cleaned her hands with solvent. Peeling off a half-dozen paper towels to dry them, Noelani jumped a foot straight up when Adam suddenly smacked his palms on top of the checks.

"I gave you conditions the other night for accepting money from you, Noelani. So tell me, have your plans changed?"

"Changed? How?" She breathed out slowly.

"You run hot, then cold, then hot on our relationship."

Exactly her earlier thoughts. "Yeah, things, uh, got pretty hot the other night."

"Quit with this stalling. I offered you a partnership in exchange for investing in Magnolia Manor. Are you ready to accept or not?"

Her eyes couldn't have grown rounder. "I don't recall you saying anything about a partnership, Adam."

"What do you think marriage is? I consider it a fifty-fifty deal. All the way down here, I asked myself what was it about me that made you think I'd take your money as a trade-off for love. I won't, Noelani. I love you. I want all or nothing."

Floored by his plain-spoken declaration, Noelani fought to keep from fainting. She dropped into her chair. The very thought of saying no this time, knowing he'd walk out of her life forever, was more devastating than her fear of saying yes, which meant she'd be saying goodbye to her beloved Maui.

"Yes," she whispered, her throat so dry that was as loud as she could manage.

Stiffening, Adam straightened away from the desk. "Say that again?" His lips barely moved.

Jumping up, Noelani rounded the desk. She threw her arms around his neck, heedless of the fact her wet jeans dripped muck all over Adam's good boots. "I said yes, I agree to your partner—"

The rest of the word was smothered under his lips. He swept her off her feet with a mind-numbing kiss. Swinging her in circles, he didn't set her down again until they were both reeling with laughter.

The first to float back to earth, Adam grabbed her chapped hands. "Are you sure about this, Noelani? We haven't discussed how this will affect a future you've had your heart set on for God knows how long.''

''I...I'm sure.'' Anything she might've added was cut short by her phone. Ignoring the ring for a moment, she implored Adam, ''If you don't get down to the courthouse and file your forms, you'll miss your chance. I break for supper at seven. Come back, and we'll have an hour to talk and plan. Maybe we could go somewhere away from the mill.''

''I think we should talk now.'' But the phone kept ringing, and then two workmen appeared at the door. Giving up, Adam crossed the room. ''I will be back. That's a promise. Seven sharp.''

Nodding, Noelani smiled at the men and raised a hand as she reached for the phone. She jerked it up just as it stopped ringing. *''C'est la vie,''* she muttered. ''Fine, hang up! Now, what can I do for you gentlemen?''

''The time clock messed up and punched us out as a.m., not p.m. workers. Joe fixed it, but he said you had to initial the error.''

''I wish all my problems were this simple.'' She signed their cards and sent them on their way.

Since her caller had apparently given up, Noelani decided this was the perfect opportunity to phone Bruce. He deserved to hear her change in plans directly from her. She hoped he'd understand, since she'd pestered him forever about buying Shiller's when he retired.

''Midori? It's me. Is Bruce in? If so, tell him I won't be put off today. Say it's a life-or-death situation. No...don't. That's not fair. Say it's crucial I reach him.''

She doodled wedding bells on her calendar while she waited. At last the line crackled and Bruce's said, ''Noelani? Midori said you sounded funny. This better be good. You interrupted my morning nap.'' He laughed in his old, jovial manner.

''Bruce, I don't quite know how to tell you this, so I'll jump in with both feet as usual. I'm not coming back to Maui. Before you say anything, I know I've pleaded and begged to buy you out. But…it's a long story. The short version is, Adam Ross asked me to marry him. I said yes.''

Bruce's whoop of delight almost broke her eardrum. ''Can't tell you how relieved that makes me. I've sidestepped your calls all week. I was offered a crackerjack deal by the truck farmers, kid. I really wanted to accept, but I've dreaded breaking the news to you.''

''Oh, Bruce. I'm happy for you, but sad for the villagers who depend on Shiller's for their livelihood. Plus, if you quit, that virtually spells the end of sugar on our island.''

''I've devoted my life to raising cane. Truth is, I've lost money hand over fist the last five years. Shipping from here is no longer cost-effective. And expanded truck farms will employ most of our people. I have that in writing.''

''Good. Quitting can't be easy for you, Bruce. I'll try not to make it harder.''

''You're like my daughter. I couldn't bring myself to hurt you. But I couldn't let you struggle like I have, either. So, when's the wedding? Maybe I'll hop a plane and walk you down the aisle, if that'd be okay with you.''

Tears sprang to Noelani's eyes. She swiped at them to no avail. In a raw voice, she said, ''We haven't set a date, but I'd like that. I've missed you and Midori, and the others so much. Bruce, will I ever stop being homesick?''

''Honey, this is your chance for a new beginning. Grab it with both hands and hold on tight. Lord knows, sugar is a hard way to make a living.'' As Bruce got choked up, too, they ended the call, promising to talk soon.

Saddened by Bruce's news, yet also feeling freer for having cut the ties, Noelani decided that if she finished her work, she might be able to leave early. She and Adam could properly toast their future together.

She tried to phone him on his cellular. Every time she dialed, she got a busy signal. Finally, she gave up. Her desk phone rang before she could call Bellefontaine and ask Aunt Esme or Tanya to find Adam for her. Thinking it might be him, she yanked the receiver up again. "Adam? Is that you?"

"No. It's Mike Arceneaux from the chem lab. I hate to bother you, Ms. Hana, but this is the third day in a row I've noticed what appears to be a fairly substantial discrepancy between the polariscope readings on some core samples and the end figures on the clarity of juice being spun out by our evaporator."

"Are you positive you're comparing results on the same cane?"

"Absolutely," he said a shade defensively.

"Mike, it's not your work I'm questioning, but whether or not there could be a mix-up in labeling core samples."

"I think that's next to impossible. These samples all come from Casey Fontaine…er…Devlin's hybrid stock. Instead of being labeled with the truck number, her hybrids carry a special code. It's a tried-and-true system, Ms. Hana. One we've used with success since Miss Casey first began planting hybrids."

"What you're telling me is…these aren't honest mistakes."

"No, ma'am. If it hadn't been the hybrids, I might not have noticed the problem as quickly. Those codes jump off the page, so I began to see a pattern."

She clapped a hand to her forehead and muttered something not at all ladylike. "Mike, this is a serious charge. Casey's family. Before I accuse her of padding core samples to beef up her quality, I'll need solid black-and-white proof.''

''I can show you proof. But that's the really odd part of this whole deal. The cane is spinning out at nearly twice the clarity as she's receiving credit for, based on her samples.''

''*What?* That makes no sense. Let me get this straight. She's personally losing money on every load?''

''Exactly. Which is why I phoned you instead of asking another tech to recheck my calculations. Frankly, there's no explanation I can see.''

''Don't go anywhere. I'm coming up. Wait. Give me five minutes. I have one phone call to make. You did the right thing in notifying me, Mike. I don't know if you're aware of it, but I have a secondary degree in chemistry. I'll be your only backup until we get some answers. For now, let's keep this to ourselves.''

''You've got it, Ms. Hana. See you soon.''

More worried than she'd want to let on to an employee, Noelani tried again to reach Adam. This time a recording came on saying he was unavailable. She slammed down the phone and rubbed her face. Should she notify Jackson?

And tell him what?

Well, she could at least alert him to expect trouble. She yanked up the receiver twice and set it back in its cradle. Why upset him when it could be an identification error or something equally simple?

Gathering pencils, a notepad and a calculator, she made her decision to recheck all of Mike's figures before bothering Jackson. And as for Adam, it didn't look as if she'd be leaving early tonight, anyway, so she might as well stop trying to reach him and catch up with him when he put in an appearance.

The labs were half a level above her office, all the way at the end of the highest catwalk. Whoever had constructed the mill had cleverly sheltered the lab from the boilers, vats, centrifuges and such. As a rule Noelani wouldn't worry about the lab's isolation. But since her fall, she took great care on the stairs. Shifting the things she carried, she firmly grasped the rail before ascending.

Mike appeared to be alone in the lab, but that wasn't unusual. The techs often staggered shifts to keep from tripping over one another in their compact quarters.

"Ms. Hana, I'm glad you came so soon. I forgot it's my turn to pick up my daughter from her dance class—it lets out at seven. If I take off now, that gives me half an hour to reach the studio. She's not very old, and I hate to leave her standing outside in the dark. The studio's not in the best part of town."

"By all means, go." Noelani set down the things she'd brought and glanced at her watch. "I had no idea it was so late. If you've left everything out, I shouldn't have any difficulty finding where you first ran across the problem. I'll double-check your figures."

"I pulled the core reports that correspond to data fed into our computers from the cooling tanks. Both batches are here." He grabbed his jacket off the chair. "Do you want me to come back after I drop Ginny at home? Ginny's my daughter."

"No. But thanks, Mike. Depending on what I find, our next step may be to have someone check calibration on the polariscopes in the core-sample room. But if you don't mind, would you do me a favor as you head out?"

"Be happy to. What do you need?"

"I'm expecting a visitor in my office at seven. I'll jot him a note I'd like you to tape to my door. It'll save me leaving my work here to run down and get him."

"I understand. I don't mind telling you, this situation has me stumped. Duke hired me straight out of college. I've turned up occasional mistakes in the nine years I've worked here. Human error. Nothing like this. Oh, if you're hunting for the tape dispenser, it's in my top drawer.''

Noelani folded the note she'd scribbled and printed Adam's name in bold letters. Running a piece of tape up each side so there'd be less danger of its falling off the door, she handed the message to Mike. ''Then, you got along with my fa—Duke?''

''He was a good man. A fair one. He visited every post at the mill at least once a day. Yvette, my wife, had a rough second pregnancy. The doc did an emergency C-section at eight months, and Yvette and the baby were both hospitalized for a long time. Duke gave me three months off and never docked my pay. He wouldn't admit it, but I think he personally paid part of our bill. Our insurance didn't cover everything, but our bill was stamped paid. Neither Yvette's parents nor mine could afford to help. Duke shrugged off my thanks then. And now the opportunity to tell him how much that meant to me—to somehow repay his kindness— is gone.''

Noelani studied the thin young man with the serious eyes. ''You are repaying his kindness, Mike. By being loyal to his family. You'd better take off. I wouldn't want you to be late picking up your little girl.''

He dashed out and she continued to stare blankly at the space he'd occupied. Most of the mill's old-timers held Duke in high esteem. She wondered how many more stories such as Mike's she'd find if she asked around. Duke might have left Bellefontaine in a financial bind, but who could fault his generosity? Certainly not her, considering the advantages he'd given her.

To Noelani's surprise, tears suddenly blinded her. She allowed herself at last to cry for the father she'd never known. She cried away what remained of her resistance.

Finally, she blotted her eyes, heaved a shuddering sigh and sank down in a chair her father had no doubt occupied many times. She'd been so angry at him for so long. Wrongly, it seemed. Perhaps this was *her* chance to repay Duke.

She switched on the calculator and began slowly plugging in numbers. As Mike said, the discrepancy jumped out at once. There were four such mistakes—if they *were* mistakes. Casey's personal account took the deficit, while the mill reaped the reward in the excess sugar milled from her hybrids. In all, the errors represented several tons of raw sugar—which equated to thousands of dollars.

Her first thought was thank God it was all in the family. But that was the most puzzling part. Chewing over what she knew, Noelani tapped her pencil eraser on the report. Her eyes felt dry and gritty. What were the ramifications here, since money lost from Casey's ledgers still ended up in the family coffers?

If Mike hadn't been so alert, if this discrepancy had fallen through the cracks, agricultural developers could scrap this particular hybrid. Or would they? Noelani was aware that Casey kept a close scrutiny on the production level of each hybrid through her greenhouse computer. Would others know that? Might the rejection of Casey's hybrid be the goal of the person pulling this sleight of hand? A saboteur in their midst who had a grudge against a cane developer? From what Noelani knew about the development process, it took approximately six to eight years to coax stalk from seed. And it was considered a coup by growers to be selected to plant developmental cane. So—maybe another grower had reason to resent Casey's good fortune.

No matter which angle Noelani contemplated, it ultimately involved the Fontaine family. For one thing, the perpetrator might plan to accuse Casey of fudging figures to let the mill pocket the profit. Another possibility—if the person or persons behind the mischief wanted to set the mill up for a huge fine or suspension from hauling to the refinery, they might charge her or Jackson with juggling figures. The most damning evidence to date was the fact that the tampering all appeared to be internal.

"Brother! Jackson will simply not believe this."

She reached for the phone to call him and happened to see the time. Five minutes after seven. Where was Adam? He wasn't here yet, although he was usually early. Maybe the note fell off the door in spite of her efforts with the double tape.

Stacking the reports she'd run off, together with the ones Mike had prepared, she bundled the lot with rubber bands. The stack was heavy, but she wanted to store them under lock and key until she, Jackson and Casey could sort out this mess.

She took extra care descending the steep steps. Feet firmly on the catwalk, she released her breath. Moving the unwieldy load to her weak arm, she dug her office key out of her jeans pocket.

No sooner had she unlocked the door than a dark-clad figure detached itself from the shadowy alcove and more or less knocked her into the room.

"Oof!" She swallowed her yelp of surprise. For a second she thought it was Adam playing tricks, trying to scare her into paying more attention to her surroundings. But as she stumbled to her desk and snapped on the lamp, Noelani realized her black-garbed visitor wasn't Adam, but Denise Rochelle.

"Denise, for heaven's sake! You scared me." Dumping the reports on her desk, Noelani turned to face the other woman. "Did you switch shifts today? Are they still having problems with the time clock? Give me your card and I'll initial it.''

''Shut up.'' Denise kicked the door closed with a steel-toed boot.

It sprang back open an inch or two, for which Noelani gave silent thanks. Denise wasn't acting like herself. Her eyes were wild enough that Noelani considered phoning Marc, one of the vat monitors who worked on the other side of the alcove. Although with her kick-boxing training—and despite her injured arm—she ought to be able to handle one puny woman on her own, if need be.

That thought hung in her mind until Denise pulled a small but deadly looking derringer from a fanny pack strapped around her waist.

Automatically edging backward, Noelani felt her thighs bump hard against her desk. She spread out her hands to show Denise she was unarmed. Fear crept in, but Noelani beat it back with determination. ''Talk to me, Denise. Whatever the problem is, let me see if I can help. But if you use that gun, there'll be no turning back.''

''Duke Fontaine caused the problem years ago when he fired my father without just cause. Oh, the big man thought he could steal our land for pennies on the dollar with none of us the wiser. Duke assumed I wasn't old enough to do anything about his highway robbery, which made the Fontaines richer and the rest of us poorer. Well, I'm doing something about it now.'' She cocked the pistol.

''Wait! You're holding *me* accountable for a situation that happened years before I even came to Louisiana?''

''You're Duke's blood. Blood tells.''

Noelani blinked. Aunt Esme was always saying stuff like that. However, Denise and Esme Fontaine differed vastly on what the telling of blood meant. ''Okay, I'll admit I'm Duke's daughter. What do you want from me? If it's restitution for property you say Duke appropriated, I can't resolve that. You need to prove your claim to Jackson. He handles the family finances.'' Noelani shifted a step closer to the phone.

"Stop! You think you're so clever. Trying to act as if you haven't made a big discovery.'' Denise laughed diabolically. "Just so you know I mean business, hear this. I didn't spend five years dating a slimeball detective for nothing. He taught me to shoot and hit what I aim at. And he taught me to bug a place like this office.'' Denise backed to the door, then she reached up and ripped a small black box off the wall.

Noelani wondered why she hadn't noticed the box before. Now she began adding things up. If Denise had this office bugged, she'd probably planted a device in the lab, too. It galled Noelani to think this hateful woman had been privy to all her private conversations for who knew how long.

Denise saw she'd scored big. Tossing the bug aside, she snapped, "I don't intend to let Duke's bastard ruin my plans. You and I are walking out of here as if we've suddenly become best pals. We'll swing past Mikie's house. Then the two of you are going for a late-night swim in ye olde Mississippi.''

"Don't be ridiculous. I'm not going one step with you.''

"I think you will. Or I'll shoot you here. Take your pick. I chose this gun for a reason. Its report will be swallowed by the noise of the equipment.''

Noelani happened to see a man's shadow outside on the door's frosted glass. *Adam. It had to be him.* Her heart galloped, then suddenly cramped in pain. The fear she'd held at bay washed over her in waves. She feared for Adam's life.

"Adam, watch out!'' she screamed as the door swung inward.

A whistling Adam Ross waltzed in, brandishing a sizable bag from a Chinese takeout. He swallowed his last note and dropped the sack, which spread cartons of piping-hot food all over the floor between him and Denise.

Needing less time to assess what was going on than Noelani had earlier, Adam dived toward the woman holding the pistol.

Anticipating his move, Denise nimbly leaped aside.

Noelani was suddenly faced with two choices. Go for the phone and punch in 911 or try to disarm Denise. Being closer to the phone, she lunged toward it. The minute she touched the receiver, Denise trained her deadly weapon on Adam's heart.

It hit Noelani like a Mack truck. Adam's arrival was no surprise to the armed woman. She'd anticipated this joyful reunion. Noelani's anger soared as she realized Denise had, in all probability, listened in on Adam's declaration of love and her own response to his marriage proposal.

As she let the receiver slide through her unsteady fingers, another momentous truth struck Noelani. *She'd never told Adam she loved him.* He'd said the words to her, but then they'd kissed and were summarily interrupted by two workmen. She could die here tonight and Adam would never know how she felt about him.

"Adam, I love you," she blurted, rising on her toes to peer around Denise and make eye contact with the man she didn't want to live without.

"That's music to my ears. Sugar pie." Their eyes locked as if they were oblivious to the danger they faced.

"How touching," Denise sneered. "You made a bad choice, Adam. We'd have been good together. I would've cared for Magnolia Manor the way your mother once did."

"Noelani, no!" Adam cried out a split second too late.

But she'd already taken a step closer to Denise and aimed a lightning kick at the woman's weapon.

The angle was bad, which forced her to kick across Denise's body. When Adam yelled, Denise whirled, not toward the sound, but toward the threat. Her weapon discharged.

Noelani stumbled, cried out, hit the desk and went down on both knees. The phone and the pineapple paperweight Adam had given her crashed to the floor. Glass splintered explosively around her.

Fearing Noelani had been struck by the bullet, Adam launched his full body weight at Denise. For so slender a woman, she was surprisingly strong and wiry. And proved to be as slippery as a wet shark.

Since the sharp sting she felt was in the vicinity of her previous injury, Noelani thought she'd probably snapped the fragile, healing bone. Gritting her teeth against the pain, she called on every ounce of her martial arts discipline to crawl through glass particles to where the phone dangled by its cord.

She prayed Adam was holding his own as she dialed 911. Following her plea for patrol cars, she asked the dispatcher to notify Casey's friend Remy Boucherand. Then she rang the vat room to get Adam some help.

"Let go of me!" Denise kicked, scratched and bit Adam. "Duke Fontaine ruined my father. I'll make his family pay and pay and pay. Adam, don't side with her! You and I can still make a deal. Listen to me, Adam. Think! Your mom lost everything to money-grubbers, too. We're alike, you and I."

"Denise, quit now! For old time's sake, I'd rather not hurt you." Adam had her arms pinned, but from the way she twisted and bucked, he was afraid she'd get loose.

"Noelani?" he panted. "How are you holding up? Did

you get the police? Are they sending an ambulance for you?''

"My arm's numb, that's all. I hit the desk when I fell. I probably broke my collarbone again.''

Two workmen from the vat room burst through the door, cutting off whatever else she might have said. One had a length of rope, which he threw to Adam. Denise spit and hissed as he bound her hands tightly behind her back. She'd clammed up completely, however, by the time the police arrived—two uniformed cops and Remy, none of whom knew the detective Denise claimed to have dated. Remy hurled a barrage of questions at her.

In weak spurts, Noelani filled them in on Mike Arceneaux's discovery. She pointed out the electronic bug Denise had ripped off the wall. "You'll probably find another one upstairs in the lab. Heaven knows where else she might have planted them.''

Adam had gone to stand by Noelani. "Ask her about the other mill accidents. And I'll bet she pushed Noelani down the stairs a few weeks ago, too.''

Tossing her head, Denise bared her teeth at him.

Adam glanced worriedly at Noelani's pale face. "Are you in pain? You're so white....''

She roused herself and said faintly, "I...ah...want Remy to...get whatever information he needs to...lock Denise up for a good, long stretch.''

"Sugar pie, they have more than enough evidence for that. Remy—'' he turned to Casey's detective friend ''—I'm taking Noelani to the closest emergency room. Will you have someone phone Jackson or Casey, and ask them to meet us there?''

"Will do. Just go before she keels over on us!''

"I'm fine.'' Noelani screwed up her face as Adam swept her off her feet, into his arms. "Poor Casey and Jackson,'' she mumbled with a grimace of pain. "They won't believe this when they hear it. The ER has become a regular family hangout."

"Denise is obviously deranged," he said. "Or maybe she's linked to Broderick. Let's hope this is the end of the Fontaines' troubles."

Noelani barely responded. Not even when Adam set her gently in the pickup and carefully buckled her seat belt. She couldn't seem to lift her arms. "I hope you're right about this ending our troubles, Adam. Funny, but the last thing Bruce said when I phoned to tell him our news—he said this was my chance for a new beginning and I should grab it with both hands and hold on tight. But—I can't seem to hold anything tight. It's like my arms won't work."

Adam backed out of his parking space. He wanted to stop and kiss her. He settled for briefly brushing his knuckles over one ashen cheek. "I think I'd like Bruce Shiller. Too bad he lives so far away."

Noelani roused. "Bruce invited himself to our wedding. He wants to stand in for Duke. I hope that's okay with Jackson and Casey," she murmured just before she slumped sideways against Adam.

Her face had gone even whiter. Adam's stomach pitched. Worse, he noticed something he hadn't seen before—blood pooling slowly on the leather upholstery under Noelani's left arm, like a macabre hibiscus unfurling its petals a little at a time.

He cried her name, but her eyes remained shut. His heart pounded sickeningly. Not knowing what else to do, Adam pushed the speed limit. He didn't care if a cop saw him. In fact, he hoped one would. She needed a police escort to the emergency room. All the while, he cursed himself for not checking her over earlier. For not phoning an ambulance himself. If he lost her... No, that was unthinkable!

CHAPTER FIFTEEN

CASEY, NICK, JACKSON AND Murray ran into the hospital emergency room. When they saw Adam pacing near the windows, they converged on him en masse.

"Should you be walking around?" Jackson hovered anxiously.

"I'm fine. It's Noelani.... She's in X-ray. The doctor's pretty sure the bone she cracked before is fractured again. She told me and the cops that she hadn't been shot. But apparently the bullet grazed her side. Her shirt's caked with blood. It wasn't until she went into shock that I saw blood on the truck seat. Thank God, we weren't too far from the hospital. If anything happens to her—" His voice cracked.

"From what Remy told us, we expected to find you both on bloody stretchers," Casey said. "Can you fill us in? Did Denise Rochelle really bug the mill and go berserk and shoot up Noelani's office?"

"One shot. I don't know if she pulled the trigger on purpose, or if the gun went off accidentally when Noelani tried to kick it out of her hand." Adam shook his head. "Marc's right about Denise bugging the office, though. And the lab."

Nick grinned in spite of the situation. "So I guess it's true what they say about hell having no fury like a woman scorned, huh, Adam?"

Casey elbowed her husband in the ribs so hard, Nick grunted and his smile fled.

"Shades of her old man," Murray muttered. "After Duke

fired Arlen Rochelle, no one would hire the soused old coot. Finally, my dad put him on the refinery payroll. With employees like that, is it any wonder our refinery went down the tubes?''

"Denise was sober as a judge tonight. I keep thinking what she might've done to Noelani if I'd shown up any later. I should've been there at seven, but didn't arrive at the mill until a quarter after. If I'd been on time, maybe I could have kept this from happening.''

"And maybe you'd be dead.'' Jackson motioned for everyone to sit. "Self-recrimination is a waste of time, Adam. Nobody gets an instant replay in life. The best we can do is put the incident behind us and go forward from here.''

"Jackson, I never knew you to be so philosophical,'' Casey said, gazing on him with sisterly admiration. "Or to have such firm opinions.''

"Yeah, well, I didn't need an opinion when Duke was alive. He handled every aspect of the business.''

Murray spun a chair around and propped up his feet. "It's always like that at my house. Business and personal. Any opinion I express is stupid, wrong, worthless or all of the above.''

Casey eyed him with some sympathy. "Is Roland on a rampage again?''

"Since yesterday. I have no clue what set him off. When he gets in these moods, it's best if I make myself scarce.''

"Maybe he's sick,'' Jackson said. "I wondered that when he missed the growers' meeting last Friday.''

Murray merely shrugged.

A moment later, Adam leaped up from his chair. "They're bringing Noelani back from X-ray. I'm going to see how she is.''

All of them filed into her cubicle, lining up on both sides

of Noelani's gurney. Adam curled his fingers over the hand lying limply at her side. Casey held her good hand, but remained silent as Adam smoothed back Noelani's dark hair.

"I guess Adam caught you up on all the excitement," Noelani said, shifting her gaze to each of the solemn faces gazing down at her.

"I left the good parts for you to tell," Adam told her as he and Noelani exchanged an intimate smile.

Casey immediately picked up on it. "You two made up? Hey, I'll bet you got engaged, or are talking about getting engaged. I'm right, aren't I?"

Jackson, Nick and Murray gaped at Casey. "How did you arrive at that conclusion?" Jackson asked. "Oh, I get it. This is some kind of women's intuition."

Noelani continued to grin at Adam, "Maybe we shouldn't keep them in suspense. We probably should tell them we *are* engaged."

"I think you just did. Anyway, I was about to explain why I was late getting to your office." Adam lifted his eyes only briefly from Noelani, then he settled a loving look on her again. "After I turned in my bid at the courthouse, I spent the afternoon buying an engagement ring. Time sort of got away from me."

"A ring?" Noelani's eyes widened, then as quickly glossed with tears. "For me? You never told me you bought me a ring."

"Man, what's taking you so long?" Nick demanded. "Give it to her."

"Honestly, Nick. Did you want an audience when you put a ring on my finger?" Casey leaned closer. "We'll go for coffee and come back later."

"No, please. I'd like to share this step. It's a big one for us. Earlier I phoned Bruce Shiller and backed out of my offer to buy his business. He wants to fly here and walk me down the aisle. Then Mike Arceneaux discovered someone had falsified core-sample reports on Casey's hybrid cane. Denise showed up with a gun. I broke the pineapple Adam gave me, and there went all our good luck,'' she wailed.

Adam kissed her. ''I'll get you another pineapple paperweight. Shh!''

Casey shot upright. ''Remy didn't say a word about my samples when we spoke about this latest incident.''

''He doesn't know,'' Noelani sniffed. ''Only Mike and me. Well, and Denise.'' Noelani filled them in haltingly on what Mike had unearthed. ''Denise admitted culpability,'' she said tiredly as the doctor strode through the door brandishing a wet film.

''Listen here, young lady. We don't allow repeat customers. Last time I saw you, your clavicle had a hairline crack. Now there's a nasty break, plus a flesh wound from a bullet.'' He held the film to the light so they could all see. ''You've got to stop whatever horseplay's going on at that sugar mill.'' His grin told them Noelani wasn't in dire straits.

''My head's okay this time. So can I go home with them?''

''I think we can shore you up sufficiently for that. I'd hate to disappoint your fan club. But perhaps I can talk everyone into waiting in the hall while I truss you up like a Christmas goose.''

That prompted a general exodus toward the door. ''Wait.'' Adam blocked their exit. ''I was about to give Noelani an engagement ring. Since you're practically one of the family, doctor, maybe you'd like to join us.''

''By all means. Engagement rings are exceptionally good medicine.'' The doctor passed the film to his tech and motioned the others back to his patient's side.

Delving in his pocket, Adam produced a small white box. He flicked it open with his thumb, extracting a solitaire—a yellow diamond set in petals of brushed gold. Before sliding the ring on Noelani's finger, Adam murmured, ''Of all the rings in the shop, I thought this warm, sunny one suited you best. But…if you'd rather have a traditional diamond, sweetheart, the jeweler said we can exchange this one.''

Noelani's dark eyes shimmered with tears of joy as she stroked the center stone. No one present in the room right then doubted she'd wear the yellow diamond for the rest of her life.

Two weeks after the family took Noelani home, Bellefontaine's upper floor rang with feminine giggles and chatter. Toodles, the lone male allowed in this feminine domain, gave all his favorite people happy licks. Esme, Casey, Viv, Megan, Tanya and Betty Rabaud were congregated in the upstairs family room to pass judgement on Noelani's wedding dress. Midori had sent it from Hawaii. Fashioned from the most exquisite Chinese satin brocade, it had a long train that rustled with each step Noelani took.

At first Toodles shied away from the noise, then he attacked the fabric, barking furiously. Aunt Esme scooped the high-strung dog into her arms. ''I've been trying to decide how to decorate for the historic home tour this year,'' she said. ''I think simple greenery threaded with yellow roses and white magnolias on the downstairs mantels, dotted here and there with flickering white candles in crystal globes. Yellow tapers on the tables. It'll be quite striking for both the wedding and the tours, don't you agree?''

Casey shrugged. ''Decorating's not my thing. Noelani?'' She deferred to the bride-to-be, who pressed a kiss against Aunt Esme's soft cheek.

''I can't believe you're all going to such trouble for me.

Adam so wanted us to be married at Magnolia Manor. Thrilled though he was to learn he'd topped Mr. Dewalt's bid, he's disappointed that he can't possibly complete renovations between now and Thanksgiving.''

"And none of us can help, what with stepping up the cane-cutting.''

Viv stretched daintily. "At least that despicable Denise Rochelle got her due.''

Tanya stirred from her spot on the floor. "Jackson says Duke never caused Mr. Rochelle to lose his house and land. And Jackson thinks Denise is crazy like a fox.''

"That's Nick's theory, too,'' Casey murmured, worry lines forming between her eyebrows.

"Please, haven't we talked that subject to death?'' Esme fussed with the scallops around the gown's off-the-shoulder neckline. "This neck is so...so...open. In my day, wedding dresses had...more material.''

Viv studied the dress. "I hope the doctor lets you get rid of this unsightly bandage, Noelani.'' She paused, tilting her head slightly. "You know what it needs as a final touch, Auntie E? A magnolia-and-yellow rosebud lei. With a simple flower crown.''

Megan, looking like a Dresden doll in her new, ruffled pink party dress, skipped over the train to hug Noelani. The girl had really blossomed after Noelani and Adam had asked her to serve as their flower girl.

"I bet you can make Noelani a lei, Auntie Viv.''

"What a good idea. We can all help.''

"Leis aren't all that easy to make,'' Noelani rushed to say. "I'll ask Bruce to bring one of white hibiscus and ginger flowers. He's flying in from Hawaii the morning of the wedding.''

"Don't order one, Noelani. I'll help Viv make one. My dress won't be ready for a final fitting for two weeks,''

Casey said. "We've got plenty of time to order extra flowers. Is there anything we're forgetting? Something borrowed. Blue. Old. New. We don't need another speck of bad luck, so I sure hope we have all the bases covered."

Aunt Esme shushed her. "Cassandra, I swear. All your pessimism will give you wrinkles—if it doesn't invite trouble where none exists."

Viv waved frantically to gain everyone's attention. "Listen, I hear heavy footsteps on the stairs.

Casey bolted from her seat on the couch and ran to block the doorway. "Who's entering our lair?" she said in her best imitation of Goldilocks.

"Only us social outcasts," Adam called. Male laughter drifted into the room as Nick and Jackson added their own comments.

"Can't any of you read?" Viv flew out the door and met the boisterous trio on the landing. "I posted a sign on the newel post below reading Women Only beyond that point. Shoo. Go away until we're finished fitting Noelani's wedding gown."

"I came to tell her it's time to go to her doctor's appointment." Adam backed off and moved down a few steps. "We have to leave in ten minutes if she wants X rays to see if they'll remove her bandage before the wedding."

"We'll hurry. Somehow that bulky bandage ruins the effect of a low-cut dress."

"Low-cut? How low?" Adam waggled his eyebrows. "And red, I hope."

"Don't be ridiculous. And don't think you'll get a sneak preview before the ceremony, either. We've already established that this family doesn't need to go hunting for bad luck."

The men retreated in a hail of raucous, good-natured commentary. But their jovial banter was short-lived.

The women, having taken off their finery, trooped after them still chattering happily. Jackson's cell phone rang just as Adam was fitting a jacket over Noelani's bulky bandage. Jackson's sudden hiss of dismay had all the friends halting in their tracks to gaze at him with troubled curiosity.

Casey reacted first to Jackson's remote expression after he clicked off and seemed to stand there looking dazed. "Jackson? Who was on the phone? Don't tell me. What now?"

He wouldn't meet his sister's eyes, and looked as if he might bolt at any minute. Noelani planted herself in his path.

Casey shook his shoulder. "Give, Jackson. If something's happened with the cane, I need to know. If it's another mill accident, that's Noelani's domain."

"Oh, no!" Noelani clapped a hand to her mouth. "I heard you mention Denise's name. Was that Remy? The cops haven't turned her loose, have they?"

"No." Jackson sucked in a deep breath. "That, ah, was the spokesman for the NTSB. He phoned regarding Duke and Maman's accident. He said their investigators strongly suspect the plane's fuel line was tampered with. He's…ah… already spoken with Remy. They've questioned both Broderick and Denise. Broderick was in jail when the plane crashed, and Denise never missed a day's work. So they're not suspects."

"Have they questioned Chuck Riley?" Nick and Adam exclaimed almost in one voice.

"Remy told the guy who phoned me that he planned to bring Chuck in for questioning. So far, they haven't been able to locate him. Beats me why Duke trusted that SOB. Remy's trying to get his hands on Duke's logbook. It may implicate Riley."

Noelani stirred. "Adam, this is awful! We'll just have to postpone our wedding."

Casey and Jackson both jerked to attention. It was Jackson who declared, "You'll do no such thing. This is a problem for the law. It has nothing to do with you or Adam."

"It does." Noelani's chin began to tremble. "I've spent twenty-eight years denying I had any connection to Duke Fontaine. But you know what, Jackson? He was my father. You and Casey aren't alone in this mess."

Aunt Esme, who'd been gripping the newel post with one arm and poor Toodles with the other, spoke up. "Noelani's right. You all share Duke's blood. And from what I've seen these last few months, you all do him proud. No matter what, I'd remind you that Fontaines keep a stiff upper lip. I say the wedding goes on as scheduled. If we have other enemies lurking about, they need to see we're made of sterner stuff."

Although the accidental siblings were obviously shaken by the news coming out of Italy, they all agreed to follow Esme's dictate.

Casey rallied first, hugging Noelani, then Adam. "Go on to your appointment. Guys, my wedding went past in a blur. I intend to enjoy every moment of yours."

THANKSGIVING DAY DAWNED crisp, cold and without a single cloud in the sky. Bellefontaine had been a beehive of activity for weeks. Betty bustled around the newly restored kitchen. For nearly a month she'd fashioned and frozen white chocolate candies and trays of canapés. That morning they were whisked out, placed on the family silver and set strategically around the dining room for the guests to enjoy.

Esme, never more in her element, flitted around the house making certain every candle and sprig of greenery looked just so.

"Auntie E, relax. No couple could ask for a more beautiful setting to be married in," Noelani chided, lovingly pressing a kiss to the woman's soft cheek. "It's time for the wedding party to dress. Will you help me with my gown?"

The Fontaine matriarch failed to hide watery eyes, but did manage a nod. With a rustle of her ecru crepe dress, she scooped up Toodles, who'd also been groomed for the occasion with a satin bow and diamond collar. In her usual sweeping manner, Esme kept pace with Noelani up the winding stairs.

A scant hour later, stunning in emerald-green silk, Casey Devlin stepped back to view her handiwork in an ornate, free-standing mirror. Her last act was to arrange a fragrant lei around Noelani's shoulders. One they'd all had a hand in crafting. "As usual, Viv, you were absolutely right. The lei and matching crown of magnolia blossoms and tiny yellow rosebuds sets off Noelani's dark eyes and black hair to perfection. Oh, isn't she beautiful?"

Blinking back tears, Casey once again flapped her hands in front of her eyes in a manner that had become familiar to Noelani. And yet the last time—in the kitchen after the *cochon de lait*—seemed ages ago. When things hadn't been so perfect...

"Blast! I knew it. There goes my mascara. Noelani, honey, you're going to knock Adam's socks off."

Impulsively, Noelani leaned close and brushed cheeks with Casey. "No tears today, please. You've all made me happier than I ever dreamed possible. I have a family. And soon I'll have a husband and a real home of my own. And these were all things I tried so hard to turn my back on."

Jackson tapped on the door casing and stuck his head in the room. Megan skipped inside, a little princess in her floor-length dress. Jackson looked as if his black tux had been tailored for his lean, runner's body.

"Are all the men in the wedding party on the landing?

Except for Adam, of course. I assume he's downstairs with the JP?'' Noelani murmured anxiously.

Jackson smiled. ''Bruce Shiller, Nick and Luc are in place. The background music's just stopped, and Murray is walking Aunt Esme and Toodles to their seats. I can't believe you bought that dog a satin pillow, Noelani.''

Her answer was to lower her lashes and adjust his already perfect tie. It'd long been decided that Jackson would escort Megan downstairs first, followed by Casey, matron of honor, with Nick serving as Adam's best man. Viv, the bride's second attendant, was set to go after them on the arm of Luc, another of Adam's groomsmen. While Tanya played the piano, a good friend of Luc's would sing a love song.

The leaders started their trek down the polished stairs. Bruce took hold of Noelani's icy arm. ''You're the spitting image of your mother today. Ah! Thank you, hon. That huge smile tells me your life couldn't be better.''

''I'm ready,'' she said. ''No matter what happens from this day forward, Bruce, nothing will change the love I have for Adam, or his love for me.''

''That's my girl.'' The man acting in her father's stead made a sweeping gesture toward the beautifully decorated hall below. They heard the faint change in the strains of the antique piano.

Noelani took a deep breath as she watched Jackson, Casey, Nick, Viv and Luc assemble in a row. Megan floated two feet off the floor. She didn't have to pretend that all was well in the Fontaine family. That was one happy child.

Leaning heavily on Bruce, Noelani prayed her knees wouldn't give out. She arrived safely at the curve of the stairs, her train a satin waterfall behind her. For the first time, she glanced down on the dearest friends of a family she'd joined by choice. Her eyes skidded across their heads to Adam's upturned face. Joy, awe and love reached across the distance separating them. Her world stopped spinning out of control and steadied on its axis when Adam stepped forward and raised both of his arms toward her. Whatever else life had to throw at the Fontaines, her place here and Adam's love for her were secure.

A fresh tune rippled from beneath Tanya's nimble fingers. The cultured baritone voice of Luc's friend galvanized every guest in the room as he began to sing "The Hawaiian Wedding Song."

"This is the moment I've waited for…"

Noelani's heart echoed the words to the haunting love ballad; she alone knew it had been Anela Hana and Duke Fontaine's special song. This small thing she would do to honor the man and woman who'd given her life.

Reaching Adam, Noelani let go of Bruce and moved into the warm circle of her soon-to-be husband and lover's arms.

"I will love you longer than forever…"

With all her heart, Noelani sensed those words would bind her and Adam for all eternity. Truly, for this moment, the family's problems ceased to exist.

*   *   *   *   *

Turn the page to read an excerpt from

JACKSON'S GIRLS

by K.N. Casper,
the third book in the
RAISING CANE *trilogy.*

CHAPTER ONE

PANIC CLEARLY GRIPPED HER, but she managed to close her mouth. Jackson Fontaine admired that. When she didn't say anything, he leaned over, reached inside and snagged her keys. In doing so, he came within an inch of her face, caught a whiff of her delicate feminine scent and almost lost his resolve. Angry at his own weakness, he fisted the keys. She pulled farther away. Appalled that he was making a woman afraid of him, he stood up.

"Are you going to answer me?" When she only stared mutely at him, he said, "Okay, have it your way."

Taking a step back, he withdrew a cell phone from his pants pocket and started hitting numbers.

"No, wait— Who are you calling?" Her words were clipped, almost strangled, but she had a nice voice, not too high, deliciously feminine.

"The police. You're trespassing on private property, lady. Since you won't give me an explanation of what you're doing here, I'll let the police sort it out."

"But—" Her left hand reached out in an imploring gesture. No ring, he noticed. "Please," she begged, "don't do that." Her eyes suddenly pooled.

Jackson had enough experience with the opposite sex to recognize crocodile tears when he saw them. As he observed the fright in this woman's face, however, he realized she was just plain scared—or the world's finest actress. Being taken into custody by the police would unnerve anyone, he reckoned, except the most hardened criminal. He wasn't exactly sure what a hardened criminal was supposed to look like, but he was certain this lovely creature didn't fall into that category. No, her fear was real, her panic coming close to terror.

He clicked off his cell phone and shrugged. "Start talking, then, and you better make it good."

Relief softened her features, though the tears didn't immediately dry up. She took a deep breath and absently closed the laptop resting on her thigh. "My name is Leanna Cargill." She retrieved the handbag on the seat beside her. "I have identification, my driver's license—"

"I'll take that." He snatched the purse from her. For all he knew she had a gun in it and was going to plug him full of holes. Again, she shrank away from him, making him feel like a goon. Playing the heavy wasn't a role he enjoyed. He'd been brought up to respect and protect women, not bully them. Leanna Cargill might be a trespasser, but she wasn't a killer. Maybe some hitmen…er…women had blue eyes, but not the look he saw in *her* blue eyes.

There was something else, too. When his hand had brushed hers, she didn't feel like someone who wanted to hurt him. What her soft skin conjured up in his mind was a lot more pleasant. Damn, he'd been without a woman too long.

He started to unsnap the clasp on the imitation leather handbag and noticed it was broken. Why did going into a woman's purse make a man feel like he was violating her? He stopped, disgusted with himself. "What are you doing here?" he demanded.

She shoved the laptop aside and took another fortifying breath. "I'm an insurance investigator for the Sugar Coalition."

He arched his right eyebrow. Her answer was certainly not one he'd expected. "Say that again."

She almost smiled, and he wished she had. Behind the anxiety and embarrassment, she was pretty, and he had a sudden need to see the worry lines fade, to see her face light up.

"I'm an insurance investigator for the Sugar Coalition," she repeated.

"Really? And what might an insurance investigator for the Sugar Coalition be doing on my property?"

She bit her lip, then said almost shyly, "Checking out an anonymous tip that raw sugar is being stored at this site illegally...."

Let award-winning author

Tara Taylor Quinn

take you back to the town
we'd all like to live in....

Born in the Valley

Life in Shelter Valley, Arizona, is pretty good,
and Bonnie Nielson knows it. She has a husband
she's crazy about, a child she adores, wonderful
friends and a successful business in this town
she loves. So why isn't Bonnie happy,
and what can she do to fix it?

SHELTER VALLEY:
Read the books. Live the life.

Available wherever Harlequin books are sold.

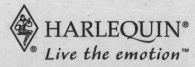

HARLEQUIN®
Live the emotion™

Visit us at www.eHarlequin.com

HSRTTQBIV

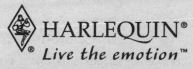

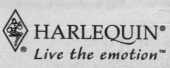

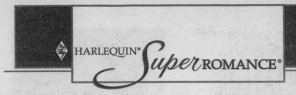

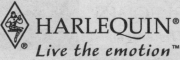